# NO GOOD DEED GOES UNPUNISHED

# No Good Deed Goes Unpunished

## WORLDS OF SHADOWS AND LIGHT: BOOK ONE

A.P. Vandy

Oceaniacom Press

First published by Oceaniacom Press 2024
A division under Oceaniacom Pty Ltd.
www.oceaniacom.com

Worlds of Shadows and Light: Book One
No Good Deed Goes Unpunished

Copyright © 2024 by A.P. VANDY
www.apvandy.com

ISBN (Print): 978-1-923113-00-8
ISBN (Ebook): 978-1-923113-01-5



Edited by Sally-Anne Ward and Alethea Van Holland
Cover art and design by Alethea Van Holland

*Shannon, this story would not exist if not for you.
And Logan, our roles have been reversed; you gave me
my voice back.*

# Prologue

*There was no fanfare of trumpets when the sleep of untold ages finally released its steely grip on her, but it was the sign of the new age nonetheless. Bards might sing of the importance of the day, but for now, all she felt was the grogginess of an artificial sleep interrupted.*

*Without conscious thought, she began to stretch—first her limbs, then her neck. Much to her surprise, her muscles were stiff and sore from her untold millennia of idleness, but otherwise, they seemed none the worse for wear. Her head was another story: after a few moments of shoulder and neck stretching, she nearly swooned in vertigo.*

*Grunting in irritation at her foolishness, she waved a front foreleg, and gentle light, such as from a star-filled night sky, washed over the cavernous room. She winced even at this minimal amount of light, but she was glad to see her surroundings, for they further helped her differentiate between the "now" and the dreamless void she had just escaped. An involuntary shudder convulsed her. Long ago, she had grappled with, and overcome, the loneliness and heartache which accompany living with other races with shorter lifespans, but the dark void 'the spell' consigned her to was an agony worse than death.*

*"But enough of that rubbish," she abraded herself out loud in a raspy, unused voice, "if you choose to walk in darkness... you will lose your way. And there are far too many ways for this to go awry."*

*With another wave of her foreleg, the room became daylight bright, and the shadows were banished throughout. The cavern was enormous, for she could not see the north or east walls nor the ceiling even with full illumination. What she could see was a table that lined nearly the whole south, stone wall, which was covered with an odd assortment of armor, weapons, staves, hats, clothing, and even multicolored vials. Everything there seemed as she had left it.*

*Nodding to herself, she turned to the west and beheld a gigantic sphere of light that spun slowly above a raised gilt-covered dais. She smiled. The orb pulled her as the moon would the waves, and she lay next to it and embraced the power and warmth emanating from it: a balm for her weary soul. It cleansed her. It warmed her. It filled her—to the point she could not help but sing!*

*She leapt into the air. Wings at her sides unfurling upon command and holding her aloft with powerful strokes. Neck extended nearly as long as the tail behind her. Claws, scales, talons, terrible rows of razor-sharp teeth—all combined in a hew of gold. Her triumphant dragon's roar had not been heard for many millennia, but that couldn't diminish its power and beauty.*

*Like all too many moments of passion, hers ended too quickly. She floated down to the space before the globe and once again embraced its healing waves. For now, she would have to gain back her strength and gather what information she could about this world around her, because soon, she would be called on to curate the new beginning.*

*Unfortunately, this golden dragon was the only being on Earth who knew the truth: the world was not as it seemed.*

# Part 1

ONTARIO, OREGON

# Chapter 1



Electricity crackled in the air like the moment before an electrical storm unleashes its potential violent power upon the earth. Or at least that was how it felt to one Dr. Zander Parks. It took every bit of self-control he possessed not to check his e-mail yet again, call Imagine Lab's receptionist, or hop into his car and drive to the FDA's Maryland headquarters and demand that they announce their decision regarding Imagine's request.

Instead of doing any of these things, the 45-year-old, greying researcher did what he always did in high-stress moments—he fished a pack of peppermint gum out of his white lab coat and carefully unwrapped the stick and popped it into his mouth. As he savored the flavor and aroma he mused, it beats smoking. But the comfortable habit provided him only a momentary respite from thinking about how much hinged on the FDA allowing them to take the next step: human trials for their "cure" for Leukemia.

Twenty years of exhaustive research… he hoped it was enough to fulfil his promise to his 15-year-old kid sister, Crystal. A promise which required him to dismiss his former career path of becoming a general practitioner, like his father. Crystal grew ill during the summer before his third year of medical school, and she was gone by Christmas. The following months were rough on the whole family. If his parents had not been there to temper his acute despondency, he would have quit medical school. But after a great deal of soul searching, he concluded he would continue studying medicine the next fall, but his focus was to be research.

But Zander was not the only family member who had been contemplating how this tragedy would mold the future. His parents, Dr. Wesley Parks and his wife, Silvia, loved Zander's new career path, but they absolutely rocked his world when they announced their new brainstorm: Crystal's Cure. The sole purpose of this organization was to underwrite a top-tier research lab in their backyard, Ontario, Oregon. Population 11,300. Furthermore, they planned to dedicate much of their retirement savings to get the charity up and running. Wes would have to work a few more years than he had wanted, but it also allowed Silvia the time to aggressively pursue donors and patrons throughout Malheur County and beyond. There were tears, but also the beginning of healing for the whole family.

Years later, Zander graduated *magna cum laude* from medical school and accepted a research assistant position at the foundation's newly dedicated facility: Imagine Labs. Both his parents were beside themselves with joy at watching their son walk around, open-mouthed, seeing every piece of equipment and the layout of the rooms and labs. But nothing could prepare him for their *coup de grace:* the door to his current office, said Dr. Zander Parks, Director of Research. Unsuccessfully, he pointed out that he was unqualified for such a role, but he found out his stubborn streak was legitimately inherited from his mother as well as his father. He accepted.

A timid knock at the door interrupted his reminiscing, "Come in."

The door opened just enough to see his colleague Dr. Lise Lorenzen's platinum blond head, "I was going to brew one of my special coffee blends and wanted to know if you are interested in a cup?"

"I grabbed some gum a minute ago, so I'm good. Besides, I have enough nervous energy between the waiting and the caffeine to run yet another marathon. Go ahead and make one for yourself if you like."

"If I'm being honest, I don't need any either, but I wanted an excuse to leave my office. Do you mind some company?"

"Love some," Zander said as he motioned her to grab one of the two plush chairs that faced his desk.

Bounding into the room with little of her usual restraint, she plopped into the left chair. *Drank much more than a little of your fufu coffee I see,* he thought and chuckled to himself. His friend was born and raised in Denmark and she prided herself on her potent, yet delicious, blend. His closest friend was a stunning woman who had turned 63 a few months back. Most people noticed her hair first, which was a natural blond so pale it appeared white and was straight and shoulder-length. Then they were struck by her diminutive height: 5' 1". Only fools commented on her stature, for Lise was one of the most brilliant doctors Zander knew, and she did not suffer idiots at all.

After a few moments of companionable silence, she said, "Do you ever think about how we got started?"

"Can't help it. So many things had to fall into place for this serum to happen."

"No, I mean the day we met."

"Oh, of course," Zander said. And he did. It had been one of the most magical days in his life. Not in a romantic way, but important, nonetheless. Both had been attendees at a medical conference featuring a gene manipulation symposium. It had only been a month since he had learned he was head of a lab, and he needed to hire a staff. A dozen people were in the final stages of the hiring process, but it was hard for Zander to sit alone in the lab, hypothesize a possible cure, and wait. So, he had signed up for the conference. Lucky for them both, they had sat next to each other and had struck up a friendly conversation during one of the intermissions.

It had not taken long for him to gush about his new project to Lise. One intermission later, they agreed to blow off the rest of the bland presentation, go to a nearby restaurant, and further discuss the possibilities and avenues of research Imagine Labs could pursue. The evening was intoxicating: the giving and taking of ideas allowed him to travel down paths toward curing cancer he had not considered. Lise was brilliant and a perfect collaborating partner. She was far more impressive than any of the interviewees he had spoken with so far in his search.

It was crazy and a bit reckless, but he tendered her a position on his staff. Maybe she was as caught up in the impulsiveness of the moment as he. Whichever it was, she said yes, with one caveat: her husband, Paul, in Portland, had to agree. Zander had suggested she call him 'right now.' Giggling with the insanity of it all, she had talked to her mate for 20 minutes before telling Zander that Paul was intrigued and wondered if Zander would like to give his "pitch" to him before heading onto Ontario. Three hours later, the three were talking in Lise and Paul's front room.

Both smiled at the pleasant memory, and Lise said, "This morning, I looked at the pad I used when brainstorming in the restaurant. Do you realize how close we came that night to our final cure? It's uncanny."

During their brainstorming, they decided to focus on a solution to the disease specifically targeting the cancer cells. Two options were clearly the most viable: (1) modifying a virus to attack only cancer cells and (2) tinkering with the patient's immune system.

After creating a pros and cons list for each choice, it was difficult to decide which avenue of research they could follow, but Zander intuitively felt that modifying the virus was the best choice. Lise had played devil's advocate for a bit, but as they debated the merits of each path, she abandoned the notion of the immune system.

"Have to admit, it was hard telling you I thought we needed to do the virus," Zander said with an embarrassed smile. "Had only been out of med school for a month and it was difficult telling someone considerably older that I was right."

"Between you and me, I'm glad you did. But if you keep making cracks about my considerable age advantage." She sat up straighter and assumed a matronly air, "I will box you about the ears, young man."

Laughing and holding up his hands in surrender, Zander said, "The drive to your place in Portland was nerve-wracking. Wasn't sure what Paul would say. Three hours is a long time to prepare a sales pitch."

"I bet, but I knew Paul was not happy in Portland. He grew up in the tiny city of St. Paul and he only moved to the big city for me. So, I figured we had a better than average chance of talking him into it. Besides, he is a good man and how could he resist your persuasive sales pitch, a good cause, and the good graces of the love of his life?" Her eyes twinkled in mirth.

"You are incorrigible; I didn't know him very well, or at least not until we drank those three bottles of wine."

"Don't remind me," Lise said feelingly in remembrance of the next morning's hangover, "if everything goes well with our cancer virus, we should come up with something that eliminates the unpleasant aftereffects of over-imbibing. Bet there's a fortune to be made there."

"Careful, we don't want to get too far ahead of ourselves."

"Trust me, I know. It's just... I don't know if I can face starting over. I'm not as young as I once was," she said as she stood. The fears gathered about her face and aged her like some supernatural leaches. *None of us is as young as we once were, Lise. Even I struggle with starting over if the FDA rejects this cure,* he thought. She went to him and held him tightly—together, they could dare their fears.

At that moment, there was a quick knock, the door opened, and two men wearing lab coats appeared in the doorway. The man on the left was Dr. Ben Mayette, who was in his late 50s, blonde hair turning gray at his temple, and the beginnings of a sedentary belly. The other was Dr. Rohit Tamboli. The doctor's dark complexion and hair belying his Indian heritage, but the most dominant facial feature Tamboli had was a ferocious mustache Tom Selleck would die for.

"Ohh, sorry, we didn't mean to interrupt," Dr. Tamboli said with a slight Indian accent.

Lise's moment of self-pity evaporated in a blink and she pivoted to a playful tease, "You hadn't interrupted anything... yet."

Zander colored and said in a rush, "Did you need something?"

"Not really, we're just biding time like everyone else in the building. Don't suppose you have heard anything yet?" Dr. Mayette said.

"Trust me, you guys will know shortly after I know," Zander said. "Why don't you guys come in, and we can wait together? It shouldn't be long."

The two doctors hustled into the office and took the two remaining office chairs. Shaking her head, Lise left and moments later brought in a chair from the reception area and created a loose semi-circle.

"Zander and I were just marveling about how many things had to go right for us to cook up our little Frankenvirus," Lise said.

"For instance, I was so lucky to find a crew of such dedicated doctors and lab assistants," said Zander.

"…who were willing to come to a small town, miles from anywhere," Dr. Mayette continued.

"…and work for less than average," Dr. Tambolli added.

"Okay, okay, I get the picture, and I will see if I can wrangle some much-deserved raises from the budget in the near future. Sheesh." Good-natured laughter filled the room. "But seriously, I recognize Lise is not the only one to whom I owe a great debt. If I remember correctly, Ben, you were the one who came up with the idea of using HIV as the delivery system for our little cocktail."

Beaming with pride at the recognition, Ben said, "I was watching a documentary on TV one night which detailed how the virus attacked T-cells. It seemed like the perfect vehicle for our cure. I was so excited that I worked through the night on a proposal: manipulate the virus to attack Leukemia cells."

"I knew you had something right away," Zander said. "And you, Rohit, are a master gene manipulator. It took you a while, but today would not be possible without your expertise. Thank you for the hundreds, if not thousands, of combinations you had to try to make it work."

There was silence for a moment as the man was overcome with emotion, but when he could speak again, Rohit said, "If the FDA approves our serum, it will all be worth it. Think of the millions of lives it could save."

But they couldn't savor the moment very long, because his computer made an innocuous chime. All eyes in the room zeroed in on Zander's computer. As he reached for the keyboard, he hesitated, and closed his eyes. *Oh God. Please let this be the one.* Reaching forward, Zander tapped a key and read the email's executive summary.

When finished, he met Lise's eyes and calmly asked, "Can you assemble everyone in the staffroom in five minutes?"

"Yes, I can, but you will not tell us now?" Lise said.

"I want to break the news to everyone simultaneously, and you all have terrible poker faces. Especially you, Rohit. Give me five minutes."

"You just told us how important we are to this team and then you treat us like everyone else," Ben said with a growl. "You can be such an ass sometimes." Then he stormed off.

Rohit and Lise gave Zander a look, shrugged, and headed off to gather the staff.

When they were gone, he printed a few pages of the email and spent the next two minutes thinking of how to break the news to his staff.

The staffroom was a grandiose term for a bigger-than-average room. Imagine employed about 30 people most of the time, and it was rarely necessary to have them all gathered in the same place at once, but gather they had. Someone at the FDA had dropped a hint there would be an announcement today, so the room was abuzz with nervous, excited whispers.

As people began to notice Zander had arrived, it grew nearly silent. Once again, he was struck by the energy and anticipation in the room. He only remembered feeling this way once before when he was younger—the space shuttle Discovery was launching after the destruction of Challenger and the nation held its collective breath.

Shuffling his printouts to hide his nerves, Zander began, "As you can guess, I have got the application results here, or at least a few of the 500 necessary pages the FDA sent me." Almost everyone laughed at the joke because they had helped him craft Imagine Lab's application, which was not less than a thousand pages. "Earlier today, I was thinking about all the fun ways I could draw out the reveal. For example, I could thank everyone who put so much hard work into this project or my new scheme for how we should assign parking spaces. But by my light tone, some of you've already surmised," he looked down at his now crumpled email pages, "…our testing has confirmed your initial findings regarding the efficacy of your Leukemia treatment. Therefore, we not only approve moving forward with human testing, but we recommend that this process be granted Accelerated Approval and given Fast Track status."

It took exactly half a millisecond for the staff to react, but react they did. In one of those little mysteries of the world, time slowed down, and like a movie montage, he floated through the room seemingly without purpose until he appeared in front of his friends Rohit, Ben, and Lise. He grabbed each in turn, wrapped them in tremendous bear hugs, and tried to communicate, over the din, how proud he was of what they helped him accomplish. He made an effort to make personal contact with everyone there, but after a while, it was hard to keep track of all the heartfelt, tender moments, slaps on the back, words of congratulations, or hugs he received. But like all moments of passion, the energy of this one finally abated.

Moments later, he called his parents, gave them the good news, and arranged to meet as soon as he could leave the office. When he hung up the phone, the enormity of the situation hit him full force, and he began to cry.

*Crystal, we finally did it,* he thought. *If we get through all the hoops for this treatment, no one will need to suffer from this disease again. No other children will die! I hope you can hear me. Miss you so much, kiddo. Love you.*

# Chapter 2

*December 16, 2016 — 3pm — Ontario, Oregon*

Though he had to travel at a snail's pace to avoid the numerous potholes in his parents' long gravel driveway, he still arrived at their slate grey-colored house before the coffee drinks could melt. Though it wasn't their normal coffee Wednesday, Zander was sure his parents wouldn't mind a second visit during the week. He knew that his parents cherished the time they spent reconnecting each week as much as he had.

Besides, they were as responsible for a viable treatment for Leukemia, if not more so, than anyone working at Imagine, and they deserved a celebratory moment as well. His father must have heard him drive up because he was heading toward the car as Zander parked. *Pretty spry for a man just shy of his 75th birthday,* thought Zander. But he couldn't deny that Wes looked older; his hair was shock white and growing sparser by the day, and a pair of trifocals was hanging around his neck on a lanyard.

However, Wes still had more energy and drive than men 20 years younger. Personally, Zander thought it had as much to do with his parents' fanatical, almost daily, squash matches as genetics. He got out of the car, greeted his father with warmth, handed him the drink carrier, and they headed to their usual haunt, the library room. His mother, Silvia, met him at the door with a radiant smile, which highlighted the smattering of freckles across the top of her cheeks and her sea-green eyes, and tenderly grabbed his hand and gave it a little squeeze. Meanwhile, Wes entered the room and passed around the treasured beverages. Duties performed: he zeroed in his favorite green recliner and sat down.

Before she relinquished Zander's hand, she took one hand grabbed his chin and peered into his eyes. Apparently, she was assured by what she saw because she nodded to herself and folded herself into her seat. Even at 73, Zander was always amazed at the grace in which his mother moved. In her early 20s, Silvia was well on her way to becoming one of the premier ballerinas with the Baltimore Ballet.

According to the romantic in the family, Wes, it was during one of her performances that he fell in love with his future wife. But according to his mother, it had taken him more than a few of her performances before he got up the nerve to approach her. Even though it took him a while to approach the beautiful dancer, the spark between them was real and they dated while Wes attended medical school at John Hopkins University. There was little money in those days, so they decided to elope partway through his father's residency.

A year later, Zander was born, and the new family moved to Ontario.

Crossing the room, Zander eased into "his" chair and sipped his frappuccino. As he savored the beverage, the calm of the familiar setting and his steadfast parents helped him regain a measure of peace, which was sorely needed after months of tension. Zander closed his eyes and savored not only the victory, but the peace of finally achieving a long-held goal. When he opened them, his parents were watching him and waiting. Somehow, he mused to himself, they always know what I need.

With a wry smile, Zander said, "I'm guessing you guys know why I'm not popping the cork on some champaign and bouncing around like a fool?"

His parents stated in unison, "Crystal."

"Am I that transparent?"

"Only to us, Zander," Silvia said.

"It's been 20 years. Why won't the pain go away?"

Like all memories that define someone, Zander remembered the day. He was nine when his parents shared their joyful news with him. A sister. He remembered their laughter when he audaciously asked why they waited so long to give him a brother or sister. His mother had grabbed his hands and told him with all seriousness she was a "gift from God." They had not expected to have another child but were excited to become parents again.

After their announcement, they waited to see how he would take the news. They shouldn't have been worried because, unlike many children who resent the news they will have a new sibling, Zander welcomed the idea. He loved Crystal the moment she held his pinky finger in her tiny fist. Without question, he continued to love her with a fierce passion until the fateful day at Doernbecher's Hospital when she squeezed his 25-year-old hands in hers as she faded away.

A single tear caressed his mother's cheek.

"Mom?" His mother made a placating gesture to continue. "All those years ago—promises to myself—promises to you two. I thought... I don't know... I thought all the pain would go away. It sounds silly when I say it out loud now, but I believed it."

"Maybe you needed to think that," his father said.

"Honey, we all were grasping at straws back then," his mom said. "We all had to find a way out of the darkness."

It had been tough on the whole family, but Zander knew it had been particularly hard on his mother. When they had moved to Ontario, she had given up her career to stay with her children. As long as he could remember, she had dedicated her incredible energies to loving and caring for her kids.

When Crystal got sick, Zander was in medical school, and Wes worked full-time in his practice. Both had offered to pause their lives to help out with Crystal's care. But Silvia would not hear of it. She would take care of her little girl. The two became even closer during Crystal's decline, but it led to greater heartache for Silvia when her daughter passed. His mother's way back to "normal" must have felt especially long.

Wes's eyes narrowed, and then he changed the course of their musings, "Your mom and I are so proud of you."

"Well, I didn't do it all myself. Besides, human trials are just the next step in a long process."

"True," Wes said, "but Zander, according to the FDA and all the data Ben and Lise have shared with me, you have a legitimate cure for Leukemia. It will happen. Don't you worry."

"Thanks. But we all know this wouldn't have happened without your support and help with med school, the lab, and... everything. It really means a lot to me that you were willing to take a chance on it all."

"Nonsense," his mom said. Her sincerity and intensity shook him. "You are our son, and there was no doubt you would give it your everything. The icing on the cake is you actually *did it.*" Her wink and wry smile were classic Silvia.

"Well, now that we have established his true parentage," Wes said with his own wink, "let's see if that bottle I have been saving is as good as they say."

The nerves remained—but now—Zander felt everything would work out.

# Chapter 3



*June 23, 2017, Wednesday — 6pm —
Outskirts of Ontario*

*It's a fine day for a stroll,* Dr. Craig thought as he worked his way around the perimeter of his ranch house. The day had finally arrived. After so many years, the next few days were critical to his plan.

The anticipation made him feel like doing a frenetic jig, but there would be time enough for dancing if all went well. Instead, he permitted himself a rapturous smile and continued his tour about the front of the house. Grunting in satisfaction, he noted passing cars would only see what appeared to be a modest farmhouse. It was important that his 'friends' would attract as little attention as possible. When he purchased the property 16 years ago, he made it painfully clear to the realtor—privacy was paramount. When this farm came on the market, he knew it was perfect for his needs. Situated 10 miles northwest of Ontario on a small rise, his nearest neighbor was at least an acre south of his home.

The surrounding farmland originally grew wheat; now—besides a huge garden—the other 200 acres lay mostly fallow, which effectively acted as a natural screen for all the homestead buildings, save the house proper. The deed was signed over within the week.

Continuing his walk about the property, he could see the metal 10-foot-high chain link fence flash as the sunlight played on its surface like a thousand wavetips on a choppy lake. Once again, to the casual observer, the barrier, like many of the neighbors' fences in this part of the country, was erected ostensibly to keep the deer out of the garden. Still, in reality, its purpose was very different.

As he made his way to the backyard, it never failed to fill him with pride. Behind the fences: not a farm but a small village. Worn-looking, tan modular trailers were logically placed about the immediate vicinity, and heavy electric and water lines now snaked throughout the compound, providing the basics for the nearly 220 inhabitants. But their community's population was in constant flux, and it depended on the number of people who occasionally arrived or left, usually at night, because no one outside of this small group realized this was the current headquarters of *Gaia's Children* or the "GC."

As he made his way to the back side of his house, he began to see many more of his people going about their business, and they affectionately greeted him with addresses of Dr. Craig, "Doc," or "Sir," depending on their familiarity with him. This pleased him. Why shouldn't his people acknowledge and respect him? He should be happy. He was happy in all ways except… for some reason, it was not enough. Like Adam in the Garden, perfection wasn't enough. Every day at Imagine, he had to face the reality that he was not the leader; Zander was.

Logically, his jealousy of Zander made no sense. The current membership of *Gaia's Children* was hovering near three thousand members and growing. They had branches up and down the West Coast and were actively recruiting followers from most of the college campuses in this region and online as well.

Global warming scared people, and Craig and the GC promised them a path toward saving the planet and her people. But the logic of numbers very rarely comes into play when it comes to people's thoughts and emotions. So, Craig stewed about Zander and Lise's popularity at the lab, but he knew it was only a temporary irritation. And he would make sure they knew who brought them low before the end. Just then, his Lieutenant Greg Mundst exited a building to Doc's east and headed toward him with two glasses of lemonade. Greg, a very fit 45-year-old man wearing a black tank top, green army fatigue trousers, black military boots, a flat top haircut, and aviator sunglasses, looked like an advertisement for 'Mercs R Us.' The irony is the man had never used a gun until recently and had yet to hurt anything besides a firing range target.

With a twinkle of his eyes, Greg handed a glass to Craig and said, "Thought you could use one of these."

Suspicious, Craig sniffed the proffered glass and could smell the whisky a distance from the glass. "Next time, you should just skip the splash of lemonade and pour me a shot. You know I have a somewhat important speech in a few?"

"Yeah, yeah. But we both know that you get nervous before you speak in public. Always. This will take the edge off. Cheers!" Craig was going to protest, but his friend's mischievous grin made him relent and clink glasses with the man before they both took a hardy swig of the beverage.

"Walk with me," Craig said.

"Aye, Captain," Greg said and sketched an irreverent salute.

"Knock it off. It doesn't look good in front of the troops." Nodding to those in the yard who were watching the two leaders. The men started at a leisurely pace toward the large barn toward the back of the compound.

"Can't help but think back to when all this started at the ole U-dub campus. What was the name of that chick who started the club?"

"Ali."

"How do you remember that crap? I can barely remember what I ate yesterday," Greg said. "I do remember her apartment was half the size of one of these trailers, and I had to sit on a plastic deck chair."

"And yet, those are some of my favorite memories while going to school," Craig said in a nostalgic mood. "How naive we were back then. Even *I* dreamed we could change the world for the better."

"Glad you took over for her. We stopped the bake sale BS and started doing meaningful things."

"Yeah, but even after I seized the reins, we didn't really do anything," Craig said. "Putting spikes in trees, dumping sugar in logging truck gas tanks, and arson: mere inconveniences to the corporations." The words were a bitter condemnation of their previous tactics. However, there was a side benefit—recruiting. Word of *Gaia's Children's* guerrilla actions spread throughout the eco-community and their numbers grew. Like-minded people of all ages, religions, and socio-economic backgrounds flocked to the GC. "Our new plan will get everyone's attention, though." Both men laughed at the ludicrous understatement.

A very small circle of GCers knew of the big news Craig would share with the membership in a few minutes, and Greg was one of them. It was a shame they couldn't postpone their solution so they could save more lives, but to wait any longer could imperil the Earth. And that was unacceptable. The way Doc saw it, the world would soon be unable to recover from humankind's desecration. The time for action was now. And it was a delicious irony that his plan's start coincided with Zander's greatest triumph.

"Showtime," Craig said as he glanced at his watch, "and someone has to lead his op team through some last-minute drills."

"Don't worry, we will be ready. And Doc," Greg said as he turned away from the stage and laughed with evil delight, *"nooothing* will go wrong with your speech."

"Prick," he said without malice and a bit of humor. Knowing his friend was trying to get him to relax before the rally.

A blond woman, his aide, approached him and said, "Everyone who is not on duty or is already in the know is present and waiting for you, sir."

A crowd of almost 200 GC was loosely gathered to his left. "Thank you, Norma. Please ensure the guards know not to let anyone in or out without my permission from now on." The young lady performed a picture-perfect eye roll. Doc chuckled. "Humor me, and yes, I'm nervous."

Like a mother with a recalcitrant child, she took the nearly empty glass from him, handed him a few notecards, and said as she turned to do his bidding, "Good luck, sir."

Normally, they would have held such an important meeting inside for the sake of secrecy, but they did not have a room spacious enough to hold their current population. The need for hiding from society was close to an end anyway. Even still, he would not give into hubris and allow fate to interfere with their plans—four heavily armed, hyper-protective guards patrolled the perimeter to keep their secrets safe. Doc stepped onto the makeshift stage, and someone in the crowd used a two-fingered whistle to quiet them down. The electricity in the air was palpable. He gazed out at the people. *His people.* And reveled in their adoration.

After a moment of pregnant silence, he spoke, "Brothers and sisters, the day has finally arrived to strike a blow for our planet. Gone are the days of sitting on our hands and doing nothing. Gone are the days of being a mosquito to the corporate entities raping this land."

The applause and shouting were thunderous and intoxicating for him. He allowed it to continue for a while and then interrupted them, "We will reclaim our birthright to have clean air, pristine waters, and to peacefully coexist with nature."

Glancing at the notecard for a moment, he said, "According to the UN, 'the Earth is in the midst of a mass extinction of life.' Scientists estimate that 150-200 species of plant, insect, bird and mammal become extinct every 24 hours. According to biologists, this is nearly 1,000 times the 'natural' or 'background' rate and is greater than anything the world has experienced since the vanishing of the dinosaurs nearly 65 million years ago."

The mob became angry, and they cursed and screamed. His speech worked them up as he had planned. They needed to have the proper motivation to do their next hard task. After they were committed, it wouldn't matter anymore.

"Your government has done nothing for this beleaguered planet. The corporations don't give a shit about anything except their bottom lines, as they poison the earth and the sky. The chemical companies create Frankenstein plants without considering whether their abominations will wipe out the natural flora humankind has relied on for sustenance for thousands of years. Cars continue to spew their poisons into the air. And lastly, too few of your fellow human beings bother to look up from their damn phones long enough to give more than a passing thought to the fact we have a garbage island in the Pacific Ocean twice the size of Texas or the frightening reality: the world's glaciers are melting at a rate five times faster than they were in the 1960s. My children… we can wait no longer for others to fix this problem. We will die before others pull their heads out. We must act today!"

If he thought the crowd was worked up before, he was wrong. It was a frenzy now.

At that moment, Craig nodded to a small group of volunteers gathered near the stage. They picked up small cardboard boxes and then handed out small vials of liquid to everyone present.

Doc recognized he would be guilty of some pretty high-handed theatrics with this next part of this assembly, but he also counted on the human desire to have a stake in something bigger than themselves.

He held up a small vial of pale-greenish solution and made a toasting motion, saying, "My friends, we have been patient and cunning. Our enemies have no idea of the audacity of our plan. Their shortsightedness allowed us to become what we are today, a force to be reckoned with. We will no longer spike log truck tires. We have a holy purpose now. The GC's leadership core authorized the creation of a virus capable of wiping out the scourge of the Earth: humankind. This weapon is fast acting, and in a matter of months, we will have this planet virtually to ourselves."

Shocked silence replaced the anger and exultation from earlier, and Craig knew the next few moments were crucial to making this all work. Eight men and women in the back of the crowd discretely held modified AR-15s at the ready. *This has to work,* he thought privately and forged through his nervousness.

"Now is no time for half-measures; as I outlined before, we are at a crossroads. We can blithely wander down the path of destruction with all the other sheeple, or we can choose a new course. Will you give Gaia a chance to heal and mend as she truly deserves? From the ashes of this dysfunctional world, we will create a new, better society that respects its home. Our mother needs our assistance! Help her! I know this is hard, but we all need to have the strength to act. Only then will we righteously deserve the title of *Gaia's Children!*"

The applause was meager at this pause, but then they grew in volume.

Raising his vial to chest level, he unstopped it and dramatically elevated it above his head. His disciples did the same with their glass tubes. "Thousands of these vials of the virus antidote have been distributed to our GC family, and soon, they will be discreetly given to those we love and trust. In a week, we will all be safe from the plague we will release upon the desecrators. There will be no more 'us' and 'them.' Every one of your descendants will praise you for your decisive action. Very soon… we kick off a new age. Have courage, my friends; we will soon be in Paradise together."

At that moment, he downed the liquid quickly and greedily watched as everyone did the same—except three. Thinking they were invisible within the crowd, these rebels surreptitiously dumped the contents of their vials on the ground.

Craig's eyes narrowed in anger, and he made eye contact with the leader of the gunmen in the back and gave a slight nod. The man had been scanning the crowd for holdouts and had observed the two men and a woman reject the generous gift they were given. But Doc could resume reveling in his moment now, safe in the knowledge their three bodies would never be found. Hopping off the stage, Craig glad-handed his GCers like he was a politician who had just won an election. Those gathered needed to feel like they had made the correct decision, and even if it was painful, it would ultimately allow humankind to survive on this planet for millennia to come.

But just in case, those four heavily armed soldiers on guard about the perimeter would stay there to discourage any further second thoughts. Fortunately, they would not have to guard the grounds for very long.

# Chapter 4



*June 30, Saturday — 8pm — Elks Lodge, Ontario*

Zander shared the FDA announcement with them two weeks ago. It had stated that Imagine Lab's Leukemia cure, Picadone, worked as promised in all test subjects except one who also suffered from Aplastic Anemia.

Dr. Lorenzen was already attacking the problem and was hopeful she could overcome this obstacle. But there would be time to finetune the treatment as they prepared to produce the viral solution for limited distribution to patients who didn't include people suffering from this rare blood disease.

Meanwhile, the world now knew a small lab on the Oregon-Idaho border had successfully delivered a blow to cancer, and nearly 400,000 people currently diagnosed with Leukemia were given hope. As exciting and important as this news was, Silvia didn't have the time or the energy to revel in her son's triumph.

Two months ago, she had decided, maybe foolhardily, to take the FDA at their word on when a decision would come through. A few called in favors secured the Elks Lodge in Ontario on the appropriate date. The only difficulty with getting the space on such late notice was they could not get into it until the Santos'

Quinceanera was finished, so the dinner would be later than usual. Now, all she had to do was plan a party worthy of this momentous accomplishment.

Fortunately, the announcement came on the 15th. Unfortunately, that left her with two scant weeks to engage a caterer, hire a band, buy decorations, rent lighting and sound equipment, and send out invitations. Thank God a small army of local saints volunteered to help out, or it would have been too much for one woman to carry out.

One way or another, it would be done tonight. She was more than tired, but it was the exhaustion one feels when much has been accomplished. She studied the hall with unadulterated admiration for their handiwork. The hall was awash in the Crystal's Cure scarlet red and white. Red had been her daughter's favorite color. Groups of 10 red and white balloons festooned each round table. The tables would hold about 8-10 people and were covered with alternating red and white tablecloths.

Her table centerpieces were the *piece de resistance* of her decorations. A long-necked glass sculpture filled with water was in the middle of each table. A single red rose was suspended in the water with two white floating candles. These were placed on circular mirrors which were sprinkled with red rose petals and white plastic gems. A nice touch, indeed. As she made her way around the hall, a bronze fire department occupancy placard caught her eye, and she grimaced. "Not to exceed 500 persons." Chief Hansen had engineered several fundraisers for the foundation and was planning to attend the gala, so she hoped he might use a little fuzzy math tonight.

The stage sat on the south side of the room. It was similarly adorned as the room tables, but a giant banner was draped above it with "Crystal's Cure," "Congratulations, Imagine Lab staff!" and "Thank you all donors, patrons, and Ontario!"

The microphones and speakers bracketed the family table on the stage for the obligatory speeches and thank you's following the meal. To the stage's left, a dozen tuxedo-wearing, big-band musicians were arranging their seating and tuning up their instruments. They would play quietly until after dinner. After the speeches, the dance would begin in earnest. Everything looked perfect. The only thing Silvia had to worry about now was how the food would turn out. She turned to her right to head toward the kitchen, when she espied a familiar figure heading her way. *Damn, Wesley looks dashing in his tux with a red cummerbund and bow tie.* Even after all these years, she never tired of appreciating his handsome looks. She beamed at him.

"Hi, sweetheart," Wesley said with a cherubic look on his face.

"Hi, my dessert hound," she said as she wet her finger and rubbed off what was most likely powdered sugar from his chin. He had the decency to look abashed for a moment and then rationalized his pilfering by saying,

"Well, someone has to taste test Cathy's hard work." Wes loved his sweets.

"You keep telling yourself that," she said as she poked him softly in the ribs, "and I will have to put this doctor on dietary restriction." They laughed at her teasing, and Wes gave her a kiss.

Then he looked about the hall in amazement and awe, "Silvia, you have outdone yourself. Everyone is going to be knocked out."

Silvia blushed and said, "I just wanted to show everyone how much I appreciate what they did to make this happen. To have a celebration of life."

"Well, they will love it. Good timing, too, because it seems like half of Ontario is at our gates." Party attendees in bright-colored dresses and black formalwear were streaming in the door and signing the guest book as they entered the room. Making an extravagant bow to her, Wes made a crook in his arm and offered it to her. She laughed and put her arm through his as they greeted their friends and charity patrons.

*Meanwhile, outside Ontario — 8:25pm.*

Greg Mundst and his hand-picked group of *Gaia's Children* parked their two pick-up trucks in a predetermined, heavily forested area just off Forest Road #138. When the engines were cut, eight men and women exited their vehicles and hung their night-vision goggles about their necks.

*It always gets dark faster in the forest*, Greg mused, and that was true tonight. But on the road, the last twilight moments provided enough light to see even without their headlights on. Soon, they would need the devices to make their way among the trees and fulfill their final objective.

Checking his watch, he grunted in approval. *Not sure why Doc insisted the op had to be tonight at this time, but who am I to argue.* His troops formed up in a line behind the trucks, and he did a quick visual inspection. The soldiers wore black from head to toe and had matching, non-reflective face paint. If he was being honest, this wasn't so much an inspection as it was a chance to look into their eyes and assess their state of mind: nervous. Well, that was okay. It would keep them on their toes and not be too complacent.

For two months, Greg molded this group into soldiers, and they had prepared for this mission during the last week and a half. He knew all their drills and practice would erase their nerves and allow them to complete their assignment. But their intensive training wasn't the only thing the GC did to guarantee this operation would succeed.

Doc did not want to leave anything to chance, so they had planted a GC operative at the site two months before they had even begun training for the mission. Their "insider" had given them the layout of the place, as well as some key details—such as the security camera placement, patrols, and other measures the company employed.

The team entered the woods in two groups. Each put on their night vision goggles, transforming their surroundings into an otherworldly ghostly green. The other team headed off to do their part: damage some of the corporation vehicles and break a few windows. A diversion. Greg's mission was far more important.

*Ontario Elks Lodge — 8:30pm.*

The party was in full swing, and everyone seemed to enjoy themselves, but Silvia couldn't relax. It was her duty to make everything perfect. Gliding among guests, she tried to make contact with everyone. But after a while, she wanted to congratulate the people responsible for making this happy occasion possible.

Finally, tucked away in one corner of the big hall, she saw the cluster of people she was looking for. As is oftentimes the case, co-workers have two nasty habits: they hang out with each other outside of the workplace, and they talk shop. This group was doing both when she interrupted them.

"There you are, welcome to my humble little *soiree,*" Silvia said with a saucy tone.

Lise snorted, which was incongruous with her elegant appearance. She wore a lavender and black ankle-length evening gown punctuated by a stunning black opal necklace accentuating her *décolletage.* "If this is humble, then I would hate to see your idea of pretentious. Would you agree, Rohit?"

Dr. Tamboli looked disheveled in his tuxedo but attempted to rise to the occasion by slicking back his black hair into a somewhat modern style. "Haven't been to many parties, but this is the best I can remember. Thank you, Silvia."

She blushed and said, "I'm delighted with how it turned out. But I do have one request for you all, and I mean this in the nicest way. Get your butts out there and enjoy this special night with your guests. They are here for you."

"I know that, but . . ."

"'But me' no buts, young man," Silvia interrupted. "You little geniuses get to hide in your lab all day. I've had to glad-hand thousands to make that possible. If I tell you to let others share in this victory. . ."

"All right, all right," Zander raised his hands in surrender, "should've known better than. . ."

"If you value your life, you better not finish that sentence," Silvia gave him her best unwavering death glare.

Everyone in the group laughed as Zander raised both hands in surrender, looked to his co-workers, and said, "Don't know about you guys, but I'm not sticking around to see if she has a Plan B for recalcitrant medical professionals."

Chuckling at the exchange between Zander and Silvia, the rest of his team backed away, much as had their retreating leader.

Silvia shook her head in amusement and went in search of other wrinkles needing ironing.

*Outside Ontario — 9:15pm.*

Giving a 'move out' signal with his right hand, Greg and his group headed through the trees at a slow lope. In no time, they reached an eight-foot-tall security chain-link fence topped with circular loops of concertina wire.

Once at the fence, they headed approximately 300 feet east of the entrance, to a spot where a copse of trees encroached on the fence's usual treeless buffer zone. Two minutes with a wire snip, and they were through. According to their intel, only a half dozen cameras were on the property, and he intended to erase those recordings before they left. The way he saw it, the only tricky part of this mission was the two-man security patrol moving about the grounds.

Doc was very specific about dealing with the guards—do nothing that would cause the company to cancel their party the following day. So, during their planning stages, they decided to use Tasers and not guns in case of a confrontation with watchmen. To make things even more interesting, the insider reported that the guards carried 9 mil handguns. Greg's team would likely have the element of surprise, but the sentinels would have an advantage in range and the amount of ammo they could fire at the intruders. Greg sincerely hoped it didn't come to that.

Needlessly, he pointed at their objective. They headed to the second largest building of the compound, the maintenance garage. The door was closed but not locked. They ducked inside. Not closing the door for fear of losing their only ambient light, two small courtyard halogen lamps. During their original planning, they hoped they could get in and out before someone noticed the open door.

Even with the dim otherworldly green light of their night vision goggles, Greg could tell the day shift had attempted to spiff up the place a bit. A wispy coating of sawdust covered the floor. Apparently, it had escaped the broom's attempts to banish it. The near wall was overlaid with peg board and was nearly covered with Sharpie pen outlines of the tools and their proper places.

The place smelt of oil or other petroleum lubricants. Further scanning the area, he counted about 20 plastic 4x8 tables and plenty of the ubiquitous metal folding chairs skirting them.

Festive cloths covered the tabletops, as well as a red and white banner hanging from the rafters announcing, "100 years of healthy forest management, here is to 100 more!" He couldn't help quietly chuckling at the irony of their hubris. His squad didn't have to move too much further into the shop before finding what they came for.

A large table designated for picnic beverages was in the corner of the room. Two orange 10-gallon coolers sat on the table along with a couple dozen plastic pitchers and enough red solo cups to satisfy any frat party organizer. One cooler was marked with a black Sharpie "Water," and the other labeled "Lemonade."

Bingo.

As Greg was taking something out of his jacket, he heard a noise outside the shop. The strike group quickly but silently found cover under tables and behind tool cabinets and sited their stun weapons on the door. A seeming eternity later, the guards and a pair of flashlight beams moved without haste toward the open garage door.

"Thought the garage door was closed last time we came through here, Sam," said one guard.

"Can't remember. The nights all seem to run together."

"Well, humor me and make sure nothin' funny's going on." The two entered the structure, and a flashlight beam searched the wall for the light switch. *So much for everything going according to plan,* Greg thought grimly as he slipped his finger inside the gun and tensed, ready to fire. His force could "handle" the guards, but there was a pretty decent chance one of the guards wouldn't get stunned by their short-range weapons. If that happened, things were going to get messy.

At that moment, everyone heard the distinctive sound of breaking glass coming from across the compound.

One guard said, "Damn kids are shooting at the trucks again. Run! We can still put the fear of God into them."

Thirty seconds later, Greg exhaled noisily as he heard the guards sprint toward the 'vandals.' He returned his taser to its shoulder harness and gingerly took out a small, padded box containing two vials.

These test tubes, he knew, were unlike the vials Doc held earlier; these were red. He had a sneaking suspicion the viruses had no colorful tint, and his friend was being a little dramatic, but he couldn't fault him for making it obvious which was which.

Opening the cooler marked "Water," Greg peered inside. *No good dumping a red fluid into an empty cooler. Some fool would wash it out with my luck.* Their luck held, though. The day crew had dutifully filled both liquid containers with either water or lemonade. He dumped the flavorless vial into the 'water,' took a nearby stirring spoon, and gave it a vigorous swirl. Same for the lemonade container.

Then, he pointed to the door, and his team exited. They ran north to the back of the administration office, entered using a key, erased the recent video footage per instructions they were given, and were out the door in minutes. He had to admit that having someone on the inside had made his job exponentially easier. According to his watch, his team was only two minutes behind schedule. The other group would have exited the compound and returned to the vehicles.

Meanwhile, Greg's platoon would take a more circuitous route back to their hole in the security fence, which allowed them to avoid all the security cameras in the yard. Once through the fence, they all trotted back to the vehicles. When the GC troops reunited at the vehicles, they were much too disciplined to talk, but there were plenty of fist bumps and shoulder clapping. They piled into the trucks and quietly departed with no one suspecting their true motive.

Adrenaline coursed through Greg's system. It was exhilarating to do something illegal and not get caught. A sign to the left of the company access road appeared in the moonlight.

It proudly announced: Forestco Products.

*The Elks Lodge — 10:05pm.*

As most of the party guests finished their dessert, Silvia moved to the microphone at the front of the bandstand and motioned to the crowd for their attention unsuccessfully; a two-fingered whistle by a bystander did the trick, and the crowd quieted and waited for Silvia to speak.

"I want to thank everyone for coming. Tonight, we gather here to celebrate life." She paused for effect. "Twenty years ago, Wesley, my son, and I sat down to talk about Zander's vision: a cure for his sister's killer. As parents, we wanted to help our son realize his dream. But you all know it would be impossible for us to fund such a project. So, we started Crystal's Cure, unsure how people would respond. We needn't have worried. Everyone's generosity truly humbles us. I'm proud to announce that since its inception almost 20 years ago, we have collected 148 million dollars..." Silvia had to halt her speech because the applause was so thunderous that she could not be heard for almost a whole minute.

"Folks, you must stop that, or my two-minute speech will take all night." The crowd laughed as she wiped an appreciative tear from her eye.

"As you all know, the FDA has given the okay for Imagine Lab's anti-cancer treatment: Picadone." The crowd clapped and cheered. "If all goes smoothly, our treatment for Leukemia will be available within the next two weeks." More applause.

"Lastly, I also have an exciting announcement to make beyond what I have already shared with you. My family and the Crystal's Cure Board have unanimously decided to provide our cure to everyone, regardless of country, race, religion, etc., for our cost. Our goal was always to help people suffering from this disease, not make a profit. This announcement will go out to the world press on Monday."

If the applause had been loud before, it seemed like a mere warm-up to the explosion of sound as the assembly rose as one and shouted and cheered.

Wesley and Zander got up from their places at the table and went to her, and each grabbed one of her hands. The three of them raised their interlocked hands in victory. Nothing could bring Crystal back, but this was the next best thing.

*Outside Ontario — 10:59pm.*

The ride back to the compound gave Greg enough time to ponder this night's activities. It wasn't the first time he thought about the implications of this action, but now they seemed more real.

It no longer was some esoteric philosophical debate. Very soon, people were going to die because of what they had done. Hitler had killed a mere six to ten million people, and he had been vilified for eighty years. Greg and his team could easily be responsible for the deaths of billions. What did that make him?

The thought was disturbing enough to make the bile roil in his stomach. *What if we are wrong?* There was still time to go back and undo the coming holocaust. No! Those were the reactions of someone weak. He needed to be strong to face this future. Craig said the Earth would become uninhabitable very soon. He believed him.

And yet, if a cosmic scale did exist, could saving the Earth balance out all those deaths? Or an even better question might be, could his conscience bear the guilt?

These dark thoughts were interrupted when someone handed him a flask and clapped him on the shoulder. Greg turned to his trooper and plastered what he hoped looked like a jubilant smile on his face, and then watched the driver turn on the truck's headlights. The sudden brightness hurt his eyes, but he forced himself to stare at the trees as the truck hurried down the road.

Taking a big swig from the bottle, Greg felt the fiery liquid burn all the way down. Once his stomach settled, he joined in the excited voices of his troops in the truck.

Afraid to be alone with his thoughts.

# Chapter 5



*June 30, Saturday — 12:05pm — Forestco Inc., North of Ontario*

*Another gorgeous day in paradise,* Janice thought without sarcasm as she drove to work on a golden Saturday afternoon. She hadn't always felt this way about her drive to work. Not long ago, she was a road warrior in the Los Angeles County area.

Back then, a good day was one in which her travel time to work and back was a mere two hours a day. Today, it encompassed one traffic light and 10 minutes of drive time. Heaven.

Conversely, acclimating to quiet Ontario took some getting used to, especially for a young lady. She still had yet to find anything resembling a dating scene within 100 miles. Although disappointing, other undertakings, such as her receptionist job at Forestco, mitigated her lack of a love life. A local logging company with a fleet of log trucks and the facilities to keep them running was located only 8 miles from town.

Surprisingly, the position took up much of her time, so it was a godsend that she treasured her coworkers and her new commute down this county road. The drive was always surprising. One day she would marvel at mighty ponderosa pines, with their soaring trunks and clouds of green needles sparsely scattered about the tree.

On another trip, the slender but tall lodge-pole pine caught her eye. During other commutes, the omnipresent Oregon Douglas fir dominated her view. And on special days, she had even seen a few Western junipers hugging the outskirts of a copse of trees.

Breathtaking.

A sudden fancy of Janice's demanded she pull her sporty, late-model, blue Toyota Prius to the side of the gravel road and get out. Dappled sunshine caressed her face, and the lack of the developed world's artificial hubbub allowed her to revel in the multitude of wildlife noises around her: bugs, bees, and birds going about their routines.

Tipping her head back, she closed her eyes and drank in as many of these delectable sensations as possible. It was sublime. Alas, as much as she would have loved to prolong her "nature break," she knew they expected her at the picnic. With a longing sigh, she got back into the car.

*No way I could've had an Emerson moment on the way to work back home. Someone would've run my ass over for certain.*

The Forestco sign appeared in moments, and she turned left onto the company road and drove the quarter mile up to the compound. A bright and cheery poster on the left-hand side of the access road announced: Welcome to Forestco's 100th birthday celebration! A nearby volunteer directed her to a grassy spot west of the entrance.

Once parked, Janice headed in. The day crew had prepared the grounds yesterday, so she had seen all their decorations and preparations. But nothing prepared her for the mass of humanity before her. The entire open area between buildings was filled with people—picnic blankets laid out, lawn chairs, sun umbrellas of every imaginable bright color, footballs, and frisbees flying, a jumpy house, a dazzling yellow dunk tank, couples holding hands, kids laughing, screaming, crying (sometimes at the same time) and smells of mouthwatering barbeque.

One item, among many, on Janice's Forestco to-do list was to hire Uncle Jack's BBQ—the tastiest food Ontario had to offer. Her boss authorized Janice to order a prodigious amount of Unkle Jack's famous smoked ribs and to slow-cook a prodigious amount of prime rib. Skip, her boss, gave explicit orders, "Order a ton! I'll be damned if we run out of food halfway through this thing!"

So, the amount of beef she ordered was stupendous, and so was the bill. But she understood his insistence because another thing on her busy agenda was to send out invitations to the event. The list included all their employees and their families, suppliers, forestry department workers, and even company bigwigs from Portland to share in the Founder's Day celebration. If everyone attended, they expected 300-500 people.

As Janice wound her way through the parked cars toward the food serving area, she saw in her peripheral vision a UFO coming at her head. Ducking, the object hit a car beside her and exploded—water and small blue rubber pieces now decorating her outfit. She whipped her head to her left and made eye contact with a horrified-looking, flaming, redheaded 8-year-old boy. A moment later, a laughing young girl appeared from behind a nearby parked car; his spitting image, brilliant hair, and all. When confronted with the authority figure before her, the miscreant's sister's smile melted like snow in the morning sun.

Upset at getting wet and having an onery streak, Janice decided to have some fun, so she asked in her most imperious voice. "Did you know those balloons are supposed to be used in the water balloon toss later this afternoon?"

The boy looked through ragged bangs up at her and said in a breathless, hurried voice, "But these are extras; they had no water in 'em; me and Sissy were worried they would go to waste. Didn't mean it... um, ma'am."

A smile tried to worm its way onto Janice's severe expression. Lucky for her, the boy was staring at his muddy feet, not her. "Well, maybe I should take you and your purloined goods to your parents, and you can explain your rationalization for larceny to your mother."

Janice put her hands on her hips and tried to imitate her mother's traditional pose for recalcitrant children. The boy looked confused until he heard the word "mother."

He blanched and started stuttering.

"Hon-ne-nest-tly la-a-dy, I didn't mean to hi-it you."

Janice couldn't maintain her stern demeanor another moment longer, and she began to howl.

The boy's confusion was complete. Was he in trouble, or was this woman crazy?

Janice put her hands on the boy and girl's shoulders and lowered herself to eye level with them, and said, "I'm joshing you, kid. What're your names?"

He hesitated momentarily because he was deciding if he could tell a stranger this information. The stranger's laughter and broad smile encouraged him to trust her. "My name is George, and this is my sister Pammy."

"Well, George and Pammy, tell you what. If you promise not to fill any more balloons until you get home, I will not report you to the proper authorities."

George looked confused again but perceived he had been spared the heavy hand of authority today. He smiled a giant grin, which was missing a few prominent teeth, and said, "Thank you, lady." Crossing his heart with the fingers of his right hand, George ran away with his sister in full chase mode.

"It's the least I can do, kid," she said to no one.

Brushing off a few blue balloon fragments from her shirt, Janice resumed her quest to get a plate full of ribs, but halfway there, she ran into her boss, Skip Jelks. A pleasant enough sort, but for some reason she just loved to pick on him. Maybe because Skip acted like her younger brother, Mason. *Go easy on him, he can't help that he has lived here his whole life,* she thought sarcastically.

"Was wondering if you were going to make it. The caterer started serving food 10 minutes ago," he said with the hint of a whine in his voice.

"Sorry Skip, got stuck in traffic." He looked at her. *Oookay, moving on,* she thought with exasperation. "Boy, you guys know how to put on a spread. Everything looks fantastic, and I could smell the ribs half a mile away."

Beaming with pride, he said, "It's better than I had expected. A lot of that is due to you. Thanks, Janice." She followed his eye when Skip paused and watched three men dressed in tailored business suits walking around the grounds smiling and shaking hands with everyone they passed. "Let's pray they're as delighted with all this as I am."

"Guessing those aren't locals?" she said with a mischievous grin.

"You got that right. Forestco decided to send out some top brass from Portland. In fact, the short man with dark hair is the owner's son, Jake Masters. Going to be our boss next year when his father retires. Wanna meet him?"

"Would I? Maybe I can hit him up for a promotion and a raise." Skip gave her a mortified look and realized she was playing with him only when she gave a throaty laugh. He chuckled without enthusiasm momentarily and then led her toward the out-of-towners.

Janice sized up Mr. Masters as they approached: an expensive, styled haircut, a nice linen suit, which seemed a little over the top for this affair but was lightweight enough not to be too uncomfortable as the day warmed up. As she watched him, it was obvious he had a politician's knack for making the employees around him feel like they were the most important person in the world. When he saw her, he smiled and shook her hand.

"Who do we have here, Skip?"

"Jake Masters, this is Janice Lesh. Been working in our office for two months and is the best." He lowered his voice to a stage whisper and added, "She is way overqualified for her post, and I thank my lucky stars to have her."

"Pleased to meet you, Ms. Leash."

"It's Lesh, but please call me Janice."

"Well, then call me Jake."

"So, Janice, what are your impressions of our little company?" Jake said.

Janice gave Skip a sideways glance and then refocused on Jake and said, "I love the people and being in the forest. After living in LA all my life, it is a marvel to gaze out my office window and see a forest. Can you tell me if you plan on cutting all these beautiful trees down any time soon?" she said with an innocuous look.

A groan emanated from Skip's direction, and when she cut a look at him, she was pretty sure he was about to have a coronary. Poor Skip. But she had been right about Jake being able to take a joke, though, because he was laughing with gusto.

"If I ever need brutal honest opinions, I know where to come. But I can appreciate someone who speaks her mind. I was going to glad-hand for a bit more, but I'm famished. Wanna join me for a bite? I'm buying." His gray eyes danced with this last comment.

"How can I refuse? You're in for a treat. Uncle Jack's the best."

The small caravan of Jake and his employees made its way to the garage and got into one of the two food lines. As they waited, Janice saw her one objective for the day. Technically, her "job" was done as soon as the strike team used her keys and intel to complete their mission last night, but Doc was always a stickler for details. He insisted she come today and perform one final task—check on Greg's team's handiwork.

Two bright orange coolers sat in the corner of the room. And before them was a continual line of happy picnickers—drinking their water and lemonade.

It was only a matter of time now.

Janice couldn't help but feel a sense of pride in fulfilling her role in Craig's plan. She almost couldn't wait to report back to him so she could sooner see his special look of affirmation and love, which made her feel invincible. *Can't let this food go to waste, though.*

Strutting up to the drink line, Janice waited her turn and poured herself two cups of lemonade. She smiled. Then, she returned to Jake and handed him the drink as he gave her a paper plate. In a mock toast, they clicked solo cups, and each took a small sip. She watched him partake of the beverage over the rim of her own while she pretended to drink.

For Janice, there was absolutely no temptation to test the efficiency of the antivirus Doc had given them. She followed Jake to the food table, grabbed a pair of tongs, and placed a short stack of ribs on her platter. *I will miss working with these people.*

# Chapter 6



*July 2, Monday — 9am — Jelks' Residence*

With silent steps, Sarah Jelks entered her tidy but small master bedroom after dropping off her two kids, Tyler and Samantha, at May Roberts Elementary School.

Normally, they didn't have to worry about taking the kids to school during the summer, but the school's principal, Tom Marx, had written a successful grant securing financing for an ambitious three-year pilot program. The curriculum was promoted to parents as a way for younger students to learn valuable study skills and time management techniques. Last year was the program's first year, and 37 young people signed up.

One year later, the maximum of 90 children was reached before the end of March, with another dozen or so on a waiting list. It was a wonderful opportunity for her kids, but it was challenging for Sarah to drive them there because she had to leave for work an hour before classes began.

Therefore, Skip had to take the kids to school, and she would pick them up. But last night, her husband was feeling so drained he called in sick, so she decided to take the day off, pamper her ailing mate, and take the kids to school.

Sarah finally reached the master bathroom, partially shut the door, and turned on the light. But her concern for waking him was unneeded because Skip hadn't moved since she saw him last or after the light hit his face. Sitting beside him on the bed, she put the back of her hand against his forehead. He was hot—scary hot. A doctor's visit might be in order if his temperature was as high as she feared. The thermometer was in its usual spot in the medicine cabinet. Now, the hard part—waking her husband.

"Skip." No response. "Skip!" Louder and more urgent. A muffled moan. "Thank God," she said as she took a second to let her heartbeat slow back to normal. "Hey honey, let's take your temperature."

Groaning, Skip opened his eyes and tried to focus. "Can't remember feeling this crappy before. What did you say?"

"I need to take your temperature. You're very hot. I heard on the news that it's hospital time when an adult has a temperature of 104 or more. Get up."

With great effort, Skip got himself to sitting. Propping him up with a pillow behind his back, she then presented the thermometer to him, and he dutifully opened his mouth and lifted his tongue. While she waited for the instrument to signal, she gave him a visual once-over. She didn't like his color, and he was sweating profusely.

After a muted noise, she removed the thermometer and checked it. 103 degrees. Frowning, Sarah eased him back to lying down, put a wet towel on his forehead, and covered him with a mere bedsheet.

"Get some sleep, dear," she said as she closed the door to their bedroom and headed to make a phone call. When Sarah got to the front room, she called her friend Dede, who was Jakob's wife—Skip's foreman.

Two rings later, Dede answered. "Hello?"

"Hi Deeds. It's Sarah. Can I ask you a question?"

"Of course. What's up?"

"Skip's had a fever since about eight last night: fever, pale, and no energy. When he talked to his secretary this morning, she told him there were dozens of employees who called in sick. How's Jake?"

"Funny you should ask," Dede said, "Jake came home from work about half an hour ago complaining of a fever. Gave him some medicine and sent him to bed. Do you think the food at the picnic was bad?"

"Don't know. It's weird; Skip never gets sick. Must be bad if he got it. Hope we don't catch it from him. Frankly, Skip is worthless as a caregiver—might notice if one of us has a bullet wound or something, but otherwise, he can be pretty oblivious." Both women laughed at the observation.

"Well, hon, I will keep you posted if anything changes with Jake. Talk to you soon."

"Okay, Deeds will do the same. Hope Jake bounces back fast."

As she hung up, Sarah stroked her throat. Was it the beginning of a sore throat? Or maybe talking about their husbands' sicknesses made her imagine the symptom. Either way, she decided she did not want whatever Skip had got, so she curled up on the sofa, just in case.

A few hours later, she was startled awake by her phone ringing loudly and vibrating on the coffee table before her. In a half-stupor, she picked up her cell and answered it.

The cobwebs in her mind immediately parted when she heard the pathetic, hurting voice of her 7-year-old, Tyler, "Mommy? I'm sick… sissy, too. We want to come home. Lots of others sick, too."

Her momma-bear instinct kicked in, and she cooed, "Of course, sweetheart. I will be there in 10 minutes. Can you be a big boy and watch your sister for me until I get there?"

"Yes, Momma. I can," Tyler said in his best big-boy voice.

Suddenly, Sarah replayed in her head what her son said earlier about other children. A sixth sense told her their sickness was a pattern and not a coincidence, but she had to test her theory. "Can you let me talk to a teacher?"

No reply. Tyler must have forgotten to answer, as the next thing she heard was a harried feminine voice saying, "This is Mrs. Phillips. Is this Mrs. Jelks?"

"It is. My son said there were other kids sick today?"

"Yes, we've had about 40 kids either get sick last night or have gotten to feel pretty puny as the day progressed. It's frightening how rapidly this is spreading in only a few hours. We are wiping down everything with bleach, but we might need to shut down a few days until this flu passes. Why?"

With each word, Sarah was more certain her premonition was correct. "Sorry to be a pain, but can you answer one more question?"

"Sure."

"Do the sick children have parents working for Forestco? My husband and some other workers there are sick, as well."

"Give me a sec and I can check with our attendance secretary." The minutes crawled by like an ant trying to traverse a highway. When Mrs. Phillips got back on the phone, she said, "You were right, Mrs. Jelks. Most of the kids have parents at the mill. Maybe someone should check into it. Hope we get a handle on this; I haven't seen anything move this quick in all my years of teaching."

"Well, if we're all going to get it, let's hope it leaves as fast as it showed up. Could you tell Tyler I will be there as fast as I can? Thanks." She hung up the phone.

As Sarah got off the couch, she suddenly felt hot.

"Crap! A lot of good taking a nap did."

After she picked up the kids from May Roberts, they were only too willing to go to bed. Taking hand towels out of the hall cupboard, Sarah soaked them with cold water and put a cloth on each tiny head. *Children done. Hopefully, Skip is doing better,* she thought.

It took a substantial amount of shaking before Skip would wake, and when asked, he only mumbled something unintelligible and went back to sleep. It was all for the better because she didn't feel like talking either. She grabbed a few more hand towels and ran them under the faucet. After replacing Skip's, Sarah lay beside him, letting the blissful wet cold soothe her flaming forehead. She awoke around 2 pm with nausea and a splitting headache. Once the queasiness subsided a bit, she checked on Skip and the kids. The flu, or whatever this was, had her family in its firm grip. This didn't feel normal. Fear struck her heart, and she was no longer content to wait out this bug.

A moment later, she was calling Doctor Parks' number.

A familiar female voice said, "Hello?"

"Silvia. Hi, this is Sarah. Hate to be all business, but is Wes there?"

"No, my dear. He is out on a call. Seems like a lot of people under the weather today."

"Don't want to add to Wes' workload, but Skip came down with something last night. It took the kids and me a bit longer to get it. Nothing makes me feel stupider than asking a doctor to come and reassure me about a cold, but is there any chance you could have your husband stop by? Something about all this seems wrong, it..."

"Don't worry, Sarah," Silvia interrupted. "I will send him your way soon. It shouldn't take long; he is out on a call. Hang in there. We'll have you 'right as rain' soon."

"Thank you for humoring me. I worry about my family."

There was a slight catch of breath before Silvia replied, "I totally understand, dear. Sometimes, a mother's intuition shouldn't be ignored. Don't worry, Wes will be there soon; I promise."

Sarah decided to read her book in her comfy Lazy Boy recliner to pass the time. Even with her headache, it was tough trying to stay awake and focused. Fortunately, she didn't have to wait long before there was a knock at the door.

"Come in," she said as loudly as her throat could handle as she tried to put the footrest down on the recliner.

Dr. Parks entered with his black doctor's bag and a practiced, comforting smile. "Don't worry about getting up, Sarah," he said as he closed the front door.

"Thanks," she said as she gave up on trying to get the chair completely upright. "I didn't know what to do. Skip is scaring me and—"

"Shhh. No need to worry yourself. I know you have never been an alarmist. Now, let me look at you." With rehearsed ease, he performed his usual series of tests to assess her condition initially.

Then, he said with deadpan delivery, "Sarah, I have to tell you that . . . you are sick." She acknowledged his little joke with a slight nod but didn't have the energy to do anymore. "That bad, huh? It's uncanny that everyone I have seen today has the same symptoms. In every way I can tell, it is the flu, though I have no doubt it feels much worse. A fever never fails to make you always feel like you are dying. Lie back and rest while I check the kids and Skip."

Wes gave her his patented everything-is-going-to-be-okay smile, which never failed to make her feel protected. Feeling sheltered from danger in his care, she snuggled further into the chair and somehow fell asleep before he could return. An indeterminate time later, she was awoken by his gentle shoulder shaking. "As near as I can tell, you all have the same bug. If you don't mind, I would like to take some blood and see if we can figure out what is going on with you guys."

"Okay." She tried to give him another of her finest brave soldier smiles.

In a heartbeat, he had returned all his implements and her sample into his bag.

"You know the drill: drink lots of water, sleep, take aspirin as needed, and go to the hospital if anyone's temperature exceeds 104."

Wes patted her on the shoulder with great tenderness and let himself out. Sleep took her.

* * *

The room was dark when she woke with a start. It was disorienting to wake up in the chair and have no idea what time it was or even what day of the week.

A faint light in the kitchen allowed her to pick up her phone.

4:02 am, Tuesday, July 3.

When she tried to get out of the chair, she realized everything ached, even her eyes. It was tempting to give in to sleep once again when she heard a noise. Only then did it hit her; the noise must have woken her a moment ago, and the sound she heard was the scream of a terrified child: *Tyler!*

Adrenaline crashed into her system like a tidal wave, and she exploded from the chair, bolted across the front room, down the hall, and leaped through the kids' bedroom door.

The bedroom curtains were open, and a small patch of weak moonlight lit the room. A sound to the right. An ill-defined dark smudge hovered above her son's bed. The sound, a throat desperately trying to gain any bit of breath. Someone was trying to kill her child!

Without thought, Sarah launched herself at the figure and screamed like a banshee: a sound born of terror and hatred. She rained a torrent of blows upon the head and shoulders. The attacker didn't even glance up, so she switched tactics and reached around the head with both hands and tried to gouge out eyes.

This new tactic finally drew a response from the assassin—a feral sound and backhand that sent her flying across the room. Her flight ended when her head and back collided with her kids' toy chest. The finale of a 4th of July fireworks display appeared before her eyes. There was no detectable sound from Tyler now.

All she could be sure of was the assailant stood, turned, and faced her. It was then she saw his face in the faint moonlight. For a moment, Sarah slipped further into the unreality of this nightmare, and she didn't believe her eyes.

"Skip?" she said with equal parts confusion, unbelief, and anger. Could this be the gentle man who had never raised a hand against her? A sound. Did he snarl?

Once again, her intuition told her this was all wrong. So wrong. Her gut told her that she would end up like her son if she didn't move. A second burst of adrenaline exploded into her, demanding she distance herself from this monster. Back against the toy box, her only quick option was to lift her butt and scuttle across the floor like a crab so that she could get some distance between her and Skip.

Her movement triggered him, and he rushed toward her prone figure. Luckily, he tripped on some forgotten doll or block that had not been put away.

It was her chance to make a break for it. She sprang to her feet and ran for the kitchen. Minutes ago, she wouldn't have considered it, but now, in this confused insanity, her only thought was: get a knife. She only made it halfway down the hallway before a body hammered her into the wall, knocking the breath from her. Her attacker closed his hands around her throat and would have killed her if not for her reflexive self-defense move: her knee exploded into Skip's genitals. There was a grunt and a loosening of his grip on her throat.

Once she could finally take a gasp of air, there was a sharp pain in her chest and her vision refused to clear. But she ran for the kitchen in a panic. A bellow of pure rage reverberated off the walls behind her, which didn't sound quite human, and it terrified her beyond anything she had ever experienced before.

Sarah careened around the hallway dining room junction and bounced off the room's west wall before correcting her path into the kitchen. The light over the sink was on, so finding the knife block near the microwave was easy. She drew her weapon and spun to face her husband. A heartbeat later, he appeared in the doorway to the dining room and stood there mutely for a moment. Hoping to give him pause in his attack, she brandished the knife in front of her like a sword.

In this frozen moment, she begged him with all her being, "Skip. Please stop. We can work this out. I love you." The stress and terror made her shake so much that it was almost impossible to keep hold of the blade, and the tears fell unheeded down her cheeks.

As he continued to stare at her with hate-filled eyes, she began to count on the fact that when a rational person saw an eight-inch butcher knife pointed in his direction, he would reassess things.

It was a dangerous assumption.

Without a word, he charged her. Sarah put every ounce of strength she had into killing her husband.

But it was not enough.

The knife was aimed at his heart, and for a moment, it appeared she would successfully plunge it into his chest. But somehow, he managed to get his left arm in the way of the lethal blade. Time slowed down, like when someone is in an unavoidable car accident. She watched the knife blade pierce her husband's flesh and felt the jar of it hitting one of his main forearm bones.

Then, the momentum of her frenzied strike continued to fillet his arm's flesh until the blade exited at his elbow, and a 11-inch section of his forearm flapped open. Hanging from his arm by skin on the backside of the cut. Bone, muscle, nerves, tendons—all laid bare. If this macabre scene were not enough, a spray of his blood hit her in the chest and face.

The moment overloaded her senses. Sarah knew she was still in danger, but her body no longer seemed to be under her control. Frozen, she could only make eye contact with this insane *stranger*. There was no trace of Skip in those eyes. The loving man she had known for the past 12 years was gone. There was no recognition or emotional expression on his face, which was scarier than the anger evident in every action he made since she had awoken from her sleep. His eyes bore into her with all the passion his face did not reveal.

"Why are you doing this!" she screamed.

But there was no response except her former lover and friend viciously grabbing her hand with the knife and crushing it with his own. Bones popped until the weapon dropped from her senseless fingers. Then he released her hand and hit her with an uppercut, which lifted her off the ground and sent her sailing into the countertop behind her. For a second time that night, she tried to shake out the cobwebs in her head, and in a disconnected way, she wondered why her legs wouldn't work.

Her back scraped terribly on the quartz as her unresponsive legs slid from under her. Back broken, she watched in hopeless terror: a prisoner in her own body. Like a mad lion, Skip leaped upon her. His weight finished dragging her fully to the ground. The only option she had left was to hope someone could hear her.

"Help! Help me! Please, someone!" she screamed, though no one else was alive to hear her.

The monster grabbed her hair on the sides of her face and began to slam her head repeatedly on the floor. Mercifully, the darkness took her after the first few times her head made a crunching impact.

* * *

*The cry of a woman in distress awoke her. It was the first but by no means the last. With great sadness, she contemplated the tremendous suffering, fear, destruction, and death caused by the dissolution of the powerful spell.*

*It couldn't be helped, but what kind of monster would she be to callously applaud as the world burned? Solarum was getting stronger by the day, but this magicless world still held dominion over nearly everything on this planet.*

*But soon, her time would come.*

# Chapter 7



*July 2, Monday — 3:54 pm — Imagine Labs*

It wasn't unusual for Wes to stop by the lab. Now that he was semi-retired, he liked to visit Imagine Labs and hear about their latest developments. Not to meddle because medical research was not his forte, but to learn from and encourage this staff he had come to respect deeply.

What was unusual, Zander noted, was his father looked nervous. Most wouldn't have noticed, but for Zander, it put him on alert. His dad was as unflappable as a lot of medical professionals. Few, if any, patients like to see an anxious doctor examining them.

"Come in, Dad, and have a seat," Zander said.

"Thanks." A long moment of silence.

"Hell of a party you guys threw the other night. It meant a lot to all of us."

"Ah, yeah, it was great, huh?" his father said distractedly.

"What's wrong?"

"Well, to paraphrase a patient I saw earlier today," Wes began, "I don't want to sound an alarm and it turns out to be nothing, but I have a bad feeling about this Forestco outbreak. The phone has been ringing off the wall since last night, and I have made about 20 house calls since early this morning. I'm exhausted, so I hope that is not coloring my judgment, but I don't think so."

"Someone said something was going around, but I haven't heard much. What are the symptoms?"

"That's the crazy part. Most of my patients assume it's food poisoning because it seems to be only affecting people who attended the picnic. But none of my patients were throwing up or had diarrhea. Also, if they ate bad food on Saturday, they should have had symptoms long before Monday. On a hunch, I called Abby down at St. Alphonsus, and she told me they have been overwhelmed by people with the same complaints as mine: chills, 103+ temperatures, body aches, headaches, extreme lethargy."

"Classic flu symptoms," Zander commented.

"Yes, but why would this flu only hit people at a founder's picnic? I called Marge at Forestco. She confirmed my suspicions; everyone she could get ahold of had reported symptoms. In fact, she was going to head home after talking with me. If this is a flu, why that specific group? Why would everyone get symptoms at the same time? None of it makes sense."

His father had logically presented his argument, and Zander had a hard time disputing the case was unusual, even bizarre. Still, he didn't have any better insights than his father. "Okay Dad, I think you are onto something. But I assume you are here for something besides dropping a Rubik's Cube in my lap."

"You caught me," Wes admitted with an embarrassed grin. Reaching into his sport coat's vest pocket, his father removed three glass vials labeled with white identification stickers and put them on Zander's desk. "These are blood samples from my last three patients. Would you be willing to check them for me?"

"Of course, we will run a complete battery of tests on them."

"Thanks, and..."

"Let you know as soon as we find anything," Zander finished, smiling.

"If you had seen how much they were suffering, I just want to do something for them."

"Which is why your patients love you." Scooping the test tubes off the desk, Zander stood and gave his father a hug, and went in search of some help.

*15 minutes later in the staff room.*

Lise, Rohit, Ben, and Zander were sitting at a table furthest from the door, and Zander had just presented Wes' medical conundrum to his colleagues.

"...so, he's asking for our help analyzing these blood samples," Zander explained as he laid the three specimens before him.

"Not sure what we are discussing," Lise said matter-of-factly. "He's one of the principal supporters of Crystal's Cure and, subsequently, us. If the man wants our help, I say we owe it to him."

"Moreover," Rohit added, "if this is some kind of new bug, it would be crazy not to get in front of it if we can before it ravages Ontario or the surrounding area. Besides..."

"Great points," Ben said without waiting for his colleague to finish his thoughts, "but we're missing the bigger picture here. The FDA will be closely monitoring the first batches of Picadone for impurities. We need to keep our eyes on what is important. Other public health agencies are better geared for dealing with this flu outbreak. Let them handle this."

"Good points, everyone, but I think we have more than enough people to do quality assurance on the production lines and do this favor."

"Would we even consider this if it wasn't your father?" Ben said with biting derision. Zander's eyes narrowed in anger, but before he could respond, Lise backed him.

"What is gotten into you, Ben? We haven't gotten this far by sniping and fighting. Less than a week ago, we had our arms around each other while doing publicity photos and interviews."

But Zander had a pretty good idea where this attack was coming from. Earlier in the day, Rohit and Ben had paid a private visit to him in his office. Not everyone on staff was excited by his news that Imagine Labs would provide the drug for cost. Zander had always believed that the foundation was established to cure Leukemia, not make them rich. It had never occurred to him that these two men wanted to patent the formula and reap the financial rewards of their labors.

Maybe it was naïve, but he assumed everyone else also had altruistic motives. Looking back at the heated discussion, Zander could have pre-emptively told his staff what would happen if they found the cure. But when the lab had first started, it seemed the height of hubris to worry about such a thing. Neither man was satisfied with Zander's argument as they stormed out the door, and it wouldn't surprise him if he lost one or both men. He would have said Rohit and Ben were two of his closest friends a day ago. Now, he felt like a fool.

"I was hoping we could all agree to perform this test..." Zander began.

"Excuse me," Lise said, "but you don't need to ask our permission. You are the director of this facility, and we will perform these tests to help all our friends and neighbors." Her eyes bore into Ben's until he looked away.

"You heard her," Zander added. "Let's get these samples processed quickly so we can refocus on distributing Picadone to all who need it.

# Chapter 8



*July 3, Tuesday — 6:59am — Ontario Police Department*

The residents of Ontario liked their sheriff.

Long ago, they stopped voting for any other candidate besides Peter Alvardo. Which was okay with him; he liked the job—helping people. A 45-year-old trim man with a thick, black mustache, an impeccable khaki uniform, and a dog-eared Stetson. Some called him "McCloud," after the old TV show, but those who respected and liked him didn't call him Sheriff or Alvardo; they called him Pete. The 25-year-veteran law enforcement officer walked through the door of his 'actual' home, as his somewhat bitter ex-wife, Karen, christened it.

Truth be told, he did prefer the station house to his trailer. Seeing Pete in the lobby, Sam, a blonde, stocky 20-year-old who looked barely old enough to shave or get into an R-rated movie, buzzed him in through the glass door at the entrance of the building.

"Heya, boss," Sam said with unexpected enthusiasm and volume for this early in the morning.

"What's the word, Sam? Actually, unless Idahoans are invading us, don't want updates until I get my first cup of coffee." Glancing at

Sam's mini-carafe mischievously, Pete said, "By the way, how many have you had today?"

At the gentle tease from his boss, Sam tried to nonchalantly hide his beverage behind the phone on the shiny, black receiving counter. "Maybe three so far, but I—err, lost track. There is a fresh pot just the way you like it."

"Keep it up, Sam, and you will go far in law enforcement." He grinned at the young man and took a big whiff of said coffee. "It's gonna be a *faaantastic* day!" Pete lifted a section of the counter, walked through to the other side, and lowered the "drawbridge" back to its original position.

He made a beeline to their kitchen, but maybe that was too grandiose of a term for a dingy sink, a microwave, and a coffee pot.

All that mattered was his mostly clean blue mug was right where he left it. He poured some of Columbia's best and took a generous sip of the boiling mixture. Pete had long ago burned off whatever nerves were responsible for notifying a person a beverage was too hot to be consumed.

Boy, Sam was right about making it perfectly. Definite potential. It was moments like these, calm before the crazy, which he treasured. The station wasn't much to brag about—institutional white walls, bulletin boards, and even an old McGruff the Crime Dog poster. But it was *his*—home.

After taking another scathing sip, he went to his modest office. The room was not much bigger than his Maplewood desk, but that was okay with him. He only needed a quiet place to work on the omnipresent paperwork, which dominated most of his time at the station.

*Stop procrastinating,* he thought to himself as he parked his butt in his luxurious office chair, it had cost him his supply budget for a month, but with how much time he spent on the damn thing, Pete never regretted it.

No sooner than he had put the coffee on a beverage coaster and pressed the space bar to "wake" the computer workstation, when the tan phone's inter-office light lit and buzzed simultaneously.

"This better be Idaho, Sam," Pete groused into the phone.

"Sorry, sir, but I think this is important. Just took a call from Marge at Forestco."

The mention of Forestco made his ears perk up. The grapevine reported there had been a severe case of food poisoning at their Founder's Day celebration picnic. Though he did not envy their next few days, he couldn't imagine what it had to do with him. "Said Skip Jelks had not rung in this morning as he should. Tried to call him on both his phones and Sarah's and couldn't reach anyone. Marge said this is not like him, so she wanted to know if we could investigate."

"Sorry bout hard timin' you earlier, Sam; you were right to tell me. Will handle it."

Pete and Skip had graduated together in '99 from Ontario High and shared a common bond in their love of deer hunting. Over the years, they bagged their share of bucks and drank far too many fireside PBRs.

During their years of friendship, Skip was never without his cell phone. Also, Skip was very protective about "his" mill. So, if he told Marge he would check in, it would take an act of God to stop him. His friend's place was two miles away. So, it wouldn't take but two minutes to be certain Skip was okay.

After one more sip of coffee, Pete grabbed his familiar Stetson, put it on his head, and headed out.

Crossing the pint-sized parking lot in a few steps, he hopped into his cruiser, a black Dodge Charger with a blue diagonal stripe at the front of the door panels and "Ontario Police" in white block lettering on the door. He turned left from the lot onto SW 4th Avenue and headed toward Skip's house.

Without thought, he turned up the police band radio and half-heartedly listened to the background chatter. Whatever he heard could be deemed more important than making, in essence, a house call on a friend.

As he weaved through what little traffic there was on this main road in his quaint little hamlet, he mused for not the first time how there were quite a few benefits to being chief of police in Ontario: 1. there was never any vehicle congestion to speak of. And 2. Most of his duties in this sleepy, remote eastern Oregon town encompassed trips like the one he was on now.

So, instead of dealing with the ugliness of some heinous crimes committed in the more suburban areas like his fellow cops, he could focus on helping others like Skip and Marge. Cosmic irony can be a bitch, though. Even though this task was not a real emergency, he punched the accelerator, hit the lights once he got out of the city proper, and headed northwest of town.

Like a kid on a scary carnival ride, he never got tired of the thrill of instant acceleration. This Charger had 264 pounds per foot of torque and the superb handling to go with it. Before he knew it, he had arrived. The gravel road was well-maintained. But he didn't want any surprises, so he took it very slow up the tree-lined road. Everything appeared normal. A white F450 diesel work rig with a large fuel transfer tank in the truck bed and Sarah's late-model, green Dodge Caravan were in their usual spots.

*That's weird. If they're home, why aren't they answering their phones?*

Stopping his sedan behind their vehicles, Pete approached the porch area of the almost-new, slate gray, double-wide trailer. Everything seemed normal. It was quite beautiful as the dappled sunshine filtered through the abundant trees on the lot.

There was a small patch of grass in the front of the house, and down the middle of it ran a gravel path and two small, bordering flower beds bursting with red geraniums so bright they almost hurt his eyes. With a grin, he remembered how much Sarah babied these plants with an intensity that bordered on mania. If memory served him right, she had won an award at the Malheur County Fair.

This reverie was cut short by a sound that issued forth from under the tiny flight of stairs leading up to the front door. He shaded his eyes from the sun and squatted to investigate the noise. When his eyes adjusted to the dim light, he saw the Jelks' dog, Astro, under the steps.

Calling to the family pet in an encouraging tone, "Hey buddy. Come see Peetey."

The animal did not move but instead growled softly—not aggressively—but rather like a scared animal. When this newcomer didn't go away or threaten him, Astro finally decided this man was 'okay' and came out from under the stairs.

Sniffing Pete's hand, the dog recognized him, then rolled onto his back and let Pete rub his tummy. The dog was a beautiful 6-year-old Golden Retriever-Yellow Labrador mix that had the floppy retriever ears but the lab's short hair. Ever since he was a pup, Astro had accompanied Skip and him on their hunting trips. Had always been a loyal and joyful companion. Because of that, it hurt Pete's heart to see the canine peering up at him in a haunted way.

Pete's gut told him something bad had happened.

Suddenly, the peaceful scene took on a more sinister feel. Pete returned to his car. Astro followed. Fishing a dozen dog treats from a bag he had stashed in a front compartment for times he was dealing with furry friends, Pete opened the back door and laid them on the seat.

The canine must have been famished because he jumped in and started messily munching away at the tasty tidbits. While the dog was distracted, Pete closed the door. If nothing was wrong, he could let Astro out later.

When he returned to the front of the house, he was struck by the utter silence of the place.

"Guess it's a good thing I came out here," he said out loud to break up the unusual stillness of the place.

The short hairs on the back of his neck began to stick up.

The only way he could have heard the meager whimper the dog had made was there were no nature or human sounds. He knew the kids were sick, but even ailing children make noise. It was tempting to take out his Smith and Wesson M&P .45 because of the wrongness, but if the Jelks were only asleep inside, he didn't want to traumatize them for life when he had a loaded gun pointed at them.

Hyperalert now, he moved quietly up the three steps, knocked on the door, and said, "Skip. Sarah. It's Pete. Is everything okay?"

Ten seconds later, he banged more forcefully on the frame, but again to no avail. Checking the knob. Locked.

"Why would the cars be here and no one answers? It's not like there's a 7-11 nearby."

At this point, he unsnapped the holster for his gun and decided he needed to call Sam and report what he had found. He reached for his shoulder mic, "Base. This is Chief Alvardo."

"Chief. Base," came Sam's enthusiastic reply. "Go ahead."

"I'm at the Jelks' residence. Their cars are out here, but they didn't answer the door. Gotta bad feeling."

"Do you want backup?"

"Not yet. It still might be nothing. The windows in the front are too high. Going to go in the back and see if I can find an open window or an unlocked door. If you don't hear from me in five minutes, go ahead and send a car."

"Let's hope it doesn't come to that, Chief."

"You and me both. Alvardo out."

Skirting the south of the home warily, he approached the back door. The lot gently sloped down to the highway below. The trailer sat almost halfway up the rise, so the backside of the house's doors and windows were at ground level and provided easy access. The dining room picture window was opaque with sun, so Pete moved up to the glass and shaded his eyes with a hand. There was blood on the kitchen floor, a lot of blood!

Urgently grabbing his shoulder mic, Pete said, "Base. This is Alvardo. Need immediate assistance at the Jelks' home. We might have a homicide. Send everyone you can. Now!"

"Understood, Chief. Backup is on its way," Sam said. This time, his rapid speech had little to do with caffeine.

Each police force nationwide has a collection of regulations that direct law enforcement officers on dealing with a situation. Even small cities, like Ontario, had a book of these rules. In a case like today, where there was a violent attack or probable murder committed, the reporting officer was to call for backup and hold his or her position until help arrived.

With a dismissive grunt, Pete thought, *Unfortunately for my sense of self-preservation, I'm not a big reader.* Besides, judging from the glimpse of blond hair, he had a pretty good idea who was on the kitchen floor, and he would not let her die while he waited for someone to hold his hand. It took less than a decision to make his decision.

Gun out, he thumbed the safety off with practiced ease, and he was running to the door before he could think better of his choice.

Testing the handle, it turned. Unlocked!

He rushed inside, screaming, "Police! I am armed! Do you need assistance?!"

Scanning the tiny mud room, gun following his eyes. No one. And no sound.

He entered the small kitchen, muscles so tight they hurt. Still no one. The source of the blood was pretty evident, and whoever it was on the linoleum would most likely never need his help. But he needed to find out if there were any survivors and secure the scene.

Urgently and carefully, Pete canvased the rest of the house and found only two diminutive corpses. The tragedy was complete. *What the hell is going on?*

Whoever did this was gone.

Holstering his weapon, he began the gruesome duty of trying to ascertain what happened to these victims. He would start with the body in the kitchen.

During his tenure as sheriff, Pete had been through a few dozen homicide investigations, but to say he had seen enough death to be inured to it would be a lie. In fact, as he got closer to what he assumed was Sarah's body—*assumed*—because the body had been so desecrated, it resembled the corpse he had seen two years ago when a cougar killed the Simpson boy.

With a cursory inspection, he would guess her assailant had smashed her head against the kitchen floor a couple of dozen times until the skull was a formless mass. If this were not enough, there were deep furrows in her face, which indicated someone had dug his or her fingernails in Sarah's tender flesh and raked them across it over and over again.

The only reason Pete thought it was her was a small swath of unsullied blonde hair, which wasn't currently covered with blood, bone, and brain matter, and the remnants of a comfortable top she liked to wear.

The gentleman in him wanted to grab a dishcloth and cover her naked, ravaged breasts and give her some decency in death, but he knew it could not happen until the Medical Examiner—ME—arrived. There would be thousands of pictures taken of the crime scene before she would be afforded the modesty her corpse deserved.

Continuing his visual examination of the body, he was struck by the violence of the scene. If he were to guess, he would say she had been dead during 80 percent of the attack. An animal could have done this much damage, but he discarded that notion quickly because of one simple fact: Sarah had been stabbed in the abdomen and chest enumerable times.

The vile weapon, a large kitchen knife, was lodged between her ribs and protruded 6 inches above her torso.

As far as Pete knew, no beast used weapons to kill. Normally, good detectives try to visually "see" the event in his or her head to get a feel for what happened. When Pete tried to do this, he could only think about Sarah's pain and horror in her final moments.

The bile rose in his throat.

Between the smell and the mental images, it was more than he could take.

He fled outside. Then, he vomited what was left of his breakfast and coffee onto a rhododendron bracketing the back door.

As he finished purging his eggs into the shrub, he could hear the siren's wail from his backup. Moments later, he could also hear the gravel crunch under the other cruiser's tires. To save face, Pete was frantically trying to find something to wipe his mouth clean before his help arrived. But before he could recover properly, his right-hand woman, Lieutenant Roxane Mollett, Roxy to her friends, came around the corner with her weapon drawn and pointing it in his direction.

"It's okay, Roxy. No one is here besides us."

Still, she didn't holster her gun until she thoroughly scanned the hillside. Almost six feet tall, Roxy had the athletic build of a woman who knew her way around the weight room. She had a dimpled chin, a cute button nose, and spiked, coal-black buzz cut. Her pale green eyes dipped briefly to the bush before him, and her police business face instantly melted into her usual impish grin. She removed a handkerchief from a breast pocket of her uniform and held it out to him.

Pete stepped away from the bush and his breakfast and accepted the cloth. After cleaning his face, he glanced her way, and she made a you-keep-it motion.

He tucked it in an evidence bag before stuffing it into his jacket and said, "If you have some mint lip balm, you're gonna need it. The kids and Sarah have been dead for a while."

"Skip?"

"Not here."

"This must be hard. You were close." He nodded. "Still, are you out of your mind? Entering a homicide scene without backup is like a death wish."

"It was stupid, but I thought Sarah might still be alive."

"Well, don't let it happen again," she said with a playful smirk. Then she grabbed her friend's shoulders and looked him in the eye, "Someday, I want to be sheriff of this town, but not anytime soon. You hear me? Be more careful."

Suddenly, a young, stocky man with strikingly red hair and a full complement of freckles appeared around the corner of the house with his nine-millimeter drawn and he too scanned the backyard and acknowledged his superiors with a nod.

"The perp is gone, Jackson, or at least I haven't seen him," Pete said in his usual businesslike manner. "Keep your head on a swivel, though. Call the ME and report we have a triple homicide here. Then grab the tape and cordon off this whole house. Make sure you watch where you walk. If you need help, get Roxy's attention. It is better to ask for assistance than messing up a crime scene. Do you understand me?"

"Affirmative, Chief." And he left to carry out his orders.

"Rookies," Roxy said with mild affection. Then, a cloud crossed her face. "Noticed you said *he* when talking about the perp. Skip?"

"Lord knows. I would love to tell you otherwise," he said. "All I know is he's not in there with the other bodies. The weird part is there are tracks in the blood, but they are barefoot. By the size of them, it seems like the footprints could've been Skip's. Have Sam call the coroner and the state troopers, let them know what happened here, and put out an APB on Skip."

"Will do. Then, I will get my camera and start documenting the crime scene." And she was gone.

Pete took a deep breath and steeled himself for continuing to examine Sarah's body in the kitchen. Inside, he analyzed the macabre tableau. A forensics genius, he was not, but he knew the clues did not add up. The head wound probably killed her, so why would the killer go to the trouble of gouging her face and stabbing her hundreds of times? A crime of passion seemed to make sense if Skip killed her, but this went far beyond catching her with another man and wanting her dead. Way beyond. He had talked to Skip a week or so ago, and he seemed happy. There were no rumors in the air about infidelity or marriage issues. It didn't add up.

"My God!" Roxy said at the sickening scene, "I had no idea it was this bad." She blanched, but to her credit, she tried to be professional and started taking pictures of the butchery from every angle.

Trying to stay out of her way, he moved to the kids' room. Both children lay in their beds. Purple bruising about their throats and burst blood vessels in their eyes made diagnosing strangulation a mere formality. But their form of execution puzzled him.

Almost all killers had a particular method they preferred to use when killing, their MO—or modus operandi. This killer did not follow a pattern. Strangulation was a rather violent, personal way of killing—face to face. But unlike Sarah's murder, Tyler and Samantha's bodies were unmolested after their deaths.

Pete's hard-won detachment slipped as he stared at the two. Tyler was such an intelligent and inquisitive boy. He was a child of a thousand questions. His sister Samantha was whip-smart and empathetic. She would have made an excellent doctor if her life hadn't been cut so cruelly short.

Now they were gone.

A silent tear slid down his cheek. *How could you Skip? Never in a million years would I have believed you could kill them.* There were too many puzzle pieces missing for Pete to even attempt the borders of this situation, let alone take a crack at the interior of this enigma.

When he returned to the kitchen, he waited for Roxy to stop taking pictures and make eye contact with him. Anger and frustration were suffused in his voice, "Hate to think it, but it has to be Skip unless we learn otherwise."

"His truck is out front, and no one has seen him since Wes' house call," said Roxy. "No word back from the APB Sam sent out. Can we assume he is on foot?"

"Probably. And he might be closer than we suspect." Pete pointed at the bloody footprints. "I'm going to head back to the station and start making some calls—to Gary and his dogs, the State Patrol, and the boys from Fruitland. Let's see if we can get Skip before he hurts someone else. You're in charge while I'm gone."

"I think I will have Jackson and Goodwin see if they can follow the tracks. Find out at least which direction Skip headed. Hope the coroner gets here soon. Maybe he will have a better idea of what happened. And Pete, I will radio when I see him if he returns."

"I know you will handle everything. Stay in touch."

Pete launched himself into the cruiser and gunned the engine before being startled to hear a quiet "Woof" from the backseat. With everything on his mind, he forgot Astro was still his passenger. He stopped the car at the highway, turned, and looked the dog in the eyes.

"Guess you are with me for a while, Astro. It might not be a suite, but we can get you some food and a warm place for the night. Looks like you will be needing a new home."

Hitting his lights and siren, Pete's Charger flung gravel into the air while the back of his rig fishtailed wildly for a moment until the tires gained traction on the highway's asphalt. The muscle car leaped like its namesake, and he tried unsuccessfully to convince himself that he was leaving in such a hurry because he wanted to catch Skip. Because in his heart-of-hearts, he knew the real motive for his urgency: to get away from the feeling of wrongness enveloping a place that would never feel welcoming to him again.

# Chapter 9



*July 3, Tuesday — 10 pm — Jelks' Residence*

Pete stared out at the quickly cobbled-together group, which consisted of six Malheur County Fire and Rescue personnel men, three local patrolmen, a half-dozen state troopers, and three officers from the nearby city of Fruitland, not to mention four of Gary Moore's bloodhounds. The men and women of the posse were gathering their gear and doing last-minute equipment checks; they would be ready soon.

The Jelks' driveway was packed tight with two dozen vehicles. Most of them still had their headlights on because sunset had been 25 minutes ago.

As he waited for them to finish their preparations, Pete thought to himself for the umpteenth time, *Skip. What made you do that to Sarah? Why hurt your kids? What made you snap?* To say he had no idea what was going on in Skip's head was an understatement. But underneath his desire to determine his friend's motive, he heard a clock ticking. Each moment they did not have Skip in custody could be a moment he hurt someone else.

Earlier, Jackson and Goodwin had followed the bloody footprints to the west a short distance until the trail petered out. They continued to head in that general direction but searched in vain for two hours. After radioing in, Pete told them to return to the house. Skip had a big head start on them, but blundering through the wilderness without the aid of the dogs would be unproductive.

So, the afternoon was spent contacting media and government agencies. Hoping to warn everyone to be on the lookout and avoid the deadly man. Beyond that, they could only anxiously wait until Gary finally returned their call at 7 pm. They had later learned he had been on a family boating trip down at Lake Owyhee and hadn't brought his cell phone.

Fortunately, this manhunt was happening during the summer. It hadn't rained for over a month now, and Pete knew from recent personal experience the bloodhounds could easily track a scent this fresh. Just last fall, the hounds made short work of finding the Shenigen's toddler, who had wandered from home.

*Time to get to it,* Pete thought as he raised his arms above his head and made a throat-clearing sound; an expectant hush came over those gathered.

Pete began, "By now, you should all be up to speed on what happened here. The coroner's preliminary examination puts the time of death for our vics at some time between 16-20 hours ago. Since our suspect's truck is still here, we assume he is on foot. An APB was issued when the bodies were discovered early this morning, but Skip Jelks has not been seen anywhere nearby at bus stations or other transportation hubs. The Oregon media has been sent a picture and a warning our suspect is very dangerous. Still, I think our best chance of finding him is *you.* The scene investigation revealed he didn't appear to have taken a bag or a coat. Not only that, but it appears he isn't even wearing shoes. So, he couldn't have made it far.

"Most of you know the region is heavily forested, so the trees and undergrowth will slow him down. But it's literally his backyard, so he's familiar with the area. We guess he can travel about a mile an hour, which gives us a range of 16-25 miles. The hounds have been given his scent, and we will head out when everyone is ready." As soon as Pete had said this, everyone became hyper aware of the canines' excited noises, and Gary's Herculean efforts to keep them from bolting after their suspect.

"You've seen the pictures of what Skip is capable of, so I don't want to see anyone playing Lone Ranger out there." There was an angry buzz as he made this remark. "And remember, we don't know the full story here. If we can, I want to bring him in peacefully. That said, if he tries anything, I don't want anyone else getting hurt tonight. Are we clear?" All of them murmured in agreement. "Now, buddy up and fan out behind Gary and the dogs."

The large, reddish-brown dogs were now baying in bloodlust as they sensed the beginning of the hunt. Straining and jumping against Gary's immovable form, they seemed like kids at an Easter egg contest starting line. When all was ready, the party moved out in an orderly, determined fast-walk due west, behind the excited hounds.

The search party had prepared for a minimum five-hour hike. They needn't have bothered. Half an hour later, the dogs indicated Skip was near.

To say Pete was confused by this discovery would be an understatement, and when he turned to ask Roxy what she thought, she gave an exaggerated shrug. It was one more bewildering detail in this ongoing enigma. Why would a man who supposedly killed his family 15 hours ago stop a mile away from the crime scene? Why would the killer choose to walk barefoot through the forest for only a mile and not expect to get caught? If he wasn't worried about being arrested, why leave the house?

There were many questions and no answers, but Pete hoped they would be forthcoming.

Grabbing his rescue walkie-talkie, he transmitted, "Converge on my position and remember, we don't know his state of mind. Keep weapons ready."

The dispersed group slowed their pace and closed ranks. Nerves taut, Pete scanned the woods for any sign of his friend. Over a dozen flashlight beams wove through the grove, and when they illuminated clumps of moss, ferns, stumps, and broken branches, they created thousands of moving shadows.

Each movement could be the fugitive they searched for. Each shadow could have been the only warning the madman was coming to kill him. Pete's hand sought his gun for the second time that day.

The dog's baying had reached an almost ultra-sonic sound, which ratcheted up the suspense and excitement. It was primal. The hunt. Their quarry appeared as if conjured from thin air, about 100 feet before the mob. Pete signaled Gary to pull the dogs back and silence them; they would only make the arrest more challenging to manage.

A man was huddled against a stately, mature pine tree 15 feet in circumference. It was relatively easy to see him in the dark, because the figure was only wearing a pair of gray sweats: now predominately a ghastly rust color. The man's torso and hair were streaked with dried blood and other viscera. It had to be Skip, but the figure had his arms in front of his face. Hidden from the bright flashlights. Now that the hounds were hushed, it seemed he heard the man growling? What the hell is going on?

The line of men formed a semi-circle around the figure, making escape impossible. Raising his gun, Pete took a few cautious steps forward. Keeping a good arm's distance between himself and the suspect.

"Skip." He infused the practiced command and calm of a policeman's tone into his voice. Pete hoped after 16 hours, his good friend was no longer angry, no longer under the influence, or whatever it was that had triggered him earlier. Unfortunately, hope was all it was.

The man screamed like an animal and leaped with unnatural speed at a nearby deputy, who had put away his weapon and tried unadvisedly to approach the suspect's left side undetected. On a normal manhunt, the deputy's bravery might have resulted in a non-lethal takedown and restraint of a prospective criminal.

Alas, the day refused even to try approximating normal. The unidentified man's leap took the weaponless lawman to the ground, and Pete could hear Sal Rodriguez gasp as the air was knocked from him. The assailant grabbed his victim's throat and squeezed his windpipe. But strangling was not enough. Skip commenced lifting the hurt man's head and commenced smashing it against the tree root below them.

The sickening crunch of the Rodriguez's skull and his subsequent scream of pain, shocked the posse out of its astonishment. To be fair, the whole attack had only lasted two heartbeats, and they now moved with resolve to rescue their comrade.

As a group, they jumped onto the madman and wrestled him to the ground with their sheer weight and mass strength. The nearly naked man gave them as good as he got, and his odds against this mob didn't daunt him. He roared again as he tried to bite, punch, and kick anyone within reach. The ferocity of the man caused Pete to wonder if Skip was on meth or bath salts: the inhuman strength, speed and ferocity was frightening.

Skip redoubled his attack every time the officers seemed to have him subdued enough to restrain him. Finally, the hail of punches and kicks from the posse took their toll on the man, and he was forced onto his belly and handcuffed. Dusting himself off with a few pats, Pete decided Skip could wait a minute while he went to check on the wounded officer.

Rodriguez was an officer from nearby Fruitland, Idaho, and they often worked together over the past ten years. The poor man screamed in prodigious pain; the paramedic reported the man had a cranial fracture, a full-blown concussion, and a pretty severe neck wound, where Skip had tried to tear out his throat as he was being set upon by the group. They would know more when they got Rodriguez admitted to the hospital. The injuries were serious enough to warrant bringing in a life-flight helicopter, but the area was too thick for the big machine to land. Fortunately, they had brought a green army stretcher. The medic administered a healthy dose of morphine so Rodriguez could handle the jostling he would soon endure.

Four of the search team were detailed to carry him back to the Jelks' place. There would be an ambulance waiting for them. Every else had their share of cuts and bruises but none warranting medical attention.

Once Pete was certain his wounded comrade was taken care of, it was time to face the next unpleasant task.

"Get him up," Pete said.

Two men grabbed the prone man, slammed him up against the tree, and held him there. A shock of hair partially covered the prisoner's face, and in the low light, Pete was uncertain it was his friend. As the adrenaline started to wear off, he could feel some sore spots, including his mouth.

Anger took him. He dragged the back of his hand across his split lip to mop up some blood from his chin and shouted, "What the hell is your problem, Skip?"

If the man before him answered to that name, there was no sign.

Closing the distance between them, Pete roughly pushed the man's hair to the side so that he could ID him. A loud clack of teeth was heard throughout the clearing. His hand was only just outside the man's range of attack.

Though he expected it, the ferocity of the response unnerved him.

Making eye contact with the officers holding Skip, he said, "You got him?"

Both men further braced themselves and nodded.

Pete pointed his flashlight in the man's face and observed him. There was no doubt it was Skip Jelks. But it also wasn't. Gone was the friend, whose face normally was friendly and ready with a quick smile, now replaced with a mask of implacable hatred.

There was no doubt that if handcuffs and two burly men did not physically restrain this man, Skip would be trying to kill him right this minute.

Stepping away from him, Pete went to Roxy and said, "What do you make of this?"

"It's spooky. Did you notice he hasn't said a word?"

"Seems to believe more in actions tonight," he said with black humor. "Even if he is high on something, he should recognize us."

"Yeah, it's almost like he is a rabid dog instead of a man."

Scratching his chin in thought, Pete said, "You know. That makes as much sense as anything."

"Let's get the other search and rescue stretcher over here and bind him to it."

"Agreed, but I also want his mouth gagged as well. No one else is going to get hurt tonight."

When Roxy returned with the stretcher, she asked, "Do you want pictures of the vicinity before we leave?"

"Nahhh, there isn't much to be seen. Besides, I think if there was important evidence, the 13 of us rolling around like a WWE show probably obliterated it. Though I want someone to tape off the area for now, and, at first light, we'll search for anything that can explain what the hell is going on."

"Will do," she answered, then spoke to the men holding Skip. "Bring him over here, and let's make him real cozy."

Taking a deep breath, Pete removed a handkerchief from his pocket and mopped at his stinging lip.

"Back to the house," he said to no one. Weirder and weirder.

The search team knew they had returned to Skip's property when the surrounding trees and shrubs were bathed in a newly arrived ambulance's red and white undulating lights. Careful hands loaded Sal onto the vehicle, and the back doors closed with a final click. Meanwhile, other officers removed Skip from his stretcher and unceremoniously "threw" Skip into the back of Pete's cruiser.

A dull thudding sound might have been the detainee's head, not quite making it below the car's roof. He should have reprimanded them for mishandling the man, but he didn't have the heart for it. They all knew and liked Rodriguez. He thanked each man as they began to leave the scene.

Finally, he jumped into the driver's seat of the Charger and rolled down the window. As Roxy walked by his vehicle, Skip started lunging forward and smashing his face into the divider between the front seat and the back and clacking his teeth in an attempt to latch onto the back of Pete's neck. She stopped, saw Pete flinch, then changed her destination.

The passenger door opened, and Roxy hopped in. Without a word, they created a new Ontario police SOP—Standard Operation Procedure—no one should be alone with this madman.

In no time, they arrived at Saint Alphonsus Medical Center in downtown Ontario. It was a fairly new building with modern architecture and was tan with a dark brown accent. It could care for most of the city's needs, and the community was justifiably proud.

Even still, if anything required advanced, life-saving equipment, the patient would have to be life-flighted to nearby Baker City.

As they pulled into the parking lot, the name of the building and a cross were lit in red fluorescent tubing. Below the sign was a covered entrance where Rodriguez's ambulance was parked. Their friend was probably already being evaluated inside. Their "passenger" did not need emergency help, so Pete found a spot in the normal parking lot.

Both officers exited the car, Roxy went inside to scare up a stretcher, and Pete didn't want to be alone in the car with the growling madman.

A few minutes later, Roxy and Rodriguez's fellow Fruitland officers, who had made the trip with Rodriguez's ambulance, were ready to transport Mr. Jelks. Skip fought them, but his previous injuries allowed the four officers to manhandle Skip onto the stretcher and secure him with multiple zip ties. Everyone took station on the corners of their prisoner's gurney and escorted him into the building.

The interior color scheme matched the exterior—dark tile and carpeting with light walls. As they made their way through the foyer, Pete glanced at the crucifix statue affixed to the wall above the balcony above him. Most of Pete's limited experience with churches involved funerals, but after dealing with Skip and his family today, he figured it couldn't hurt, and he crossed himself.

Technically, they had entered the building from the back, so they had to travel down the main hallway to get to the admittance desk.

Dr. Abigail Gallagher smiled and warmly greeted them as she shook their hands. She was of average height, and had shoulder-length, dirty blonde hair, which always needed taming. Lastly, she wore black rimmed glasses with thick lenses which mostly hid her sky-blue, intelligent eyes.

Then she noticed their 'charge' on the stretcher nearby and added, "Hello, Skip."

Their prisoner neither acknowledged the greeting nor bothered to make eye contact. Abby raised an eyebrow, and Roxy gave an exaggerated shrug.

"Okaaay. Let's move him to Room 2." Without another word, she motored toward the room without checking to see if they would follow.

Pete grinned. The woman gave orders to everyone and expected them to be followed, even if the directions were given to the sheriff or the mayor. Her behavior would have been irritating if she was merely ordinary, but he would bet Abby was the most competent medical doctor in this part of the state. Pound for pound, she was every bit as medically brilliant as Dr. Parks. However, Wes had her beat in bedside manner. But she was an ace at diagnosing patients, which made her the best fit for Mr. Jelks here.

Abby was methodically washing her hands in the sink as they entered the room. She paused long enough to point toward the inspection table. They removed the ties to the stretcher, but they did leave the handcuffs on him. The two deputies resumed their post on each side of their ward. A hand on each shoulder. While they did this, Abby grabbed two small latex gloves, put them on, and turned toward them.

"Dr. Manly is working on the deputy in Room 1," she said. "The poor guy is going to have an unenviable headache for a while, but the chunk torn out of his throat was the most immediate life-threatening injury of the two. Already had to use a few units of blood on him. It will take Dr. Manly some time to get him patched up, but at least the deputy is stable now."

Her patient did not seem to show any remorse about the injuries he inflicted. His eyes darted around the room like a caged animal.

"Don't take this wrong, but you people look like crap. Told John to brew us up a fresh pot of coffee. Would you guys like some?"

"Sounds wonderful, but just to be safe, not until you are done with Mr. Jelks," Roxy said.

"Probably a smart plan." Turning to her 'patient,' Abby smoothly transitioned from folksy friend to consummate medical professional. "Well, Mr. Jelks, you appear to be having an unpleasant night. Do you recognize me?"

Skip growled at her through the gag.

"Take that as a no." Turning to Roxy, she asked, "Can we remove that? I need to ask him some questions?"

"You saw what he did to Rodriguez, and Pete's lucky not to be missing a few fingers. Be careful, doc; he's quick." Roxy moved behind Skip and removed the muzzle.

Dr. Gallagher then continued with her litany of admittance inquiries. "Have you been drinking? Have you taken drugs? Have you been sick? I heard Forestco had some problems with food poisoning at their picnic."

When it became apparent that she would not get any answers from him, she grabbed her ophthalmoscope—a device used to check for pupil dilation. When she moved closer, Skip bulled through his guard's shoulder grips, lunged forward, and tried to bite her hand. In surprise, she cried out and fell back onto the floor.

"Are you okay?" Pete asked as he helped Abby up.

Brushing imaginary dust off her posterior, she said, "The only thing bruised is my pride, and in all likelihood, my tailbone. Should have taken your warning more seriously."

"Do you want us to put the gag on again?" Roxy held up the restraint in her left hand. "Or do you want to sedate him? It's your choice."

"Usually better to have the patient awake, but I'm not sure I can safely examine him or draw blood without him being a little less—ah, feisty. Hold him down."

It took some doing, but the four officers pinned Skip to the table while Abby expertly applied the sedative. There was no rush to complete the examination, so Abby was content to let the anesthetic take full effect before she would evaluate Skip again. And to be doubly sure, they resecured Skip to the table. Only then did she deign to continue the exam.

"...has two broken ribs, a fractured wrist, contusions over much of his body, blood under his fingernails, which will be tested, and a sprained ankle. His heart and respiration are both elevated above the norm. Until we get the toxicology lab back, we won't know what is causing it. I will have John run all the samples up to Baker City tonight. Can I assume you want answers yesterday?"

"Yeah, this has got heaps of people nervous," Pete said.

"Well, I set his wrist, but that is all I can do for him now. No reason he can't be your guest tonight. If you have any problems with him, give me a call. Meanwhile, I'm going to see if Dr. Manley needs any help. Thanks for keeping my evening—interesting," she said with a lopsided smirk.

"You went above and beyond tonight, Abby. Next time I'm in Portland, I'll get you a dozen VooDoo Donuts. Night," Pete said as he tipped his worn Stetson to her.

"Frankly, not a big sweets gal. If you want to show your appreciation, I would prefer a nice bottle of Pinot Noir. Maybe you could bring it over later?" she said with a twinkle in her eyes.

Cheeks suddenly warm, Pete mumbled, "Ahhh, sure thing, doc." And he beat a hasty retreat.

After dumping the now unconscious Skip in a wheelchair and escorting him to the car, Roxy quietly did her best Dr. Gallagher impression, "Oh, sheriff maybe you could bring it over later."

The Fruitland deputies and Roxy had a hearty guffaw at her dead-on impersonation. Even Pete chuckled at her good-natured ribbing. Not that he wouldn't enjoy giving her a little payback in the future. It didn't take them long to get the unconscious prisoner back to the police station and under lock and key.

"Just between you and me, boss," Roxy said, "now that he's behind bars, it feels like a weight is off my shoulders. We have dealt with our share of crazies and druggies, but they didn't scare me half as much as him."

"Between us? Me too."

Skip's cell was the furthest from the holding area door. They chuckled as they walked past the makeshift home they had created for Astro. The dog now had a water bowl and a few chew toys to play with. A police station could not have a pet wandering around, so they had secured the door. Astro lay on the mattress with his head between his paws.

"Night boy," Pete said in a friendly tone and moved to turn off the holding area lights.

Astro growled.

# Chapter 10



*July 4, Wednesday — 7:16 am — St. Alphonsus Medical Center*

*A rough night,* Abby thought as she surfaced from her dreams, *and an even rougher morning.*

"Ughhh." Everything ached, and she seemed to be moving and thinking in slow motion.

She rubbed her palms into her eyes and massaged the crusty sleep from the corners of her eyes. Feeling a bit better, she braved opening them and saw her desk across the small room. Then it hit her. *That's right, was going to close my eyes for a few.*

The hospital had called her in at 11 pm last night—after working a full day shift. *You're not a young intern anymore,* she thought with a touch of wistfulness. But as her memories of last night returned, she had to be honest with herself. Last night scared her. She had always been a fiercely independent woman, but it was even more true after her divorce. But the thought of being alone in her empty house last night was too much.

Skip had tried to kill her. Dead eyes. The growling lunges. The clacking teeth.

All on a continual feedback loop. Reason told her it was a mere happenstance of her day, but her heart told her she had brushed against evil. And she had barely escaped.

As the bright light of the early morning shone through her window, she said aloud, "Enough of this foolishness."

She threw off the gray hospital blanket, stood up, stretched, moseyed down to the staff room, and put on a pot of java. While she waited for the coffee machine to do its thing, she went back to her office and booted up her computer to check her e-mail for Skip's tox screen. The results were not there.

*"Patience is a virtue,"* some would say, but it surely wasn't something Abby possessed in overabundance. She tapped her manicured nails on the keyboard's space bar with nervous energy. After a brief pause, she grabbed the phone and hit speed dial 8 to call the lab.

A bright male voice said, "Saint Alphonsus Medical Center. How can I help you?"

"This is Dr. Abigail Gallagher from the Ontario branch. I sent some blood samples to you guys' last night for a toxicology screen. Can you check to see if they have been finished yet?" she said with some asperity, but she realized she was not talking to the responsible party and added a belated, "Please."

"Sure thing, doctor, let me send you to the lab department. Can you hold while I transfer you?"

The operator did not wait for her reply before she heard the soothing sounds of Barry Manilow in her ear. A moment later, a friendly soprano voice replaced the canned music, "This is Pamela. How're you today, Abby?"

"Fine, Pamela. Hate to bug you, but I really want to know what the results are for the tox screen we sent you last night. Is it finished yet?"

"It is, but it didn't reveal much. Let me send you the report really quick." Silence except for the clicking of keys on a keyboard in the background. "Didn't mean to make you wait, but since the sample came in so late, we figured you wouldn't be in so early. Besides, we wanted to make sure of the results, so we triple-checked it," the young lady said.

"Thank you for being thorough." Abby felt a private stab of embarrassment for judging the lab tech, but she forged on. "What do you mean I won't find many answers?"

"Well doctor, we didn't find anything." The frustration was evident in Pam's voice. "Heard about that poor family down there, and we figured you were looking for some chemical reason for it all. But nothing."

The computer chimed, and Abby checked the data for herself. "There is nothing out of the ordi—wait a minute... he has an elevated white blood cell count?"

"Yeah, that was the only thing abnormal about the blood sample, but those cell concentrations could be caused by a simple cold or flu. I'm no doctor, but I've never heard of a violent homicide being caused by elevated white blood cells. So, nada."

Despite her lack of caffeine and sleep, Abby felt the pieces start to fit together. "Interesting, now that you mention it, we have had a bad flu outbreak in the area. Seems like everyone who has come through the hospital the past few days has had it. Most attended our local Forestco Founder's Day Picnic, so I assumed one of the families passed a nasty bug around. This can't be a coincidence. Hmmm, wait a minute, I forgot Jelks is the manager at Forestco. Betcha a raspberry cheesecake there has to be a connection there. When I spoke with Silvia Parks yesterday, she said Wes had made numerous house calls. Apparently, he was baffled by it and figured it was some virus. Maybe I should call him and see if he learned anything more."

"Actually," Pamela interrupted, "Doctor, I remember getting a sample from Dr. Parks a few days ago." Keys clattered in the background once again. "Yep, we sent him the workup yesterday. If he sends us a release, we could CC it your way. Keep me in the loop either way, doctor, and let me know if we can assist you any further."

"Sure thing, Pamela. Thanks for all of your help."

As soon as Abby hung up the phone, she speed-dialed her good friend, Wesley Parks. It rang three times before she glanced at the clock, 7:24 am. *Crap, should've thought about him being retired.*

She started to hang up when she heard a groggy male voice say, "Hello?"

"Sorry, Wes, I didn't notice the time. Can call back later."

"It's okay, Abby. Seems like sleeping is all I can do now. This flu that's been going around has got its claws into Silvia and me. I would have guessed I was immune to everything by now. Feel pretty miserable, but we should live. What can I do you for?"

"Well, I have a strange case, Wes. Last night, a patient literally tried to bite my face off."

"Are you okay?"

"Thank God this old gal has a little bit of spring in her yet."

"Can't imagine what that has to do with me."

"The tox report came in a moment ago, and everything was negative except a high white blood cell count. Your wife said you examined a few of the Forestco personnel the other day, and my attacker works there. Trying to figure this puzzle."

"Yes, I was unusually busy that day, but they only had the flu. By the time I saw Skip and his family—"

Abby interrupted, "You went to see Skip Jelks?"

"Why, yes. Been their doctor since I can remember; gave the whole household the once over. All had it, whatever it was: fever, chills, lethargy, and headache, you know—the classic symptoms. Food poisoning would've made more sense since everyone at the picnic got it, but the timing made no sense for that. Also," Abby heard the shrug, "Silvia and I couldn't have second-hand bad potato salad. So, I figured a very contagious flu."

"Well, I hate to break this to you, Wes, but you're my late-night patient's doctor. Skip tried to kill me last night, and he's in jail for his family's murder."

The pause after her revelation continued until Abby thought the connection must have been lost. But eventually, Wes said in a heartbroken voice, "Can't believe that. Wouldn't hurt a fly, and he adores Sarah and those kids."

"Sometimes things change," Abby said with a heavy heart.

"I guess," Wes said, "Sylvia will be crestfallen to hear the news. Sarah created the Crystal's Cure website, and they were great friends. Wish I could be more help—"

"You can," she interrupted him a second time. "Can you tell Pamela to release the Jelks' blood sample findings to me?"

"Boy, this thing is muddling my brain worse than I thought," Wes said with a touch of self-recrimination. "Of course, you can have them. There are three specimens, but they all came back the same."

"Even still, I still want to see how they compare to Skip's."

"Done. I will send the form after this call."

"Take care, you two, and let me know if you get any worse, and you know what they say—"

Wes groaned, "An apple a day keeps the doctor away." Then she heard his chortle across the miles of telephone line. "It's a good thing Silvia doesn't like apples."

Even under the weather, Wes' quick wit made her smile, though it was fleeting. For she had to follow up on her 'patient' downtown, but not before grabbing at least one cup of coffee. She hoped her friend was correct in his diagnosis, but Skip's behavior last night baffled her. A simple flu, it was not.

Half an hour later, she was walking into the Ontario Police Station with a sense of purpose: to get to the bottom of this mystery. But as she entered, she was overcome by a strident wall of noise.

"What the hell?" she asked Roxy, who was behind the front counter.

"You must see it to believe it, doc! Pete is back in holding."

Abby had thought the cacophony was bad when she first walked in, but when she opened the holding door, it was exponentially worse. In the cell directly to her left, a good-size dog was barking in a frenzy. It kept leaping and hitting its head and body against the bars, with no apparent concern for the damage it was doing to itself. Ostensibly, it was trying to get to Pete, who was on the other side of the cage, and it was willing to kill itself doing it. If she was not mistaken, the Golden Lab had the same desire to kill in its eyes as Skip did last night.

It—was—terrifying. But the most disturbing part of the surreal scene in front of her was not the canine but the man two cells down from the hound. The man's behavior mirrored the dog. However, Skip was shrieking instead of baying. And for a long enough duration, he was starting to go hoarse from his exertions. After Skip had bounced from the bars once, he noticed her and switched from wanting to kill Pete to trying to slaughter her.

In horror, last night's nightmare came alive again. She froze. Then someone grabbed her elbow and directed her back to the station's main room.

"Glad you are here, doctor!" Pete had to shout to be heard. "Was getting ready to call you because poor Skip there is going to off himself at this rate! Have you found out what is going on with his bloodwork?"

Shutting the holding door diminished the caterwauling a bit.

"Wish I did, but the toxicology report came back negative for any drugs we test for."

"Almost wish something had turned up," he said. "At least then we would know it would wear off."

"Know what you mean. Pamela in Baker City said Dr. Parks had sent in some bloodwork, too. Talked with him a few minutes ago, and he said he had visited Skip a few days ago."

"So, we could compare the two samples," Roxy said as she approached them.

"Already did," Abby said, "and they were the same. And according to Wes, Skip and his family had the flu."

Rubbing the day-old bluish colored shadow growing about his face Pete said, "I would be lying if I wasn't hoping you had a magic bullet for this mystery." The sheriff obviously had not slept last night, and the lack of sleep and stress were taking its toll.

"Did Wes note anything strange about Skip when he saw him?" Roxy asked.

"Not that he mentioned. The only thing he thought was suspicious was how everyone at the picnic got sick. We all know no virus is 100 percent contagious, but this one seems to be. It got Wes and Silvia, too." *Maybe Skip has had some kind of psychotic episode related to the fever, but that doesn't explain why there are two "creatures" in the holding area that seem crazy or rabid,* she thought. "What's the story with the dog in there?"

"Skip's pet, Astro," Pete said. "Didn't have the heart to leave him out at the place without anyone to care for him. Figured we could tend to him for a few days. Lucky for us, we kept him locked in the cell so he wouldn't be peeing on the carpet in here or getting in our way. When I went in there 15 minutes ago, he came unglued and tried to kill me. Remind you of someone else we know?" He nodded his head in Skip's general direction.

"Lord knows I'm no vet, but it looks like it has rabies."

"Not gonna rule it out, but don't you think it's a strange coincidence two of my friends want to kill me?"

"Not that strange," Roxy said sarcastically. But their laughter was subdued. The barking and screaming demanded it.

"On the surface, their behaviors are very similar, but I don't know if you understand how unusual it is for a pathogen to jump the human-animal barrier," Abby explained. "It's not completely unheard of, the bird flu or even TB to name a few have done it, but to say it's rare is an understatement. Besides, the only abnormal thing about Skip is an elevated white blood cell count. Hardly something someone gives to his dog."

"Can't speak to what is causing what, doc, but I have a feeling we will have two dead patients before too long if we don't calm them down soon."

"I can give Skip some Ketamine and see if we can't negate the hysteria and keep him from hurting himself or others. Barring that, we have a full-body restraint at the hospital. Can't help you with the pooch."

"I'll call Dr. Tobin Letterman at the Human Society and see what he can do for Astro," Roxy said.

"Well, if you can get Astro settled too, I want to get a blood sample. It will be interesting to see if there is a connection between the man and his pet."

"We will send you the blood sample as soon as we can. And Abby..." He paused to give her an exaggerated, mischievous wink. "Have a fun Fourth of July."

"Think we've enough excitement in this town without adding a bunch of rednecks tying more than a few on and lighting off illegal fireworks at each other. Don't you think?" Abby groused.

They all laughed. As Abigail headed for the door, she couldn't help thinking a set of fresh eyes might pierce this riddle—and she knew the perfect pair.

# Chapter 11



*July 4, Wednesday — 8:40 am — Dr. Zander Park's Residence*

Zander rolled over to glance at the alarm clock and groaned. He wasn't concerned with showing up for work late; it's good to be the boss, but it had been another night of restless tossing and turning. Initially, he believed that when the FDA's decision came down, he would finally be able to stop worrying about what could go wrong. Now, he understood: different day—different worry. The phone on his bedside table began playing the Firefly series theme and rumbling against the hard surface. Grabbing it, he thumbed the answer button.

"Zander?" A feminine voice said.

"Yes. Who is this?" he said, morning grogginess in his voice.

"Dang it! I woke up another Parks this morning, didn't I? Sorry. Should I call later?" Zander finally recognized Abby's voice.

"No, I'm already up now," he said with a touch of sarcasm.

She returned the playful banter, saying in a sultry voice, "Good, because I really need you—"

"Ummm, ah, Abby, I'm not sure—"

But her deep-throated laugh interrupted his embarrassment. "—to solve a mystery, and I was wondering if you could lend a hand?"

He gave a shaky laugh of his own before saying, "Well, I love a good riddle as much as the next guy. Shoot." The last vestiges of sleep melted away like snow in the springtime sun.

"Well, before we start this, I have to warn you, according to HIPPA regulations, we have to keep names and the details of their health records confidential." His friend was such a stickler for rules, which wasn't an altogether bad thing, but it still made him smile.

"Send the form to my secretary," he said. "Now get to the juicy details."

"You heard about what happened out at the Jelks' place?" she asked with a touch of sadness.

"Yes," he said soberly. "The grapevine is alive and well in town. Did they find out who did it?"

"Didn't you hear?"

"I did, but I was hoping I heard wrong. Do they know his motive?"

"It's all speculation at this point, but Skip seems to be incapable of speech. Even worse, he tried to bite my face off last night at the hospital after Pete brought him in."

"Oh my God, Abby! Are you alright?"

"I'm fine but can't say the same for Skip. This morning, I found him slamming his face and body against his cell's bars in an attempt to kill Pete. His toxicology came up negative on everything except leukocytosis, which shouldn't cause this kind of psychosis. The lab told me your dad had sent them some blood work."

"My dad has been busy. This thing must have bothered him more than I thought, because he dropped three blood samples off at our lab and wanted us to give them the onceover. Would've loved to have found something for him, but there was nothing. Haven't had the time to let him know the results."

"You might want to hold off on that. When I talked to him this morning, he sounded like this flu did a number on him. Tried to downplay it, but he was struggling."

"He hates to get sick. No wonder he hasn't been bugging me about that sample. Maybe I will move up our weekly coffee date. Thanks for letting me know."

"No problem. Hope they get through it fast. Do you mind if I send you Skip's sample?" Abby asked. "Maybe something changed between when your father drew his blood and when I did. Don't want to assume they are the same."

"Well, Abby we are *reallllly* busy with the FDA right now—" After a short pause he laughed.

"Zander! Don't make me bring your mother into this."

In mock horror, "Ahhh, let's not get hasty!" They both chuckled. "Is this afternoon convenient for you?" Zander offered.

"Perfect. Thanks."

Their call had ended on a light note, but the tension was working its way through his belly. In less than half a week, two of the most brilliant, steadfast medical minds in the area were worried enough about his or her medical dilemmas to enlist Zander's help. Neither would have raised an eyebrow by itself, but this was different.

In 20 years, neither doctor was concerned enough to bring him samples, let alone the day they collected them.

But was he reading too much into the situation? A trio of grisly murders in the small community of Ontario was not unheard of, but it was rare. And that a dear family friend committed it made it much more heartbreaking.

Then, there was the barely hidden note of terror in Abby's voice as she spoke of her near-death experience. Others might buy into her tough-as-nails doctor's persona, but Zander had been with her through the tears during her divorce.

And now, Mom and Dad had whatever was going around. There wasn't much he could do with Dad's samples, but he could try to use his Parks' magic to come at this thing from a different angle.

# Chapter 12



*July 4, Wednesday — 11 am — Wesley and Silvia Parks' House*

It had been a restless morning at the lab. Zander intended to work through the puzzle before him, but his brain wouldn't cooperate. It was frightening how fast this "flu" was spreading, and his parents were of an age when it could turn deadly. So, he had called 20 minutes ago and moved up their coffee date. Ostensibly, to check in with them.

The house was lifeless looking.  Not shocking, considering most sick people aren't gardening or playing squash, but it goosed Zander's unease. Parking his blue Jeep Wrangler in the drive, he headed to the side door with his usual tray of drinks. Before he could try the knob, his mother opened the door. He was shocked.

It would be unfair to say that Silvia was a vain woman; it would be closer to the truth to say she wanted to project a certain appearance: an urban, confident, stylish woman.

Sure, there were days she didn't meticulously apply her make-up or wear a cocktail dress for breakfast, but more times than naught, she appeared more ready to take over a Fortune 500 company rather than watch *Days of Our Lives.*

Somewhere in the back of his mind, Zander knew both his parents were growing old, but they always seemed vigorous to him. Yes, they occasionally forgot things, but he did, too, and he was only halfway through his 40s. So, he knew he would have to face their mortality someday, but he hoped that day wouldn't happen soon.

Hope wasn't enough. His mother gave him her special smile. But it did little to hide the dark circles under her eyes or the pain crinkles that tightened around them. Her disheveled hair and worn robe completed her appearance. Like a parent whose child was sick, all he wanted to do was hold her and comfort her, but he knew she was a proud woman who wouldn't want pity.

So, instead, he gave her his brightest smile and said, "Are you guys still okay with me coming to visit for a few minutes today, or should I deliver the ambrosia and leave?"

"You know we always love seeing you, but I wonder if it's smart to risk giving it to you? This thing, whatever it is, seems to be very contagious and not much fun to go through."

"That would worry me more if I hadn't seen Dad after he was exposed, or the fact we have a few people at the lab come down with it already," Zander shrugged. "So, I'm willing to chance it. Don't worry, I will only stay for a few minutes."

With practiced steps, they headed for the study. She grabbed a chair, and he set the drinks on an end table. In the meantime, his father came into the room and endeavored to hide a slight grimace as he inserted himself into his recliner. His father appeared to be in the same beleaguered state as his wife. Zander handed each a frappuccino and took a seat. As they waited in companionable silence for someone to speak, he attempted to surreptitiously gauge if his parents were suffering from more than a simple flu.

He finally asked, "Have you considered going in to see Abby? I'm concerned; you two look like death warmed over."

"Glad to see you, too," Wesley said with a chuckle and became more thoughtful. "Been around for a while. Don't you think I would realize we needed medical help and ask for it? Still, I would be lying if I told you I feel great, though. Think my aspirin is wearing off."

"Don't mean to be a mother hen," Zander said, "but I worry about you two after Crystal. I guess I—I'm afraid of losing you."

Silvia turned to her son and said, "We don't want anything bad to happen to you either, but we can't treat each other like we're porcelain dolls. If Crystal's death is to positively influence our lives, then let's hope it taught us to appreciate the blessings God gave us. For the most part, I believe our family has done its best to *carpe diem* since your sister's death. Even so," she said with an onery look in her eyes, "your father and I are bound and determined to spend your inheritance before leaving this world."

They laughed and raised a frappuccino in toast.

Once he was certain his parents were down but kicking, Zander said, "I didn't intend to come and wear you guys out, but I do need to share two things with you."

Wes made a continue motion with his hand.

"The blood samples you gave me two days ago were completely normal. In fact, we didn't even see any elevated white blood cell counts, which is weird now that I think of it."

"Thanks for checking. That makes me feel better about whatever we caught," Wes said.

"We are happy to help," Zander said and then screwed up his face in disgust, "or at least most of us are glad to do our part." Silvia gave him a look, but Zander waved it away. "Just office drama. Actually, that's not true. A few team members think we have no business working on anything except the cure," Zander remarked.

Wes raised an eyebrow and said, "Do these staff people know who the favor is for and who it benefits?"

"Trust me; they know I'm not happy about their objections. So, when Abby asked us for a favor this morning; test Skip's latest blood sample, I couldn't jump at the chance fast enough. I guess that makes me petty, but I talked to Pete after he found Sarah and the kids."

"Thank God. We have only heard the barest of details..." Silvia started to remark but then trailed off into silence.

"There's just no explanation. Pete and Abby both figured there had to be some pharmacological reason for Skip's behavior, but the lab work came back negative. According to Abby, if it weren't for some heavy-duty tranquilizers, Skip would have already crushed his skull against his cell bars. So, if drugs didn't cause him to have a psychotic episode, what did?" Turning to his father, he asked, "Did you notice anything unusual when you examined him?"

"If you mean, was he trying to hurt me, then no," his father said. "The fever had a grip on him for sure, but he seemed to be his normal self. What did Abby's sample reveal?"

"Haven't had a chance to process the sample she sent this morning, but I doubt it will do much good."

Scratching his chin whiskers in a thoughtful pose, his father suggested, "You have to remember the first rule of medicine: once you eliminate the impossible, whatever remains, no matter how improbable, must be the answer."

"Pretty sure you cribbed that from Sir Arthur Doyle," Zander chuckled.

"Maybe I did, but does it make it any less applicable to medicine? Are there any assumptions you are making which hurt your results?"

"Hmm. Well, we know at the time when you saw him, he was mentally fine, and he was infected with whatever this bug is." His father and mother nodded. "And we can all agree this violent behavior is atypical for Skip, so there has to be some physiological trigger. Therefore, something has to be in the sample." When

Zander struggled with the next step, Wes made a keep-going-with-that-thought motion with his hands. Zander worked through the problem a few times before his face lit up. "Sooo, it's impossible for it to be clean. I don't know how, but our sample must be tainted. It's the only answer." Zander stood. His revelation demanded immediate action.

"Glad to be of help," Wesley said with a proud grin on his face. "I knew you'd figure it out. Sometimes it's hard to get out of your own way and think the thing through. Regarding your consultation fee, I think 50 bucks sounds about right. You can pay my lovely receptionist on the way out." His mother held out her hand, awaiting payment. They all chuckled at the family in-joke.

"How about I continue to be your frappuccino dealer?" Zander offered.

"You drive a hard bargain," Silvia said as she turned her hand from palm up to vertical to shake Zander's hand.

Without thinking, he almost shook her hand to make the "mock" deal when he thought better of it. His mother's knowing, sad smile accepted Zander's caution, but then he realized hurting her, even in this inconsequential way, was not worth two figs. He shook her hand once and pulled her in for a heartfelt embrace. When enough time passed, they broke the embrace with love in their eyes. Then, he knelt by his father's chair to hug him, but Wesley grunted in irritation. He got to his feet and hugged his son.

"Thanks, Dad, for the assist. Wish there was something I could do to help you through this," Zander said as he entertained the notion of nursing them back to health.

"There's nothing you can do, hon," his mother said, "Go test that sample and see if you can help Abby. That is where you can do the most good."

"I know, but I want you to know how much I love you both," Zander said, tears threatening to spill.

"We love you too, sweetheart. More than you can fathom," his mother said.

"Love you, son," Wesley said as Zander drove away. It seemed somehow inadequate for all the things he wanted to say.

*20 minutes later at St. Alphonsus.*

"…Dad reminded me of a truism he uses, if something is improbable that doesn't mean it is impossible. When he said that, it blew me away. Over and over, I have been wracking my brain as to why we didn't find anything in Dad's sample. Maybe I didn't want to face reality—someone I trust sabotaged the samples."

"You know what this means, Zander," Abby said as she pushed the vial of blood in circles around her desk blotter.

"It means I can't let this sample out of my sight or let anyone else touch it," he said in misery.

"I'm sorry, Zander, "Abby said with brows furrowed, "it's never easy when someone betrays your trust." Zander tried to interrupt and ask about her hurt, but Abby pushed through. "Get this sample processed, and let's see if we can stop this thing."

"The staff will be leaving around 1 pm for the holiday. I will wait until they are gone before I run my tests. Will let you know as soon as I learn anything definitive."

# Chapter 13



*July 5, Thursday — 4 am — Alvardo
Residence*

"Hello?" Sheriff Pete Alvardo croaked into his phone. He was not sure how many times it had rung, but he felt like there were at least two layers of sleep fog between him and true consciousness. A film-coated his tongue, and his throat felt like molten gravel. Grabbing his water glass from the nightstand stand he drank what was left.

"Pete?" A familiar female voice asked. When he made no reply, she forged on. "Hey. Sorry to wake you, but I need you to come to the station now."

He fumbled to find his alarm clock in the dim light of his bedroom. "It's 4 am, Roxy. I didn't get any sleep last night, and I'm dogging it. Can you handle it for three more hours?"

He knew it was selfish, but the past few days had been trying, to say the least, and sleep had been in short supply. Then, it registered: Roxy sounded scared and panicked. He knew she would have done anything to not call him right now, so it must have gone into the crapper.

"Never mind, Roxy, that wasn't fair. What's happening?"

He could hear her exhale in relief as he took charge of the situation. "Thanks," her gratitude meant on several different levels.

When she resumed, her voice was professional and efficient as she began her recitation of the night's events. "There are three different reports of a homicide or attempted homicide called into 911 dispatch within the past 15 minutes."

The news hit Pete like a sheet of ice-cold water, and he bolted out of bed while exclaiming, "Did you just say *three* murders?!"

"Yes. And there are only three of us on shift tonight. Sam and Jackson are on patrol, and I'm manning the front desk."

There was no fog now as Pete gave instructions, "First, contact the Oregon State Patrol, then Fruitland and Baker City PDs. Tell them about what we are facing, and we need any help they can lend. Will be there in 15."

"Will do, Chief." Then, dial tone.

'The Sheriff' walked into the station 14 minutes later. And Roxy greeted him with a sympathetic expression and a steaming mug of joe. Two swigs later, Pete sighed and smiled.

Then, without preamble, he moved his other hand in a circular give-it-to-me motion as he continued to sip his coffee.

Grabbing the tablet on the counter, Roxy presented the pertinent details in her efficient but somewhat snarky manner, "We now have four reports of violence in the past 30 minutes. The first was a call from a Jeff McCallister. According to him, without provocation, his wife tried to play T-Ball with a baseball bat and his head. Her scream beforehand was his only warning of the attack, but it was enough for him to block the shot to his head with his arms. Even still, she got a couple of substantial swings into his body before he ran for the bathroom and locked himself in. Lucky for him, Jeff's cell was still in his pocket when he sought refuge from Hank Aaron, and he was able to contact 911. The operator tried to stay on the line with him, but it went dead a few minutes later. I sent Sam and Jackson out to his place to try to sort everything out.

"The second call was from a"—she briefly checked her notes—"Vera Hopkins out on Barnes Road. Some sort of ruckus woke her from a sound sleep, so she decided to check it out. It sounded like her new neighbors, Trish and Noah Schaal, were having a spat, so she was going to head back inside when something crashed through a window. Now she could plainly hear screaming, like cats going at it. And what sounded like a body crashing into walls. Then silence.

"She was scared to death, but she wanted to see if they were okay. Made it as far as the front bay window, before she saw a pool of blood soaking into the linen light shade of an upset floor lamp. Vera was done Nancy Drewing for the night, so she scampered back home and called 911. The operator said Vera was breathing pretty hard, but otherwise, she was okay. Hiding in her bathroom.

"I wanted to check on the Schaals, but with Sam and Jackson heading to the McCallister call, there was no one but me." Pete glared at her. "I know you don't want us going solo on domestic disturbance calls, but at the time, it seemed my only choice."

She hurried on with her report, "As I was saying, I was going to head out the door when I got another dispatch call. That's when I knew everything was heading to the shitter, so I called you. Had just hung up with you when someone came in the lobby and claimed he found multiple dead bodies."

"You did the right thing, Roxy. What were the other two?"

"According to dispatch, the third call was from Jacob O'Malley. He reported that an unidentified man was banging on the front door of his house and screaming, 'Let me in. Someone's dog is trying to kill me.'" Both officers turned as one in Astro's general vicinity. Now quiet. "Jacob got his pistol out of his safe, but no Cujo or vic to be found. When he hit the porch light, there was blood on the step but nothing else.

"And if the night weren't bozo enough, Logan Francis ran into the station shortly after I called you. His wife, Ava, works as a bartender at the Hill Topper just off 84. Normally, she comes home from work around 1:30. So, when Logan woke at 2:30 to take a pee and didn't see her anywhere, he tried the bar's number and cell with no luck. He freaked and drove to her bar.

"But instead of finding her stuck working late, he found Ava, the dishwasher, and two customers lying dead in the kitchen. Said there was blood everywhere and no one around. He checked her pulse. She was gone. He bolted and drove here like a bat outta hell. He was a real mess. Had one hella time trying to even understand him. Finally, talked him into taking a seat on your office couch. Did I miss a full moon or something?"

Things were worse than Pete thought. On the best of days, he didn't believe in coincidences. So, having potentially four homicides in half an hour only two days after Skip's violent outburst looked a hell of a lot like a pattern—a pattern that was getting exponentially worse. The hairs on the back of his neck pricked, and he didn't think it had much to do with the fever he was starting to get. Whatever "this" was, they couldn't handle it within the department even if they brought the other eight officers in.

He was not too proud to ask for help. "You did the right thing, Roxy, and I will check on him in a minute. But first, I need to know where we stand with the cavalry."

"Baker City and Fruitland are going to send us two patrolmen each, and OSP will shoot us a couple of troopers, though it will take them a while to get here."

"When they get here, issue them one of our radios and have them head to the Hilltopper ASAP. Let them know we have four suspected homicides there and no killer. Call the state troopers and tell them to go to Jacob's house and see if they can puzzle out this dog attack. Maybe we will get lucky, and it's only an every-day animal assault." Roxy gave him an incredulous look. "Hey, on a night like tonight, gotta be an optimist. While you make those calls,

I will have a quick chat with Logan and see if I can calm him down a bit. Then you and I will head out to Trish and Noah's and see what happened out there. You got 10 minutes. Make it happen!"

He quick-stepped it to his office, the coffee and adrenaline made him feel as if his feet didn't touch the ground, and he knocked on the door. It felt a little foolish to be knocking on one's own door, but the poor man had enough shocks for any night.

There was no answer.

When Pete opened the door, what he found was shocking. Logan was curled up asleep on the couch. Apparently, the combination of the shock and a warm, safe, boring room was too much for the man. So, he slept. Pete was not a psychologist, but he knew this probable widower would have very little peace in the coming weeks, so he turned off the lights and shut the door behind him.

Grabbing a memo pad, he wrote his phone number and a brief message, in case Logan woke before they got back, and then taped it on his door.

There were a handful of minutes left before his self-imposed deadline, so he decided to use them to check on his charges in the holding area. Both man and dog were in a less-agitated state than earlier. They slept soundly in their darkened cells.

*If only my city would do the same. Now, Pete, don't start drumming up more trouble than already exists. Who knows, maybe these incidents aren't as dire as they seem—yeah, right, if you have faith in that, then you probably think Big Tobacco believes their cigarettes don't cause cancer either.* Some days, it was harder for him not to have a dark sense of humor than others. It was his defense mechanism, he kept telling himself. Sanity didn't have handrails.

When he returned to the main office, Roxy was getting off the phone. "Perfect timing; let's go," he said.

Five minutes later, they knocked loudly on Vera Hopkins' door and announced they were the police. There was a distinct pause as she checked the peephole before opening it for them. Vera was a plump 60-year-old woman who was wearing an 'old lady sleeping dress' covered in flowers, a pair of slippers, and her blue, plush robe.

Her gray hair was cut short, and her nervous eyes darted about. "Boy, I'm so glad to see you two. Not much I can tell you I didn't say to the 911 operator. 'Cept haven't heard a peep since I looked into their window. Not much I could do for them here but pray."

"Thanks, Vera," Pete said with an awe-shucks smile. "We appreciate your help." Her blush was apparent, even in the poor light of the porch light.

"Glad you are okay," Roxy said with a reassuring smile. "Stay here and lock the door behind us, dear."

Once they were sure Vera was safe, they crossed to the well-manicured lawn of the Schaals'. Stopping at the front room window, they shone their flashlights inside and saw a female body lying sprawled on the floor in a pool of blood—limbs askew.

They ran to the nearest door. Pete readied his gun while Roxy moved to the side of the door jamb and tried the knob.

Unlocked. Most people in this small town did not bolt their doors.

They made eye contact, and then Pete silently counted down from three.

Throwing open the door, Roxy then drew her gun and followed Pete into the house as both screamed, "Sheriff officers! Drop your weapons and come out here with your hands up!"

The announcement was unnecessary: no one was alive to hear it. They found Trish's body first, and after a quick pulse check, they continued their sweep through the small house. Partway through their search, they found another victim. A male body lay on the floor in the front bedroom, unmoving. Roxy covered Pete as he entered the room, turned the body over, and checked for the man's pulse.

Joining Pete beside the corpse, she said, "That's Noah. He worked out at my gym and seemed to be a nice guy."

"All we can do now is try to figure out what happened here. I'll work this room; you work the front room. See what happened to Trish."

"Okay. Yell if you need me," Roxy said as she left.

A .38 was lying on top of a pile of clothes near the body. Near the gun were several spent rounds and the acrid smell of gunpowder. Vera had said she heard yelling and banging but no gunshots. Maybe she was already sequestered in her bathroom by then. If this was a domestic disturbance, then the argument had escalated into a gunfight. Noah must have gotten angry enough to pull a gun on her and threaten to kill his wife. What didn't make sense was if he had time to fire off two shots at his wife or attacker, why wasn't she dead on the floor here instead of him?

Were there two attackers?

Did he wound his attacker?

Was it Trish?

And how did a man with a loaded gun get killed by someone tearing out his throat?

Two weeks ago, Pete would have guessed the damage had to be caused by an animal. Now, he couldn't be so sure. If this case wasn't weird enough, domestic disturbance calls were usually straightforward. Every experienced police officer will tell you these stops are some of the most dangerous, but when it comes to figuring out what happened, the officers only have two combatants and their versions of the truth. So, the clues seemed to point to Trish, but Trish was dead too.

Therefore, the evidence would point to an outside attacker, and yet Vera said she had heard the couple shouting. Why would Trish do this to her newlywed husband, or even more disturbing, how *could* she do this to him?

Pete didn't want to be a sexist, but Noah, a US Marine, had recently returned from a tour in Afghanistan two months ago. The man had to be a well-muscled 220 pounds man, who appeared to be fully capable of 'taking care of himself' with or without a gun.

Pete had known Trish for years, and she was barely 5'2" and 100 pounds soaking wet. She was a preschool teacher at her church and had worked as office manager for Forestco for the past two years.

It was nearly impossible to imagine her doing something so barbaric as chewing someone's throat out. Maybe that was why she overcame her husband; Noah probably thought his wife couldn't hurt him even if she wanted to. For the second time that week, the case details made no sense. And yet, Pete felt there had to be some connection. Pulling a pair of latex gloves from his back pocket, he started to put them on when he heard a cry from the other room.

He ran.

"Almost missed it," Roxy said as she removed her two fingers from the woman's neck, "she has a weak pulse, and she's alive!".

Pete rushed over, and they quickly turned her onto her back. Obviously, one of the two bullets Noah fired had hit his wife. Blood was bubbling from the now uncovered, ragged hole in her thigh. Lucky for her, the bullet missed the femoral artery, or hydrostatic pressure would have caused her to bleed out long before they arrived.

Even still, a wound this large could kill if not treated, so Roxy immediately covered the injury with her hands to try to staunch the blood flow. It continued to seep through Roxy's fingers and add to the two-and-a-half-foot wide lake that was forming on the hardwood floor around her body.

The wound was far enough down Trish's leg that Pete figured they could use a tourniquet on her. He removed his belt and cinched it down hard above the bullet's entrance. The bleeding slowed to a trickle.

Searching for a sufficient dressing for the wound, he discovered a well-used, lavender lap blanket on a nearby couch and placed it over Roxy's hands. She repositioned her hands long enough to put the coverlet in place and then reapplied pressure to the wound.

Grabbing his shoulder mic, he said, "Sheriff to base."

No response. Then it hit him: there was no one at the station. He took out his cell and dialed 911. The operator picked up on the second ring. "This is Chief Alvardo. We have a 30-year-old female with a gunshot wound to the thigh. Lost a lot of blood and we have applied a tourniquet. Tell Alphonsus we have no time to wait for paramedics. We will transport. ETA: 5 minutes!"

The operator acknowledged the message and hung up.

"Her breath is shallow, and her color is getting worse," Roxy said. "Grab her feet, and let's get her into the back of the car!"

Time fast-forwarded. It seemed he blinked, and then they were speeding down the road. His partner was in the backseat, keeping pressure on the wound. She screamed his name so she could be heard over the wailing siren, then she added, "Something occurred to me."

He wanted to give a sarcastic reply, but he bit his tongue and said, "Hit me."

"Don't Skip and Trish work together at Forestco?"

Suddenly everything clicked into place for him; like playing spider when only a dozen cards were left on the table. Everyone in the area knew people who had attended the Forestco picnic had succumbed to either food poisoning or a rather unpleasant flu. In a moment of intuition, he knew this sickness was much worse than rotten eggs in a macaroni salad. He goosed the gas pedal even more, feeling like he was trying to outrace whatever this thing was pursuing them.

Three minutes later at the St. Alphonsus Medical Center the tires of the Charger mildly squealed as he negotiated the covered, half-circle emergency entrance. The moment the car stopped, Abby, wearing a mask, and a nurse, John Lange, rushed to the back door of the cruiser and opened it.

John had a stretcher, which he moved to the right of the back door of the car. Pete launched himself out of driver's seat, and was going to open the driver's side back door to assist moving Trish, when Abby shouted rapid-fire instructions.

"John, grab her under the shoulders; Pete, get over here and help with her torso when he gets her out far enough; Roxy, take her legs. Keep her level!"

In a heartbeat, their patient was loaded on the stretcher and being whisked to a surgery suite.

As they headed across the lobby, Abby said, "Three is prepped for surgery. Get her in there, stat!" She ran to another room, ostensibly to do final preparation for the operation.

Meanwhile, Roxy, John, and Pete each grabbed a corner of the sheet that covered Trish's stretcher, then lifted and deposited her onto the operating table. Then, John snatched a pair of scissors from a nearby counter and expertly removed Trish's blood-soaked top, bra, and jeans.

Meanwhile, Roxy and Pete grabbed a pair of latex gloves from a nearby dispenser and put them on. Roxy snatched a large clear plastic forensics bag from a nearby cubby hole, collected Trish's clothes, stuffed them into the container, sealed it, and then put the evidence on the stretcher for later.

Pete ran to a nearby cupboard, grabbed several fresh stacks of gauze pads, and laid them next to Trish's wounded thigh. Roxy made eye contact with him, when he nodded, she removed the blood-soaked blanket. Pete pressed six pads firmly on the wound just below the tourniquet/belt. Roxy grabbed some nearby wipes and tried to clean the blood off the patient while John focused on smearing a bright orange antibiotic solution all around the gunshot wound.

As he was finishing up, Abby entered the room wearing a full, green, surgical gown and mask. Briefly, she lifted the dressing Pete was holding in place, nodded to herself, and replaced it. Once she had examined the wound, she assessed her patient's overall condition. Abby knew her business and wasted none of Trish's waning minutes of life on overthinking or dithering.

"Lost a lot of blood. Whoever applied this tourniquet gave her a chance, though." This she said out loud to no one in particular. "Pale and shocky. John, let's get some plasma into her before she goes into cardiac arrest."

It almost seemed like John was inserting the needle in Trish's arm before Abby had completed the command—the duo in perfect synch.

"Probably gave her a chance by calling this in and rushing her here. Had her blood type on file: A positive. Didn't waste precious time," Abby said as she lifted Trish's wounded leg and probed for an exit wound. "Damn, bullet is still in there."

Even as she spoke, John moved a ubiquitous IV bag holder to the head of the bed. Two bags of liquid hung from its arms: one plasma, the other saline.

"One last thing. Roxy, can you apply those EKG pads on her chest?" Nodding to the far counter, she then turned on the bright operating lights, brushed Pete's hand and bandages to the side, and grabbed a pair of telescoping glasses to visually reassess her surgery site. Moments later, the EKG machine was tracking Trish's faint heartbeat.

"Thank God, I insisted you guys take advanced medical training classes," she told the two law enforcement officers. "But you need to leave it to John and me now. Will let you know as soon I know anything." Abby got to work.

Roxy took a few wobbly steps as they left the operating theater and stopped. The evidence bag containing Trish's blood-soaked clothes was firmly pressed against her chest. Pete made it partway down the hall and turned to comment to his friend. He realized she was not following him to the car. Completing his turn, he saw she was suddenly pale, shivering, and close to tears.

He returned to her and softly said, "Hey, you, okay?"

Without a word, she gave him a ferocious hug. He returned it. She was shaking, but then he realized he was too. Their adrenaline spike wearing off, the horror of the crime, and the beginnings of shock were a potent cocktail that neither could master. Eventually, the horror and fear resided enough for both to face the next thing—they broke their embrace. As they did, Dr. Manly rushed by them, giving them a grim nod. Then headed into the surgery suite without a word.

"Let's take a breather," Pete said as motioned toward the hospital staff break room.

"But we are in the middle of a crisis," Roxy said quickly with a hint of desperation in her voice. "We need to get back out there."

Chortling, Pete said, "We will, tiger, but we're no help to anyone if we are both in shock. Besides," pointing toward his shoulder mic, "they will let us know if they need us."

They entered the small room. Roxy turned a plastic chair backward and sat facing the six-person table as Pete went to the coffee pot and poured them a few cups. Taking a seat opposite her, Pete waited for her to speak while sipping his lava-hot beverage. The wait was not long. Her tight shoulders suddenly eased as she grabbed her cup and sipped.

Then, like the sun peeking through the clouds, her usual smirk appeared, and she said, "Sorry about—"

"Nothing to be sorry about. Yes, you missed her faint life signs, but when you did catch your mistake, you didn't freeze. If Trish lives, it's because of your actions, and I couldn't be prouder of one of my team," Pete said with sincerity.

Her blush was sudden and brilliant. "I was so scared…then when we were done… it hit me. I should be more…"

"Human?" Pete interrupted her again. "Give yourself some slack. If you couldn't tell, you weren't the only one with the shakes afterward. We are a stronger team when we have each other's backs. So, stop second guessing yourself, because I need my right-hand woman."

"Sure know how to give a girl a pep talk. And thanks." Her sincere smile alluded to a time when everything would return to normal, but both would have their share of nightmares before then.

"Are you up to—" Pete began but never finished.

Their radios squelched, and Sam said, "Pete, Jeff McCallister is dead. His skull and most of the bones in his body are broken. Victoria took a swing at us when we came in the door. Gave Jackson a first-rate bruise on his shoulder, but better his shoulder than his head. Even with a head as hard as his." Sam chuckled and then sobered up. "I can't believe how strong she is. Can't be much bigger than my little sister, but it took everything we had to hold her down and cuff her." Pete shared a meaningful glance with Roxy. "Heading to the station with our prisoner now. Any further orders?"

"Not right now," said Pete. "But sounds like you handled things well. Good work. Roxy and I are at the hospital now. Trish and Noah Schaal must have had a hell of a row as well. Noah is dead, and Trish is hanging by a thread, .38 sized hole in her leg. Abby is working on her now, but her prognosis is poor. Heading back to the station in 10 minutes. Once you get Victoria in holding, grab yourself a coffee and wait for us. We'll figure out what to do then."

"Sounds good, boss," Sam said. "See you in a few."

"Are you starting to notice a pattern to these murderers?" Roxy said.

"You mean the one where loving, stable people become monsters?" Pete said with sarcasm. "Yeah, my expert detective skills helped me kinda pick up on that one."

"It's more than that, Pete. It's almost like they are high on something. How are they becoming psychotic killers, who can't feel pain, and seem to have superhuman strength? I know doc ruled out drugs, but what is it then? This is not getting better Pete, in fact, it seems to be getting worse."

"Agreed, but we don't have enough information." Mopping his forehead with a handkerchief, Pete sighed and said, "Think you have something with the Forestco angle. As soon as we get all this buttoned up tonight, let's do a little look-see up at the mill. Maybe we can figure out the connection."

"You are of course assuming we have a break anytime in the near future," she said. Pete raised an eyebrow. "Heard there were about three hundred people at the picnic. If their shindig is ground zero for whatever this is, then tonight is just the beginning of one hell of a shitstorm."

Giving a theatrical shudder, Pete said sarcastically, "Thanks for those wonderful words of comfort, Sally Sunshine."

She stood up and jauntily pushed her chair under the table and said, "Hey. I'm not just the eye candy in this partnership."

Chuckling, Pete got up and followed her out to the cruiser. Seeing her return to her usual jocular and crude self was heartening, but he couldn't help feeling that her observation was dead on.

If it was, it was going to be a long day.

# Chapter 14

*July 5, Thursday — 3:01 am — Gallagher Residence*

She awoke in a pool of sweat. The pounding within her head and a wave of chills quickly sent her in search of relief. Abby grabbed two aspirins from the bathroom cabinet and tried to get back to sleep. But sweet oblivion was not to be found.

Instead, her doubts and fears chased themselves round and round like a litter of playful puppies. The more she tried to sleep, the more elusive it became. Finally, she got out of bed to make some herbal tea. While she waited for the water to boil, she reflected on her predicament.

Being a scientific, dispassionate observer was one thing: she collected data, consulted colleagues, and perused related medical articles. It was altogether another thing to know you were a part of the second wave of an epidemic. But before she could become too maudlin, Pete called to warn her about the unprecedented wave of violence crashing into Ontario.

The only golden lining to his heads up was she could focus on something besides self-pity. She was heading to the hospital 15 minutes later.

*St Alphonsus Hospital — 9:33 am.*

The phone on Abby's mahogany old-fashioned executive desk taunted her, daring her to pursue action. If she accepted the challenge, call the Center for Disease Control (CDC) and report this as an outbreak, she could no longer cling to the fantasy that everything would be okay.

Unfortunately, as much as she wanted to believe the fiction, her clinical, rational mind wouldn't let her. The facts available to her all pointed to a scary conclusion: her sleepy little town was ground zero for a possible catastrophic pandemic. She lifted her hand and rested it on top of the phone, unable to pick it up.

Questions.

*Why* Ontario? No idea.

*How* did it get started? No idea. There might be a tenuous connection between humans and animals, but it didn't feel like the answer.

*When* seemed to be the only answer she had so far. *The picnic.* But it seemed to be such an artificial, specific starting point. Something was wrong there. Could that be enough to raise the alarm? Could she explain it to them sufficiently?

*Would* they trust her instincts? No.

So, she released the phone and wiped her damp brow again.

Six murders were committed in three hours. Even now those facts better suited a place like Chicago than Ontario. In her bones, she knew she could no longer ignore the relationship between the flu-like symptoms and the insanity that followed. But there simply was no medical explanation for the violence, no physiological evidence to lead her toward a possible avenue of exploration.

Not only that, but Pete had found Skip and Astro's dead bodies in their cells after taking Trish to the hospital. She had doubted

Skip would have regained his faculties. His death, though tragic, presented her with an opportunity to have a thorough physiological picture of what happened to the man by way of the coroner's autopsy. Until its completion, much of the enigma would remain.

The old-fashioned clock on her office wall ticked off each second in the near silence. *Just do it!* she admonished herself. *Better to be an alarmist than let someone open Pandora's Box.* Then, grabbing the phone handset with resolution, like a parachutist approaching a plane door, she almost lifted it when it rang, filling the room with its instant clamor.

Her hand leapt from its perch to her breast, as if it would defend her heart from the sudden shock. She took two deep, cleansing breaths before daring to seize the receiver again.

"Hello?" she asked in a breathless whisper.

"This is Pete. Are you okay?"

"I'm good. Had to run to catch the phone," she lied. "What's up?"

"Wanted to get your opinion on our situation here. I don't like to admit it, but this whole thing is snowballing out of control. Yesterday, I had a psychotic Skip in a holding cell. Now, less than 24 hours later, I have eight more prisoners, and they are all exhibiting the same symptoms as Skip. There are only five cells, and these people do not play nice together. Been thinking about kicking this to the next level, but I don't know if I'm overreacting. What do you think? Is this thing gonna get better?"

Abby sighed in relief and said, "So I'm not crazy. We are thinking along the same lines; I was picking up the phone to call the CDC when you called me. All our hospital rooms are taken by those injured the past few days. Starting to have people brought in who had the flu but now have slipped into comas. Once that gets out—" She didn't need to finish the thought. Both knew there would be widespread panic.

Zander walked into her office wearing a mask. Abby had one below her chin, and she moved it to cover her nose and mouth. "Hold on Pete, Zander is here, and I want him in on this, so putting you on speakerphone."

"Heya, buddy," Pete said, trying to disguise his obvious exhaustion, "Glad you're helping us on this one."

Zander gave her a meaningful glance and asked, "Are you okay?"

"Got woke up at 3 am this morning. Had to deal with more violent assaults and homicides in the past 10 hours than I have in my whole law enforcement career. Got three hours of sleep in the last 48, wish it was only that, but it started with a sore throat this morning, and got worse half an hour ago when the chills and aches hit. Whatever it is, I got it. By the way, why do you guys sound muffled?"

"I don't know about Abby, but I started coming down with the flu around dinner time last night. So, I'm wearing a mask to try to limit the spread of this thing. Abby just put hers on so I'm guessing she has it too?"

"You got that right," she said with a scowl. "Near as I can tell, sometime after I went to bed last night is when I got sick. Which fits with all the data I have on this thing so far. Looks like symptoms appear about 12-36 hours after exposure. Did you learn anything from Skip's second sample?"

Rubbing his neck with vigor, Zander said, "Certainly did. I learned two things: the first sample does not match the second."

"So, you were right, I'm so sorry Zander," Abby said with a touch of sadness in her voice. She explained to Pete, "I gave him the blood sample I collected from Skip the night you brought him in. Neither one of us could figure out why Skip's blood was clean in the sample Wes gave him."

"Hrm, this just went from a mystery to a criminal case pretty damn fast," Pete said.

"You got that right. The second thing I learned is someone had to have stolen my research."

"What?!" Abby and Pete exclaimed in unison.

"Not only was the second sample a different blood type, but it contained several elements of biological material we used to create Picadone."

"What pieces?" Pete asked.

"Well, you all know we used a modified HIV strand to attack Leukemia cells, and I found an exact replica of it in Skip's blood."

"So, can I assume it would be impossible for someone else to create this same virus combination coincidently?" Abby asked.

"Winning Megabucks with the Powerball—twice—would be more likely," Zander said despondently. Abbey knew how proud Zander was of his staff. Now, he not only had to acknowledge one of them betrayed him, but he was faced with the reality his cure for cancer was being subverted into something that could kill hundreds, if not thousands, in Ontario.

"But it couldn't just be HIV. Could it?" she tried to ask Zander gently.

"No. HIV is devastating, but it can take years for it to compromise the immune system. So, it would be impractical to have a treatment for Leukemia which didn't immediately heal the patient."

"Um," Pete interrupted, "unsure I want to ask, but how did you speed up your virus?"

Moments ticked by while Zander tried to work up to his answer, but finally, he said, "Ebola."

"We have *Ebola?!* God above!" The speaker on the phone crackled as Pete shouted.

"Calm down, Pete, no infected people are bleeding through their pores here," Abby said.

"She's right. Ebola was only a part of this new virus, and it has been heavily modified. There were other things I didn't recognize," Zander said. "I can try to figure out the other pieces later, but I wanted to get this to you guys, ASAP."

"Did the right thing," Abby said. "Now, we must figure out how to stop it from spreading. Usually, Ebola is transmitted by blood or bodily fluids."

"There was a lot of blood flying when we took out Skip," Pete said.

"Don't doubt it, but I'm sure Wes and I were careful with our patients," Abby said. "It's got to be something else."

"Pretty sure I didn't come into contact with contaminated blood either," Zander said. The silence spooled out as they worked their way through the knot before them. Finally, Zander added, "Wait. My dad came to see me on Monday. Maybe that is why I got sick before you guys."

"Could be. Whoever engineered this thing modified its attack vector, too," she said. "Hmmm. I'm only spitballing here, but I didn't wear a mask. Zander, do you think this could be spread through the air?"

"Well, you know as well as I do, there are many disease microbes which are dispersed by breathing the air others have exhaled. If I wanted to create something that would spread quickly, that's how I would do it."

"But why release it at Forestco?" Abby asked.

"Got a guess," Pete said. "They suffer more vandalism and get more death threats and hate mail, than any person or business in the county. The thing I can't figure out is why would some eco whackos release something like this in their own backyard? They had to know it would spread beyond the mill."

"Why does anyone create biological weapons?" Abby asked. "There is always danger they could backfire on you."

"Okay. So, some whacko created this thing. Why are you sure your lab is involved beyond the sample tampering? Is there anyone else in the area who could create this thing?" Pete asked.

"Maybe two or three in the state," Zander said. "We are the only ones capable in this area."

"Then my investigation should begin at Imagine immediately. Can't take too long to interview 20 scientists and lab techs. Hopefully, whoever created this thing isn't batshit crazy. If we catch them and they have an antidote; we're good. Right?" Pete asked.

"I don't think you understand how much trouble we're in Pete," Abby said. "Assuming this is an engineered virus, one designed to have hosts try to infect others instead of just hunkering down and dying. If I were to guess, I would say half the population of Ontario has been infected in less than a week."

"Oh my God," Zander said in horror. "Whoever created this thing doesn't want to just hurt Forestco or Ontario. This could become a worldwide pandemic!"

"And if that is not bad enough, we haven't even addressed the fact that Skip's dog went as nutso as his master. There have been reports of several unusual animal attacks during the past few days. Can something like this spread to animals?"

Zander shook his head negatively, though Pete couldn't see it. But he addressed the question.

"As I said, Pete, there is no precedent for this pathogen, and only rarely in cases like HIV and bird flu do we see a disease cross the human-animal barrier. Not only that but if we have truly guessed the culprit's motives, it makes no sense. Why kill animals?"

Abby couldn't stay quiet any longer, "I have a hunch we are getting closer to the truth, but I think we shouldn't wait any longer to ask for help. Before talking to you two, I was worried about crying wolf. Now, I think we need to call the CDC and the governor and get the National Guard involved this minute. I recommend we get a quarantine in place as soon as possible, maybe we can still save thousands, if not millions of lives."

"I agree," Pete said. "Will call the governor and have him send us some troops. Hate to admit it, but my staff is working at about half capacity right now, and we can't handle normal business, let alone this."

"Half of your officers are out? What happened, Pete?" Abby asked him with concern in her voice.

"More accurately, I should have said they are half as effective. Roxy had her arm badly broken trying to bring down Bill Bradly 30 minutes ago. She should be there soon. And all of us have our share of bumps, bruises, and sprains from the new homicide case and two new assaults we had this morning. And we're all sick. We need help."

"Don't worry, Pete; we will take good care of her. Meanwhile, will you talk to Mayor Hill about commandeering Treasure Valley Community College after you call the governor?" Zander headed to the couch and plopped down in exhaustion as the two discussed logistics. "Once we secure the college, we need to stop the spread of this contagion, so let's gather all the Forestco employees and detain them. Zander might be right; we might be too late to contain the initial infected group, but we must try. Once things are set up, I will arrange a skeleton crew here at the hospital, then the rest of us will head over to 'TVCC.'"

"Just told you," The exasperation in Pete's voice was evident even across the phone line, "we were shorthanded, and now you want me to deliver 600 scared and angry people to the community college?"

She chortled at his acerbic comments and said, "McCloud, I didn't say this minute. But we need to do it ASAP, before any hopes of containing this thing gets out of reach. I know you will try your hardest."

With an overly theatrical sigh, Pete said, "All right. I'll see who we can scrape up before the guardsmen get here. Honestly, I'm not sure I have the jurisdiction even to attempt to incarcerate hundreds of townspeople based on what you guys said was shaky evidence at best." Pete took a deep breath and started again in a calmer tone, "If we agree this thing is airborne, do you think paper masks will guard the uninfected people I bring in?"

"Doubt it." Abby loathed asking Pete and his crew to become infected with a dangerous biohazard voluntarily, but she wouldn't lie about the danger either. There were no other options. Stop it now, or the genie would leave the bottle. "Those masks are not intended to shield someone from an airborne virus. There are thousands here, and we could provide them to anybody who wanted one, but they would offer little besides providing a feeling of safety.

"There are devices designed to protect the wearer, and we have a handful. The military also has them, but their stockpile doesn't help us in the short run. Of course, everything we came up with was pure conjecture, and a paper one might be acceptable. Regardless of whether the masks are a viable protection or not, I can tell you this much: if we don't try to quarantine these people now, it will spread across the country. If you can communicate how dire things are to your troops, they may be willing to risk it."

"Appreciate your honesty, Doc," Pete said. "I will present them with the facts and let them decide. They're good officers, and I would be surprised if it made one damn bit of difference to them. But I won't trick 'em into coming here."

"Fair enough," she said. "My staff will take charge of caring for the sick and procedures for the confinement. Your people will be handling all the traffic and movement of patients. Unfortunately, we are both aware you might have to physically restrain them if they have moved into the third stage of the disease. There is a small supply of tranquilizers at the hospital, and we will bring most of them to the college. I would like to use those sparingly, considering I don't have many. And as you pointed out, it might not be 100 percent legal to restrain and 'knock-out' people who haven't done anything wrong." She grimly grinned at the massive understatement.

"Probably know the answer already, but shouldn't we be on the list of people being detained at the college?" Pete asked.

Abby winced at the implication. *This can't be the way my life ends. So many things I thought I would have time to do. Now, all I have is my job, and I can't even leave on my terms.* "Technically? Yes... but who will run the asylum?" Her rhetorical question was filled with such sadness no one dared reply. Or her two friends were mentally traveling down the same bleak roads. Eventually, she broke the silence, "The CDC might quarantine us when they get here, but for now, I say we do our jobs. Besides, I want to see if I can contribute something meaningful to stop this outbreak before this bastard virus tries to take me down."

"Couldn't agree more," Zander said with an angry burst.

Pete asked, "Is there anything you can give us that will help keep us on our feet during all this?"

"I wish I had a magic pill for you," she answered. "But honestly, popping a few aspirins every couple of hours is your best bet for the time being."

"Had a feeling you would say that," Pete sighed. "Well, you two let me know as soon as you learn anything more, especially if it's *good* news."

"We promise," Zander said. "Take care, Pete."

"Hang in there, Pete; only need to hold out for another day or so." Hitting the disconnect button, she gazed over at Zander. "Well, you heard most of that. What do you think?"

Zander paused a moment to pull out a pack of gum and pop a piece in his mouth. Once the ritual was complete, she could see the hurt in his eyes. "I think we are going to lose a lot of good people before we can find a cure. It's funny, I can be cavalier about my own life, but when it comes to others—" he left the rest unsaid.

Her heart went out to him. It was one thing to talk about casualty rates and how many would die, but it was something altogether different when it hit this close to home. "I'm sorry, Zander. I should have acted sooner. Maybe I—"

He cut her off. "The time for self-condemnation might come someday, but neither of us can afford that luxury now. I better go."

The rebuke stung, but it put some steel in her spine. Her face hardened with resolve as she reached for the phone.

# Chapter 15

*July 5, Thursday — 12:02 pm — Imagine Labs Staff Room*

The last two hours were some of the toughest Zander could remember—and that included med school. First, the virus had taken its best shot at him, and there wasn't anything he wanted more than to curl up and sleep. Second, now that all the testing and sleuthing were done, he had to face the fact, someone in this building, and possibly in this room, had taken their recipe for Picadone and perverted it into a contagion which could kill millions.

A quarter of an hour ago, Pete called. He told Zander he opened an investigation into the blood sample tampering but also admitted that any personnel they would have committed to the case would first be used to corral Forestco families. For now, it would be up to Zander to ferret out the traitor(s) in his midst. He had arrived in the staff room a few minutes before the noon starting time.

Grabbing a chair at one of the front tables, he tried to muster a little strength to help him through this imminent, difficult chore. But the constant throbbing of a low-grade headache made ordering his thoughts for the meeting feel like he was an eel wrangler trying to capture one out of hundreds.

Lost in his misery, Zander was brought back to reality by someone clearing her throat, and he glanced up at his staff.

"Sorry." The mask caused the sound of his voice to be muffled and weak. He rose from his seat, but the room spun, and he almost had to sit down again before he regained his balance enough to place two palms firmly on the table. "What I wouldn't give for Dr. McCoy and a medical tricorder right now."

If Zander had thought this line would bring chuckles or lighten the mood in the room. He was wrong.

*Their* friends, family, and neighbors were getting sick, and they were scared. They looked to him for much-needed answers; he would give them what he knew. "Most of you know our lab has been working with local police and health authorities. It is not a secret that we found nothing in our first samples. But you may not know I ran a second set of samples from the same person and came up with totally different results."

Murmurs arose at this revelation.

"My independent test revealed there is a virus in the victim's blood, and it contains elements very similar to our modified HIV and Ebola manipulations. We didn't create this thing, but someone who works here did." Shocked whisperings were replaced with angry mutterings as the staff came to the same conclusion as Zander.

"It gets worse, folks. Apparently, this thing has a 100 percent infection rate and Dr. Gallagher thinks this virus might be spread through the air."

His staff felt death's chill hand grasping for them. They worked with dangerous pathogens for a living, but they knew with proper handling, their risks were minimal. Unfortunately, what Zander had just revealed was, each person in the room was sick. It was only a matter of time until they showed symptoms. In effect, they knew a death sentence had been served to all in attendance—maybe everyone on the planet.

"So, let me get this straight," Lise said with anger in her voice. "Someone here switched the vial of plasma with another and someone created a mutant virus that most likely will kill us all?"

Righteous fury swept over the room. It was too much to take in. They wanted to find the traitor in their midst and ask why. Zander felt as helpless as a sailor caught in a hurricane. Lise saw her friend falter. She rose, moved to his side, put a hand on his shoulder in sympathy, and then turned to *her* troops.

Righteous fury flaring in her eyes as she spoke, "You are right to feel scared, betrayed and angry, but none of that matters! Let the sheriff handle hunting down and taking care of the twisted piece of trash who did this." A low feral sound of agreement emanated from most throats at the table. "For now, our job is to find out everything we can about this new superbug. Time is not on our side, but we know what is causing this epidemic. Let's do what we do best: create an antidote. From now on, we will not waste another minute. Food and cots will be brought into the facility. There will be mandatory sleep periods, and no one will leave this building or be unaccompanied at any time. Yes, I mean *any time.* By God, I will not allow whoever is responsible for this to scurry off like a cockroach."

Lise's words enheartened Zander, and he felt himself stand up straighter and added, "Most of us got into this business to save lives, and we're damn good at it." He lifted a stack of manila file folders and said, "Here are copies of everything I have found so far, and the tainted blood samples will be made available to everyone. And obviously, all Picadone work will be shelved for now. I can't tell you how proud I am of everything we have accomplished, but we must do it again."

The walk to his office was a blur, and he didn't remember picking up the phone or dialing the number for one of the most challenging calls of his life. "Abby?"

"Zander? You sound terrible."

"Trying to hold it together long enough to work one more miracle."

"Wish I could give you more encouragement, but the more we learn about the progress of this disease. The more I think whoever created this thing made our job damn near impossible. The victim can become infected and infect others in less than half a day."

"My God! That's faster than I thought," Zander said. "No wonder it has swept through town so quickly."

"That's not the worst of it, 2-3 days later the infected enters a coma-like state."

"A coma?" Zander said in surprise. "First I've heard anything about such a stage."

"Not surprising. From what we have begun to piece together, the coma only lasts about half a day or so. Most first-hand accounts from Treasure Valley believed their sick were sleeping hard, but found out, if the caretakers lived, they were mistaken. Once we knew what data to consider, we could analyze the readings from a few of the Forestco employees in the hospital. We had assumed something was triggering their aggressive, non-verbal stage. Now we know the infected's vitals become depressed for some time, then dip to the point their breathing and heart rate are nonexistent. It's like they experience a momentary death, and when they wake up, they exhibit the same symptoms Skip and the others did."

"So, you're saying during the coma, something happens to them physically?" The pieces were starting to fall into place, but they were coming too fast for his fevered brain to handle like a car on black ice.

"Knack for understatement," she chuckled. "When the first victim came out of her coma, she tried to take a bite out of John's arm while he checked her vitals. Fortunately, she was restrained, and he didn't get bit, but I'll bet you a steak dinner he never trusts a patient to be merely asleep again. You should have seen his face when he got loose from her and fell on his butt. I laughed so hard I cried."

"Has anyone ever told you that you have a dark sense of humor?"

"Don't worry, Zander, I'm still sane." It was almost like she had read his mind. "It's—well, he has been teasing me mercilessly since Skip tried to take a chunk out of me. Just desserts and all. Still, I'm glad he didn't get hurt."

"Can I assume this victim does not speak or seem to recognize anyone, too?"

"It's like their intellect or personality has been wiped. In fact, I got Skip's autopsy results back a few minutes ago. It's bad. According to the report, his brain had been devastated, somewhat similar to Mad Cow Disease. It is safe to assume there is no return to normal if an individual reaches this stage." There was an uncomfortable silence on both ends of the call. Abby eventually forged on. "Another interesting physiological change was he had off-the-charts levels of testosterone and adrenaline in his system."

"So, whoever designed this virus wants it to spread throughout the population aggressively," said Zander. "We have seen Skip infect at least two dozen others in a few days. Speaking of Skip, any idea why he died when he did?"

"As near as I can tell—and I hate using that qualifier—Skip's injuries seemed to have hastened his end. Based on the autopsy, our best guess is this animal-like phase lasts for approximately two days. The reason this stage is so short is simple: the body needs fuel. Pete reviewed the holding area footage, and neither man nor animal ate or drank. Between the adrenaline and the sickness beforehand, the body burns up. Skip died from a massive heart attack. This is all preliminary; we will know more as other autopsies are performed."

"It's amazing how much you have figured out."

"Well, I might have a little self-interest in figuring this out," she laughed. But then her tone melted into resignation and sadness, "I have to tell you something. Wish there was another way, but your parents were brought in to St. Alphonsus about half an hour ago. Sorry."

He knew it was inevitable they would reach this stage, but somehow it still sucked the air from his lungs. In a surreal way, Abby's announcement catapulted him back to the day his mother told him about Crystal's diagnosis.

"What happened?" Zander could barely speak.

"Pete's deputies went out to check on them and found them unresponsive. Gave them our last free room, they deserve so much more for all they have done for Ontario. I'm so sorry, Zander."

The silence beat at him with silent wings. With Abby's help, he now knew the basic progress of this disease, but knowing he would never share one more moment with them opened up a terrible abyss before him.

Abby interrupted the blackness, closing in on Zander: "I don't want to pile on, Zander, but I'm not sure I will be in this fight too much longer. The mind is willing, but the body is weak." A half-hearted laugh traveled achingly across the telephone line. It threatened to overwhelm him. "I'm having a hard time concentrating. I might be closing in on the coma phase, my friend." There was a pause in which he was not sure she would continue. But then in a voice so different from her usual, a scared, little-girl sounding voice, she asked, "Zander?"

Faced with all this sudden loss, he found he could not answer her. All he could manage was a choked sob, which encompassed all of his terror and grief.

"Zander. Hon. This is not over for any of us. All we can do is try to stop this here and now."

The tenuous life-line she threw him allowed him to fight back to the surface of his anguish. "Abby, I'm sorry, I'm overwhelmed. I'm not in much better shape, but can I do anything for you?"

"Nothing except pull out a miracle and try to save as many of us as possible. I will try to do the same with what time I have left."

They shared a moment of tacit understanding in the quiet.

"Would it be too much for me to ask you to do something important for me?" Zander dared to ask.

"No. What can I do?" she asked.

"If you are correct, and Mom and Dad are gone—for the love of God, please don't let them wake up." Every word was a dagger stabbed into his heart.

There was a long pause before she replied, "My Hippocratic oath prevents me from purposely harming a patient. Haven't broke that once in 28 years, and I'm sure as hell not doing it in my last few days. Not even for a good friend."

"No, Abby. You misunderstand. Not asking you to kill them, just give them a tranquilizer like you did for Skip. Please."

Her voice softened with understanding. "Oh, of course. One way or another, they will die peacefully. I can promise you that."

He almost collapsed in relief as he said. "Can't tell you how much that means. We will give everything we got to stop this virus."

"I know you will. Now, go rescue the world." And she hung up.

All thoughts of curling up on his bed and waiting for his inevitable end fled.

# Chapter 16

*July 5, Thursday — 5:24 pm — Treasure Valley Community College*

Sheriff Pete Alvardo witnessed complete chaos as he drove into the parking lot. Cars, trucks, police cruisers, buses, national guard vehicles, ambulances weaved around the throngs of people like a slow-motion, surreal ballet.

There were flashing lights everywhere. And hundreds of angry, scared, sick people were talking, screaming, begging, and threatening those around them. The cacophony battered his ears through his open driver's side window. It exacerbated the throbbing pain of his ever-present headache to the point it almost overwhelmed him.

Taking a long, cleansing breath, Pete tried to focus on the Herculean responsibility before him. If he had his druthers, he would be curled up into the fetal position somewhere. But he would be damned if people remembered him doing anything but his best for them. So, he would do his duty for as long as his body let him.

Well, first things first. This fubar situation could devolve into a dangerous riot if order was not quickly restored.

He had to come to a complete stop mere feet into the lot because hundreds of people were wandering without thought of the vehicles around them. *What the devil is going on?* he thought.

Earlier, Roxy had begged him to let her out of the station to help out, he relented, not letting her in the field, but leaving her in charge here. Now, he wondered if giving her leave to run things here had been such a great idea. *Looks more like a Walmart Black Friday sale than an orderly processing of Forestco personnel.*

Pete grimaced at his biting observation. *She has a newly broken arm for Pete's sakes, and she is out here trying to keep a lid on this mess for you. Least you can do is stop judging and lend a hand. Damn virus is wearing me out.* Properly self-chastised, Pete began scanning the spectacle before him with a practiced eye.

In the distance, a few black Apache National Guard helicopters menacingly rested on a berm. Before them, soldiers in grayish, brown fatigues with blue paper breathing masks carried containers marked with red crosses. Meanwhile, other guardsmen moved with purpose between the parking lot to the gym and other outlying buildings. There was some semblance of order here, but the mob masked it.

Suddenly, one of the local TV news crews appeared before him.

"Just peachy," he said with weary resignation, but to be honest, they were only doing their job.

If the police were rounding up over one thousand locals, it was big news. Unfortunately, it made his job that much harder.

"I don't have time for this crap," he said as he hit his lights.

Unlike hundreds of times before, the blazing blue, red, and strobe flasher bar atop the cruiser accomplished exactly—nothing. Not only did it not clear a path for him, but the news crew moved in front of the hood of his car.

A pretty, blonde reporter gave him her best winning smile, which instantly changed as he hit the siren. The poor woman and her cameraman jumped a foot into the air. But once they landed, they scurried to the side of his vehicle with remarkable haste.

He felt a little embarrassed for a moment, but he had no time to worry about ruffled feathers. The throng before him now parted as if he were a modern-day Moses. *Well, a Moses with a 124-decibel siren and a "bright as the sun" bar of blue and red, LED lights,* he mused to himself with a cynical chuckle. Inching his vehicle past the traffic gauntlet, he found a parking spot, donned a mask and his worn Stetson, and moved toward the gym with purpose. As he progressed through the scrum, he thought he spotted a familiar coal-black buzz cut and headed in Roxy's direction.

The persistent young reporter had regrouped and charged at him from Pete's right.

Her shouts of "Chief Alvardo!" resulted in his dipping his head and touching the brim of his hat with a finger.

She ignored the polite dismissal and closed the gap between them. Cameraman jogging to her side for the shot, she was about to shout her first question above the noise around them when she looked into his eyes. Apparently, the look Pete gave her did not invite her to start the interview, as she took an unconscious step backward and pretended she was interested in talking to someone else.

Grunting in satisfaction, Pete resumed course for his lieutenant. She hadn't moved, and now he could see she was in an intense conversation with a medium-built, brown-haired female major. Neither noticed his arrival until he cleared his throat loudly.

Turning in his direction, Roxy's face lit up. "Pete, errr—Chief, so glad you're here."

A blue, canvas shoulder sling and a soft cast encompassed most of her arm and although she had a smile, he could see the effects of the fever in her eyes. He nodded at her limb. In response, she tried to shrug, but a grimace interrupted the gesture. She had no business here under normal circumstances, but he doubted telling her to go home would have any effect.

Then, with a lop-sided grin, she used her uninjured hand to motion between him and the military woman and said, "Sheriff Alvardo, Major Bressan."

Touching his finger to his Stetson, he said, "Major."

"Sheriff," she said as she shook his hand with a firm grip.

It had surprised him Bressan was willing to shake his hand when she had to know almost all townspeople were infected, which spoke to her unflappable nature. And yet she wore a face mask, so she was not foolhardy. There was no doubt in his mind this competent woman could be a valuable ally.

"Your lieutenant and I were ah—*discussing*—the most efficient use of our manpower." The word "discussing" seemed chipped from a substantial block of ice, and its frostiness and aloofness were exacerbated by the blue paper mask, which cut off half the major's facial features.

Roxy bristled at the woman's tone and characterization of their conversation. So, that was what all the fireworks were: two headstrong women determining who was the alpha at this three-ring circus. His well-developed instinct for self-preservation told him to back away and let them resolve this. But they needed the National Guard's help, not a pissing contest.

*Well, you get more from honey,* he mused as he affixed his best politician smile in place and said, "Major Bressan, you and your people are a godsend, and the Ontario Police Department truly appreciates your *assistance.* What was your advice?" This time, he was the one emphasizing a word.

Major Bressan's hands barely clenched at the gentle reminder of the scene's chain of command. This was his jurisdiction until circumstances warranted his removal. Which would not be long if the CDC and governor's office inserted themselves, but he had the ball for now.

"I was telling your deputy here," Bressan pointed without need at Roxy, "we need to establish a perimeter, as soon as possible, to stop the spread of this thing. My people are best suited for the duty. Therefore, I suggested she handle things here while we set up the blockades."

The battlelines were coming into focus now. In an innocuous tone, he asked, "Major, how many personnel have you brought with you?"

Scanning a sheet on her clipboard, she said, "Two hundred and thirty-six on station."

"Excellent." Turning to his subordinate, "Roxy, would you agree we need nine roadblocks to stop everything going in and out of the city?"

Her eyes were thoughtful momentarily, and then she nodded after making her calculations, "I would say nine would cover them for now. Some mule trails around Ontario exist, but only certain trucks could access them."

"Excellent," Pete said with feigned enthusiasm. "Major, what is the absolute minimum it would take to man nine blockades?"

"The least possible number I would like to have per blockade is 20—" She stopped her assessment when she saw him fold his arms and give her a hard stare. Then, with a shrug, which eerily mimicked Roxy's earlier movement, she backtracked, "Okay. For a time, we could get by with far fewer." The major's alto voice lowered in desperation, "It sounds like you have one nasty bug here, and I don't want to be the one who lets it out. Too much depends on keeping this contained."

"On that, we are in complete agreement, Major," Pete said. "Could you get by with only 10 per blockade? Scuttlebutt says we have a small army headed this way as we speak," he said with a conspiratorial wink. "Reinforcements from other inbound National Guard battalions can back fill your crews, meanwhile, we would have a little less than 150 to control the campus and collect local infected people."

The clipboard again magically appeared in her hands with a practiced motion, and her eyes lost focus.

It seemed, to him, a good sign she had not rejected his proposal outright, so he added a little more honey to the pot. "Can I assume, Major, your troops have extensive training that prepares your people for handling the logistics of hostage-prisoner control and the movement of civilians in an emergency?"

Pete assumed she smiled with pride because her eyes lit up. However, he could only guess with her damn blue mask in place.

"Dealing with those duties is one of our company's primary functions, which is why we're usually first on the scene." Her voice was filled with pride. "There are enough rations, restraints, medical supplies, and cots in our transport trucks to deal with everything I have observed so far, and as you say" —she nodded her head toward the west— "there is a small army heading our way."

In a complete breach of military etiquette, she winked at him. It was safe to assume the pissing contest between their two fiefdoms was over.

Roxy's shoulders relaxed.

"Thank you for your cooperation, Major. Please feel free to move whatever materials you need into the gym and surrounding buildings," he offered. "It might be easier for your medical people to set up a triage tent here closer to the parking lot. There are medical staff in the physical education building who would love to see your corpsmen, and we can send the more critical cases to our hospital. Once you get settled, I will get you a map with appropriate places for roadblocks marked." He turned to Roxy and said, "Please continue to provide the Major with whatever assistance she needs to integrate her people."

"Aye aye, Captain," Roxy said with her usual hint of irreverence.

Turning back to the Bressan, he asked, "Would that be acceptable?"

"More than satisfactory," she said as she reached out and shook his hand, then she turned to Roxy and offered her hand. After the shortest hesitation, Roxy smiled and took the solidly built woman's hand.

The major turned to leave when Pete interrupted her.

"Ahhh… Major, could you do me a favor?"

Turning back to him with a raised eyebrow, "Am I not already— never mind. Shoot."

"Could you impose some military order on our loading and unloading area?" His arm swept behind him.

"That, my good man, will be my pleasure." She glanced with disdain at the reporters and looky-loos nearby, "And don't worry; it won't cost you a thing." Executing a perfect about-face, Bressan headed toward a group of her people gathered on the manicured lawn nearby.

Pete turned to his friend and ribbed her. "Don't take this the wrong way, but shouldn't you be sitting in a cozy hospital room eating green Jell-O to your heart's content?"

"What and miss all this overtime?" she shot back at him. "Come on, you know something as minor as this" —she lifted her arm and sling but ruined her display of bravado with a wince— "it will take more than this to sideline me."

"There was no doubt in my mind you would help me get through all this, but I still want you to know how much it means you are here." In a rare show of affection, he lightly placed a hand on her hurt shoulder and gave her a sincere look.

She covered his hand with hers and said, "I couldn't let you do this alone." She squeezed his hand with tenderness before they moved apart.

Resuming a more businesslike manner, he said, "Figured we would have gotten more help from the vicinity by now, but I guess the scuttlebutt has people scared. Can't say I blame them; we don't know what it is—or even how it spreads. However, the station told me two state troopers and a policeman from Baker volunteered and are on their way here, even knowing the potential danger. Thank God, Major Bressen is here, but it would be less ominous if our locals were picked up by local law enforcement, instead of a soldier. But with only three of us still active—"

"Why only three?"

"There is no easy way to say this, Roxy." An involuntary image of his young blond friend, who always had a big grin on his face and a ubiquitous coffee mug, caused him to choke up. "Sam is dead. Went out with Jackson to bring in another Forestco employee. Well, he didn't spot the woman or her screwdriver as he approached the house and was stabbed through the throat before Jackson could even warn him. Lucky for Jackson, the assailant gored Sam three or four more times before turning to attack him, but by that time, Jackson drew his weapon, shot twice, and killed her as she lunged at him. Jackson tried to staunch the wound with his shirt, but Sam died before the ambulance arrived." Pete took a moment to compose himself. He wasn't used to losing staff. When he felt like his voice was his again, he continued, "Once Jackson got back to the station house, he lost it. Told him to take some time. Honestly, not sure he will be back."

"We all have been through so much the past few days. I hope we can find a way through all this."

"Well, I promise we will give him a proper wake if we do."

"I will miss him," she said. "Let's make sure we lose no one else."

"That is something we agree on," Glancing at his watch, he noted, "Just need to hold out a few more hours until the National Guard and CDC get here."

"Does anyone else see the irony?" She laughed with a hysterical edge. "Here we are, just two infected cops collecting infected people and incarcerating them."

"Trust me. If my splitting headache ever went away, I would chuckle like a loon about the inmates running the asylum. But today, I don't feel much like laughing, even at the insanity of this situation."

Suddenly, Roxy slapped her forehead and said, "Almost forgot. Guess what we know about the virus now?" Wearily waving his hand to indicate she continue, "Abby called and reported that Zander found the virus in Astro's blood, too. So, unless we hear otherwise, she said we can assume the dogs can infect us the same way people can."

The implication of an animal population as dangerous as people was starting to overwhelm him. There were so many unknown variables to consider.

Roxy asked, "Should we start euthanizing and disposing of all the infected pets in the area? And if animals are hosts for this disease, can we still contain this thing? Those roadblocks the Major is setting up might be as useless as a child at the beach trying to bring water to her sandcastle's moat using a sieve."

Pete didn't remember sagging to the grass at their feet, only the blackness enveloping his vision.

When it receded, Roxy repeated his name in desperation, her eyes wide in terror. She must have assumed his disease had progressed to the next stage, and she had lost him.

When he opened his eyes, she cried joyfully and asked him. "Are you okay?"

But damned if he had an answer to her question or the multitude of problems they faced. He had pinned all his hopes on containing the virus in Ontario. A lot of good people would die, but it would stop here. Now he knew he would have to swallow that hope like the bitterest of pills.

"No. I don't think I will ever be okay again."

Roxy grabbed her shoulder mic and reported an officer down.

# Chapter 17



*June 30, Saturday — 10 pm — Portland, Oregon*

*A few days earlier.*

Jake Masters was tempted to take his father's advice about staying in Ontario another day, but the mill would not be open again until Monday morning. So, besides postponing the trip back to Portland, there was not another reason to stay in Ontario.

Traveling south on I-205 from Portland International Airport, he knew coming home was the right call. The past two days had been beyond exhausting: there had been two commuter flights, a mill inspection, looking over their books, a hotel stay, and all the glad-handing at the picnic. A sign warned Lake Oswego Exit 8 was coming up in a quarter mile, so he edged his late model Lexus into the right-hand lane and prepared to leave the thoroughfare.

It began to sprinkle, and he turned on his windshield wipers as he snickered. No need to complain about rain, it was ubiquitous, you might as well whine about air.

The last few miles between the off-ramp of the highway and his neighborhood went by in a mild haze, in which he didn't really wake from until the car seemed to park itself in his driveway automatically. The front room lights were on, meaning Megan was waiting for him. *Okay. Sleeping in one's bed is the second-best reason to come home,* he thought with a sudden lecherous grin.

The overnight bag can be taken care of in the morning. They must have been on the same wavelength because Megan met him at the door in his raincoat. And nothing else, if her mischievous smirk was any indication. The light from his still-on headlights reflected like fire on her copper-colored bobbed hair.

She grabbed his hand and pulled, "Hurry, lover, get in here. We don't have much time. My husband will be here later tonight."

"Okay, baby," he replied with enthusiasm.

Once inside, they were drawn together like a magnet and steel, clinched in bliss and passion. The moment ended with both breathless and longing, but Jake needed to take care of one fatherly duty first. "Honey, I want to look in on Ginny and Cassy for a minute, then we can, ah—continue my homecoming celebration."

She smiled in understanding and said, "The girls would love to see you. They were disappointed. I wouldn't let them stay up to see you. But don't take too long—" Her hand caressed his chest, drifting lower, enticing. Megan gave him an impudent grin before she turned and seductively swayed her hips as she sauntered down the hall to their bedroom. Damn! It was tempting just to follow her; his children would see him in the morning. But Jake missed them, and it wouldn't take long to reconnect with them for a few minutes. The girl's room was the first door on the left, which he opened with care so he could spend a contented moment listening to their quiet breathing. There was something pleasing about watching them sleep, maybe it was they were so angelic and peaceful when they slept.

For a minute, he was tempted to let them continue sleeping, but he selfishly wanted to whisper goodnight to them. So, he entered the room, shuffling his feet, there was no sense tripping on the multitude of toys and outfits which were always strewn across the floor. Halfway across the room, his foot bumped against the first mound of clothes, and he chuckled at his recent supposition.

When Jake got to his 6-year-old's bed and sat on the corner, the movement caused Ginny to move a bit, but otherwise, she continued to sleep the slumber of angels. Unbidden, his hand moved of its own volition and brushed the hair from her forehead with great tenderness, and then he gave her a butterfly-light kiss on her brow.

A moment later, he did the same for his other daughter, Cassy. Unlike her heavier-sleeping sibling, Cassy awoke and tentatively asked, "Daddy?"

"Yes, sweetheart," he whispered.

"We have a goldfish," she said with growing excitement as sleep faded and elation replaced it. Then, she pointed to the nearby night table.

"It is a superb fish." In truth, he could only see a shadow of the bowl in the near darkness. "Tell me all about it tomorrow?" With big eyes, she nodded. "Give pops a hug and kiss, and then you get some sleep. Okay?"

"Okay, Daddy." She enfolded him in a fierce embrace that lasted, to him, many glorious moments. For good measure, he kissed her forehead again, and finished tucking her in to bed.

Backtracking out of the room, he quietly closed the door. He smiled contentedly as he made his way to his room. The door to the master bedroom was open just a crack, and gentle candlelight dipped and bobbed. *Glad I gave Megan a courtesy call when I arrived at the airport. It's good to be home.* Remembering his wife's admonition, he dashed to their door.

He would've never left Ontario if he knew what he had just done to his wife and girls.

*July 1, Sunday — 1:49 pm — Forestco Corporate Headquarters, Clackamas, Oregon.*

*Should have taken the day off,* Jake thought with increasing regret. Sunday was supposed to be a day of rest; Megan reminded him when he told her he would work today. When he resisted her 'suggestion,' she had hidden his car keys until he swore, "I will only stay for a few hours." In truth, it wasn't a hard promise to make, but he hated starting the week behind.

Glancing at his inbox organizer on the right-hand corner of his desk, he had made a considerable dent in his stack of paperwork. If he were to guess, only an hour more. The tedium of work was soon replaced by a familiar tickle in the back of his throat.

Deep down, he knew exactly what it meant, yet he hoped it only indicated he needed to drink more water. Walking to the office cooler in the hall, he grabbed a paper cup, drank two cups worth, and prayed that was all it was. But the relief was temporary, and his throat felt worse as the minutes passed.

With sudden ferocity, he shouted to no one, "Give me a damn break! This is July, and I shouldn't be sick now."

Though, if he was being honest with himself, the past month had been a trial. There had been too many days of getting little sleep, fast food, and vending machine fare. And worst of all, the stress.

In the back of his mind, he hoped he didn't have to see his doctor, or there might be a pointed discussion about his blood pressure. So, his sudden outburst was less about railing against the heavens than being sidelined for any time by something as pathetic as a cold. Well, I will plow through this and pretend it isn't happening. Unfortunately, being an ostrich didn't help him one bit during the next hour.

*July 2, Monday — 6:45 am — Masters' household, Lake Oswego, Oregon.*

Jake opened his eyes and wished he hadn't. Even his eyelids hurt. Then, with burgeoning clarity, he recalled getting sicker as the night progressed, no matter how much Zinc he consumed. Sleep had been poor, but at least the hurting muscles and throbbing headache were only a vague sensation. He wanted nothing more than to roll over and try to eke out a bit more rest, but then he remembered his resolution from the previous night: soldier on.

But upon standing, he found the floor seemed to shift, and he had to grasp the nearby bedstand with both hands to stay upright. Just when he felt it was safe to let go, his face flushed like it was on fire. Rushing to the sink, he splashed some cold water on his face and contemplated taking yet another dose of aspirin. *Maybe a shower will make me feel better.*

But before he could remove his boxers, Megan waltzed into the room and playfully commented, "What is taking you so long, sleepyhead? Normally, you are out the door." She stopped when she saw his condition. "Oh, hon, do you feel as terrible as you look?" Lines of worry crinkling her beautiful brow.

"Wow, you have a way of making a guy feel special." His teasing smile intended to cover his pain.

Megan bought none of it; she applied the back of her hand to his fiery forehead and went into full-on 'Mommy Mode.' She pulled her hand back like she had been burned and instructed, "You're going to march back into that bedroom and get into bed right now."

He recognized that tone and knew she would brook no debate, so he returned to bed. He could hear running water in the bathroom a moment later, and then she placed a cool, damp hand towel on his forehead.

"Don't worry, I will phone your dad and tell him you are not coming in. Get some rest and feel better." She gave him a brilliant, sympathetic smile, turned, then closed the door. For the thousandth time, he wondered at his luck in finding this wonderful woman, and then he let the cold compress soothe away his headache and drifted off to sleep.

*July 3, Tuesday — 2:45 am — Lake Oswego, Oregon.*

The police cruiser sprinted down the barren streets of Lake Oswego. Lights flashing. No siren. Tension permeated the cabin of their patrol car.

With each new breath, Officer Maria Reyes felt like there was not enough air left to draw another. Her job had its share of tense moments, but every police officer dreads hearing dispatch broadcast a code 273.5—a domestic violence call. She couldn't help wondering if this encounter would be the one to spin out of control?

Her teachers back at the academy stressed that even if they did everything according to the 'book,' they might become part of a lamentable statistic. Domestic violence calls result in 25 percent of all officer on-the-job fatalities. All she could do was breathe.

Glancing over at her partner, Byron Stowell, who sat in the passenger seat nervously scanning the road ahead. Short of stature, Byron had a severe military-like haircut, which was so "tight" the color wasn't obvious. The hairstyle and many of his mannerisms originated from his two tours in Afghanistan. He always had his head on a swivel, so it didn't take long for him to sense her scrutiny and turn toward her. She gave him a reassuring smile before turning back to the road. If there was someone to have her back, it was him. But she would bet a six-pack that Byron would prefer the straightforwardness of a traffic stop or a criminal investigation to this call's fuzzy rules of engagement.

Everything seemed quiet when they arrived at the 911 caller's address, but it seemed unnatural. Or was the odd quietness a projection of her fear? Seeing no apparent danger, they exited the vehicle and made their way to the door, and with a self-assured knock announced. "Lake Oswego Police!"

The door opened, revealing a 70-year-old balding man with a paunch.

"My name is Officer Maria Reyes, and this is Officer Byron Stowell. You reported a disturbance next door?"

Holding the screen door for them, he said, "Yes, I called. Name's Raymond Milner. Come in, officers. There is someone you need to speak with before heading over."

Before Maria stepped into the foyer, she noticed a shotgun propped up against the inside wall and raised an eyebrow at him.

With an uncomfortable shrug and a guilty look, "After hearing the girl's story, I felt like it way only prudent. Bring her in Constance!" he shouted.

An older woman, wearing a robe, obviously his wife, led an eight or nine-year-old blond girl with puffy red eyes and a runny nose into the room. The terrified girl whimpered, her little eyes darting from side to side as if expecting an attack. This waif would need a gentle touch if she were to trust a stranger.

With her off-hand, Maria motioned Byron to hang back while she tried to talk to the little girl. Removing her fitted ball cap, Maria slowly strolled into the spacious Milner living room, which was dominated by a crystal chandelier and a black, shiny grand piano.

When the girl started to inch behind Mrs. Milner, Maria stopped her approach, got down in a squat, and smiled her most reassuring smile. The bedraggled moppet watched Maria with interest but made no further move to hide. In this moment of *détente*, Maria observed there was a significant amount of blood not only on the youngster's face and hair, but also smudged on her dark colored clothes. With sudden alarm, Maria glanced up at the steel-gray-haired, matronly woman, who made an almost imperceptible shake of her head.

Without thought, Maria grabbed the crucifix under her uniform and soundlessly thanked God.

"Honey, you are about the same size as my little girl," Maria said in her best mom-will-make-it-better tone and continued, "Her name is Olivia. Can you tell me your name?"

There was no response as the traumatized child buried her face in the older woman's robe. After a short time, the girl peeked out and decided between the reassuring uniform and this lady's gentle voice; she might be safe to talk to.

"My name is Cassidy, but everyone calls me Cassy." Remembering who had called her Cassy, her lower lip started to tremble, and a pair of tears slid down.

Maria's heart went out to the poor girl, but she desperately needed to know what her partner and she would be walking into. So, she started slow. "What a pretty name, Cassy. My name is Maria. Do you know what my job is?"

"You are a policeperson," she said with assurance. "Daddy got pulled over for speeding one time. Said some bad words when he drove away."

Laughing, Maria said, "Don't worry; I'm not giving any speeding tickets today, yet there are some questions I must ask before I head over to your house. Would that be all right?"

"Yes'm," Cassy said in her best grown-up voice.

"Can you tell me what happened tonight?" The 8-year-old started to cry anew, but Maria interrupted the waterworks this time before they could start in earnest. *"Mi corazón,* I know it hurts, but I need you to be a big girl and tell me what you can."

"Mommy said Daddy got sick at work. Got all of us sick," she wiped the back of her hand and half her forearm across her leaking nose. "Said, the doctor told Daddy he had the flu, and he could do nothing about it. So, he stayed in bed and slept a lot. Me and sissy and Mommy got sick yesterday, so she said we had to stay in bed. I heard Daddy finally wake up; he was really angry."

"Did he say something which made you think he was angry?"

"Didn't say nothin'. But he came into our room. Mommy was sleeping with sissy, and he started hitting Mommy," she sobbed. "She was screamin' and tryin' to protect her face. He grabbed her hair and she felled down on the floor. Sissy was crying, and I was *so scared."* The tears were falling steadily. "Daddy was hurting sissy, and I heard Mommy make a noise on the floor. Wanted to help her, so I got on the floor. There was lots of blood on her face, on the ground, in her hair, on her hands." In horror, Maria made eye contact with Byron, but the girl couldn't stop her narrative now. "Wanted to help her, but she whispered to me. 'Run away. Get help.' Mommy used to say, 'If there is trouble, call 911 or come over here.' So, I runned out the back door, came here, and pounded on their door."

At the conclusion of her tale, Cassy's eyes seemed lifeless and hollow. The beginnings of shock setting in. Standing up, Maria made eye contact with Constance, who nodded and enfolded the wounded little girl in a warm embrace.

Meanwhile, Maria moved to the foyer, and in a hushed voice updated the dispatcher.

Once done, she returned to Cassy's side and squatted down to her level. She turned the child toward her with tenderness and grabbed Cassy's shoulders. "You have been incredibly brave, but I need you to be brave a bit longer. Can you do that for me?"

The waif nodded. In a moment of inspiration, Maria took a foil gold police star sticker out of her left breast pocket and presented it to the survivor. "Good, then I will make you my deputy. Deputy Cassy, I need you to watch over the Milners until some nice people come here for you. Can you do it?" Maria asked. Without hesitation, Cassy nodded, and Maria added, "Meanwhile, my partner and I are going to see if we can help your family."

Wordlessly, the little girl launched herself at Maria. Her short arms were long enough to wrap around Maria's neck. With a mother's automatic reflexes, Maria stroked the fragile girl's hair and nearly cried herself.

"Okay, Maria." And Cassy let go.

As Maria stood up, she realized Raymond had moved to Constance's side and put a supportive hand on his wife's shoulder.

Maria opened her mouth to confirm their willingness to temporarily care for Cassy when she was interrupted. "Don't worry. We'll take care of her," Raymond offered.

"Lock the door behind us. Someone will be here soon." Smiling, she shook both their hands. Then, turning to her partner, she said, "Let's move."

An insistent clock continued ticking in the back of her brain. Some people might criticize her decision to take the time to talk with the girl before investigating the house, but domestic disturbances were dangerous enough without heading in blind.

The information Cassy gave them helped clarify things, but it didn't make any sense. Sick people could be crabby when they felt poor, but why would her father go into an unprovoked murderous rage? Also, the girl was insistent that her father never spoke, which was confusing because a verbal altercation usually triggered these domestic situations. Why walk into the girl's room and begin beating up his wife? It sounded like they were sleeping in their room—not bothering anyone.

Damn! There were more questions than answers.

Maria grabbed Byron's arm two steps down the Milner walkway, brought them to a halt, and asked. "What do we know?"

"Our backup is still 10 minutes out." She gave him a burning glare as he held up his hands placatingly. "Hey, don't blame the messenger. What should we do?"

It was obvious Byron didn't want to play it 'safe.' He might not have taken point with Cassy, but he had two boys and a newborn girl at home, so Cassy's recounting of events had to have hit him as hard as it hit her. His hand wandered to his pistol grip and came to rest.

Putting a hand on his chest, she made him stare back at her,

"Byron." She peered down at his white-knuckled grasp of the butt of his weapon. "Pull back on the anger; I need someone under control watching my back in there. Can you handle it?"

A heartbeat elapsed, he took a deep breath, and then nodded.

"Don't misunderstand me, soldier. If a little girl and woman are in danger there, then I have no desire to wait for backup. But if we go in alone, we must be smart about it. You got me?"

A look of relief washed over his face when she told him of her intention. The book said they should keep their hands in their pockets until sufficient help arrived.

"I've got your six. What's the plan?" he asked.

"Call me crazy, but I don't think this guy is a normal perp. If he was, I would say you take the back, and I will take the entrance. I feel like we need to work together on this. Let's go in the front with a standard cover pattern."

"Okay, let's go."

Once they had decided, they ran north across the two well-manicured lawns and approached the cover portico of the light-gray, modern, expensive residence. The curtains were closed, but lights were shining around the edges of the drapes.

Pausing at the door, Maria checked the knob. It was open.

They prepared to rush the entrance by drawing their guns and holding them high. Maria used a silent finger countdown. At zero, Maria slammed the door back as Byron jumped past her, and they both yelled as loud as possible, "Police! We are armed and will shoot if you don't get on the floor now! Do it now!"

The luxurious front room was empty, and their probable suspect, Mr. Masters, was nowhere to be seen. The adjoining kitchen and dining room were likewise deserted. The absolute silence, no disturbed furniture, or a deranged madman helped ratchet the tension to a fever pitch. Using another hand signal, Maria indicated she would take point as they headed down the narrow hallway. The first door on the left was open, but there was no light. Rushing into the room, searching for a light switch, the space was revealed with a click: a computer and office room. After checking the closet and other imaginable hiding spots, she returned to the hall and shook her head in the negative.

Byron took point and traversed the distance to the next doorway on the right with practiced and confident steps. This interior door was closed and silhouetted around the four edges by a gentle light. Byron took no chances of being attacked as he entered. His size 11 combat boot was sufficient to breach the flimsy interior door easily. But he needn't have bothered. The master bedroom was empty, too. There was one last door, which had to be the girls' room. Chances were, the room would only contain victims, yet there was no reason to take any gambles.

Since there was no longer a need to guard the hallway, they would enter simultaneously. Once again, using hand signals, Maria indicated he should take low, and she would take high. The silent countdown, the rush, lights turned on, revealing two bodies and more blood than she thought was possible. The chance either person was alive was minute, but they couldn't assume.

"Check them!" Byron yelled. "Got your six."

Training taking over, she holstered her weapon and was going to a knee by the woman on the floor. When the next thing she knew, she was airborne. The surreal feeling ended when her back slammed into one of the single beds. The air exploded from her lungs in a whoosh, but that was the only sound besides an animal growl near her ear. She turned toward the sound and nearly lost her nose when her assailant noisily snapped his teeth a millimeter from her face.

Fear gripped her, and she begged her partner, "Shoot him! What are you waiting for?!"

Somehow, she leveraged her forearm under the ambusher's chin before he could make another attempt. Dead eyes tried to find a way past her defenses. Teeth violently clacking together again and again.

Suddenly, she could hear the dull thumping of body blows falling on her attacker's back and shoulders. The reverberations transferred through the man's body to her—but to no seeming effect. The ever-nearing teeth started to nip the skin of her throat as she strained to move her head away from him. Her forearm should have provided her with the mechanical advantage to maintain the distance between them, but inexplicably he kept moving forward, despite her best efforts. Her muscles were shaking with effort, like a weight-lifter at the end of a superset. She knew they would fail any second, and then the man pushed off her and launched himself at Byron.

Scrambling to her feet, she noticed Byron no longer possessed the nightstick he had pummeled the man with earlier, and both men were grabbing each other's shoulders like wrestlers. The impasse was broken when Byron used one of his Marine unarmed combat moves. He ducked under the man's grip and spun him until he had the assailant in a powerful bear hug.

The submission hold should have been enough to subdue their assailant. Byron could still play linebacker in college if he needed to. His hold would have worked on 99 percent of the perpetrators he wanted to take down.

Unfortunately, Masters was a member of the one percent. Instead of trying to break Byron's iron grip, Masters started pistoning his legs in a backpedal, which carried both into the wall behind them.

There was an explosion of air as Byron connected with the solid barrier, but Byron maintained his hold. The lack of oxygen getting to Masters' brain must have triggered a berserker-like rage because he began to rear back his head repeatedly.

The first blow destroyed Byron's nose and slammed his head into the wall. Subsequent head butts further inflicted grievous wounds.

Blood exploded everywhere.

The handcuffs in her hands seemed less than useless now, so she threw them on the ground and reached for her gun. The holster was empty. True terror threatened to freeze her in place. That was until she saw Byron's eyes roll up in his head, and he slunk to the floor.

Primal anger surged within her, and she wanted nothing more than to tear Masters to pieces with her hands. Fortunate for her, she was not so far gone in her rage that she thought she stood a chance against their assailant. If Byron couldn't handle him, she would be in trouble.

With laser-like focus, she scanned the floor, found her .38, and brought it to bear on Masters. Now that he was free, he turned to bite her partner.

"Freeze dirtbag or I will fire!" she screamed.

It had as much effect on their attacker as expected, but she wanted to give Masters a chance to stop this madness. Without glancing back at her, Masters continued to lunge at Byron.

Aiming her gun center mass, she fired one incredibly loud round into Masters' back. The bullet should have killed him or at least dropped him in agony. It did neither. But the impact of the bullet did get his attention because Masters released Byron's unconscious form and spun around toward her.

Growling, he rushed her. Without hesitation, she emptied the rest of the magazine into the man's chest. For the second time in so many minutes, he barreled into her and took her to the floor. This time, though, she knew she was dead. She was pinned beneath him, and there was no way to defend herself.

Eventually, the terror receded enough for her to become cognizant of her surroundings again. The only sounds in the room were her heaving breath and the mechanical clicking of the gun's trigger as Maria kept pulling it incessantly.

Taking a steadying breath, Maria could remove her finger from the trigger, but when she concentrated on her hands, she realized they were covered in liquid. That and the pain of her gun and hands crushed against her sternum by her attacker's body. Then the realization of what fluids were hitting her. She screamed in revulsion. With a mighty shove, she heaved the body to her left side.

A host of new smells assaulted her then: gunpowder, death, and a multitude of bodily fluids and viscera hit her like a tidal wave, and she turned her head to the side and retched with vigor.

Stomach empty, Maria grabbed her shoulder mic, "This is Officer Reyes! There is a man down. I repeat, Officer Stowell is down! Need immediate medical assistance now!"

She winced as she let go of the mic. *Might have a separated shoulder.* She arose with a groan and hurried over to Byron, who was still slumped against the bedroom wall. Weak pulse—but he was alive.

"Hang in there, Byron. Help is coming," she said as she slid him from his sitting position to the floor.

The welcomed wail of a nearby emergency vehicle siren flooded the house. She continued to evaluate her partner's condition.

There was blood flowing from Byron's nose as well as the back of his head, so she scanned the room for something to staunch the bleeding. Everything in the room was soiled, so she quickly went to the bathroom and grabbed a handful of large, fluffy towels. One she soaked with water from the faucet, then returned to her partner. The dry ones she put under his head for a pillow and to staunch the blood flow. With mother-like care, she dabbed at the blood covering Byron's face, but blood continued to flow from his damaged nose. Giving up, she used the towel as a compress for his face.

The room began to get a little hazy around the edges. *Must be shock,* she thought.

Then she heard someone entering the house.

"We're in here!" she shouted.

Four men in blue paramedic uniforms rushed into the room. One of them grabbed her and led her to the front room as if she were a little girl. After a few preliminary tests, the medic decided she was well enough to wait until they transported her to the hospital for further evaluation, so he returned to the back bedroom.

Forgotten for the time, Maria suddenly wanted to leave the house and get some fresh air. She barely made it outside before she threw up again, this time in a nearby azalea bush. There definitely wasn't much left in her stomach this time around, so she was gripped with dry heaves for an indeterminant time. Finally, her stomach stopped its contractions, and she gathered herself. Wiping her mouth on her sleeve, Maria leaned against the outside wall of the house in exhaustion. The adrenaline surge was wearing off, and the wounds she received during the battle started to sound off.

In particular, a few ribs might be broken; she probed with her fingers. *Yep, broken for sure.* Trembling fingers trailed up to her facial lacerations and hooked on her crucifix necklace.

She held the cross between her thumb and forefinger with reverence, gazed up at the stars, and asked, "Why, God?"

Little did Maria know, a fellow police officer in a small town, far to her east, was beholding the same stars and asking the same question.

# Chapter 18



*July 6, Friday — 9:49 am — St. Alphonsus*
*Medical Center*

The first surprise was—he woke up. The second—everything ached. Emphatically! But after 'knowing' he was going to slowly lose his brain and die after a day or two, Zander discovered that he didn't mind experiencing terrible, glorious pain instead.

With tentative care, he opened his eyes and was promptly blinded by the sun-bright illumination of the—hospital lights? Lifting his hand to shield his eyes from their intense glare, he discovered to his dismay, his hand stopped far short of its goal, and he felt metal 'bite' into his wrist. Momentary confusion was replaced with understanding. *I was Stage Four. Must be handcuffed to the side rails of a bed,* he thought.

The metallic rattling had alerted the attendant in the room, who then moved to his side. The figure loomed above him with an ominous air, but at least he or she was blocking out the bright lights. When his eyes finally adjusted, he could not determine much about the figure beyond the fact that he or she was wearing a bright orange hazmat suit.

"Do you know who you are?" A muffled male voice asked.

"Zander Parks. Who are you?"

"Dr. Latrelle Mack, director of the CDC field team in Ontario. A staff person told me you might be waking up soon, so I scooted down here to check on you. How do you feel?"

"Feels like someone took a bat to my whole body, but beyond the overwhelming pain, I'm peachy." Once again, Zander proved the old dictum: doctors make the worst patients.

"Heard you were a smart ass," Dr. Mack said with a frown. "Considering what you went through, I'll cut you some slack. This time."

"Thanks," Zander said in an arid-dry tone, then scrunched up his face in confusion. While it was true, he was in a great deal of physical pain, it was also true that the fugue he had been in the last couple days had lifted. With this newfound mental clarity, Zander worried that whatever time he was down would keep him from finding an answer to this virus. He needed answers now! "Why am I not dead? Doesn't the disease infect everyone and kill them? Did the virus mutate? Are there other survivors? Where am I? If I am okay, why am I handcuffed?"

The urgent questions peppered Dr. Mack like the spray of automatic gunfire.

"Whoa, slow down, Dr. Parks. I will try to clear things up for you. For starters, we have no idea why you and some other people have escaped this bug. And believe me, we will ask for more than a few blood samples from all of you. At this point, there is only conjecture as to whether you are biologically protected from the virus's full effects or whether the virus indeed mutated to your version."

Zander's analytical mind wanted to delve into the medical conundrum, but something the doctor said a moment ago had to be cleared up.

"Dr. Mack—" Zander couldn't finish the question as his breath wouldn't come.

The man misinterpreted Zander's pause, "Please, call me Mack; we can compare med school diplomas later, champ." The orange-suited doctor's laugh sounded like the braying of a donkey through the speaker.

"Okay, Mack. Are my parents—?" He couldn't say the word for fear of it acting like an incantation, calling forth a nightmare.

Mack finally understood the question and said, "They're gone. Once they entered the coma stage, they were not allowed to regain consciousness, as per your instructions to Dr. Gallagher. Some of my colleagues believed it was inappropriate to induce an artificial coma in this circumstance, but your friend was—*ahem,* very energetic in presenting her side of the debate. In fact, I think her exact words were, and I quote, 'I will kneecap anyone who tries to come into my hospital and tell me how to practice humane medicine.' End quote."

Mack's face was somber for half a second before he busted out laughing. Zander was shocked by this man's lack of decorum. On a different day, he might laugh at the absurdity of his diminutive, fever-ridden friend threatening CDC doctors with gang violence. But today would not be that day.

Mack continued, "If Hall and Perry weren't wearing their suits, I bet you could have seen them shaking. It was priceless, and I believe she meant it, too. Damn, man, I heard you people in Oregon were still cowboys; thought it was a romantic notion. Guess I was wrong."

"She *was* a good friend," Zander said as he remembered Abby's kind face. "I will miss our talks."

"Then you are in luck; she is still with us. Do you want to visit her?" Zander raised his arms until the handcuffs jangled against the bed rails. "Sorry." It looked like Mack was attempting to shrug within the suit. "Private! Come in here and unlock these restraints." Moments later, Zander massaged his wrists and ankles. He was happy that at least a few parts of his body were starting to feel better. "I will be outside. Let me know when you are ready to see her."

Zander's first step toward the recliner next to the hospital's window was shaky, but he felt stronger as he went. The buttons and zippers conspired against his sense of urgency, but finally, two stressful minutes later, he exited the room. On the way to Abby's room, Mack sketched out what trifling amount the CDC had figured out about the virus since Zander entered his coma the day before.

Dr. Mack revealed that the original assumption that the virus killed 100 percent of its victims was obviously wrong because of its limited sample size. The disease did kill all the earliest victims, but as the infection spread, it became obvious even this virus couldn't be engineered to be perfect. Of the original 600 Forestco picnic attendees, 46 had survived. After analyzing Zander and the other survivors' blood, they discovered that the virus was somehow unable to attach itself to their T-cells. So far, there has been no explanation for *why*. All they knew was the immune townspeople seemed to come down with the flu and the coma—like their peers— but for some reason, it neither destroyed their brains nor was fatal to them. It would take some time to see if they could replicate this immunity for others.

They arrived at Abby's room.

It was a mirror of his own, with vinyl flooring, white walls, beeping machines, restraints, and a hospital bed with rails. As they entered, Zander stumbled and came to a stop when he saw her in the bed; she aged 20 years within a few days. He was not yet privy to how the CDC knew who would survive the disease or not. It might not be exact science though because he had been handcuffed to his bed. But it was obvious his friend was deep in her body's struggle to survive, her bruised eyes were closed, faced flushed, respiration shallow.

The only sound in her room was the rhythmic, artificial murmur of the heart monitor and the breathing machine. He couldn't help but feel guilty that his death sentence had been commuted, but apparently not Abby's. For a moment, he was worried they had arrived too late, but as he glanced at a nearby monitor, it was obvious her vitals had not crashed into coma territory yet.

It was tempting to allow her to sleep undisturbed, but selfishly he knew she was one of the last survivors of his circle of friends, family and coworkers. Soon, they would all be gone. If she was not lucky enough to be a fellow survivor, he knew the insidious virus was systematically pillaging every neuron and dendrite of her brilliant mind. When it was done, the only brain functions that would operate were autonomic and adrenal. In essence—a rabid animal. For his sanity, it was imperative he say goodbye properly to at least one of his kith and kin. There had been too much loss—too little closure—to maintain his mental equilibrium.

"I'll wait for you outside," Mack said as he left the room.

Zander ignored him. Pulling a chair to her bedside, he sat. A sigh escaped him. Even this small trek had taken quite a bit out of him. He gently put his hand on top of hers.

Her eyes fluttered and opened. There was puzzlement in her expression until her eyes found focus.

"Zander?"

"Yes, Abby. It's me. You look great."

"If I knew your poker face was so atrocious, I would've invited you to our game night long ago," she cackled at her quip until a fit of coughing took her. When she could speak again, she grabbed his hand and said, "I know I'm dying, so you don't have to pretend otherwise. Do me one last favor, though." He nodded. "Tell me, how are you here? Thought *your* bug was 100 percent fatal?" Zander rocked back as if struck. "Now I've gone and done it." She stroked his hand in apology. "It's so hard to concentrate. Please forgive me."

"Of course; I understand."

"Let's try that again. I'm so happy you are alive, but how is it possible? They don't tell me anything. Treat me more like a patient than a doctor now." Zander wasn't sure which hurt her more, dying or being replaced in her own hospital.

"To be honest with you, I'm not sure I understand it much better than you. I woke up 15 minutes ago, and Dr. Mack gave me a quick snapshot. When he told me you were alive, I was so surprised. I had figured—well, I had to come right away."

She nodded in understanding.

"Guess I'm too stubborn to *go gently into the night.* I'm glad you came." Her fragile, wistful smile transformed into a sympathetic expression, and she reached out and grabbed his forearm. "Sorry about your parents. Did all I could for them."

"My new 'friend' here," indicating the orange-clad figure in the hallway, "told me you had a rather colorful exchange with some CDC doctors."

"Told 'em to go to hell, is what I told them." Glancing mischievously at Mack. "Well, they had it coming. The nerve of them turning up here and trying to tell me what to do with my patients!"

"You made good on your promise. Thanks. As to why I'm alive, I guess we both should have known nothing is 100 percent. According to our numbers so far, one in 10 are immune to the virus."

"Even with our small sample, we should have made that observation sooner. Damn it!"

"Don't blame yourself, Abby. The symptoms are virtually the same for both groups." A disturbing thought hit him, and he frowned as he asked, "What if we didn't realize there were uninfected because those in Stage Four had killed them?"

"My God, why didn't we think of that before? Of course, we wouldn't know about the uninfected until we brought everyone in and monitored them."

"Well, we know now so that we can protect those unaffected by the disease. According to Dr. Mack, the only thing the CDC knows about the survivors is the virus can't corrupt their T-cells. They are working on a way to identify better who is immune."

"Well," Abby said, "they lucked out. Your expertise in this field should be invaluable. Do you think they can use the antibodies from your blood to design a vaccination?"

"No luck there. My body never created antibodies for the virus. It recognized a foreign organism, and I got 'sick' fighting it off, but it didn't target that virus," Zander said as he massaged his aching back. "So, besides some minor cell damage, which they haven't figured out yet, I'm no worse off than before. They say I should fully recover."

"I'm glad. At least some of us can carry on the fight."

"Hang in there; we will create a cure for you soon."

"Stop—Zander." She grabbed his hand again and held his eyes with a knowing gaze. "Can't say I don't want to live a bit longer, but I have made my peace with this." A serenity settled about her. "One thing?" She reached up and with the utmost gentleness cupped his face in her soft, feverish hand. "When this is over, will you say a prayer for me? For us?"

"I swear it." He covered her hand with his own and squeezed it with meaning. At those words, the energy in Abby's body seemed to exit her body like air from a deflating hot-air balloon.

"Thank you. Now get out of here. There isn't much time." She gave him a final brave face.

Zander held her hand for another moment, stood up shakily, and then turned and left her. As he walked down the hospital corridor, a tremendous sadness—like a colossal tidal wave—threatened to crush him.

After the euphoria of waking up and finding out he had literally dodged a bullet, it hit him. Mother, Father, Lise, Pete, Roxy, Skip, and most likely everyone at Imagine Labs were gone. Whoever had created this virus had killed them as surely as if he or she had held a gun to them. And what had he done to save them? *Exactly nothing.*

The abyss of despair opened before him. It called to him seductively. And like Odysseus strapped to his mast, he listened to the sirens and heard their sweet song of oblivion. The darkness could erase all the pain. It would be so easy—

Suddenly, he was drawn into a bright light, and he felt transported from the hospital to—nothing.

A moment of panic.

Then, his senses slowly came into focus. He seemed to float above the ground.

Warmth surrounded him, as did the smell of freshly baked bread with a hint of cinnamon. Lastly, his vision cleared, and he looked about in wonder.

The room was so vast he couldn't see any of the walls, but one, or the ceiling. But what drew his vision was an enormous sphere. It was dazzling, but unlike staring at the sun, brought no discomfort from gazing at it.

Also, the closer he observed the globe it was not a pure white light, but actually more of a spectrum of all colors. Without conscious thought, he was drawn forward. As he neared the object, he noticed it slowly turned above a gold platform and seemed to be the source of warmth.

No, that was wrong. The light/heat seemed to penetrate him beyond just his skin. The darkness which had nearly enveloped him moments ago melted like frost on a window in the morning sun.

And still, the light continued to work through him until nothing remained of the stain of despair. He felt rejuvenated and at peace, so much so that he reached out to it. Wanting more than anything to join with it.

But as he touched it—he transported back.

* * *

*In the shadows, she smiled. In time, she would be fully revealed. But for now, it was good enough to help him continue his journey unfettered.*

# Chapter 19



*July 6, Friday — 11:11 am — Imagine Labs*

His little journey, if that truly was what it was, had not lasted long. Afterward, when Zander asked obliquely if Mack had seen anything strange earlier, the doctor said no. So, it would be easy to chalk it up as a daydream or hallucination except for one thing: the crushing hopelessness had dissipated. Completely. In fact, he felt a newfound strength and enthusiasm, which had caused him to turn to Mack in that hallway and insist that he *would* help them find a cure.

It was then that Zander had learned the government had appropriated Imagine Labs, and they would welcome his assistance. Minutes later, they were on their way to the lab.

*It's weird being driven to his work,* he thought. *It's even weirder being driven to work in a military Humvee—by people in bright orange hazmat suits.* But Zander didn't mind. Being chauffeured by anyone afforded him the luxury of focusing fully on everything Mack was throwing at him.

"—and we were lucky to find the drink coolers at Forestco undisturbed." Mack's glasses reflected the sunlight as they turned a corner, but they might as well have represented the transformation of the man's total demeanor as he got into his element. Earlier,

Zander had taken an instant dislike to the man. He had seemed cold and alien.

To be fair, the space suit didn't help, but the man seemed to be more concerned with Zander the *specimen* than Zander, the grieving son who barely escaped death. This feeling was further exacerbated by the sting of Zander's encounter with Abby. But inexplicably, Zander now seemed to see the man more clearly. Mack was a detective with a world-class mystery before him. It wasn't that Mack didn't care about the people around him as much as he focused on solving this medical conundrum. In an epiphany, Zander wondered if the excited man before him wasn't that different from himself.

"—the residue within contained our bug," Mack continued. "The FBI and some of our best counter-terrorism specialists have been called in. We will nail whoever released this within a day or two. If we are lucky, they might be crazy but not stupid. They will have created an antidote."

He nodded, but Zander did not share the man's enthusiasm. "But what will happen if we can't find them, or they have destroyed their cure?"

Mack's face darkened. "The projections are bad. Our latest computer workup predicts that left unchecked, it will blanket the country in months and kill millions. It is imperative we don't let that happen."

"Agreed. Have you made any further progress with identifying how to stop this virus?"

"Unfortunately, there has been no shortage of bodies to autopsy at this point." Dr. Mack stopped and seemed human for a minute before continuing. "Though the pathology has been consistent: the HIV aspect of the virus no longer targets T-cells, but frontal lobe cells, while the Ebola element batters the body. As near as we can tell, the destruction of an infected person's brain begins as soon as they contract the disease. By the time of death, their brains have shrunken to three-quarters of their original size and resemble an advanced Alzheimer patient's. It is believed that the coma stage signals the destruction of a person's upper cognitive brain function. In essence, the person is gone."

"Hence their animalistic behavior."

"Exactly. The desecration of their frontal lobe is hidden by the average victim having a headache, feeling fuzzy, and sleeping a lot."

"I detected stray DNA code I failed to recognize in the infected blood samples. Have your people identified any of those elements?" Zander asked.

"I wish," Mack said with unfeigned zeal. "To be honest, that is more your people's bailiwick than ours." Zander's eyebrows rose at the admission. "Don't get me wrong, I'm flying in the 'big guns' as we speak, but they still lack the familiarity with the virus you and your team have with a good portion of this contagion. They will be starting from scratch because your Picadone? formula is not public knowledge. So, having you aboard is quite the windfall for us."

"I can appreciate that, but some of these modified viruses are not behaving as we created ours. Believe it or not, our Picadone Leukemia cure is not an infectious pandemic," Zander said in a desert-dry tone. He wanted to like this CDC newcomer—it was critical they work together—but it rankled him that everything was a calculus equation for him and not a humanitarian crisis.

"—err, wasn't insinuating, doctor." Apparently, the man wasn't completely oblivious, Zander mused. "Anyway, another interesting thing we learned from the autopsy is the cadavers all had off-the-chart adrenaline levels." Mack smiled and enthusiastically added, "It really is quite remarkable how they created the perfect vector for distributing this virus."

"Excuse me, doctor," Zander almost shouted. He took a deep breath and tried to continue in a more reasonable but sarcastic tone, "for not sharing your admiration for the creators of this thing."

Mack winced as he tried to look contrite, "Sorry." Then he hurried on with the debrief, still looking every bit as excited as before. "Near as we can tell, the final stage of the virus ends when the host's body runs out of energy, usually within three to four days. Unfortunately, this period is more than sufficiently long enough to infect significant numbers of people around them by either breathing on them, biting them, or getting other bodily fluids in their mouths or eyes. Fortunately for us, people in Stage Four don't have the mental capacity to operate guns or other sophisticated weapons. Still, they have used knives, bats, or furniture to stab and batter their victims."

"At least we have that going for us," Zander said. "But what have you learned about how it affects the animal population?"

"Not much more than you had guessed. Obviously, most of our resources are focused on stopping this in the human population. Still, we have autopsied a few infected domestic pets and found the same pathologies as their human counterparts. Right or wrong, the police and soldiers have left creatures, domestic or wild, to their own devices. Nothing else will matter if we don't get ahold of this thing in the human population."

Mack shrugged his shoulders, but Zander's eye caught movement to his right. What he saw made his mouth fall open in wonder. Imagine's parking lot was now a bustling medical community: canvas, khaki tents with their distinctive red crosses peppered literally almost every flat spot in the area; dozens of assorted military and CDC trucks and cars, and a few menacing-looking helicopters, crouched on the blacktop bracketing the shipping building next to his.

Beyond this impressive array of vehicles, hundreds of people moved in and around the parking lot, doing their business. There were techs, doctors, nurses, scientists, and the ever-present National Guardsmen with weapons at port arms. Peppered amongst the masses were people wearing bright orange hazmat suits, similar to Mack's, while the majority wore respirators designed to protect against viruses.

The paper, ineffective masks used before the CDC arrived were gone. Of the personnel present, only the guards remained motionless. The majority were dashing, if not running to their destinations—giving the impression of a wasp's nest after being poked by a stick.

The driver of the Humvee navigated the scene deftly and came to a stop—ironically in Zander's parking spot. Mack excused himself to check in with his staff, which was okay with Zander. He would be damned if he wasted one more precious second, whether it be on this CDC narcissist or on the tomfoolery of waiting for someone to lead him around *his* lab.

After all the crazy changes in the past 24 hours, seeing his office was unchanged was shocking. Silence filled the halls until—he got to the lab and was ecstatic to learn he wasn't the only Imagine survivor. However, the initial joy of seeing familiar faces was quickly replaced by the sadness of not seeing—his best friend and most valuable team member—Lise, before him.

"Ben! Rohit! What are the chances we would all make it through? It's awesome to see you!" The men were bent over some Petri dishes doing some prep work, so they had not seen Zander arrive. They both jumped in surprise and turned toward him.

"Zander!" Dr. Rohit Tamboli said with a broad smile as he reached out and shook Zander's hand with vigor. Rohit's smile did little to hide his rough condition—cheeks somewhat sunken and significant dark circles under his red eyes.

To be fair, Zander was glad Mack hadn't provided him with a chance to glance in a mirror. He had a feeling he was no sleeping beauty either. The virus had left its mark on them, even if it was a glancing blow.

As he reached for Dr. Ben Mayette's hand, Zander was surprised to observe that Ben seemed to be in better shape than Rohit. Maybe the man had recovered sooner? Before they could clasp hands, Ben apparently changed his mind and pulled Zander into a happy embrace.

When they drew apart, Ben said, "We bucked the odds with the three of us surviving. What amazing luck." Then his expression clouded, and he added in a sympathetic tone. "Did anyone tell you what happened to Lise?"

After a slight pause, Zander shook his head in the negative. "All I know is she didn't make it."

"I'm so sorry, Zander; I know how much she meant to you." Ben looked him squarely in the eyes. "When she thought she had reached the end, she said goodbye and went home. She said something about leaving this world on her terms. Roxy went to check on Paul and her the next day. Looks like they OD'd on something. She left a letter on your desk when you are ready."

"Probably shouldn't tell you this," Rohit added, "but I wish you would have been here sooner so you could have said goodbye to her. The CDC now checks people in Stage Three with an Electro-encephalograph or EEG to determine if the frontal lobe is fully active. Apparently, they knew you would survive, but you hadn't awakened yet. Lise tried to wait for you, but—"

The darkness again threatened to consume him, but he was prepared to push it back this time. Even still, he had to swallow hard a few times before trusting himself to say, "Thanks, you wouldn't believe how important it is to hear that from friends." He recalled Dr. Mack's handling of personal news earlier.

As much as he wanted to give all the dead more time, the clock continued to count down. He only hoped there would be time to mourn later.

He plastered a somewhat convincing, confident expression on his face, clapped Ben on the shoulder affectionately, and asked, "What do we know?"

They got to work.

*Six hours later, in Zander's office.*

Working his gum fiercely as he sat before his computer, though at the moment he was unaware how hard he was chewing, until he gnashed his teeth together. The scritch of teeth grinding, like fingernails on the chalkboard. Another distraction forcing him from his contemplative reflection of the problem before him.

The gum was completely flavorless. Taking the Wrigley's wrapper from his pants, he neatly deposited the tasteless mass into the wrapper. Then "shooting" it into the nearby waste-basket. Reaching in a different pocket, he found—to his dismay—it was empty. Lucky for him, he always kept a reserve pack in the top drawer of his desk for such emergencies. When he scooted his chair back to get to his gum stash, he saw *it*. A regular-sized envelope. In a familiar hand, *Zander* was scribbled in big letters. His heart clenched as he snatched the prize and tucked it into the breast pocket of his coat.

Out of sight, he found he could breathe again. After a cleansing exhale, he retrieved a new package of gum from his desk and let the mint flavor and practiced motion allow him to focus on his task at hand, untying the Frankenvirus' Gordian Knot. A 3-D graphic of the thing lazily spun on its axis on the monitor before him.

He knew many people in the tight-knit, medical, scientific field considered him a wizard. Under his leadership, Imagine had accomplished something other labs, which were far better staffed and funded, hadn't even come close to creating a cure for Leukemia. This community's praise did not go to his head, he knew their whole discipline was littered with brilliant men and women, who possessed multiple PhDs from formidable, prestigious colleges.

No, he knew his genius lay in his ability to make connections others were either unable or unwilling to make, which allowed him to better circumnavigate obstacles.

After much trial and error, Zander learned these leaps tended to come to him when he could isolate himself from everything and everyone and focus all his energies on the problem. It was not unusual for him to look at the clock and realize the better part of a day had been spent in contemplation.

Over the years, Zander's staff learned two significant things about their leader's notorious brainstorming sessions.

One: most of the time, he emerged from his self-exile slash meditation with a solution, or at least a direction in which their research could proceed.

Two: if someone interrupted one of his free-association periods, he was not timid about sharing what he thought of the person or his or her questionable parentage.

A mysterious sign appeared on his door shortly after someone interrupted one of his meditations. It was a miniature yellow traffic sign that proclaimed in bold black letters, "Caution Mad Scientist at Work."

It was meant as a gentle dig, but he loved it so much he would affix its suction cups to his office door each time he needed to work. In no time, it became an office institution.

*The sign became a tradition and stuck*, chortling to himself at his little pun.

As he gathered himself to try to focus on the problem-at-hand he chided himself. *That virus must have taken more out of you than you thought. You can't focus worth a damn.* So, he tried again to stare at the screen before him.

Usually, concentrating on something—like the computer model of the microbe—helped him, but the fatigue acted like a wall of ice between him and his goal. Not letting him settle down. But people were counting on him, so he rubbed the bridge of his nose.

Zander glared at the screen and finally started to feel himself sink into a familiar meditative state. There was no magic to his intuition. All he needed was time.

Suddenly, the door to his office opened and sailed into the wall behind it—making a dull thudding sound. The orange-suited CDC doctor barged into the room and made an unnecessary throat-clearing sound, which sounded ridiculous through the suit's speaker.

Zander couldn't help looking to the heavens and thought with consternation, *Really, God? You have one warped sense of humor.* With belligerent slowness, Zander glanced around his monitor and glared at Mack, and then nodded in the direction of the yellow sign swinging on the door.

The man seemed on the verge of an angry outburst but was held in check by his total confusion regarding Zander's behavior. Only then did Zander realize the sign on the door held no significance to this newcomer.

Even this absurdity did not assuage his anger at being interrupted when he finally had found his focus.

"What can I do for you?" Zander said with the short, clipped words only hinting at his annoyance at the man's lack of common courtesy.

"Frankly, I had hoped you and your team would've integrated your research more with our ongoing investigation," Mack raised both hands in a wait-a-moment movement as Zander tried to respond. "Hold on, I won't insult you by suggesting you don't understand the gravity of this threat, but we expected you and your crew to live up to your reputation as top-of-the-line geneticists. Instead, your men are working alone, and you are holed up in here incommunicado."

"If I can be as frank with you, Dr. Mack," he said. "We have made several attempts to work with you people, but you are too worried about following precise CDC policies, protocols, and procedures. We don't have time for that crap. My team and I have worked together for the better part of two decades, and we know how to work quickly and efficiently." Dr. Mack tried to interject, but Zander rolled on. "Don't get me wrong, I know your rules are there for a purpose, but they don't work for us. This is personal. Trust me when I say that no one wants to find the cure for this more than we do. So don't try to bully us into conforming to your overly bureaucratic, dawdling system."

"How dare you try to dictate terms to us," Mack said with barely restrained fury. "Far be it for an unimportant organization like the Center for Disease Control of the United States to impose 'useless' protocols on a country doctor such as yourself."

Now Zander could feel his hackles raise.

"You may have enjoyed a measure of success with Leukemia, but we have created a bevy of antidotes to innumerable public health emergencies. And using these time-tested methods, we will create one for this virus, with or without your help."

"Well," Zander's voice also increased in volume, "this country doctor and his team have only worked on genetic manipulation for 18 years. There are protocols we abide by as well, but we don't slavishly worship them. Sometimes, you must follow your instincts.

My God, man, we were on the verge of creating the cure for cancer! We know how to do this. Let us do it!"

The whipsaw emotions Zander was experiencing—since awakening on the hospital bed hours ago—made it difficult for him to control his anger. He wanted to punish someone for all the pain he was feeling, and it was all too easy to strike out at the man before him. A man who, even now, was gathering himself to return Zander's vitriol.

But Zander interrupted him, "Mack, I'm sorry. It's not your fault that less than half a day ago, I learned—43 members of my staff of 45 were dead, including my best friend. Those of us that did survive are not at our finest." He gave a guilty shrug.

With Zander's admission and apology, Mack's anger deflated, and the CDC doctor gave a terse nod of acceptance.

"Glad we can patch that up. Now, about integrating you and your team—"

"You misunderstand me, Mack. I shouldn't have taken out my anger on you, but that doesn't change how we'll move forward."

Mack opened his mouth to protest, but Zander continued, "Let me finish. I swear to you on a stack of Bibles that we will do our utmost to assist you. And I can assure you that the moment we have anything actionable, we will contact you."

The promise hung in the air for a minute until Mack nodded and said, "Guess we all have our little fiefdoms." Now, it was his turn to give a guilty grin and shrug. "I should have been more sensitive to the fact that we are Johnny-come-lately and might have started throwing our weight around."

Zander nodded. Sensing this was likely the only apology he was to get. "Have we learned anything new?"

"Just got off the phone with the President. Never talked to the man before, afraid our lack of progress didn't impress the man much. Let's hope my career taking a nosedive is all we have to worry about." The man's sardonic tone surprised Zander.

*Maybe,* Zander reflected, *I'm not the only one feeling overwhelmed and underqualified to lead this thing.*

"You know," Zander wanted to change the topic, "maybe we are approaching this all wrong."

Mack made hopeful eye contact with him.

"We have been manipulating HIV since almost the beginning but considering all the familiarity we have with the microbe; we could never generate an antidote for HIV. It's true our research wasn't focused on curing HIV, but if it was something within our ability, we could have saved millions of lives. So, if we didn't have the aptitude to fashion an antivirus during the past 15-plus years, how could we expect to have the time to create an antidote now?" Mack started to protest. "Hear me out. Just talking out loud. I'm not giving up. Listen, don't you think the world medical research community would have created an answer to HIV or Ebola by now if it was possible? So, the problem, as I see it, the problem is that this virus is neither of those things. Even if we were lucky and somehow came up with a cure for HIV, then the Ebola part would still maim or kill us."

"As much as I hate to say it, my team concurs with you," Mack said contemplatively. "The magic bullet everyone wants is possible, but only after years of research, which obviously we don't have. If you aren't giving up, then what do you propose?"

"This is all conjecture." The excitement in Zander's voice reflected his love of problem-solving. "But as I stared at this screen, I thought about changing the paradigm. What if we changed our focus from generating an antidote that protects the host from a specific pathogen to creating an immunity booster that marginally alters the body chemistry?" His eyes blazed in excitement. "The autopsies prove the virus very specifically focuses on certain brain cells and T-cells, so its targets are very narrow. What if we create some way of slightly altering these two cells? It's sort of an artificial version of what happened to Rohit, Ben, and me. In essence, we differ from most of the population by an infinitesimal degree. I don't think anyone has attempted to do this before, but I'm betting it's easier than creating a combination antivirus."

"Change the body chemistry? Don't think I've heard of that approach before. It might work." Mack's forehead furrowed as he paused to think. "Over the years, our focus has been a long-term solution to the problem: a vaccination. Your idea is a short-term solution, but that is all we really need. Do you really think it could work?"

"Never know until you try. All I know is if we don't come up with a solution quickly, I doubt we'll be able to stop it. So, by attempting this, we are simply bypassing the impossible and moving on to the merely improbable."

"You didn't just plagiarize Sherlock Holmes," Mack chortled as Zander feigned indignation at the accusation. "At least your new solution to this virus might get us to stop wasting time trying to shoehorn a vaccine into this outbreak. I will pass this proposal on to Atlanta and see if we can get everyone moving toward creating a temporary physiological change." In his excitement, Mack started toward the office door and was almost through when he stopped, grabbed the door frame, and asked with mischief in his eye. "Promise to keep me in the loop?"

With an onery grin, Zander replied, "Of course, my good man—err, Mack. We're on the same team, I swear." Raising his right hand, Zander mimicked an old hand sign and said, "Scout's honor."

"You're so weird," Mack said with a lopsided grin and the first hint of warmth in his voice since Zander awoke from the "dead." Then he shook his head and turned to go.

"You have no idea—no idea at all. Now be a good chap and let yourself out." Zander didn't bother to see if the man complied or not. His Moriarty was taunting him from the computer screen before him.

# Chapter 20



*July 6, Friday — 6:56 pm — Imagine Labs*

With nervous energy, Craig had completed his third lap around his office when he stopped in front of the nearest beige wall and had to physically restrain himself from putting his fist through it.

After taking a few deliberate breaths, he unclenched his fists and tried to force himself to calm down. But this temporary composure was an illusion, and he resumed his pacing. The back of his throat tickled with a primal scream he badly wanted to release but wouldn't dare. *Can't have undue attention given to me. That would never do.* The angry thought bubbled up from deep inside.

If he believed in such a thing as a god, he would have to say that the bastard was messing with him—hard. Everything had been going so well that it was scary. That is, until it went into the crapper. The virus was spreading according to the projected computer models they had created months ago.

In fact, he wasn't sure the transmission of the mutant contagion could have gone any more perfectly, up to the point when Zander was raised from the dead.

The worst part was Craig had no idea Zander was alive until the man walked into the room. Even thinking about it now made him clench his fists so hard that his fingernails almost drew blood. He forced his hands to relax. *I thought we had the perfect weapon!* All their data concurred: the virus was 100 percent fatal once contracted. Of course, they now knew their data was wrong. In the final stages of completing the hybrid contagion, a few of his followers lured a dozen homeless people to the compound outside town. Each was given the experimental disease under controlled conditions in one of the 'out trailers.' Each had passed through the four steps of the disease, and each had died.

Looking back, it was hubris to think a dozen hobos could predict how the virus would work in a population of millions. He now knew the mortality rate was running at about 90 percent. Knowing nine out of 10 infected would become mindless killers who likely would kill anyone who would survive the virus was his only solace.

He took a deep cleansing breath.

But then, his thoughts returned to the logic loop he was stuck in. Some people might call *Gaia's Children* extremists, and to be honest, they were, but being fanatical did not equate to brainlessness. One reason they delayed releasing the hybrid so long was that once they created it, they needed a vaccine. The GC had no intention of going down with the ship—as it were—they just wanted to remove all the truly crazy people who were so busy destroying their only home.

So, he had inoculated himself and all the GC who wanted to survive the coming cleansing. Craig was pleased with how relatively few of his *Gaia's Children* declined to take the vaccine. Not one on their administrative council dared challenge him when he voiced his opinion that any recalcitrant members would be quietly removed—permanently.

After they released the virus, Craig faked being infected. Pretending to be sick and dying was fun. Every moment gave him the pleasure of metaphorically sticking his fingers in all their eyes. And they were too simple to understand that he was even in their midst until the end.

When Sheriff Alvardo finally caught on that someone was working against them. Craig had been so sure it was already too late for them to do anything to the Gaia's Children timetable. So, he stayed to finish the 'game.' How could he know that the National Guard would secure the building after everyone was questioned? Most likely he could have escaped, but 'GI Joe' would come looking for him. But the longer he stayed in the lab, the more and more Imagine staff started dropping off. Eventually, there were so few survivors the Guard decided guarding a mostly empty building was not a great use of resources.

So, shortly after Lise left, he had said his goodbyes and had slunk off. The plan had been to sit in his bunker discreetly, and like Cicero, settle back with a drink in his hand and watch the world burn.

*Unfortunately, the best laid plans, yada yada yada...* he thought as he made another circuit about his office. *Let's be honest, buddy boy. This had nothing to do with bad planning and more with plain old curiosity.* It had taken almost no time for him to go stir crazy at the compound.

Craig had held two full-time jobs for the past 18 years, and being pushed to his limit suited his personality to a T. What other people considered free time, he viewed with disdain. The GC was his baby. Much like a human child, it needed his constant attention. He thrived on tweaking even the smallest details of the organization's day-to-day operations to mold the GC into his perfect weapon.

So, sitting on his hands was not in his DNA therefore he decided to see firsthand how his delightful little microbial bug was doing. Hence, his foolhardy trip into the office.

The guards outside Imagine had given his credentials barely a glance before allowing him entrance, and he began to wander amidst the delicious chaos and panic around him.

Blithely, he made his way to the main lab, supremely confident there was no danger of being caught until he was. *Pride goeth before the fall,* he thought with vicious self-recrimination. Rohit was there yesterday. On the fly, Craig told a tale about his own resurrection that sounds eerily similar to Rohit's. Craig couldn't just leave, so he again fell into the role of dutiful coworker-friend.

For now.

Resuming his pacing about his office, Craig took another angry turn around his desk and stopped short. An epiphany struck him like lightning. Could it be possible? Maybe he wasn't *trapped* as he initially thought, but instead he had been insinuated into the organization which would try its darnedest to stop him and his virus.

It would present him the perfect opportunity to frustrate any attempt the CDC made *and* satisfy his intellectual curiosity about the progress of his hybrid. The Cheshire cat's smile threatened to swallow his face.

The door opened, and Zander walked into his office.

"There you are," Zander misinterpreted Craig's smirk as friendly. "Was searching for you, buddy."

"What can I do for you?" Craig couldn't help putting a few less watts in his smile and replying with some tightness at the intrusion into his moment.

"Sorry," Zander said when he realized he had barged into the office without knocking. "I talked to Dr. Mack a few minutes ago, and I think I found something! Wanted to run it by you and see what you thought. I didn't mean to interrupt. Come see me later when you can, okay?" He turned to leave.

"Stop." Zander turned back to him. "Sorry, I would love to hear your idea." *You have not the slightest inkling how much, my friend,* he thought with supreme irony.

Indicating with a gesture to a plush chair opposite his desk, Craig took to his seat.

"Spill it," he said with his best encouraging grin.

With a boyish smile on his face, Zander came alive with the need to share his newest discovery with his friend. Plopping into the seat he started, "I was talking to Dr. Mack a minute ago about how we should forget the antidote approach, so we can focus on something we have a hope of completing in less time."

Zander recounted what he had discussed with Dr. Mack. And Craig found himself slipping into yet another role: collaborator. Over the past 15 years, there had been more of these brainstorming sessions than could be counted. It was so comfortable and easy.

Zander would emerge from one of his mad scientist meditations with an 'idea,' which he would then throw at Craig. Normally, 'Doc' would then try his best to poke holes into Zander's hypothesis, and in return, Zander tried to defend his brainstorming concept.

This bouncing of solution and counter notion often led to the discovery of a new remedy or the confirmation and proof of Zander's original brain-storming fix. This byplay most resembled watching someone toying with a Rubik's Cube: the individual starting with a jumble. Still, after manipulating the puzzle for a time, he or she handed it to you completed.

It was irrational to hate someone because they were a better puzzle solver than you, but Craig was self-honest enough to admit his jealousy.

If Zander had worked in another lab, it wouldn't have been such a thorn in Craig's side. But because he did, Craig had a front-row seat to his mediocrity. It was infuriating. The ultimate irony was even though their debates humbled him; he would never give them up. They were intellectually challenging and exciting. They gave him the chance to play in an orchestra first chair, as it were.

Not only that, but Craig reveled in the fact that Zander did not go to Lise or other doctors for their help—he chose Craig. Their skull sessions were pivotal to the creation of a cancer wonder drug. Regardless of all that, he knew Zander was the composer and conductor of this 'band.' Eyebrows lifting without thought, Craig could think of at least two ways this crazy solution might be accomplished quickly. Best not to help his old 'friend' too much though and volunteer them.

*Holy Hell! How does he do this?!* Craig thought in exasperation but sobered a moment later when he realized his forethought might allow him to thwart Zander and the CDC before they unraveled the GC's plans any further.

"My God. How do you come up with this stuff? It's a brilliant if not unconventional approach. Creating a blocker, or maybe more accurately, a masker, would be infinitely easier than the vaccine," Craig gushed. Okay, maybe he was laying it on too thick, but Zander's face lit up as he had hoped for.

"Thanks, but it is only an idea right now. The first thing I was thinking we could try is to use some radioactive isotope which would combine with the specific cells temporarily—" Electricity crackled in the air as both men shot ideas back and forth in a furious volley, which seemed to operate outside time. But after an indeterminable time, they set down enough basic parameters to satisfy Zander.

"—bet most of the ingredients could be found here in Oregon," Craig said. "We would just need to figure out the dosage."

Zander took some final notes and said, "That had to be one of our best sessions. We went from a vague notion to something we could present to the CDC." He looked Craig in the eyes and said, "I don't know if I have told you this enough in the past, but I appreciate all you have done for Imagine and especially me over all these years. I owe you one. Better get this to Dr. Mack, ASAP." With that, he was out the door in a rush.

"Anytime, Zander," Craig said to an empty office.

As the door closed behind Zander, Craig's smile evaporated. He dialed his home number once he was sure Zander wouldn't barge in again.

On the second ring, the phone picked up, but there was no greeting. "This is Doc. I have run into unforeseen circumstances." He outlined what he had learned about the virus' progress, Zander's arrival, and the CDC's headway so far.

"I can't return to the compound yet," he explained, "it is better if I can stay here and monitor things. As a contingency, I would like you to tell Greg to prepare a strike force. There are National Guardsmen everywhere, but we can't afford to let these people interfere. Wait for further instructions."

"Acknowledged," was the terse reply.

Then, dial tone.

# Chapter 21

*July 6, Friday — 9:11 pm — Imagine Labs*

As he left his office, Zander had to continue to remind himself to walk fast instead of sprinting to find Mack. Then he marveled, *I must be finally getting this virus out of my system. I didn't think I would ever feel like running again.* He burst into a broad smile. *That might be part of it, but let's be honest. It feels good to come up against a problem and come up with a viable solution! I didn't think I would get another chance. Damn, it feels good! Now, I wonder where that CDC director is holed up. Bet he's in that maze of a parking lot.*

He exited the building and gazed out at the sea of CDC tents. Zander took a few hesitant steps before he was literally run over by a startled lab tech, who was paying more attention to his clipboard than where he was headed. Both men went down in a tangle of arms and legs, but neither were hurt, and they got to their feet.

As the man started apologizing, Zander insisted he was fine but asked where he would find Dr. Mack. The man in a white lab coat pointed to a tent and scurried off.

Once Zander got to the entrance, he almost laughed aloud. *Do I knock?* After a moment, he decided the best way to enter a CDC command tent was simply to walk in unannounced, if for no other reason than that technically, they were on his property.

Moving the tent's flap to the side, he entered and saw the shelter was dominated by a sizeable gray plastic table in the center of the space. Other smaller makeshift counters were pushed up to the pavilion's sides, and these 'desks' were cluttered with various computer workstations and what he assumed was communication gear.

There were enough wires and cables linking all this equipment to give an OSHA inspector a heart attack. Luckily, this was not their first deployment, so a hideous—but effective—brown indoor-outdoor carpet hid everything: grass, electrical wires, and communications lines.

He still needed to be mindful of the occasional ripples on the floor. Other wires snaked up to the "ceiling" of the 10-foot-tall tent, where he could see six make-shift lights situated around it, affording adequate illumination of the workspace.

Once his eyes adjusted from the July sunshine outside, he could finally discern a dozen people within. Mack sat at one of the side desks, toiling away at a workstation.

As Zander approached, Mack looked up and grinned.

The administrator beckoned for him to grab an empty seat kitty-corner to his own. "It's good to see you, Dr. Parks. Tell me you have something for us." It was almost comical how the man's nonchalant tone was at complete odds with Mack's eager body language and nervous, wringing hands. "Atlanta is breathing down my neck."

"Might have something." Mack's face fell, but Zander continued, "But we're pretty sure our ideas are theoretically plausible. Would love to have your people vet them."

Zander pulled out a yellow notepad covered with neat handwriting and gave Mack a rundown of what their masking agent would do and possibly its composition. Mack interrupted him a few times for clarification, but otherwise, he let Zander make his pitch.

"This is good—very good," Mack said with excitement. "The way you first presented it, it didn't sound promising. But this is amazing! Don't take this wrong, but when we spoke earlier, I thought you were full of yourself—a self-important prick telling the CDC what to do." He shook his head in wonder. "I'm big enough to admit; I was wrong. But tell me. A few hours ago, you had nothing. Staring at a screen. Now this? How?"

"I told you earlier, our methods may seem unconventional to you, but we have honed them down to a science. What you have in your hands there has been independently corroborated by both of my colleagues, and they concur: my quirky solution, inelegant as it is, is probably our best chance to stop this thing."

"Atlanta needs to see this post-haste. Excuse me," Mack said as he stood and disappeared into the scrum behind them.

For the first time since waking in the hospital not a day ago, Zander didn't have anything to do. He knew there had to be a cot somewhere nearby. Unfortunately, he knew from much experience, the adrenaline coursing through his veins wouldn't allow any respite until the creative process worked itself out. So, he tried to bide his time by watching the constant parade of people moving within and from without the command tent.

Before Zander had a chance to get bored, Mack returned, "Pitched your idea to the brass. I even added my recommendation—for what it's worth—that we follow your lead."

Eager to get started, Zander interrupted, "Good. So, we should—"

"Whoa, there, cowboy," Mack said with a grin. "I know you are used to doing things your way, but the CDC is not your lab." Zander made to argue, but Mack continued, "I can recommend all I want, but in the end, I'm a grunt on the scene. Someone a few pay grades above my own will have to make the ultimate decision. Sorry."

The emotional roller coaster Zander was on sharply dipped again. Only moments ago, he still hoped they could stop the virus in time, but now—more foot dragging. "Mack, I *know* this is the best chance we have at saving millions of lives. Who cares if you are a lowly on-scene CDC director? Who better to analyze the outbreak—"

One of the nearby assistants stepped up to Mack agitatedly and noisily cleared her throat.

Mack interrupted Zander, making a face. "Excuse me for a second. What is it, Sims?"

"Sir, you have a call from the White House. It is the President." Without waiting for any acknowledgment, the aid handed him a cell phone.

Shrugging, Mack had the grace to appear sorry, but it was obvious he wasn't asking for Zander's permission to interrupt their conversation. "Have to take this."

"Sure," Zander said as he raised his hands in the universal signal for surrender and took a few steps back for good measure. Unsure where he fit in the national security picture—he needn't have worried because a heartbeat later Mack waved Zander back.

"Yes, Mister President," Mack said, still speaking on the phone. I have Dr. Parks here now, and I am switching us to a FaceTime conference call on my laptop now. One moment."

Mack put down the cell, grabbed his computer from a nearby table, and turned the screen toward the two of them. A few keystrokes later they were logged in and Mack had opened the appropriate app.

Instantly, Zander saw the eagle on the blue background of the presidential seal encompassing the display. "Waiting for Transmission" blinked in the center of the screen until a familiar face replaced it: the most powerful man on earth.

The man wore the obligatory dark blue power suit with a red tie and American flag lapel pin, yet the intelligent, ice-blue eyes drew you in. It was surreal for Zander to be looking this man in the eyes, but then he saw something shocking.

The President's hair was disheveled. His tie was loosened, and his top shirt button was undone. But the most disturbing detail of all was the dark bruises forming under his eyes. In a moment of lucidity, Zander realized he had been given a peek behind the curtain, as it were. In normal times, this man would have guarded his projected persona like the Hope Diamond. But the man before him knew full well the danger his country faced, and consequently, it permitted him neither sleep nor peace the past two days.

*It's funny how quickly your life can change. Two weeks ago, I was a nobody. Then, the world learns about my cancer treatment, and I get inundated with hundreds of media requests. And if that isn't enough, I nearly die. And yet the thing I get wigged out most by is participating in a conference call with the President of the United States?* He couldn't shake the unsettled feeling he was Alice in free fall down the rabbit hole. *I wonder where I will be in two more weeks?*

"Dr. Parks? Can you hear me?" the President asked.

Had the President already tried to talk to him and here he was philosophizing about life—an inauspicious start.

The President waited impatiently.

"Yes, Mr. President," was all Zander could muster in response.

"My advisors tell me you have a cure for this thing?"

"Cure might be a strong word, sir." The President's brows came crashing down, but Zander hurried on. "My colleagues and I feel that this new avenue of research is our best hope for a timely intervention, but honestly, it is up to the CDC and the medical and scientific research community to move it beyond the theoretical stage to an actual solution. We just need the resources and time to make it work."

"I wish I could," the President said. Rationally, Zander knew he had no right to expect everyone to see it his way, but he couldn't keep the disappointment from his face.

"Mr. President," Zander said in desperation, "I know you have other options, but I believe this will work. Give us a chance. Please."

The President momentarily looked confused, but then he offered a lop-sided smile. "Sorry, I have not been sleeping, and I guess I could have been clearer. The US government—with all its considerable resources—will be placed in your hands, but what I failed to communicate a moment ago effectively is: you have almost no time to perform your miracle. Local law authorities in Portland have reported a rash of violent attacks involving three different men." Zander couldn't see where the President was going with this apparent non-sequitur and could not keep the confusion from creeping onto his face. "All three work for the same company: Forestco. When contacted, Todd Masters, their CEO, told the police his son and the other two men had attended a company function in Ontario on June 30th. I was notified less than two days ago. We are almost out of time, gentlemen."

The President's unkempt, grim visage made perfect sense now, and a feeling of dismay nibbled at the edges of Zander's sanity.

"The plan was to get a masking agent created ASAP," Zander explained. "But we thought we would have a bit more time. These things take time. We knew going into this that, unfortunately, most of the population of Ontario was going to be lost. Our only consolation was that at least it is contained in a city of 11,000. There are 2.5 million people in the Portland metro area!"

"We are well aware of that," the President said with some asperity, "but the news gets worse—one man was found dead in his home, but the other two are unaccounted for at this time. Luck was with us in one respect. The local authorities had assumed these were three unrelated homicide crimes until one alert policewoman re-membered the CDC bulletin and made the Forestco connection. So, we know about the new outbreak, and there is a colossal manhunt being conducted, but so far, the men have not been apprehended."

"This outbreak in Portland changes everything," Zander said.

"You have a knack for massive understatement," the President said dryly. "All state governments have been notified in a five-state area in case this bug jumped our line somewhere else. But as I was saying before, more time is something I can't give you." The man's presidential façade broke, and he seemed very vulnerable. "Knowing that, it is imperative I back the right horse; you gave me qualifiers earlier" —he raised his hands in a hear-me-out motion— "I know those are necessary in your trade, but I need to know, can you make your solution work?"

The enormity of what the man asked Zander hit him hard. If what the said was true, this virus's threat level had increased expo-nentially. The implications were terrifying. What would happen if he failed? This thing had caused the deaths of almost everyone he knew: his mother, father, his close friends, his co-workers, and even his own 'death,' all in just a week. In all ways that were important, this thing had beaten him. It would kill over 90 percent of the pop-ulation of Ontario, but he had hoped their ultimate sacrifice would allow them to create a solution in time.

In his heart, he knew they could fashion a masking agent if they had sufficient time. But something arose in him—anger, yes, but also the resolution to fight. It was like how he felt when he learned of Crystal's prognosis—it demanded action from him.

With determined resolution Zander said, "We will create a counter to this virus Mr. President, but, as much as I hate to admit this, my modest lab and what's left of her staff is not best suited for creating and synthesizing a mass antidote in your time frame. Another facility is necessary."

The President gazed at Zander, once again taking the measure of the man he would place such an ultimate trust. After an indeterminable time, he grimly smiled and said, "It takes a big man to admit he needs help. Say no more doctor, I meant it when I said you will have the full backing of every resource I have at my disposal. Wait one, I need to make a quick call."

Without warning, the display returned to the presidential splash screen. Collapsing into a nearby chair, Zander tried to gather himself after the intensity of the past conversation.

Finally, he said, "Mack, when you said a few steps up the food chain, I figured you were trying to pawn off the decision. The President accuses me of being a master of understatement—little did I know—you were the team's captain."

Both laughed out loud heartily, as much as to release stress than because the observation was hilarious.

The President's face popped on the monitor without warning.

"Gentleman?" the President asked in concern.

"Sorry, sir—a private joke," Mack said while trying to tamp down his grin a few watts.

"Well, anyway," the President shook his head in annoyance, "I just spoke with the CEO of Horizons Pharmaceuticals. After briefly sharing the gravity of our situation with him, he agreed to lend us his facilities and any personnel we could use. The two closest labs are in San Francisco—and coincidentally—in Portland. Do either of you have a preference?"

"Yes, sir," Mack said. "As you pointed out, time is a luxury we do not possess. Let's not waste time flying to San Francisco. If we create our masking agent, we need at least some preliminary testing before mass-producing it. In Portland, plenty of citizens will soon be willing to take a chance on our inoculant. Also, I'm surprised we have been able to sit on this story for as long as we have. Someone in the Portland media is going to figure out the city's new violence outbreak has nothing to do with whether people use plastic shopping bags and everything to do with a new deadly virus. When it hits the news, you will have a panic. If we create the masking agent in San Francisco, we cannot guarantee we will be able to deliver our remedy when the roads are full of panic-stricken motorists."

"Valid and cogent points Dr. Mack, I will call Joe back and request their Portland facilities as soon as we are done here. Meanwhile, I want you running point on our new operation in Portland. Get one of your assistants there to handle things in Ontario. Sadly, I don't think there is much they will be able to do at this juncture. Is there anything else I need to know about?" There it was. In a handful of words, the President had affirmed that virtually everyone in Zander's hometown was a casualty, and no one even knew what the purpose for killing almost 11,000 people was.

"Mr. President," Zander dared to add. "I have a few coworkers from Imagine Labs who survived the virus, too. Their expertise in virology is immeasurable. Could I bring them with me?"

"Yes," the President said without hesitation. "Gentlemen, I will not waste any more of your valuable time. Godspeed."

The screen returned to the presidential seal again.

"Inspiring pep talk," Zander said with unrestrained sarcasm. "What is the plan?"

"How fast can you download your files and be ready to travel?" the CDC director asked.

"Most of the pertinent data is already downloaded and printed. Give me 20 minutes?"

"Make it 10," Mack said with a snarky smile. Then he turned to a nearby Guardsman and began giving orders.

*Nine minutes later.*

When Mack announced they would be 'wheels up' in minutes, Zander hadn't had time to ponder how they would get to Portland. There was barely enough time to grab a meager overnight bag of essentials and his computer in the time allotted by the CDC director.

Fortunately for Zander, his laptop and two redundant backup drives constantly mirrored Imagine Lab's research data, so he only had to disconnect them from the server and stash them in his brown, leather over-the-shoulder bag. As Zander stood outside the CDC command tent waiting for Mack, he took a moment to gaze in wonder at his lab.

In some ways, it had already become unrecognizable—the lights, the sounds, the personnel. But behind all this bustle, the Imagine Lab's Street sign testified to what this building meant to his parents, to Crystal's Cure supporters, to all the victims of Leukemia. . . to him. *Who knows*, he thought to himself, maybe we'll all come out okay on the other side of this thing. *Maybe everything we worked so hard to do will still have meaning.*

It was a comforting thought, but deep down, Zander felt like this was goodbye. There were too many ghosts here ever to call this place home again.

At that moment, a hand clapped him on the shoulder. Zander nearly jumped a foot into the air and turned in annoyance to see Mack with a wide grin on his dark-skinned face. Gone was the ubiquitous orange suit. Apparently, the man had decided the thing was overkill. An understated viral mask hung around his neck.

His gold-rimmed glasses flashed as he said, "Follow me—I've got a little surprise for you."

Zander patted the shoulder bag to assure himself he had everything he needed for this trip and shadowed Mack.

He had assumed they would jump into another Humvee and take a commuter plane from the Ontario Municipal Airport two miles west of his lab. He assumed wrong. Rohit and Ben joined him as they traversed their lab's lot and hopped a low concrete divider.

Beyond it were a dozen lit flares dropped in a loose circle around the perimeter of this empty section of blacktop. Their red light casting an earie, surreal light on seven or eight alert, armed guardsmen and a whining Black Hawk helicopter.

When they approached the craft, Mack shouted, "All aboard!"

Each newcomer was then handed a helmet and given basic airship safety instructions. As they entered the cabin, the turbo started ramping up to a roar slightly muted by their now-donned helmets. A helicopter crewman appeared as he entered and gently but insistently grabbed Zander's elbow and maneuvered him to a pod of jump seats situated back-to-back and mounted to the metal decking in the midsection of the aircraft.

Looking out the open bay door, he observed the gently drooping blades beginning to spin.

In no time, the spinning wings began whirling so fast his eye could not fully track their movement. It reminded him of old reel-to-reel movies, which seemed to jump from picture to picture in fits and starts. The air began to swirl about the cabin violently, and the propeller vanes seemed to ache to wrench the Black Hawk from its terrestrial bondage. This awesome noise only abated somewhat when a black-clad crewperson slid the side doors shut. He found his black canvas seat surprisingly comfortable, and—in two shakes— the nimble flight crew had him belted in.

The dim green light of the cabin took a while for his eyes to adjust to, but he still gawked in wide-eyed wonder at all the bells and whistles of the multi-million-dollar aircraft about him. That is, until the Black Hawk shot up vertically in the air like a missile, and much later, his queasy stomach joined him. The increasing thunder of the engine above them escalated until they finally reached their top cruising speed.

"Yep. Not how I thought this day would go at all," he said to no one in particular.

A nearby speaker crackled as the pilot announced their flight time would be a little short of two hours. He also warned them they might see the running lights of their escorts—two heavily armed Army gunships taking up station to their port and starboard. *Guess the President is not taking our security for granted.*

Easing back into the airship's spartan seat, Zander was determined to grab a little shuteye. He was not unaccustomed to long, grueling hours, but coming back from a brush with death was not something he faced every day. His jacket bunched up as he leaned back into the pillow the flight crew had handed him upon their embarking. When it did, he could see a bright white paper partly exposed, and he sighed deeply. There were no pressing matters to attend to, and he warred with himself over whether to read it now.

On the one hand, he ached to hear his friend's last words. On the other—he knew it was irrational to feel this way—but it was almost like Lise wasn't gone if her final message went unsaid.

Curiosity and the fear of being alone warred within him. Longing to hear from her one last time won out. Zander removed the letter from his pocket and laid it on his lap.

The envelope's only salutation was "Zander," which was written in the flowing script of a poet rather than the messy scribble associated with most doctors.

Without thought, he began tracing the elegant symbols with the tip of his right index finger. *Stop stalling,* he scolded. With resolution, he broke the seal and opened it. When he removed the single piece of her distinctive stationery—adorned with roses across the top—a photo fell to the airship's deck.

In a panic, he lunged to pick up the precious gift but was brought short by the flight harness, which crisscrossed his chest. Ungainly fingers tried to work the belt's release mechanism in the green half-light of the helicopter's cargo area. He grew frantic. Afraid the precious thing would pass into nothingness if he left it in the darkness too long.

The buckles finally released him. Rummaging on hands and knees about the deck, he found the memento. Resuming his seat, Zander squinted, yet the muted illumination was so poor, it was hard to differentiate the various shades of color in the photo. So, he groped the panel above him for a light switch or knob, hoping they built these machines like commercial aircraft.

Finally, he found a button. A pocket-size pool of light illuminated his seating area.

The photograph was taken at the Elks Lodge celebration—could it have been only a week ago? He understood why Lise had picked this particular photo. The man in this picture appeared to be standing on top of the world, a man who could take on an insurmountable foe and win.

It memorialized the moment Zander had joined his mother on the stage after her rousing speech. As was only fitting, his mother was in the middle, flanked by his father and him, Lise, Ben, Rohit, and some of their staunchest supporters—including Abby. The band of heroes had linked hands and were raising their arms in rapturous triumph when the photographer took the picture.

Now, all he could taste were the ashes and emptiness of losing most of them.

Blinking away unbidden tears, he opened the letter.

*Zander,*

*I had hoped to give this to you to commemorate your triumphant night. Little did I know it was a good thing I had Pete send me a copy the day after the party—otherwise—well, enough of that. I just found out you will survive this thing. I'm so happy for you, but I won't sugarcoat this. I know the road ahead of you is going to be difficult, if not seeming impossible. I want this photo to remind you of all the people who believed in you from the beginning. Their faith in you wasn't misplaced then. Trust yourself now. It was my privilege to be your friend, and I have never regretted a moment since attending that conference in Seattle so long ago. I'm glad we got to have one night of victory.*

*Love,*

*Lise*

*P.S. My only regret was. . . I didn't have time to photoshop my hair. I look like freaking Cyndi Lauper in a windstorm.*

When he read the postscript, a chuckle—not a grief-stricken sob—bubbled to the surface. In the future, the black chasm in his heart would need healing, but for now, it was a luxury he could ill afford. So, instead of focusing on the hole in his heart, he focused on Lise's intense dislike of her hair's waywardness and smiled. Their friendship had meant everything to him, and it was so typical of her to worry about someone beside herself during her waning moments of life.

Her message to him was clear: *don't give up.*

What would he do without her unwavering support behind him?

After a moment, he folded the letter and gently tucked it back into its protective sheath. Then, as he was going to stow the picture in the envelope, he hesitated—deposited it in his breast pocket—and patted it lovingly.

The loss was sharp, bitter, and new. But under that wound—was hope—a last gift from the past. When he put the photo in a different coat pocket, he felt a familiar, comforting bulge. The package of Wrigley's materialized, as if out of the air, in his hand, and as was his wont, he meticulously unwrapped the gum and began to chew.

Revitalized by Lise's letter, Zander removed his laptop from his bag and powered it up. The overhead light reflected off his screen, so he switched the penlight off. He fully intended to get a jump on his blocker, but unfortunately, his body had other plans. The darkness and sway of the cabin were the perfect combination. . . for sleep.

# Part 2

## PORTLAND, OREGON

# Chapter 22



*July 6, Friday — 10:56 pm — Horizons Pharmaceuticals*

When he awoke, Zander was doubly happy to find his laptop still safely lying on his lap and the crushing fatigue he had felt earlier gone. Triggering his helmet mic, he asked where they were. The co-pilot said they were near Troutdale and would arrive at Horizons Pharmaceuticals in minutes.

Craning his neck to the right, he could view the Columbia River as they raced beside it. The pilot throttled back the engine and gained a little more altitude than the paltry 200-foot height they had been traveling while above the sparsely populated areas of Oregon. The light and darkness below shifted from intermittent to the almost constant glow of the Portland metro area.

Another announcement: arrival imminent—stow gear and prepare for landing. He placed the laptop into its protective case and clutched it to his chest. Breath held in expectant trepidation.

The Black Hawk seemed to come to a stop in midair before alighting dead center of the well-lit helipad atop the 12-story south tower of the Horizons' research facility. He could see the east bank of the Willamette River and the University of Portland campus beyond his window. Above him, he could hear the lethal machine's engines powering down. The cabin crew went about their business of helping their passengers exit the craft in a timely manner.

Once deposited onto the tarmac, Zander looked around and spotted a well-dressed man and woman to the east of their helicopter. Head down, Mack was checking his phone for messages and hadn't noticed them yet, so Zander tapped him on the shoulder and indicated they were being watched. As if Zander's pointing were a signal, the welcoming committee exited the relative safety of the shelter created by a small elevator outbuilding and approached their visitors. Mack smiled in genuine warmth as their hosts approached. The rest of the Ontario CDC contingent remained a step behind.

The woman strode in front of her colleague, bowing her head to avoid the still spinning blades, largely unnecessary because she was well beyond their reach. The aristocratic-looking woman was of average height and very slender. Her grey hair caught up in a tight bun just above the collar of her smart business suit.

"Cora Vanderbilt, executive director of operations in Portland! Dr. Mack!?" The engine and rotor noise nearly drowned out her clipped New England accent.

"Yes, ma'am, may I introduce my colleagues!?" Mack bellowed as well.

She shook her head in the negative and pointed to the craft. "Later."

Then she grabbed Mack's elbow and ushered him toward the elevator outbuilding. Zander couldn't help stealing a glance at his friends, who, too, were chuckling at their no-nonsense host. The group moved to follow.

Once the elevator doors had shut, Ms. Vanderbilt said, "My staff is assembled in the conference room below, and we can make introductions then, but we have already reviewed your dossiers." As if to make her point, she turned her piercing aquamarine eyes toward him and said, "Dr. Parks, I do hope we get a chance to discuss your team's recent breakthrough."

"Ahh, I-I'm, I'm looking forward to it," Zander stammered. The woman smiled, but he couldn't shake the feeling she was taking measure of him. Finally, she nodded and returned her attention to Mack. He wasn't sure what conclusion she came to about him, but he was glad to rid of her basilisk stare.

Being around someone with her intensity was fascinating and just a bit terrifying. This woman was the master of her surroundings and exuded supreme confidence in herself and, consequently, her little slice of the world. He couldn't help but feel a touch of envy. Although he held the same title at Imagine Labs, he felt like a pale shadow of the woman. But he could put those feelings aside because right now, they could use every bit of her and her facility's excellence and competence to create their virus masker in a timely manner.

"Thank you so much for your cooperation in this matter," Mack said, trying to be diplomatic.

Ms. Vanderbilt laughed sardonically, "Not sure it's cooperation when the President of the United States—in essence—conscripts my people and my resources. Seems more like an order to me." Raising her hand to stall Mack's objection, she said, "Didn't say I wouldn't do what you need; I'm just saying—"

The elevator opened, and she moved to exit, but then she paused in the doorway and turned toward her guests.

Several emotions warred on her tight face. Then it melted into a genuine smile, and she said, "Guess I'm just as guilty of wanting things the way I want them. We were on the threshold of finishing a very important drug we'd spent years developing. Sorry to take it out on you. I know it's in our best interests to work together."

With that, she exited the carriage and headed down the brightly lit hallway to their destination.

*Well, this should be an interesting partnership,* Zander thought as he glanced between their host and Mack and followed behind the pack. They walked for less than a minute before Ms. Vanderbilt veered to her right, ostensibly to a meeting room. For some irrational reason, Zander anticipated it to be roughly the same size as his own, which was why he was unprepared for—the reality.

A Horizons employee hurried by their party and entered a door their host had passed. Apparently, their entourage would be taking the main, center aisle double doors.

Once inside, Zander could clearly see the other two aisles flanking their own, which gave occupants easy access throughout the space. The chairs, which rivaled the luxury of any first-class airline seat, were upholstered with a burnt red leather seating surface and black leather armrests. Many attendees had already unfolded the small table before their seats and plugged their laptops or notebooks into power and network connections at each work area.

Their troop proceeded down the aisle to the full-sized stage below. More than a few people glanced at Zander and the other newcomers, but they only had a passing interest in these interlopers.

All their eyes followed the woman before him, and without any signal or word, attendees who loitered in the aisle made way for this woman: a modern-day Moses. Upon arriving at the stairs leading to the dais, Zander covetously surveyed his surroundings. An almost luminous mahogany podium dominated the space. It was equipped with a multitude of glowing switches and a teleprompter.

Beyond it was a view screen, which spanned the full wall behind and was bracketed by massive speakers. To top it off, a sizable bank of theater lights of all colors and intensities surrounded the platform. A dozen chairs ringed the back of the stage, facing the audience. He was led to one by a courteous aide.

With nothing better to do now, he gazed about the 'conference room.' If he were to guess, this stage could easily hold his Imagine Labs' conference room back home. And that didn't even account for the approximately 300 nearly-filled seats in the auditorium. *Close your mouth, Zander. No sense in making these people chuckle at the country bumpkin,* he mused a tad sourly. Deep down, he couldn't help but be a little jealous of what Horizons had in the way of facilities, but ultimately, he wouldn't go back and change a thing.

The foundation may not have provided much beyond the necessities, but he could look every Crystal's Cure donor in the eye and tell them his or her money was well spent. Virtually every dollar donated to the charity went into life-saving equipment and personnel salaries. And if not for this damn virus, they would have achieved their purpose: eliminating the scourge of Leukemia. So, much like when a person sees an impressive sports car and looks longingly at it, Zander could appreciate Horizons' luxuries without second-guessing his choice to pursue his cure as an independent.

These thoughts were interrupted when several well-dressed individuals dashed onto the stage and sat around him. There was no time for introductions because Ms. Vanderbilt got up from her seat and approached the podium.

The room fell into immediate hush.

Zander could see attentive faces awaiting her address—that is until the room dimmed, and five brilliant stage lights focused on the podium and those assembled on the stage. The screen behind him lit up, and Zander glanced back to see a bigger-than-life video headshot of Ms. Vanderbilt.

Without preamble, she began, "Ladies and Gentlemen. Most of you are now aware," she smirked at the tacit understanding that a secret this vast was impossible to keep, "of the tragic viral outbreak in Ontario, which now has spread to Portland. According to the

CDC, this Frankenstein pathogen's DNA is a combination of HIV and the Ebola virus."

She let this terrifying thought marinate for a moment before continuing.

"The President of the United States has asked for our help, and I assured him that we will do everything possible to help stop this deadly contagion. So, until you hear otherwise, you will drop all current projects and work exclusively with the CDC and these doctors." She waved generally in his people's direction.

Turning to face her audience again, she began to tick off salient points on her fingers. "Until further notice, there will be unlimited overtime; we will set up sleeping rooms in each section of campus. Arrangements have been made to have a local tour bus establishment pick up everyone's immediate families and bring them to Horizons for their safety. The cafeterias are trucking a few months' worth of provisions in as we speak. Lastly, we will have a company of Oregon National Guardsman arriving within the hour, ensuring our work is uninterrupted and providing on-site security."

Vanderbilt's face tightened. "The President also said the FBI has confirmed the release of this virus was not an accident, and they are pursuing leads as to who is responsible. It is highly unlikely this 'group' knows about us here, but we can't afford to assume."

She let them be human for a few moments as they vented their astonishment and anger at this atrocity, and then she raised her hand like a conductor in front of her symphony—and they quieted.

"Therefore, we must maintain building security, so the military will be provided with your company photo and what rooms you should have access to. Always keep your security badges on your person. Your families will be afforded temporary IDs and are expected to stay in designated berthing areas and out of all working spaces. This is not a prison, so you can visit with them during your few off hours. We didn't ask to be put in this position, but I know you'll rise to this challenge as you have in the past. When this emergency is concluded, on my personal authority, Horizons will award each of you an extra month of vacation time."

She paused for a moment and smirked, "Lastly, I'm told Uncle Sam will cover any 'reasonable' expenses you and your family incur during this crisis."

The woman's charisma was palpable. As she gazed out at her audience, Zander could feel her willing them to accomplish this impossible task. It was then that he realized Vanderbilt was not that much different from himself. She might be no-nonsense and gruff, but underneath, she was a leader who genuinely cared about 'her people.'

"Now let's get down to business," she said, and there was the sound of bags and briefcases opening, papers shuffled, and various electronic devices being turned on. "A compendium of the pertinent information on the virus and the avenue the CDC wishes to pursue has been loaded onto our server. After this briefing, we will break into teams. But before we do that, I would like Dr. Mack, head of the CDC mobile ground team and our liaison with the President, to say a few words."

Ms. Vanderbuilt relinquished her podium and deigned to sit in a chair to his left. The complete silence that met Mack's introduction instead of the normal applause spoke volumes about the state of mind of everyone in the room.

In a warm tenor voice, Mack began his exhortation with, "On behalf of the President of the United States, I wish to thank you for all the sacrifices you and your families are about to make. It is no hyperbole to say that if we are successful, we could save human-kind from extinction. The current computer projections predict the virus will infect every continent and major human civilization within six months. Furthermore, according to the data we have collected from the Ontario hot zone, 100 percent of the population became infected—of those—nine out of 10 progressed to Stage Four and subsequently died."

The Horizons' audience knew of the outbreak, but Mack's predictions and statistics foretold a dire future for humankind. A nervous murmur ran through the previously staid audience.

"If those numbers weren't bad enough," Mack plowed on, "our empirical evidence from the site confirms the virus has broken the animal-human barrier. The CDC's investigation of this virus is less than a week old, and we don't know every detail about it yet. So far, we know household pets are affected, but we don't have the personnel to check on animals in the wilderness. Our disease modeling experts are assuming that animals are carriers, too. If that is the case, then our computers predict that only people in the world's remotest areas have any hope of surviving this unscathed. The numbers are always being updated, but current projections are that fewer than one billion people will survive the virus itself. Unfortunately, the final stage of the contagion causes its host to act like a rabid animal. Undoubtedly, these infected victims will cause millions of further deaths among the virus' initial survivors. Therefore, we have downwardly revised our estimate from one billion survivors to fewer than 500,000 worldwide."

This news hit his audience like a blow to the solar plexus. Zander heard nervous whispers and agitated movements from the crowd as they caught their breath.

Attempting a reassuring smile, Mack continued, "We are not dumping the world's fate at your feet; you are but one part, albeit a critical part, of the solution. In a few minutes, the CDC will contact most of the world's preeminent scientists and doctors in research medicine. Revealing to them—with the strictest warnings of secrecy—the existence of the virus and our conclusions about what it will do to the Earth's population. For those who join us, we will distribute an address for a secure FBI website, which will help us pool our data and observations. You know our field tends to be quite guarded, but if we are to survive, we must collaborate on a scale never attempted.

"Obviously," Mack grimaced, "telling so many people such a thing means that it will get out to the general populace no matter how much we would like to keep this under wraps. The potential for this news to create panic and hysteria is tremendous. Therefore, we would like to postpone the release of this information for as long as possible to minimize disruption of travel and communication. Both would make our work exponentially more difficult. So, we ask that you only tell your immediate families about what we have revealed today. As you can see by our projections, there is no 'safe haven' they could escape to. There might be parts of Alaska left unscathed by this thing, but there will be no safe place in the continental United States. It's up to everyone involved in this project to formulate and implement a solution to this virus.

"You are free to pursue our objective as best your company sees fit. The President will receive hourly reports from me on our progress, so during this operation, all department heads will report to me at the top of the hour. Each group supervisor will be given my command center location and contact number. All information should be funneled to them. I would like the man who conceptualized our virus masking strategy to say a few words—Dr. Zander Parks."

*I can't believe I let Mack talk me into this,* he thought as he stared into the bright lights. "Talk to the troops," he had said. "Tell them what the basics are. No need to prep." Without thinking, Zander's left hand strayed to his pants pocket searching for his familiar, comforting package of gum.

He was tempted to indulge himself even with all eyes upon him, but then he chided himself. *You have done this hundreds of times back home. Just give them the basics and be done with it.*

Even with his less-than-stellar pep talk, his knees felt rubbery, and sweat quickly broke out about his person. Gripping the podium tightly, he took a cleansing breath. As the seconds ticked by, he finally decided to stop dithering.

"Umm, thank you, Dr. Mack. You—ahhh—might be asking yourself the question, 'Why are we following this guy's plan?' It's probably because we"—Zander pointed in Ben and Rohit's direction—"are intimately familiar with this virus. It was a bitter pill to learn that someone stole and corrupted our research—turning it into this *thing*," Zander couldn't help but instill all the vitriol he could muster into that last word.

"Our lab in Ontario had 65 staff members. We three are all that's left. Nearly everyone we knew has succumbed to this virus." He let that sink in. Lastly, we have spent more than a week already trying to develop a cure for this pathogen. Unfortunately, we did not have enough time to create something, and I'm fearful that even with global resources and all our medical acumen, we still might not have enough time to finish before the clock strikes midnight.

"My solution is simple—and in my opinion—and it's this simplicity which gives us the best chance at stopping this virus in time. If creating a vaccine that targets this Frankenvirus is too time-consuming, then why try? Instead, why not create a physiological barrier? This disease targets and destroys a person's T-cells and brain cells. Block 'em. My colleagues and I believe it to be possible to alter our bodies on a molecular level temporarily. However, we have no idea how we can do this without causing permanent damage. So, even though Dr. Mack might give me credit for the scheme, I'm hoping that there is a solution to be found between you and the world medical community.

"On your screens, you will find a folder labeled 'Imagine Labs.' There is a copy of all our research so far. You are all highly qualified geneticists, so I will not insult you by explaining our work to you. Besides, I would appreciate fresh eyes on our data anyway. Please don't hesitate to bring me any questions you might have, and I look forward to working with you."

Once again, there was no applause from those assembled, only an uncomfortable silence and the bright lights in his eyes.

After his impromptu speech was complete, Zander stood there unsure about what should happen next, his embarrassment mounting until it was interrupted by a tap on his shoulder.

He turned. Zander beheld a woman who looked to be in her late 40s—every bit as tall as him—and wearing a black, conservative dress, which did nothing to hide the trim, athletic figure beneath. Her sandalwood-colored skin was perfectly highlighted by jet black hair, which hung to her mid-back. But what drew his gaze most were her eyes: large and chocolate brown. He could stare into them forever, but doing so now was quickly becoming uncomfortable.

*What should I say? Something witty. Something intelligent,* he thought.

But what he actually said was, "Umm—hi—"

This reminded him of painful middle school dance memories. He was startled when his voice boomed out of the room's speakers. Apparently, this brief encounter had not only been faithfully reproduced in full HD quality on the stage-wide screen behind them but also in Dolby surround sound.

The audience's snickering filled the silence after his painful greeting. His first impulse was to flee the room and seek out the nearest cave, where he could promptly die of terminal embarrassment. But then the skin around her eyes crinkled, and did he see the hint of an amused smile? Trance broken—he shuffled to his chair, sat down, and pretended no one existed behind the bright lights.

The self-assured woman approached the microphone with practiced ease and, in a smoky alto voice, said, "You have heard the basic outline of the situation and the plan; now, let's get down to brass tacks. Our normal organizational structure supported 17 diverse undertakings, which would be grossly ineffectual for this project, so I created three new discrete groups. The appropriate file has been downloaded to each person's workstation. Open it now."

She paused for the briefest of moments. "As you can plainly see, the groups should have a nice balance of skills and experience, therefore maximizing our efficiency."

It was impossible for Zander not to gape dumbfounded for the second time in the past 15 minutes. A scant two hours ago, the President had called with the news that Horizons would be dropping everything and taking on this massive project, and here this woman had completely restructured her 300-person staff based on how well they worked together in time to make this presentation? Astonishing!

"If you're in Alpha group," she continued in a short, clipped delivery, "your responsibility is to work out a solution for blocking the virus's attacks on T-cells. Beta group, your concern is preventing attacks on brain cells. Lastly, Charlie group, your task is formulating a dispensing method for the two blockers. I think a liquid injection would be simplest to create and administer, but we should not also rule out aerosols or inhalers. Alpha and Beta teams, if we can combine the two remedies, that would be optimal, but if we can develop two antidotes quicker than one, then we will pursue that avenue."

Stopping momentarily, she let the note-takers catch up with her rapid-fire instructions.

"Initially, Ms. Vanderbilt and I thought working as a group in a room—such as this one—would be most beneficial, but upon further contemplation, we think operating in pods of four with periodic debriefing sessions would allow more comfort and flexibility. Open up the second attachment now. The room location of your pod, its members, and the group leader should be listed. When I'm finished with this debrief, you will meet with your respective groups in this room first, then move to your pods. If you have any questions, direct them to your facilitators, and they will bring them to Dr. Parks or my attention." At this point, she stopped talking and glanced at Vanderbilt, who nodded. "Dismissed."

Like a well-oiled machine, the Horizons staff switched from passive observers to active participants. With a click, the stage lights and video screen dimmed and then went out. The room was abuzz with activity except for Zander and his team; they looked around the room like lost high school freshmen on their first day.

He was about to ask where his team should go when a young, slender blond woman with a generous spray of freckles across her cheeks and nose approached him and said, "Dr. Parks, my name is Tabitha, and I was asked to show you around the facilities before you got to work. Would you please come with me?"

"I don't want to seem ungrateful but is that really the best use of our time?" he said as he waved his arm toward Ben and Rohit.

"Don't worry, sir. It will take our new groups some time to get set up. Besides, Ms. Vanderbilt felt you would be best served to be familiar with this building and our telephone and computer resources before things heat up." She gave him a warm smile.

Zander turned to his right to make sure Rohit and Ben had heard what was happening when he noticed they had also been assigned a chaperone. Again, he was impressed with this whole organization's effectiveness and general competency.

The leadership of these two powerful women was undoubtedly reflected in the machine-like efficiency around him. Even though his management style was much more laid-back, it didn't keep him from appreciating the military-like precision of this operation. Of course, there was always a danger in such a managed organization: creativity could become stifled.

Returning her smile, Zander motioned with his hand and said, "Lead the way."

The informative tour proceeded logically through various labs, the cafeteria, a rec room, and other less grandiose meeting rooms. Each was as well-appointed as the initial conference hall. At first, he couldn't help being jealous of their facilities, but then he decided to revel in seeing what a fully funded lab was like. Besides, if he was to be honest with himself, he wasn't as concerned about the building as he was in learning a certain detail.

"Tabitha," he tried to ask nonchalantly. "Can I ask you a question?"

The young woman had been a half step ahead of him, so she stopped and turned to face him. "Of course, doctor."

"This is ah… embarrassing, but I never caught the name of the attractive Asian lady who spoke at the end of our briefing."

The young woman opened her mouth to speak but then paused in surprise. Zander didn't know what to make of Tabitha's silence and was going to ask her what was wrong when he was startled by a feminine voice behind him.

"The pretty Asian lady's name is Dr. Grace Wu. Why?"

Though Zander had only heard her rich alto voice once before, it could only belong to one woman. Mortified, he turned to see her behind him. Her arms were crossed, and she didn't seem to be amused by his previous comment.

Zander excused himself to no one in particular: "Err, I think I need to splash a little water on my face before we get started." It was a feeble attempt, but it was all Zander could come up with. "I think I remember the way back to the washrooms. Excuse me, ladies."

In his mind's eye, Zander would have liked to call his flight to the restrooms a careful, tactical withdrawal, but honestly, it was more like a prison break from Alcatraz. Female laughter echoed down the passage as the bathroom door closed behind him.

The cool water was better than any salve for his burning cheeks, though he could have sworn the first few splashes evaporated upon contact with his skin. Looking in the mirror before him, he chided, *Well, Zander, you succeeded in making this working relationship —interesting—as in the Chinese curse 'may you live in interesting times.'*

Eventually, he knew he couldn't postpone the inevitable without looking like a coward, too. So, like a convict facing his sentence, he dried his face and hands and trudged back to his guide.

# Chapter 23



*July 5, Thursday — 3:10 pm — East Portland*

It seemed like only yesterday that Jazmyn Perez-Salazar had walked with her class at UCLA, but in fact, she had worked for the local FOX television affiliate in Portland for a little over a year.

It was weird. Everyone knew you were supposed to hate this part of your career—a time when a person spent as much time being a coffee gopher as she or he ever did as an actual reporter. But she didn't. Not that she would dare tell anyone that. So, she dutifully played the time-honored role of put-upon rookie whenever her journeyman coworkers were nearby.

*Besides,* she thought, *even if a lot of what I must do is grunt work, I still have learned more in the past year than all those years at UCLA.* KPTV had her working the police beat, which most people erroneously assumed involved Jazmyn cruising the mean streets of Portland, ferreting out crime stories with her uncanny sleuthing abilities.

The reality was that she spent an unhealthy amount of time sitting at her desk and studying the face plate of her trusty police scanner. Hoping for anything to happen. There were times when she felt guilty for wishing there were more robberies and assaults in town, but the only way she would get noticed by the higher-ups would be to get as much 'face time' on the air as possible. As of late, though, the old Yiddish curse was making itself felt—*May you get what you wish for.* She thought the TV van's window was less than clean for the seemingly hundredth time, but somehow, Jazmyn forgot to mention it when they returned to the station.

Once she sank her teeth into a story, there was room for little else, as her cameraman Liam, who was currently driving them to a homicide on East Burnside, could attest. There was no mistaking the crime scene when they arrived. At least a half-dozen police cruisers stood guard around the Safeway parking lot on their right-hand side, along with enough yellow caution tape to cordon off everything.

Traffic on the busy thoroughfare had come to an almost complete standstill as looky-loos macabrely craned to see if they could see any titillating details.

After an interminable time, they neared the supermarket, and Jazmyn pointed to a building half a block up from the Safeway, "Liam, could you pull over just to the left of the laundromat?"

He gave her an aggrieved glare.

"Please," she added.

With practiced martyrdom, he huffed and did as she asked. The station had nominally given her leadership of their 'team,' but honestly, Liam had 10 years of seniority on her. So, she couldn't blame him for resenting a 'cub reporter' telling him what to do. Even with that caveat, it didn't change who was responsible for creating her segment for the newscast tonight. So, all too soon she had to direct his actions once again after they were parked.

"Try to get some outside shots of the store in which some of the pretty flashing lights will give our audience something to gawk at," she said.

Liam made as if to protest, then gave up and went about getting his gear from the back of the van.

Flipping down the visor, Jazmyn checked the condition of her shoulder-length black hair and makeup. It was perfect. Then, she had a strange out-of-body experience.

Instead of seeing herself in a mirror, she saw a mature, sophisticated, mid-twentyish woman—a woman-mature and respectable—which, she thought sardonically, *It's the reason I spend more on hair styling and beauty products than most spend on their car payments. At least I don't have to spend money on tanning.* She mused as she admired her golden-brown skin tone, which was courtesy of her Guatemalan heritage.

Pleased with her appearance, she removed her press badge from her purse, affixed it to her dress, and exited the vehicle. A group of policemen and women gathered in the lot's southwest corner, so Jazmyn made a beeline toward them. Once she snuggled up to the tape, she assumed an air of nonchalance while she tried to eavesdrop.

Experience taught her that they would talk only loud enough for her to catch brief snippets of their conversation, but she had to 'play the game.' Even still, these bits and pieces would not have provided enough detail to get a scoop, which meant she had begun to build relationships with a handful of officers.

Every beat reporter worth their salt knew their police contacts were worth 10 telephone tips. It was important to nurture these relationships so they would be willing to go off-the-record with her occasionally. If it was really a good day, they might even share an official report. It was not lost on her that most of her informants were male. So, Jazmyn was willing to engage in a little harmless flirting if it meant she got a news anchor job someday soon.

While trying her hardest to be inconspicuous, one of the officers in the group made eye contact with her and smiled. The policeman was about average height, but his uniform almost seemed one size too small for his muscular build. With a swarthy complexion, a square jaw, and black wavy hair, Grant Metzger just happened to be her type.

She smiled back. Then, he subtly nodded toward the opposite side of the parking lot. Metzger continued to talk with those about him. After waiting an appropriate time, Jazmyn nonchalantly strolled to the other side of the police SWAT truck; Grant arrived a minute later.

"What's going on, Grant?" she asked, removing a small notepad from her bag. "The scanner said this is a homicide. Seems like a lot of hardware for just a shooting."

"Doing great. And, how are you?" he asked with a devilish grin.

"Sorry," she winced and shrugged guiltily. "The adrenaline gets flowing, and I lose myself."

The twinkle in his eye said it all. "I can't help yanking your chain." But then the playful banter abruptly stopped, and he said, "The excessive hardware is here because this is much worse than your average homicide: eight dead in the store, not including the assailant."

Making quick notations on her pad, she then asked, "What type of gun did he use?" It sounded heartless, she knew, but she had learned early on in her career that the window for this kind of exchange of information could be inconveniently short.

"This was not a shooting," Metzger paled at the recollection. "The killer used everything except a conventional weapon. Tore out the throats of two of the victims with his teeth. Five of the vics were killed by blunt force trauma, probably caused by having their heads blasted into the floor over and over again, and one decapitated by having his head repeatedly slammed into a freezer door."

"Oh my God," Jazmyn said in horror after having her professional detachment stripped from her.

"According to eyewitnesses, he threw all his victims around like they were rag dolls, and one was impaled by a shard of glass created by the victim being thrown into a frozen foods' door. This is the *most* disturbing crime scene I have ever seen on the job—bar none."

There was a slight hitch to his voice as he recounted the horror he had witnessed, and she glanced up from her pad and really considered his appearance. If he wasn't in shock, then he was close. Reaching up, Jazmyn put a reassuring hand on his arm, and he grinned weakly in return.

"It sounds like he was abnormally strong," she said, trying to steer the conversation back to something safer. "Was he on crack or something?"

"There's no way to tell until we get the tox report later. I can tell you this, when we arrived, we assumed there would be a hostage situation, but we were dead wrong. We heard screaming and figured we had to move before anyone else got hurt. Six of us charged the building entrance. The assailant was a short distance down one of the aisles, slamming a victim's head repeatedly into the floor. We shouted for him to get on the ground and lace his fingers. You know what he did next?"

"No. But I'm almost scared to hear if it has you this shaken up."

"He roared at us! Sounded like a freakin' gorilla or something. There was blood covering his mouth and chin and two or three bodies on the ground. He must have been eating them or something.

"Then he charged. No other word for it. Can you believe that? Six policemen in riot gear—guns ready—and he rushed us?" Metzger couldn't keep the incredulity out of his voice.

"We fired at least a dozen rounds into him. He rag-dolled, but it was almost like he couldn't feel pain. And still, he came on. He took another barrage before he finally fell. I tell ya, Jaz', it was unnerving. Even someone coked up on something will go down with enough holes in him," he said with grim regard.

"When I went to check for a pulse, the guy freakin' woke up and tried to *bite* me. Here's his blood pooling all around him—body torn to shreds. This freak has no strength to do more than move his bloody mouth and his neck a little, but it was enough to try one last time to kill me." Metzger took an immense, shuddering breath and continued, "I had been squatting to check him. When he lunged, I popped back and fell right on my ass. I never moved as fast as I did then. Got to one knee and pointed my gun at him. It was then I realized there was nothing he could do to me. But he still wasn't dead yet. His eyes were locked on me. Kinda blank. Like no one was home." He pointed at his head.

The blood on his uniform and his shaken state now made sense. "That is so creepy. How's it possible someone hurt so bad could or would keep trying to kill you?"

"Trust me, Jaz. There's a lot of things not making sense today," Metzger said with feeling. "If you take a dozen 9 mm rounds to your body, you are not going to be worrying about anything except dying."

She continued to jot down notes in her notepad furiously. "Is there anything else you can tell me?"

"Yeah. As if all this weren't bizarre enough, this guy apparently had no motive for killing any of those people. According to the few eyewitnesses left alive, the man wandered into the store, stood next to the registers, and just kinda swayed. Didn't make a move until the assistant manager walked up to him and asked if he was all right. One witness said it seemed like something triggered when she got close enough to him. One second, he was standing there; the next, he was tearing a chunk out of her throat. The poor woman didn't even have a chance to cry out.

"Except for a few customers and a checker at the front of the store, no one knew what happened to the manager, so there was little warning for the other shoppers. The attacker killed victims as he came upon them. Or those who investigated the screams and glass breaking. The video evidence we briefly viewed supports witness accounts." Jazmyn opened her mouth, but he interrupted, "And no, you can't get a copy."

Metzger shook his head firmly. "Anyway, none of the witnesses had seen this man before. It's so weird, Jaz, we almost never see true random violence. The pattern oftentimes can be difficult to spot, but normally it just takes time. Maybe we will figure it out as we gather more info, but for now, this baffles us." The shaken man ran his hand through his wavy hair like he was trying to cleanse something from his person.

"Thanks, Grant. And I'm really glad you are okay. Owe you." She paused in thought and then smiled. "I have to talk to the station and see if I can get something put together for the five-clock segment. I'm sure you need to do some paperwork and get cleaned up. What do you say to joining me for a late-night supper? I make a world-class lasagna. You bring a bottle of cab? It looks like you could use some comfort food and a friend."

"You know, I might take you up on that," he said with a haunted smile. "Have a feeling I will be twiddling my thumbs."

"Administrative leave?" she asked. He nodded. Fishing her business card out of her purse, Jazmyn wrote her cell number on the back. "You better call me sooner than later. Okay, mister?"

He couldn't help but smile at her tone and expression. Not wanting to get him in trouble for talking to her, she turned to go.

Before she could take a step, he grabbed her arm and turned her back to him. "There is something else you should know; we have recently seen an uptick in violence around the metro area."

A tingle ran up Jazmyn's spine.

"How extensive of an uptick are we talking about, Grant?"

"Well, we have had more murders in the city during the past two days than we did all of last year."

Her breath caught—there had been 20 total homicides last year in Portland. Eight of those 22 murders had occurred this afternoon, which inflated the total, but 14 deaths in two days were shocking for a usually subdued Portland.

"Remember what I said about patterns?" Metzger asked, and she nodded. "None of the murders involved guns. All the killers have used their hands or blunt objects to kill their victims. The department originally thought it was something like the Bath Salts overdose we saw in Florida earlier, but all the tox screens performed on the perps have come back negative."

She already knew some of this from her own reports, but she had been so busy reporting the facts that she had not had the time to connect the dots yet. Then, with horrible certainty, she realized this was not just a scoop but something far more dangerous. Why were people suddenly going berserk and murdering random strangers and not seemingly caring about themselves?

"Oh my God, Grant! Don't take this wrong, but why are you telling me this? This sounds like something interdepartmental, not something you share with a reporter." Jazmyn knew if this leak was traced back to Grant, he would at least lose his job and quite probably be prosecuted for interfering with an ongoing investigation.

"The captain wants to keep a blanket on this until we know more, but some of us don't like where this is heading. I don't want to go behind his back, but people need to know. Promise me this, though, wait for one or two more days before you broadcast anything. Keep your ear to the ground, and if this gets worse—as I think it will—maybe we can do something about it."

"It's a deal," she said. "I'll find out what I can in the meantime."

*5 o'clock news headlining story.*

She always felt a little vulnerable when the bright camera lights popped in front of her. When the cocoon of bright light enveloped her, the whole world seemed to evaporate. It was just her and the camera.

"Good evening. This is Jazmyn Perez-Salazar reporting live from the scene of a multiple homicide at the East Burnside Safeway behind me. The assailant killed eight victims before dying in a hail of police gunfire."

# Chapter 24



*July 7, Saturday — 12:12 am — Horizons Pharmaceutical*

Conference Room 235. It's such an unassuming-sounding location. After literally sharing the stage with all the 'big' players in this little drama, it felt like a demotion to be shuffled off to some random room away from the action.

Zander knew it was petty, but after making all the important decisions in his little fiefdom, it was tough to be relegated to being a grunt in a back room. Then he chuckled to himself. He was as prone to a temporary pity party as the next, but for the most part, he believed that a person controlled his or her destiny.

If he didn't like his position in life, he knew he could do something about it. So, he knew himself well enough to understand that this "dithering" was his way of dealing with a colossal case of nerves. It was far easier to whine about his being left out of the leadership of this project than to contemplate what their failure would mean to millions of people, not to mention betraying the trust of the President.

Moments ago, Tabitha had left him here and told him someone would be along shortly. As she left, did he detect the hint of an amused expression? *Oh God, between the initial briefing and the faux pas in the hallway earlier, they will never let me live this down.*

The conference room was good-sized, but it seemed far from his definition of what a command center should look like. The geek in him wanted the room to have lots of impressive pieces of equipment, dials, and electronic sounds—resembling NORAD from a James Bond movie.

Instinctively, he knew NORAD's command center probably didn't look that cool, but a nerd can dream, can't he? Instead, this room was painted a nondescript beige and was dominated by three spacious, utilitarian 5'x15' tables, which formed an upside-down U as a person entered the room. A dozen black leather work-desk chairs were tucked under the tables, and he grabbed one and sat.

His computer bag bumped against the armrest as he did, reminding him it was still attached to his person. Shaking his head, Zander unslung the strap, removed the laptop, and placed it on the table before him. As he booted it up, she walked in with a cart of—what he assumed were—her materials.

Behind her came no less than five techs in work overalls with "Horizons" stenciled in red on their right breast pockets. Their carts were loaded with electronics to almost the tipping point. Fifteen minutes later, half a dozen landline phones, two printers, a fax machine, and at least eight workstations were set up and ready to be used. Not a word was spoken, nor a smile broken before they left the room.

The scene reminded Zander of old cartoons in which an automated house had its robots appear, do their work in record time, and then disappear behind a flap in the wall.

Meanwhile, Grace acted like he was invisible. She said nothing as she unpacked her cart: placing her workstation in front of her, plugging it into LAN ports located in the center of the table, logging into it, and creating several discrete stacks of paper files and notes. Lastly, she put two—one pink and one yellow—sticky pads, an expensive pen and a mechanical pencil in a specific arrangement about her workspace.

Apparently, she disliked chaos, and the table in front of her was a microcosm of how she liked her world. In a moment of insight, Zander realized this woman was perhaps not angry with him, per se, but more with what he represented.

Horizons and Grace Wu had been happily making their cutting-edge pharmaceuticals when the President and the CDC had the audacity to demand their help. If the tables were turned, he would be just as irked.

If the government were to mandate that he put his Leukemia cure on hold, even if it was for a very good cause, he would be fuming.

With this epiphany, he laughed quietly.

"What's so funny?" she asked with just a hint of exasperation in her voice.

He tried to make eye contact with her but had no luck, so he continued anyway. "Believe it or not, I was thinking about what a goober I am. Here, the CDC and I bully our way into the middle of your operation and expect you to be okay with it. Then, I make a fool of myself. Can't apologize for the CDC, but for my part, I'm sorry." Taking a pack of gum out of his pocket, Zander held out his peace offering while giving her his most winning smile.

Long moments ticked by as she stared at her computer screen without moving. But he wouldn't give up on her so easily.

"Gum? It's spearmint," Zander said.

The corner of her mouth twitched before it broke out into a genuine grin. To him, it rivaled the beauty of a cloudy spring day when the brilliant sun was finally revealed.

"You're such a dork."

"Wait a minute, you aren't mad?"

"No, but dammit, now I owe her a buck."

Zander looked confused.

"Tabitha bet me I'd be smiling at something you said or did in less than two minutes." She shrugged. "Anyways, why would I be upset? It's not like you were rude to me; I just happened to catch you when you complimented me. My God. You should have seen your face when you turned around in the hall. It was priceless. It's part of the reason I couldn't make it for two minutes. I can still remember that bright shade of red you turned."

Her laughter was hearty and genuine. "Never seen anyone spontaneously combust, but I was worried about you for a second there. My aide made a bet with me while you were in the bathroom; guess she knows me better than I know myself."

With her admission, she brazenly snatched a stick of gum from his pack, unfolded it, and popped it in her mouth.

"I will have to settle for the booby prize," she noted with a sparkle in her eye.

Even though her amusement at his discomfort felt like a backhanded compliment, Zander didn't care because even a doofus like him could tell that teasing was better than cold detachment.

"Not sure if I should be relieved or feel picked on," he said with feigned injury.

"Come now, doctor, you must admit you have a certain knack for breaking the ice." She paused dramatically and gave her best starry-eyed look, "Hi."

Then, they both laughed at the absurdity of it all. A small chip of Ontario ice about his heart broke away. For a brief moment, Zander could believe the pain of his losses would someday ease.

The moment passed, Zander looked around uncomfortably and said, "I feel like I'm out of my element here. Could you let me know how I can best assist here, Dr. Wu?"

"First off, please call me Grace," she said.

"Of course, and I'm Zander. If you say, Dr. Parks, I look around for my dad," he said with a touch of sorrow.

"Well, according to Ms. Vanderbilt's debrief, you are a solid researcher, but your forte is your almost prescient vision." This was high praise from a peer, and he nodded in acceptance of her compliment. "So, I think you should collate our information and keep us on point. As for Dr. Tamboli and Dr. Mayette, I think they could serve us best by working as advisors for the Alpha and Beta teams, respectively. They are familiar with the virus and they have the advantage of knowing you and your vision for this blocker. Our groups could function more efficiently, and they wouldn't have to interrupt you with their questions. What do you think?"

"Well, if my forte is vision, yours is organization," Zander said. Earlier, I was taken aback by how you reorganized your whole company in an hour. And all this in a few hours? All I can say is amazing. I'm pretty sure I couldn't do that."

It was Grace's turn to nod graciously at the compliment. "I'm glad you think so. Others have remarked that I am mental." Zander made to protest. "Don't get me wrong, I know I have some pretty strong OCD tendencies." She nodded at the table before her. "But they have served me well here, and you never know when life will throw you a curveball."

"Boy, you can say that again. Less than two weeks ago, my only concern was getting approval for human trials. Now everything and nearly everyone I loved is gone." He looked down at his lap as his eyes threatened to water. *Way to go, Zander. You know this woman for five minutes and start telling her your troubles. She probably thinks. . .*

His thoughts were interrupted by Grace putting a comforting hand on his arm.

"I heard a bit about what happened in Ontario. Can't even imagine what you have been through." When he dared to glance up, there was no judgment—no mocking laugh—only her warm chocolate-brown eyes.

Even after admonishing himself moments ago, he couldn't stop sharing his burden, even with a stranger.

"Can you believe I was coming out of a coma only a day ago? Sometimes, I think I'm still dreaming, that all this is just one long nightmare." He brought his left hand up and dry scrubbed his face with it before continuing. "Even if it is, I know I am responsible for it all, and I need to clean up my mess."

Grace gave him a searching look, so he stopped before he gave away too much. Just then, Rohit and Ben walked into the room. With this interruption, Grace withdrew her hand and averted her eyes to the laptop before her.

"At least I haven't lost everyone." He smiled warmly and asked, "What can I do for you two?"

Ben spoke first, "There is a problem." Then, both men glanced in Grace's direction and then back to Zander.

"Guys, if we are going to work together, we can't keep secrets from each other. Dr. Wu is our host and liaison. Who could be better for handling any issues here?"

Both men looked unhappy, but Ben continued, "Zander—Rohit and I have been talking, and we think our original team shouldn't be split apart. Fifteen plus years of working together means we can finish each other's sentences. We are most efficient working as we always have. By putting us by ourselves," he nodded in Grace's direction, "we negate that advantage."

Rohit bobbed his head in agreement.

Zander's heart wanted to do exactly as they asked—advocate for them against this enormous bureaucracy. How comforting it would be to have the three of them together again—the three musketeers saving the day once more. But this could not be about him. Too many lives were at stake. But he had to handle his two friends gently.

"Ben, I can't express how important you and Rohit are to me. Without your help, Imagine Labs couldn't have completed half of what we did. I rely on you two more than I can tell you. Just because we're in a new lab doesn't mean that's changed. I need you to follow Dr. Wu's assignment—go to your respective groups and share our knowledge with these people. The efficiency you talked about will occur when you divvy up what we have learned about the virus this week, as well as the genetic work we have done over the years. Go out there and show why we are some of the best in this business. In the meantime, though, I must stay here and direct traffic." He tried to give them a smile that conveyed his sense of pride, but it was lost on them.

"Fine, Zander," Rohit said with little esprit de corps, "Don't like it, but I can see your logic."

"Keep us in the loop; you owe us at least that much," Ben growled.

"Hand to God, I will keep you updated with how things progress. Now, can I count on you guys?" Zander begged them as he stood.

"Sorry," Ben said with an impish grin. "I tend to take things personally. It's just—I don't want to be shuffled to the side. I want to have a hand in beating this thing. You know, for the others." The bluster left the man, and his shoulders sagged.

Without conscious thought, Zander crossed the conference room and wrapped Ben in a warm embrace.

Then, pulling him back to arm's length, Zander said, "I had those same thoughts minutes ago, Ben. Trust me when I say—you are an asset we can ill afford to waste. Make me proud."

With this dismissal, Rohit left without a word. He didn't appear to be angry, but he still seemed unsatisfied with Zander's handling of the situation. They spun about and left the room.

When he turned back to the table, Grace gave him an appraising gaze. "What?"

"You handled that adroitly. Maybe your dossier should showcase your ability to combine data *and* your leadership skills."

Ducking his head to try to hide the red-hot embarrassment he felt at her sincere compliment, he said, "It is easy to lead when dealing with good people."

"Well, enough of the mutual admiration society," Grace said with a good-natured smile. "How about I show you the ropes?"

"Thought you would never ask," Zander said as he returned to his seat.

"Why don't you move your laptop here?" She indicated a vacant spot to her right. "You will be able to see both our screens simultaneously, so navigating the network should be easier."

He took the proffered seat, and she began her tutorial: "We have created a username and password for you already, and your Horizons clearance will extend to anything we feel will be necessary for creation of the blocker."

Grace handed him a yellow Post-it with his information. He found her to be an excellent teacher, and in short order, he understood the rudiments of the network, the filing system, and the phones well enough to be self-sufficient.

As they wrapped up, she remarked, "Not sure if you caught it before, but I'm director of R&D for our Portland branch."

"Sorry, I was a little preoccupied with wanting to crawl under a rock and die when you were introduced." His grin was a smidgen less awkward than before. "And Ms. Vanderbilt?"

"Horizons Operations administrator for the West Coast. She was the one who 'suggested' that we work together. It's funny, now that I think about it. Her speech to me was almost a word-for-word rendition of what you said to Drs. Mayette and Tambolli," Grace gave him a lopsided grin. "Naturally, I felt more comfortable working with my team, but she thought it would be more beneficial for me—and the project—for us to collaborate. Cora can be a demanding boss, but I think you'll find we will walk through fire for her." Grace glanced his way thoughtfully and said, "You remind me of her."

"Well, I'm not a natural leader. Someday, I could tell you a story about an over-his-head newly minted doctor attempting to lead a research lab. It was brutal," he said, moving the conversation back to the task at hand. "Can you tell me why she felt we needed to work together?"

"Before this conversation goes any further, I must warn you—what I am about to reveal to you is not to be shared with anyone outside of our company. In fact, you need to sign this nondisclosure form before I can say more."

"Done," he said as he signed it without reading it.

"A select few outside our company know our campus' focus is primarily on creating an inhalant that will block certain viruses. Testing for this medicine is in the final beta phase, and it promises to block most cold-causing viruses. As you can imagine, Horizons stands to make billions, if not trillions, on such a drug."

The implications of this revelation staggered him.

"I can see by your reaction that you understand the creation of our partnership was not by luck, but rather, providence," Grace winked conspiratorially at him, "or barring that, possibly the President of the United States or a top-level CDC administrator. Whatever you want to call it—someone is looking out for us because it seems we have spent untold dollars and hours developing exactly what you need to stop this epidemic.

"Honestly," Grace added, "we both know your cure, although better than the alternative anti-virus solution, would be nearly impossible to develop in that brief time frame."

"This is incredible! What do you need me for? Let's get this onto a production line," he enthused.

"Whoa there! We still have not created the perfect blocker for a cold Zander, let alone one for an Ebola/HIV hybrid. At least we know the basics of how to create one, but now we need to somehow tailor our solution to your virus." He flinched like he had been struck, and Grace asked with concern, "What's wrong?"

"Nothing," Zander lied. "I was thinking about how many people are going to die while we try to figure this out."

"Like I said, I think we're close. There are many similarities between this pathogen and the cold virus, so we hope your expertise with the bug will accelerate our research."

Zander's face lit up as the conversation wandered into a territory he was intimately familiar with. Working the puzzle was something he understood and relished.

He unconsciously began working it out loud, "Well, our lab dealt extensively with HIV in the construction of our Leukemia cure, but our focus was not on stopping HIV. But during one of my skull sessions, I might have schemed a few ways to tweak that bad boy." The concepts burst from him in a frenzy.

Grace grinned.

"Okay, wunderkind, give me a second." She wrote notes furiously on her yellow paper pad. When she was satisfied with organizing his ideas, she said, "Here is what I have come up with."

As she shifted to her computer and pushed a group of tidy files to his machine. While he began to read them, Grace fished a few notebooks from her bag—looking for other data that might help them further. A delicate dance ensued. Each contributing to and evaluating the other's data. Hypotheses were put forward and rejected. New ones from different avenues took the old proposals' place. So, intent on this process, neither realized nor cared when five Horizons' personnel joined them in the *command center*. The dilemma and its solution were the pairs' only concern.

# Chapter 25

*July 7, Saturday — 12:30 am — Horizons
Pharmaceutical*

*A few minutes earlier.*

Mack walked into Conference Room 235 and sat at the table opposite Zander and Dr. Wu. He would have joined them, but even he could tell that he would be disturbing something significant and delicate. To say they were engrossed in each other was an understatement, but from where he sat, it did not appear they moved beyond an acute awareness of the other. Both acted as professionals and knew the consequences of their failure if they didn't stay on task.

But these high stakes seemed to create an almost palpable energy about them—really about the whole room. He stole glances at the other staffers and noticed they were fascinated by the sublime by-play before them: point, counterpoint, gesture, inspiration, challenge, clarification, hypothesis.

All were in play.

What made it a thing of beauty was that there were no usual pauses, interruptions, or arguments that normally pepper a creative brainstorming session. And then it hit him. The normal tension that exists between problem solvers was replaced with—romantic undertones. There were stolen glances, extra-boisterous laughter, and furtive touches. Not that Mack blamed Zander for his infatuation, Dr. Wu was undoubtedly one of the most attractive women he had ever personally met. But he would have to say from watching their byplay for the past few minutes that beauty had not drawn him—or at least not her only appeal to him— Zander had found a kindred spirit.

Neither appeared to be a master or teacher to the other. Mack had read the paltry bio the CDC had constructed for one Dr. Grace Wu while on the way to Portland. There wasn't much beyond the obvious; she was head of R&D here—and based on the list of patents she held or cosponsored—he would have to guess her aptitude ran along the same lines as Zander's. Besides that, she was a superb manager who led by example. Her 80-hour workweeks set a very high bar for her staff. Some of her critics might say she reached this level of success by sacrificing her personal life. But those who stayed at Horizons seem to have an almost fanatical devotion to Ms. Vanderbilt and Ms. Wu.

Conversely, Zander inspired devotion from his team by treating them like family. His team was unwilling to let him down, so they approached their goal zealously, matching their Horizons counterparts. Two approaches, same result: eminence in their field. As Mack continued to listen in on their animated repartee, it became obvious to him there was one last way these two complemented each other. Dr. Wu's specialty was applied science; she looked at things as an engineer: work the problem. And it created a *spirited discussion* when Zander had another insight about their blocker.

Mack had been exasperated in Ontario with Zander's laissez-faire attitude about CDC rules and protocol, but he sure couldn't argue about the results. One minute, Zander was as lost as everyone about approaching this epidemic, and the next, his was the President's handpicked strategy. And, according to Drs. Mayette and Tamboli, this was routine behavior for the man: innumerable times, Zander had emerged from his office with some wild proposal that seemed ludicrous but turned out to be a 'dead on' solution.

It was a skill only one in a million possessed, and Zander had been on the cusp of solving one of humankind's deadliest killers with a budget and staff—perhaps a tenth of other organizations. Zander would be a vital link in it if they were to stand a chance at creating this blocker in time.

If Zander was the muse of this Greek drama, Dr. Wu was Athena to continue the Greek analogy. According to her file, her IQ was off the charts, and she had completed a good portion of her BS in biology before her teenage peers finished high school. By the time she left academia, she had accumulated undergraduate and postgraduate degrees in microbiology and life sciences, a PhD, and even an MBA. There were boundless opportunities for her within the private and public sectors. But for whatever reason, she chose Horizons and stuck with it. Skyrocketing to her current preeminent position. *As much as I hate to break this up,* he thought, *I better find out if they have figured anything out.*

"Ahem," he cleared his throat loudly, hoping to get their attention. Nothing. Okay, subtly, not effective.

"Doctors," he said out loud.

Still, there was no reaction from his audience.

*It's time to resort to desperate measures.* He grabbed a piece of paper before him and crumpled it up into a ball—hoped it wasn't important—and threw it at Zander and Dr. Wu. Startled from their reverie, they turned to him in consternation at the intrusion, which turned to embarrassment when they finally saw the CDC director before them.

"How goes it?" Mack asked as he tried hard not to smile.

He heard several in the room chortling at the comedic scene.

"Sorry, didn't see you arrive," Zander said as he glanced at the ball of paper—sitting between the two laptops—then back at Mack. "There have been some, err—disagreements about how to go about this project, but overall, we are making some amazing progress."

"Far be it from me to interrupt," Mack said with a healthy amount of sarcasm, "but the President expects updates every hour, and he outranks me by this much." He held his forefinger and thumb barely apart.

"Well, he's going to love your first report," Zander moved forward in his seat, and his face became animated. "I was worried we wouldn't have the time to create a vehicle for the virus blocker, but Grace and her team have already perfected it! This will make something which should have been almost impossible in the timetable allowed to merely challenging."

"The inhaler has been tested with near-perfect results," Grace added, "now we need to modify our anti-virus serum so it will block any virus."

"So, any idea how long it will take you to create it?" Mack asked. This news was much better than he could have hoped for.

"Well, we said we don't need to start from absolute scratch," Dr. Wu said, "but this is still going to take some time. If we could have whipped something like this up in a few hours, don't you think someone in the pharmaceutical world would have created it, marketed it, and made a bundle?"

"I understand." Mack tried to keep the exasperation out of his voice. He hated being lectured to, even if they sported 40 more IQ points. "But can you give me something I can tell the President?"

"It could be an hour—it could be two years from now," Grace said with her profession's normal equivocation. But we can hope having the world's resources behind this effort will speed up the process." Much as he tried, Mack couldn't keep the dismay from his face. "Hey, I didn't say it would take years, but I can't tell you how many times Horizons asked for a specific deadline, and we didn't meet it."

Zander stroked his chin, adding, "If it makes you feel better, I think Grace's estimate is pessimistic, but telling everyone here that the President expects a cure in a day is unrealistic and could be detrimental to the group's morale. If I were to guess, I would say we should be able to figure something out within two weeks."

Mack blew an ample breath through partly closed lips and said in relief, "If it's all the same to you, I think Zander's estimate will be exponentially more palpable to the President."

"The workstation to our right," Dr. Wu pointed to the machine, "is formatted for you, Dr. Mack. Of course, you may feel more comfortable with your computer, but this one is connected to our company-wide network. Also, I took the liberty of assigning a room adjacent to ours for the new Georgia CDC personnel, who I'm told will arrive within the next few hours. These people," she indicated the staffers on workstations with a wave of her arm, "are tasked with continually updating our developments and the feeds from the FBI/CDC secure website. They are totally at your disposal during this operation, and they'll bring you up to date as we learn anything. If that doesn't keep you busy enough, you could join us in bouncing ideas off each other."

Under normal circumstances, Mack would have found her automatic assumption of authority—grating. According to his charter, this whole facility was nominally under his jurisdiction as director of this operation, and some in the CDC would have put her in her place. But he had successfully worked his way through 18 years of bureaucratic politics and considered himself a good judge of character. This woman was not grinding his knuckles in a steely handshake. If he were to guess, Grace hadn't realized she had overstepped her authority; she merely saw chaos, and she organized it.

So, he grinned as he replied, "How very thoughtful of you, doctor. Can I assume your segue was meant to deter me from focusing on nailing down a timetable for the President?"

The blank expression she gave him said it all. Then they both chuckled as she gave Mack an appraising look.

Winking at Mack, Zander said, "The jig is up, Grace; he caught you." She shrugged and tried to hide a guilty smile.

"Well, I can see working with you two is going to be interesting," Mack said with the practiced patience of a parent. "Please, Dr. Wu, call me Mack."

"You may call me—Dr. Wu." But her severity was ruined by the return of a dimpled, impish grin.

*Five hours later.*

Rubbing his lower back, Mack tried to relax tired, stiff muscles. Once they became merely sore, he did slow circles with his neck. The hourly updates, which had once been exciting, now assumed the dread of receiving a root canal or taking the eight-hour Medical Licensing Examination—without studying first.

The President's people were understanding but were under pressure to produce reassuring results, too. Calls made to Atlanta were not much better, but at least they were mercifully short. So, as it turned out, Mack had time to help Grace and Zander in their efforts. He was no medical research slouch, but most of his time had been spent dealing with infectious disease outbreaks—not solving them.

Therefore, he quickly realized he was swimming in deep water when he joined one of their *skull sessions*. It would have been easy, and human, to be jealous of their ability to work the problem. Still, Mack decided just to be glad the dynamic pair's skills allowed them to see the obstruction and access many resources—to see patterns and fit them into a coherent solution. Their creative bond was even more obvious from up close. Their roles solidified, communication truncated to its most necessary, and the constant back and forth of ideas—two people very *comfortable* working together. It was mind boggling to think Zander and Grace had known each other for less than half a day.

The only problem was that the two of them might kill him before they found the solution. Earlier, he had thought Vanderbilt's assessment of Grace's work ethic to be hyperbolic; he was mistaken. In the five hours they had worked together, neither had taken a break, eaten, drank, or seemingly blinked.

"Hey, you guys ready for a short breather?" Mack asked as he squirmed in his seat, hating to be the first to blink. "We have been at this forever."

"No," Zander answered without glancing up from his screen, "I'm good. Thanks, though."

Apparently, Grace wasn't even going to waste the energy replying.

*"Ooookay,"* Mack said with an exaggerated air. "Well, I'm going to see if I can find some food and some caffeine somewhere."

Glancing up in embarrassment, Grace said, "Sorry, Mack, I'm a horrible host. My people know I get a smidgen single-minded when I'm working on something, so they try not to bother me." Her lop-sided grin was infectious. "Dial 7 for the cafeteria; they will bring up whatever you need."

"That's great, but I really just needed an excuse to use the facilities and move around a bit."

"Bathrooms are down the hall, left-hand side," she said while writing a notation on her yellow pad.

"What do you say, Zander?" Mack asked.

Zander stopped his work for a moment and seemed to reconsider. "Now that I think about it, moving around a tad would do me good. I still ache from not using my muscles much. Let's go."

Walking the halls of the gorgeous facility, Zander couldn't help remarking, "Can you believe this place? My old lab had everything we needed, but I can't help wondering what we could've accomplished with facilities like these?"

"Ditto," Mack added with feeling. "I work for an organization where all building projects go to the lowest bidder. My 'office,' he snickered as he made air quotes, "might be as nice or as spacious as a janitor closet around here, but I doubt it."

They laughed. Their envy gave them commonality. They rounded a corner and saw a small crowd gathered around a flatscreen TV in a break room. As they got closer, the group seemed agitated.

"Wanna see what the hubbub is?" Mack asked, and Zander nodded.

As they walked up, a beautiful female reporter was amid saying, "—incredible uptick in violence about the city. This new wave of random brutality has been perpetrated by the most unlikely of culprits: assailants who don't have any violent criminal history. What's even stranger is none have used a gun; they only kill with their hands or crude weapons." She glanced at her notepad and back up at the camera. "At approximately 7 pm, a man entered the Powell Boulevard Bi-Mart store and assaulted or slaughtered five people before an alert sport and outdoors clerk, Shawn Shiply, loaded a 12-gauge shotgun rifle with buckshot and killed the attacker. According to him, it took both shells to bring the man down. Other witnesses said the assailant didn't say a word and either grunted or screamed like an animal.

"This attack is almost identical to what was witnessed earlier at the Safeway on Burnside. According to an inside source, the

Portland police have no idea what is causing this outbreak and are worried about what will happen if the number of attacks increases. My source further said that staffing will become an ever-increasing issue if it continues on this trajectory. This is Jazmyn Perez-Salazar for Fox News. Back to you, Tad."

The woman's face disappeared and was replaced by the news anchor.

"Thanks, Jazmyn, for another insightful report," he said. "In other news, our next story is coming in from our Pendleton affiliate; they are reporting National Guardsmen are blocking all roads and highways leading to Ontario. This is footage taken earlier by one of their mobile crews."

The screen shifted to another camera view, which was obviously taken in a moving vehicle being slowed by a man and two women—in dark fatigues and carrying rifles—stationed in front of an old-fashioned wooden barricade.

The female sergeant approached the news vehicle in an officious manner and said, "Folks, you need to turn around."

An off-camera voice is heard, "Why do we have to go around? We need to get to Idaho."

The soldier replied, "Well, there was a diversion three miles back, and this time, follow the signs."

Off-camera again, "Can you tell us why we can't go through? The press is responsible for letting the American public know what is going on."

At that moment, the soldiers adjusted their M16 slings so that their barrels pointed directly at the camera/news van. They didn't say another word, but apparently, the news crew understood them perfectly.

Off-camera voice: "Whoa, sergeant! No need for violence; we're turning around."

The TV screen switched back to Tad—the unflappable anchorman—and he made a less-than-astute observation: "Something is going on out there, and we will let you know as soon as we have more information. In possibly related news, we have received unconfirmed reports indicating a higher-than-usual National Guardsman presence in the Portland area—"

Both men said at the same time, "Oh shit." Turned, and quickly walked back to the conference room.

"We need some damage control," Mack said.

"Hate to break it to you, but public relations might be the least of our worries."

"Granted," Mack said. "But what will happen to our efforts if every highway, freeway, and airport is crowded with scared people? As this thing spreads—and we know it will—it will only be a matter of time before society breaks down. So, I'll try to keep a lid on things, but ultimately, you guys need to work your magic, preferably post haste."

"Guess break time is over," Zander said.

They ran the final 100 feet to Conference Room 235.

# Chapter 26



*July 7, Saturday — 1:05 am — Horizons Pharmaceuticals*

Getting up from his workstation chair, Craig told his group members he needed a smoke. He was a stranger, so no one volunteered to join him or glanced up as he departed. It was just as well because he wanted to be alone.

Eschewing the covered smoking porch to the left of the cafeteria loading dock door on the SW corner of the south tower, he headed toward a sizable oak tree 75 feet from the entrance. Once under the ponderous limbs, he pulled out a bummed cigarette and lit it. After he took a shallow drag on it, he tried his damnedest not to cough. He had toyed with the habit back in college, but it had been years since his last puff. Now, it was only a stage prop. With his offhand, he pulled out his phone and called a number.

The phone rang twice before someone answered with a terse—"Yes."

"There is a problem: I can no longer monitor the neighbors and their plans. It sounds like they have had more success than we thought was possible in this short period. Tell our friends to join us in town and let them begin to prepare an exciting housewarming gift for our neighbors. Have our friends phone me, and I will give them the details of how to set up the party. Call me at 0600 hours."

"Understood." The line went dead.

If the government decided to monitor his cell phone, the *Gaia's Children* code would not be hard to decipher, but he would be damned if he made it any easier for them than he had to.

Dropping his cigarette in the bark dust, Craig crushed it underfoot and headed back into the building. Soon enough, his time for hiding in the shadows would be over.

*15 minutes later, at the Gaia's Children compound in Ontario, Oregon.*

There were two sharp raps on Greg Mundst's door, and then someone exploded into the room. Always a light sleeper, Greg's hand found the Glock secreted under his pillow and pointed it dead center of the intruder.

Then Greg heard a familiar hearty chuckle: "Oh, good, you're up, Mundst. Guess calling you would have been safer."

The lights popped on, and he groaned as he put the gun on his nightstand before closing his night-blind eyes to the harsh light. Before he could ask her why the hell she was waking him up, she chuckled again.

"That's not the only thing that's up. Musta been a good dream?"

Opening his eyes, Greg reached behind his head and threw the pillow precisely at the intruder's head. Deftly, the woman sidestepped the projectile and gave him a beatific smile. He moved the cover sheet over himself during the distraction, but the damage was done.

"Just lucky," he groused, "I was not going commando tonight."

"Funny, not what I thought, but the night is still young, lover boy," she said with a sparkle in her eye and a provocative leer.

Greg was not sure what her game was—*yet*. In the GC's loose command structure, Violet Springsteen was the GC military commander of the military aspect of the GC and nominally his superior. But she was a relative unknown from the Seattle chapter, who had arrived only two days ago. The grapevine believed she had been called to the Ontario compound to ostensibly 'fix' the problem the CDC and Dr. Parks were causing their overall plan.

Now that his eyes had adjusted to the light, he could plainly see Violet did not resemble her namesake in the least—unless the flower was a 5'4" woman without an ounce of fat on her. The woman was no stranger to working out, which was evidenced by her well-muscled arms and shoulders, which compared favorably to Michelangelo's David. Now, she was wearing body-hugging black yoga pants and a skin-tight green camo tank top, which did little to hide her lack of cleavage yet still left little to his imagination in other perky ways.

His frank assessment of her had taken too long, and she chuckled, saying, "Take a picture; it lasts longer." But there was something more than mockery in her voice, and she looked away as she said, "Meeting in the front room in 30. Don't make me wait, Mundst."

Without pause, Violet did an effortless about-face and left the room.

As soon as she was gone, Greg sat up and searched the floor for his discarded pants. Something soft—but thrown with considerable force—tagged him on the side of his head, making him rock a bit and his ears ring. But that wasn't the only thing he heard: mischievous female laughter rang out from the hallway. *This should be an interesting arrangement,* he thought as he placed the pillow at the head of the bed and resumed his search for his wayward jeans.

*Ten minutes later.*

Greg and his 12-man team shuffled into the meeting room. Of course, Violet was already there and sitting in a chair close to the front door. It was clear the woman was evaluating each soldier as he or she entered the room, and it was equally obvious by her expression she approved of their professional appearance and apparent readiness. He knew the military didn't have a monopoly on playing head games with soldiers. She gave him a brief nod of approval, and he grabbed a recliner that faced the room's two entrances and settled in.

Even after giving Greg an absolute deadline, Violet appeared to be in no hurry, which didn't bother him. It gave him a moment to shake out the last few cobwebs of sleep and gauge his team's readiness. Most sat upright and leaned a bit forward in anticipation of whatever news was coming down the pike. Throughout the ages, soldiers had to deal with the extreme dichotomies of their lives. On the one hand, during peace, endless drilling and inactivity could steal one's soul, but on the other, no one wanted to die. So, they waited.

With warning, Violet leaped to the front of the room and said without preamble, "We received a call from Doc" —she glanced at her black military watch— "thirty-four minutes ago. As you all know, he is embedded with Dr. Parks and the CDC in Portland currently. Ostensibly, to keep tabs on their progress and warn us if they got too close to manufacturing a miracle cure. Then, we could ahhh. . . *intervene.*" They snickered. "During the call, Doc confirmed they had cut him out of their loop. And even more disturbingly, they seem to have a workable solution to our little virus."

Violet began to pace in front of the room like a caged panther. A facet of this stranger's personality suddenly became apparent—she longed for a chance to cross swords with this enemy. Though he appreciated her enthusiasm, he couldn't help feeling her zeal might put his troops in needless danger. *I will have to keep my eye on her,* he thought as he chuckled almost silently to himself.

The memory of the lewd, promising smile she gave him returned to him unbidden. Greg tried to refocus on Violet's instructions with difficulty.

"—there is no longer any purpose for him to remain at Horizons Pharmaceuticals. So, Doc is planning a diversion for the Guardsmen, but we must execute a smash-and-grab. The building floor plans were obtained when we learned of the CDC's move to Portland, and Doc has surreptitiously sent us soft troop numbers. I called Seattle and ordered the Alpha team to meet us at the rendezvous in Portland at 0600. Bravo team will join them there. Our quartermaster is loading our vehicles with appropriate kit for a week-long deployment, which will entail pre-op surveillance and achieving mission objectives." She turned to Greg and asked, "Any questions, Mundst?"

"No, ma'am," he responded in his best military bravado.

"Then, everyone has 15 minutes to ready their gear and get on a transport," Violet said. "Dismissed."

# Chapter 27



*July 7, Saturday — 4:00 am — Horizons Pharmaceuticals*

For the seemingly 51st time, Zander rubbed the heels of his hands with light pressure against his closed eyelids, and they felt marginally better. But now his computer screen was a blurry mess. There is not enough caffeine in the world, he lamented to himself, and he snickered as he rolled his stiff neck from side to side.

"Care to share?" Grace asked with a warm smile.

"I'm just thinking about how many all-nighters I pulled in med school," Zander observed. "Over 20 years ago, but—"

"—it seems like only yesterday," she finished for him.

Despite his fatigue, he smiled warmly at her. Their rapport was so natural and effortless that Grace could anticipate and complete his thoughts. The earlier awkwardness was long forgotten, or at least he hoped it was.

There had been a handful of women whom he had dated over the years, but something always got in the way of a more permanent bond. He had always chalked it up to the notion that he hadn't yet found his "soul mate." Whatever that meant. But there were some very dark and lonely nights when he had to face reality: his compulsion to find his cure was more important to him than romantic love. And as he approached the midpoint of his life, he began to doubt if there would ever be a special love in his life.

Fortunately, he had a friends and family support group, which gave him almost everything he needed emotionally. Lise had pulled him out of more than a few emotional funks. She would make one of her special coffee blends for them and listen. There never was anything romantic between them, but their bond of friendship was nearly as strong as the bond he had with his parents. Losing that core support group cut Zander the deepest.

In his mourning, Zander couldn't help but reminisce about the night he met Lise so long ago. And in doing so, the parallels between that magical night at the conference and tonight struck him hard.

He could sense her loneliness in the abyss below the surface—or at least a surface she could never expose to anyone. And that hurt mirrored his own. Yes, he had chosen to erect the walls holding love at bay, but at this moment, had he made a mistake? Was it foolish of him to hope for love at a time when the world teetered on the brink of human extinction?

Zander resolved one hundred times to keep things business-like and forego the excitement of finding a kindred soul, but he had never experienced a creative process like this before. It was intoxicating. In the past, Ben had always tried to find holes in Zander's theories, but Grace's role was that and much more. She did not take on the adversarial role—like Ben—of disproving his ideas, rather taking them, and improving upon them in ways Zander wouldn't have even considered. She was his equal in theory and innovation.

So, there it was—he knew their romantic byplay was wrong, and she most likely did. But neither wanted to fight this thing while staying safely behind the partitions of their making. Both willing to chance something new, even if only for a few days.

A few ebony strands of wayward hair tickled her nose, causing Grace to stop typing with one slender hand, tuck them behind her ear, and resume typing again. It was something she probably had to do dozens of times a day, but in its simplicity, it drew his attention to her natural beauty.

When he looked in the mirror earlier, he thought he could easily pass for a 65-year-old—after an all-night bender. How does she do it? She looks fresh—like she just got here minutes ago. Her suit looks perfect: not a wrinkle.

"Wish I had your stamina, Grace," he said with true admiration.

"Don't be so hard on yourself. From what I read about what happened to you in Ontario, I wonder how you can do all this." She nodded at his section of the table.

"Well, not sure how much longer I can keep this up." Zander closed his burning eyes and made another rolling, circular motion with his head, trying to loosen his upper back and shoulders. When they were sufficiently loosened, he let his head hang and kept his eyes closed. He didn't think he fell asleep but heard someone clear his throat.

Zander opened his eyes and saw his friend Rohit pushing a food and beverage cart into the room.

"Guess I didn't get here soon enough, but this will fix you right up. Break time. Doctor's orders." Then he looked down at his name tag and laughed at his joke, which caused his bushy mustache to ruffle for a moment.

"Thanks, but I'm good," Grace said.

Good-naturedly grinning at them both, Rohit said, "Now, Dr. Wu, I know you have bamboozled all your underlings into thinking you are a cyborg—impervious to human frailties. But it so happens that I know a little about human physiology, and everyone needs to take breaks and replenish their calories and nutrients. Lucky for you, I've something special."

Rohit produced a café-brown carafe from the storage shelf below the cart top. With a flourish of an imaginary cloak, he then turned the lid partly off so some steam would escape.

The unmistakable smell of lemon and peppermint permeated the room as he continued, "This is a special recipe my grandmother has used since she was a little girl in India. Nani swore her brew had magical powers, which could restore and rejuvenate even the most exhausted person. Try it."

Rohit beamed with pride for good reason. There were many late nights at Imagine Labs, and Rohit treated his fellow staff with his special beverage every time. Maybe it was the placebo effect, but Zander had to admit the tea refreshed him more than mere coffee could.

"Everyone else has loved it, Dr. Wu; I hope I didn't leave anyone out," Rohit said.

"Give it a taste, Grace," Zander suggested. It gives a nice boost, and it tastes like the nectar of the gods. How did you come up with the ingredients here, Rohit?"

Grinning like a little boy at Zander's endorsement, Rohit said quickly, "I called down to the cafeteria, and a wonderful young lady went to the local herbal store and picked them up. There are enough supplies to last us at least a week."

Pouring two steaming mugs of his concoction, Rohit gave one to each of them and looked on in anticipation. The ceramic mug was a comforting warmth in his hands, and Zander paused momentarily before drinking to allow the aroma to work its magic on him. Delicious.

"Well, let it not be said that I went against the recommendations of two prescribing physicians," she said good-naturedly. "Give me a mug." She reached for the aromatic beverage.

Unconsciously, she mimicked Zander, closed her eyes, and inhaled. Then she brought the drink to her full lips and gently blew on it.

Satisfied it was safe to drink, she took a small sip and beamed. "Rohit, this is delightful; you have done your grandmother proud."

As she took another drink, Zander had a sudden, terrible thought. With everything that had happened since he awoke in the hospital, he had forgotten that they had never caught the person who stole their work or doctored the first blood sample. And then an even more terrifying idea occurred to him: if Rohit had distributed this to the whole building, then this could be another Forestco. *Oh my God! If I'm right, then he has already infected everyone in the building.*

Zander was tempted to stop Grace from drinking anymore; if the virus was in this beverage, Grace would already be infected. It was only a hunch; however, if he was correct, whoever was behind this contagion struck a terrible blow to their efforts. He discreetly watched Rohit—desperate to determine if he could detect a hint of wickedness in the man. But like the millions of people before him, Zander could find no visible sign or mark of evil upon his long-time friend. Still, he couldn't help but suspect him.

"Did you say you already served everyone?" Zander feigned forgetfulness.

"Yes," Rohit said. "You are the last on this floor. Ben is serving the others. Why?"

"It's so good. I was hoping you'd leave us a carafe," he lied.

The man beamed with pride. "Here you go."

After Rohit left, Zander waited five agonizing minutes before he excused himself, telling Grace he was heading to the restroom. By that time, she was already back at her computer, engaged with their latest technical problem.

Carrying his mug with him, he made his way to the nearest elevator. *Please be wrong about this, Zander.* The lab was two floors down. So, in no time, he convinced a surprised tech to prepare a slide using a tea sample for their electron microscope. Once the slide was prepared and inserted in the machine, Zander felt déjà vu as he pressed his forehead against the padded rest and focused on the sample. It took little time for him to locate the malicious virus.

Time froze, and a small voice within him cried, everyone in the building is infected! *Ninety percent of these people will be dead by week's end if we don't come up with something fast!* His heart began beating out of control, and it was getting harder to breathe as the world seemed to collapse around him. Now that Zander knew one or both of his old friends was the saboteur, he needed to mitigate the damage done and eliminate, if possible, the danger to their finding a cure. They were *so close.*

Taking out his cell phone, Zander called a number, "Meet me outside by that huge oak out front in five minutes? No, I can't explain. Trust me. Thanks."

Several stressful lifetimes later, Zander arrived at the majestic tree only a few moments before the CDC director. While he waited, he picked up a small tree branch from the ground and fiddled with it.

"Wanna tell me what all this cloak and dagger bullshit is about?" Mack asked with a touch of asperity to his voice.

"Almost everyone in the building who drank Rohit's tea is going to die," Zander said without preamble. "When he told us he gave it to everyone, it reminded me of the coolers at Forestco." Mack paled at Zander's implication. "I checked a sample of the drink myself. There is no doubt it was laced with the virus. With everything that's happened, I completely forgot we never found our saboteur. Damn it, we brought him or them to Portland with us!"

A kaleidoscope of emotion passed over Mack's face until his expression resolved into helplessness. "Noooo, it can't be; Zander, I drank two mugs of that stuff."

"I'm so sorry, Mack. I shouldn't have let this happen."

"What do you mean? What did you have to do with this?" Mack's eyes blazed with anger.

"When I asked the President to bring Ben and Rohit with us, I inadvertently compromised this lab. You have to believe that if I had any idea it was one of those two, I wouldn't have vouched for them. I'm such an idiot."

This second betrayal felt worse than the first. At least the first, he had no reason to expect someone close to him was trying to kill him. In a fit of anger, he swung the brittle branch against the tree. It made a loud crack and exploded into satisfyingly small pieces.

Shoulders slumping, Mack's anger dissolving with resignation, "I was trying so hard to take every precaution."

Mack made eye contact with him and nodded. "As much as I want to blame you, I always knew this could be a dangerous part of the job."

"I know it sounds like a comforting platitude, but we are getting very close. We could very well get this thing done in time."

"Well, I will notify the President," Mack said with sudden resolution. "It appears we will have an even more highly motivated staff. We better make the most of what time we have."

A sense of déjà vu passed over Zander. This time, he would be safe. Not so for everyone else.

"Of course, this lab and everyone on campus must observe quarantine protocols. I will arrange things with Ms. Vanderbilt and the National Guard commander, but before that, I will have to talk with the President about this operation being compromised. I will recommend we copy all data and try to set up a mirror site, maybe in San Francisco."

"What about Rohit and Ben?"

"Trust me." Mack's glasses flashed as they reflected a nearby streetlight. "One of the alphabet agencies will soon be coming for a little chat with our 'friends.' If we are lucky, we might finally get a break and find out who we're up against."

"All I know," Zander said, "is if you figure out who is the traitor, you better keep him under heavy guard because there will be quite a few of us that would enjoy some payback." His anger felt like something alive within him, trying to claw its way out.

"I will be in line right behind you, Zander. But point taken. Will mention that to the commander."

Putting a hand on Mack's shoulder, Zander looked him in the eyes and said, "If it is possible, I will do everything I can to fix all this! I swear it." With that, he stalked off with a punishing stride.

After their conversation, Zander didn't want to return to the conference room before Mack had his official discussion with Grace and her people. He knew it was ridiculous, but he felt personally responsible for endangering everyone at Horizons. This was irrational because every soul in Portland and nationwide was in danger: they were in peril whether it was caused by his staff person or not.

But this truth would give him little solace if she died, and what if she blamed him? There could be no deflection, which would have allowed him to maintain her high esteem. He wanted to scream to the heavens—vent his wrath.

But he had no target.

He took this little "walk" to clear his head and give Mack time to do his thing. But deep down, he didn't want to be there during the announcement. He didn't want to see the accusing eyes. He didn't want to color in shame and embarrassment before them. There were no more sufficient words of consolation for them than there were for Mack. He took another angry turn around a corner and almost knocked over a Horizons staffer. He mumbled a lame apology and stamped on.

And then the hallway was no more, and he was again transported to the "cavern."

It was still mostly shrouded in shadows, and the bright sphere still held its place of prominence. But he felt... a presence this time. Similar to when he could feel someone behind him on the street. He scanned the darkness, eager to assess if he was in danger. He almost laughed out loud at the absurdity of his last thought. If someone had the power to transport him from one place to another, he or she could certainly overcome him. So, he did the only logical thing.

"Hello?" His voice slightly echoed like he was in an amphitheater.

Enough time passed, and he started to think he was mistaken in assuming someone was there when a golden-haired woman 'floated' from behind the orb of colors. One slender hand of hers was always in contact with its surface, gently touching like a loving caress. Her garb was a diaphanous gown, which was hard to define. Actually, now that he paid more attention to it, everything about her was difficult to pin down.

When she initially appeared, he would have guessed her age to be entering womanhood, but now she seemed to be in her midforties. Her hair's length also changed, but it was always golden. The effect would have been discomforting except for one thing: her eyes. There was no color discernable. If he were pressed, he would say they seemed slightly luminescent, like a bright star in the night sky.

"Zander." A thrill ran up his spine when he heard her voice for the first time. Without words, his heart begged her to continue speaking to him.

"Who are you?"

"A friend. All will be revealed soon enough. We only have a little time," she said in a voice distinctly female, but it seemed to encompass a range of tones between alto and soprano. It sounded like a perfect chord in a woman's chorus.

"Why am I here? Why don't we have time? What is this place?" The questions poured forth in a torrent.

He was surprised by a melodious chuckle. "Over these long millennia, I had somehow forgotten how inquisitive you are, my friend. Trust me when I say all your questions will be answered soon. But for now, you need to listen." Any compulsion to interrupt disappeared. "I know it is important to you to 'fix' this virus. You feel responsible for all the deaths, especially of your friends and family. This is a blame you cannot place upon yourself. The guilt for them is another's."

"Who?" Zander said with a fierceness that would scare those who knew him.

"Let it go, *True Heart*. This was all predetermined ages ago. It had to happen." Her tone carried a sense of acceptance but also great sadness. And it was only now that he stopped focusing on her eyes and took in her whole delicate face. He couldn't point to one feature, but overall, she seemed profoundly sick at heart. The room seemed to dim, or maybe it was the globe.

"I will try," he offered.

"That is all I can ask of you." She smiled in understanding. Now, for the most important thing. You and your friends must drop everything and come to me." Zander interrupted, but she would not be deterred. I know it goes against everything you know, but you must trust me. There are forces that wish for your destruction. That cannot happen. But I cannot protect you there. Bring Grace, Mack, and Ollie to me."

The room began to fade.

"Come to me," she said, raising her hand above her head. A flash of light came forth from it, and the room disappeared.

And—

He was in the Horizons' tower hallway again. He shook his head again to clear out the cobwebs.

*Am I going crazy?* It all seemed so real. He could remember every word, every moment, every movement. *I guess an insane person would think that.* He looked wonderingly down at his hands, and that is when he felt it. He turned his right hand upright and opened it. An impossibly gold pendant and delicate chain lay on his palm. He picked the chain up with his left, and a sun medallion twirled at its end, catching the overhead light with bright flashes.

Zander's panic abated, and he shook his head in wonder. Without thought, he lifted the talisman above his head and let it gently fall around his neck. Then he tucked it under his shirt and returned to the command room. His heart unburdened. He smiled and then whistled a tuneless melody.

*At least now I know I'm only partially crazy.*

Room 235 resembled a hornet's nest. Now dozens of people were in the room, and it seemed like everyone in the building was there—except her. After making two circuits around the room, Zander broke down, asked if anyone had seen Grace, and pretended not to notice several looks and a quiet chuckle. No help there.

*Where would you go if you just found out you had four days to live?* he wondered. The building was locked down, so going home was not an option. Would she seek out friends here at work? If not, where would she go? Grace struck him as a private person. If he were to guess, he would say she would want to grieve without scrutiny—her office.

After getting directions, he hurried to her suite and knocked, but there was no answer. Trying the handle, Zander found the door unlocked, so he opened the door and stuck his head in. There was the sound of running water and maybe something else. Did he dare to interrupt her privacy? Would she welcome his intrusion?

Zander took a few hesitant steps into the room and closed the door. In the silence, he could discern something beside the rushing water: crying. The raw grief of it stabbed at Zander's own mending heart. He must help her or flee before the sorrow overcame him. The door to her private washroom was ajar, and he could see the sink beyond. With resolution, he entered.

"Grace?" he asked. Except for delicate hitches, she stood still like a statue in front of the washroom vanity, eyes vacant. Tapping gently not to startle her, Zander asked again, "Grace?" Still, no answer. The faucet continued to flow before her without notice, much like the tears that threatened to fill the sink with sorrow. Zander shut off the water. The sudden silence enhanced the rawness of her despairing cries. "Are you okay?"

Without warning, she launched herself at him and crushed him in a desperate embrace. He decided that keeping his arms at his sides was decidedly awkward, so he held her as she wept. Eventually, her tears and fears subsided. When they did, Grace gently but firmly pushed away from him. Zander took the hint and took a few steps back to give her room to collect herself. Meanwhile, Grace grabbed a few tissues from the box on the counter and tried to clear away the runaway mascara from her cheeks.

Finally, Grace broke her silence and said, "Sorry, I don't know what came over me." Even though she was no longer sobbing, an occasional tear bespeckled her sandalwood-colored cheeks. The Kleenex never stood a chance, so Zander fished a handkerchief out of his pocket and proffered it to her. Smiling in thanks, Grace dabbed at the tears and makeup lavished about her face. "I hate when I blubber."

"Nothing to apologize for. In fact, I have a general rule that states: when a beautiful woman wants to cry on my shoulder, I let her." His lame attempt at humor had the desired effect; she smiled. "Seriously, Grace, I was in your exact shoes a week ago, and let me tell you, I did not deal with it stoically, either."

"You cried?" she asked with genuine curiosity.

"Hey, I'll have you know I come from a long line of blubberers. I blame my father." Zander winked at her.

"Isn't it funny?" Grace dabbed at the last of her tears and tried to give it back to Zander. He made a you-keep-it motion. "As medical students, we are coached on how to help patients work through getting devastating news, and yet, when we are faced with dying, we cry like babies?"

"We are human, Grace—you are human. It's okay to step away from your doctor 'persona' and allow yourself to grieve. It's healthier than to not." Knowing now was not the time for sage advice, Zander tried to steer the conversation in a new direction. "Speaking from recent experience, when the odds were stacked against me, I wanted to poke them in the eye. You strike me as someone else who hates to admit defeat. We have 96 hours to work with. What do you say?" He gave her his best you-and-me-against-the-world smile and motioned to the hall door.

"Go ahead," Grace said. "I will clean up a bit and join you."

"Will do," Zander said as he headed for the door.

"Zander," she said in a hushed voice. He turned. "Thanks."

"Any time—that's what friends are for."

# Chapter 28

*July 7, Saturday — 11:13 pm — KPTV Portland*

Portland was her city. There is something to be said about choosing a thing, whether it be a man or your home. Like so many other Oregonians, Jazmyn grew up in California, specifically LA, a city with 3 times the population of the entire state of Oregon. Nobody could dispute that 'The City of Angels' had far more attractions and distractions than the beaver state, but for all that, it had no soul. The city cared not a whit about her dreams nor her hopes. Looking back on her life, she had pretty much followed the course her parents had set out for her: prep school, cheer team, and UCLA.

That all changed when she visited some friends during spring break two years ago. Jazmyn couldn't pinpoint the moment, but it didn't matter anyway—this town stole her heart. So, when she saw the posting for a TV reporter position in Portland, she packed up her car and traveled north up I-5 before even applying for the job.

The interviewer was impressed with Jazmyn and her initiative. It had been a three Long Island iced tea celebratory night. Since then, she would have to admit that most news stories were not of the most life-affirming variety.

It would be so easy to focus on the assholes who littered her crime beat. But she sensed that was the path of cynicism and burn-out. Instead, she focused on the fringe elements: the noble majority—or that was the way she chose to view them. The good people who deal with the tragedy forced upon them. It was this focus that uniquely equipped her to know when *her* city and its inhabitants were hurting. Something *had* changed.

She still loved Portland, but like an abusive boyfriend—it scared her. A little over three hours ago, she returned to the TV station after reporting on a harrowing crime scene.

When she had arrived at the Washington Square Mall's parking lot, there were 20 black body bags lined up along the southwest corner. The police did not have enough of the PVC coroner bags on hand for all the fatalities, so they covered the other 12 with yellow plastic tarps until the dead could be taken to the morgue. Even now, she could recall the terrible smell of death and the unidentified bodily liquids that seeped from beneath those coverings.

Appalling though the sight was, it had been one of many during the past few days. Her beat was beginning to feel more like a war correspondent's—death and carnage were becoming the norm. Beyond the dead lying beside the curb, 48 injured had been prepped for triage. Apparently, there were only two ambulances sent to the scene.

Later, Jazmyn that learned all the others in the vicinity were responding to other calls. So, when she arrived, there were only four beleaguered paramedics running from body to body, evaluating the wounded—then giving instructions to first responders and even bystanders.

As Jazmyn was heading to the police staging area outside the Macy's store, she walked past a screaming patient. The paramedic saw Jazmyn and waved her over. Then, he grabbed two blue rubber gloves from his waist bag and put them into her hands. She couldn't pretend she had better things to do, so she donned them.

"Come here," the dark-haired medic instructed, "and kneel next to her." He indicated the moaning, pale, early 20ish attractive brunette wearing a red blouse and black slacks. The woman was clutching her stomach and grimacing in obvious pain.

The exasperated medic interrupted Jazmyn's evaluation of the victim: "Miss, we don't have time for this!"

Jazmyn tried to comply, but to her embarrassment, she found her pencil skirt was too tight to get to a kneeling position. It was ludicrous, but she had to sit almost sidesaddle on the ground not to grind her bare knees into the blacktop.

The green-eyed paramedic made eye contact with her. "I need you to be strong. This woman will not survive without your aid. Do you understand?"

Jazmyn mumbled and nodded.

Then he turned to the prone woman and said, "Miss, I need to remove your clothing so we can give you medical assistance."

The woman, through clenched teeth, said, "Okay."

With care, he moved her hands and ripped the front of the woman's blouse open. Only when the top was opened did it become obvious to Jazmyn that it was not red but a rich cream color, much like the victim's lacy off-white bra.

The paramedic instructed her, "Grab her hands and hold tight while I probe the injury."

As he began to press his fingers into the woman's abdomen, the mutilated, terrified woman screamed and fought Jazmyn. The poor woman nearly broke free from Jazmyn's grip when, suddenly, the woman's strength melted. And a moan escaped her lips.

The abdominal wound was about the size of a human fist and looked like someone tried to gouge a chunk out of the poor woman using his or her fingers. The paramedic took an antiseptic wipe and wiped the wound dry, but the blood pooled in the two-inch deep depression as soon as the towel was removed.

The paramedic covered the grievous hurt with a folded-up linen sheet, and he glanced at Jazmyn's white, shocked face.

"Hey," he said with his best reassuring smile, "what's your name?"

"Jazmyn," she said past the bile rising in her throat.

"This woman will die if you do not help her, Jazmyn. Do you understand that?" The man said, "God willing, other paramedics will arrive and take over for you, but until that time, I need you to place your hands over mine and firmly hold this dressing against her wound. You must not let up on the pressure or remove the bandage. If it soaks through, try to get someone's attention, and put another dressing on top of this one. Do you understand?"

"Yes," she said with resolution. Her eyes must have held enough steel for him to move on. And then he was gone.

The woman before her was still conscious—her terrified, pain-riddled eyes were darting from side to side.

"Hey there. My name is Jazmyn. What is yours?" she asked, mimicking a doctor's tone and assurance.

"Halley," the woman said, grimacing. "Am I going to the hospital? Why did the paramedic leave?" Halley spoke in quick gasps as if she had just finished a battery of wind sprints.

"A lot of people got hurt tonight, Halley. It's just you and me for the time being. Can you tell me what happened in there?" As far as Jazmyn was concerned, caring for this victim took precedence over her reporting, but she wanted to distract the poor woman from her agony.

"My sister Kathy and I were clothes shopping. It is her birthday tomorrow, and I was treating her to a new outfit. Then, the next thing I knew, this woman came from nowhere and tackled Kathy. It was weird. Here we are in a busy mall, figuring we are safe." A wave of pain suspended Halley's narrative.

"Don't worry; conserve your strength, hon." The woman was very pale and shivering now, and Jazmyn stopped a passerby and asked for a blanket. Finally, the person returned with one, and Jazmyn covered Halley and tucked in the edges with her free hand.

"Are you a reporter?" Halley asked. Jazmyn nodded. "Good, people need to know they are not safe. Maybe if we had heard sooner, Kathy—anyway, the attacker growled like an animal and bit Kathy on the neck. It was Kathy's screaming that shocked me into action. There was nothing to use as a weapon nearby, so I screamed and swung my purse as hard as I could at the woman's head. The lady fell to the side, but then I saw she had part of Kathy's throat in her mouth. The bitch was grinning at me with my sister's blood covering the lower half of her face.

"Without thinking, I jumped on her, but she was amazingly strong. I tried to choke her, but she stiff armed me and punched me hard in the stomach. Suddenly, I was incredibly weak, and she pushed me off to the side. In no time, she was on top of me, and she was trying to pull the same biting stunt on me." Tears flowed more freely, and Halley struggled to finish telling her story.

"Shhhh. You can tell me more later."

Terrible understanding was in Halley's eyes, "No, I need to do this now." She swallowed her pain and continued, "Would've died if not for a man who came along and shot that motherf'er in the back with one round. Not sure why he only fired one; I suppose he didn't want to hit me. Heard the gunshot and felt her body twitch from the impact. I thought it was over—I was wrong. The next thing I knew, the woman pushed off me and ran at him like there wasn't a four-inch hole in her. Guess I wasn't the only one surprised. I didn't hear more shots, just a lot of screaming. Woke up out here." With desperate eyes, Halley begged, "Did my sister make it?"

"Don't you worry, Kelly is all right. You saved her," Jazmyn lied, hoping to comfort this poor woman. "They took her to the hospital. So, you need to hang in there. You'll be with her soon."

The news had a singular effect: Halley's whole body seemed to relax, and she smiled. "It's freezing. Can you get me another blanket?"

"Sure thing," Jazmyn said and looked for another good Samaritan, but there was no help to be found.

Glancing at Halley's midsection, Jazmyn had to clamp down on her emotions. The covering was soaked through with blood, and it was pooling out from Halley's body.

At that moment, Halley's hands slackened. The young woman whispered to her angel with a pain-free smile and sightless eyes, "Thank you."

Emotion overwhelmed her; Jazmyn's keening was loud, coarse, and seemingly never-ending. It was interrupted by a concerned policeman, who asked if she was one of the victims and whether she needed help. Since she was covered in copious amounts of Halley's blood, it was an easy mistake to make. She shook her head in the negative, so he moved on. Removing her gloves, Jazmyn slowly closed the lids on those sightless eyes.

"Sleep well, Halley."

The pencil skirt gave up and tore almost up to her hip as she tried to get off the ground. *It doesn't matter,* she thought with bitterness. These clothes would be tossed whether there was blood on them or not. As she arose, she nearly fell because her legs had gone to sleep on her. Once the tingling subsided, Jazmyn searched for her cameraman, Liam. Then, the shakes hit her as she walked around the mall parking lot. The memory of Halley's trusting eyes boring into Jazmyn's soul.

Shell-shocked, she wandered through the macabre scene. Someone grabbed her shoulder and spoke. It took her a moment to realize it was Liam. If she really focused, he seemed to be asking if she was okay. He quickly scanned her for injury when he saw the amount of blood on her hands, arms, clothing, and the ragged condition of her skirt.

"I'm okay," she managed to say, and in a few short sentences, she recounted Halley's tragic tale. "Let's get to work."

He looked at her like she had grown a third eye. "You are going nowhere except back to the van." She tried to object, but he hushed her. "This time, you will listen to me," he said with a victorious grin. Opening the door, he told her, "Get in."

"But I will get blood on the seat."

Shaking his head at her, he firmly guided her onto the front passenger seat and said, "Rest for a moment, and we'll see if you want to head back out there."

He made a broad sweep of his arm. When he saw she was staying put, he went to the back of the van and opened the door. She could hear him rummaging around for something. She looked down at her blood-covered hands and thought about finding something to clean them with.

That is when she saw that her skirt was torn up to her belt, and her white panties were in full view. She was trying to move her dress so that a flap would cover her when Liam returned and handed her a black coat with the station's logo. She snugged the long parka up to her neck but snuck a glance to ensure it still covered her nether regions.

"Thanks," she said.

"What partners are for." He gave her a protective-brother smile in return.

On his way to the driver's seat, he must have called the chief sub-editor because she could hear Liam yelling into the phone. It didn't sound like their boss was so happy to learn there would be no report to add to the night's news. It also sounded like they were expected to come back to KPTV immediately.

Liam wore a lopsided grin when he entered the van, "Hear any of it?"

"Umm, we're in big trouble," Jazmyn said. "And we need to return to the station ASAP or sooner?"

"Ding, ding! The young lady wins a prize," Liam said with glee and continued, "Might have mentioned that he had questionable parentage, and we would be in only after you have a chance to freshen up. So, if you don't mind, I need to know where you live." The twinkle in his eye was unmistakable.

"That was tough." Jazmyn gave him her most sincere smile, "I owe you one."

"Yes—yes, you do. I'm thinking coffee and donuts for a year would be a good spot to start," he said as he started the engine and put the vehicle in drive.

Jazmyn playfully punched him in the arm, smiled, gave him directions to her place, sat back in her seat, and breathed deep. Later, a too-hot shower and another set of clothes did much to restore her equilibrium.

When they did arrive at the TV station 45 minutes later, the first thing Jazmyn did was call Grant Metzger and ask what the police had learned so far about the Washington Square attack. According to him, the situation at the mall was over, but there were now 49 people dead. Three attackers—all dead now. Witnesses said it did not appear to be a coordinated strike. Each assailant entered the building from separate doors and at different times.

If this was truly just a giant coincidence, then the implications for the future were terrifying. Switching topics, she told him about Halley and what the now-dead woman told her about the assault.

Her account fit with what he had heard, but he would add it to their write-up.

Then, Metzger's voice shifted from professional detachment to concern, and he casually suggested she might want to leave town while she still could. Asked to elaborate, he clammed up and excused himself.

As she sat and stared at the police scanner before her, dark thoughts began to crowd her. Earlier, she had compared this city to an abusive boyfriend. Now, *Portland* seemed more like a vicious serial killer than a city she could call her own.

# Chapter 29



*July 8, Sunday — 1 pm — White House*

When the President looked out of the Oval Office's window at the rose garden, it usually made him smile. In his opinion, nothing was better than a summer's day, with all its sunshine and beauty. An overall feeling of accomplishment magnified the exquisiteness of the moment.

In a mere six months of the first term of his presidency, he had proposed, and with a great deal of horse-trading, forced through a federal balanced budget amendment. It had not been easy, but on the coattails of his overwhelming presidential election, congress had been compelled to acquiesce.

The reflection of his smile and tired eyes on the windowpane melted like snow first touched by the sun's first rays as his thoughts traveled back to the last report sitting on his desk.

More than a few people had asked him on the campaign trail, "Why would you want to be President? It is such a thankless job."

He had always dismissed the question as too cynical. The way he saw it, the United States government needed a new path, and he was willing to be its usher. To that goal, he contributed several million dollars of his money and dedicated at least 12 years of his life to achieving the objective of having a fiscally responsible administration. But today, for the first time, he cynically questioned the sanity of anyone who would ever want this job.

The universe had played one of those sick jokes on him and his administration with the events playing out in Oregon. In a casual swipe of her cosmic wrist, she might make trivial all he had done to create a fiscally responsible America—all for naught. Momentary self-pity was replaced with righteous anger, and without thought, he punched his fist into the nearest inanimate object, which happened to be the headrest of his luxurious chair.

His fury was quickly forgotten as the piece of furniture rather noisily caromed off the adjacent oval office desk, and an alert secret service agent poked an unobtrusive head in through a nearby door. She noted the spinning chair, nodded to him, and then disappeared.

Arresting its gyrations, he then checked the clock again.

It was time.

He had just reached the door when a startled aide who had been sent to bring him said, "Mr. President, they are ready for you. Please follow me."

With a wave, the President indicated the staffer should proceed. Now that he thought about it, it was more than a little silly that someone needed to show him to a room that was technically in 'his' house, but it did give him time to ponder how he got into this situation.

Unlike some of his predecessors, he was not attracted to this job's power or prestige. It sounded corny—even to him—but he wanted the world to be a better place when he left it. Eventually, a few former students talked him into speaking at a few political forums. He hadn't felt like his message of equality for all, taking personal responsibility for oneself, and fiscal responsibility was that revolutionary, but it was enough to garner quite a few influential backers.

Looking back on his initial whirlwind senatorial race, he thought there was no chance he could have won—he was wrong. What had once been a lark became a senate seat less than a year later. Ever since he could remember, his father and mother had always insisted that half-assing anything was unacceptable, so he had put his heart and soul into being the finest junior senator he could be.

His best was much better than most of his contemporaries around him, and in no time, he gained the admiration of those who worked with him and his constituents. Two years into his last term as senator, his party asked him to run for President. In for a penny, in for a pound, he had figured, so he had accepted their nomination. During the campaign, it became obvious that Americans were tired of the cynical, do-nothing politicians offered up to them every four years.

It had been one of the most significant landslide victories in US presidential election annals. The people gave him a public mandate to implement his vision and implement it he did. For this reason, he was now one of the most popular sitting presidents in America's history. Unfortunately, all the political momentum and cache would mean absolutely nothing when dealing with this crisis.

The aide announced the President to the meeting room, and everyone present stood. Duties completed; he left. Closing the door behind him. The President assumed his spot at the head of the massive oak table, told his staff to sit, and then surveyed the various men and women in attendance. Some wore military attire, others wore business suits and dresses, but all wore steely masks of determination. Their demeanor may not have revealed their thoughts, but he had a pretty good idea of what his cabinet would recommend, and he didn't like it—not at all. He might as well get things rolling because he would not learn anything from these professional politicians that they didn't want to reveal.

"Shall we get started?" he asked. They opened their black, prepared meeting notebooks simultaneously, and he nodded to the recording clerk. "Let's start with a short overview from our Secretary of Health and Human Services."

The sandy-haired, ascetic 50-ish director gave a concise yet comprehensive evaluation of the recent situation in Oregon. There weren't many surprises, considering the topic was at the forefront of everyone's agenda. Next, the President turned to the dark-skinned man wearing thick glasses, who was the current Centers for Disease Control and Prevention Director.

"Can you give us the latest on what the research community has gathered on the virus, doctor?"

Once again, there had been little 'news' since the last daily meeting, but the man covered what there was adroitly. Reports from around the world were being collected and collated from their new website and from Dr. Mack.

When the CDC administrator finished, he turned to the President and said, "It looks like we have the original virus outbreak contained in Ontario. However, the cross-contamination between animals and humans makes it likely that all our efforts at containment are moot. But if it's all right with everyone present." The man said with a sardonic smile, "I would prefer to continue using the optimistic assumption that we can still contain this."

The heads nodded in agreement. There was no other option for those present. They could believe the fabrication, or they might as well go home and spend the final days with their families.

"If," the CDC official continued with a grimace, "we assume Ontario is secure, then Portland is another story. It's a Pandora's Box there. If we try to cordon off every road leading into and out of the city without explanation, we will start a *panic*," he leaned into the word hard. "Also, we all know how people in that state will react to the federal government declaring martial law and forcing them to stay in Portland. The riots and protest parades will be legendary."

His snide comment drew some subdued chuckles, but the dark humor seemed to fit the general mood of the room and relieved a modicum of tension for the moment.

"Seriously, every conspiracy nut with a pickup and his or her stockpile of weapons could create a war zone within our borders. But if we don't, Interstate-5 alone will be moving thousands of infected people up and down the coast. Somehow, we must devise a way to delay this impossible situation there. According to" —he looked down at his notes for reference— "Dr. Mack, they are very close to coming up with a viable vaccine. Now we all know that you can't rush science or medicine. What seems to be very near could be months off, but if the virus continues unabated, in sixty days, all this," waving his arms expressively, "won't matter any longer."

The President watched his ministers react in dismay to this brutal assessment. Of course, they all knew the harsh realities of this situation, but strangely, knowing something and having it laid out for them in black and white was another.

Letting them have their minute, the President took control of the meeting again, "You are all here because I value your knowledge and ability in your respective fields. The United States and the world rely on us to make the correct call. So, I want us to put all options on the table now but let me clarify one thing—*I* will be making the final decision. Who wants to start this?"

After much discussion—and quite a bit of heated debate—his advisors arrived at the following solutions:

1. Do nothing and hope the doctors devise a solution in time.

2. Use neutron bombs on Portland—and the surrounding area— and sterilize Ontario. Bring in the rest of the CDC and the National

Guard to destroy any infected animals and corral all individuals who have broken containment.

3. Cordon off all roads leading into and out of Portland using US Military forces and declare martial law. A little over 2 million would die, but over 200,000 would live, and the virus would be contained.

Once they determined their three unpalatable courses of action, each cabinet member was given the floor to present the pros and cons of every option—as they saw it. The discussion remained civil, but most in attendance felt strongly about the repercussions of the various solutions for their administration and the future of humanity.

Eventually, the whole bitter conundrum was set out in all its ghastly glory before them. *Well,* the President thought bitterly, *went about how I anticipated it.* Not that he got any satisfaction for his prognostication.

As expected, most of his cabinet voted for the second option. He risked a public schism with his ministers by letting them air their thoughts and opinions for the record, but he would be damned if he digressed into a virtual dictator now.

Clearing his throat, the President said, "Thank you for attempting the Herculean task of determining which is the least offensive of these choices. But after hearing all the arguments, I think we only have one real option." He paused to emphasize his decision. "As long as I'm President of this country, it will never be acceptable to declare it our 'best interest' to summarily execute two million innocent American men, women, and children."

Some proponents of choice two gave him sullen stares, but more than a few abashedly looked down as he made eye contact.

It would have been easy to say, "Because I say so," but he wanted them to understand his call too, so he added, "Did you know that we have lost 1.2 million women and men of various armed forces during all the wars the United States has fought since its inception? If I picked the second option, I could kill in one presidential executive order twice that number. And I think we can all agree those doomed to die are not soldiers but rather fellow civilians. If I perpetrated such an atrocity on them, how would I be any better than Hitler, Saddam Hussein, or Stalin? I won't do it!

"On the other hand, I also think it would be a travesty to just sit on our hands and do nothing, so the first option is not viable either. So, we are left with number three." Turning to his Secretary of Defense, the President asked the stolid, red-haired woman, "How long will it take to muster and deploy the bulk of our soldiers to Oregon?" She thought for a moment and then said they could have boots on the ground in as soon as two days, but for any real numbers, it would take a week.

"We will enforce the Portland blockade in three days. The straggler units will reinforce as they arrive on the scene. The CDC will coordinate with all West Coast healthcare providers. If anyone so much as sniffles, I want them in an isolation tent. Understand me?" All nodded in assent. "Keep me apprised of every aspect of this operation. And God bless this nation of ours in these difficult times. Dismissed."

There was no talking as each left with grim purpose.

At last, the President slumped down to his chair. Drained. There were no good options, but he had tried to listen to them all impartially. If there was one positive from this whole mess they no longer sat on their hands. Whether his decision turned out to be good or bad, at least things were now in motion. Only history could evaluate whether his decision was the correct one.

*Assuming we have a history after this.* The bitter observation cut him to the bone. Bowing his head, the political visionary, husband, and father said a fervent, silent prayer.

Only those in Portland would know if it would be answered.

# Chapter 30

*July 7, Saturday — 6:00 am — Horizons*
*Pharmaceuticals*

The call came at 0600 on the dot. Craig had only been 'smoking' by his designated tree for five minutes before his mobile vibrated in his pocket. There was no need for either party to identify one with the other. Only two people besides him knew the number of his burner phone. It was virtually impossible to tap into their conversation, so they skipped the silly code they had been using.

In concise and precise language, he outlined the patrol schedule in and around Horizons buildings and campus. It had been difficult because he had duties within his pod, so he could take only so many breaks without drawing suspicion. Even still, he had gotten a few curious looks from the roving soldiers on watch. A true smoker would not have used such varied and circuitous routes to fulfill his or her hourly fix. Lucky for him, there were fewer patrols within the buildings.

The guardsmen were mainly concerned with an attack from outside. So, he would let the Alpha and Beta teams do their own more covert external reconnaissance of the campus. He gave them three days to plan their raid. Until then, he would keep his head down until they could extract him.

The connection was broken, and the burner phone was pocketed. There was a certain appeal for Craig to have his troops come in guns a-blazin', but he discarded it. If the GC destroyed the building now, the government would still have the research on the net and could probably create the antidote without Dr. Wu or Zander. Also, the FBI had to have a file on *Gaia's Children* members, and any idiot with facial recognition software could connect the dots. They had waited this long; they could afford to be patient and do it right. The trick was to make it impossible to solve his virus, so it was imperative to destroy the network and his 'friends' simultaneously. The problem with destroying the research net was the nasty NSA firewall built to keep out people—like them. Once they were past it, corrupting the data would be a breeze. The smug bastards couldn't even conceptualize there might be someone out there who would want something besides stopping the virus.

Grabbing another burner phone, Craig called an altogether different number. "Is it ready yet?"

A testy voice on the other end answered, "I am working as fast as possible. If it were simple to get past the firewall, the Russians and Chinese would have done it long ago."

"Trust me, I don't think it's easy," Craig said, trying to keep his anger in check. "But we do have a timetable here. It is a very real possibility that our friends will come up with a solution at any minute. The surprise we are planning will happen in three days. There can be no further delay. Can you do it before then?"

After a moment's pause, the hacker replied, "I would say there is an 80 percent chance of breaking it by then."

"Excellent, call Violet as soon as it is done. If we can move up our plans sooner, I want to."

"Understood." The phone clicked as the discrete man hung up.

Throwing the cigarette on the ground, Craig smashed the butt with his heel and searched for the window, which he knew hid his former friend. No plan went without a hitch. Intellectually, he comprehended this truism, but the reality of the situation was much more infuriating. He had nursed a private fantasy in which the GC would release the virus, and then he could sit on his butt at the compound and watch the world burn.

*Well, that little dream was shot to shit.*

Somehow, he was living a cosmic joke in which his resurrected boss was unbelievably still calling all the shots and telling him what to do. To say it was difficult for him to smile and act like he was excited to destroy his brainchild was an understatement.

His hand itched with the desire to call his GC brethren and openly declare war. There would be great satisfaction in letting them all know it was him. But the moment passed, and he moved his hand away from his pocket. There was no question in his mind that he would win; it would just take a bit more time and patience.

As he returned to the building, he pretended to stumble. At that moment, he discretely dumped both phones in the garbage can. As he righted himself, he began to whistle an aria. Then, a thought came to him, and he removed the mostly empty pack of cigarettes and tossed them into the can.

His only possession left—a smug grin.

# Chapter 31



*July 9, Monday — 9:30 am — Horizons Pharmaceuticals*

As Zander made his hourly refreshment lap around the building, he couldn't shake the feeling of déjà vu. The faces and buildings differed, but the sense of urgency and purpose were the same. And just like before, fear and desperation lurked below the calm. Everyone knew their hours were numbered before they succumbed to the enemy.

Well, not everyone.

There were new guardsmen, with their ubiquitous facial gas masks, and his fellow survivors from Ontario. And although those latter two didn't fear the virus, they were not without peril. The Federal Bureau of Investigation saw to that. The three of them had been taking a rare break together in one of the cafeterias early Saturday morning when a female and male agent wearing navy-colored business suits and earpieces casually approached Ben and Rohit and politely 'asked' them to come with them. As they did, Zander glanced behind the feds and saw four guardsmen with their firearms drawn.

Apparently, the federal agents had been expecting trouble from his 'friends,' and they were unwilling to take a chance on letting a suspected terrorist cause any more damage than had already been done. Both men protested their innocence and begged Zander for help. It broke his heart to know one of these men was a lifelong friend, but the other was something entirely different. Even now, the betrayal roiled his stomach and conjured black thoughts. *Godspeed,* he had silently wished the FBI investigators.

Once things were cleared up, he could apologize to the aggrieved, innocent man, but he had only looked down at the tabletop and pretended he was invisible. Once his 'friends' realized Zander could not, or would not, help them, they left in resignation. The agents escorted them to some other part of the building.

Later in the day, Mack said the interrogators had gotten nothing out of either man so far. Still, beyond that, he was not at liberty to say anything more about an ongoing investigation. Interrupting his route for a moment, Zander grabbed a pack of gum out of his pocket and assiduously popped a stick in his mouth, breaking his worry cycle involving Ben and Rohit.

A harried, white-coated woman brushed against him and mumbled an apology without even making eye contact with him. Yep, déjà vu all over again. The only difference between then and now was that this time, he didn't feel like his head was going to explode, and every atom of his body was on fire. These changes magnified his overall effectiveness by at least a factor of five, but unfortunately, they did not make his dealing with the human element any easier.

In fact, watching everyone at Horizons go through the virus' progression was agonizing. For perhaps the hundredth time during the past two weeks, he shouldered the yoke of responsibility for every death the pathogen caused. It was neither a healthy attitude nor rational, but it didn't matter one wit. People were dying as an indirect result of his research. It crushed his soul, but Zander had no time to wallow in self-recrimination. There was a small window where he could redeem himself by creating the virus blocker. *Please God, let us be in time.*

Somehow, Zander found himself transported to the command room entrance. It had always fascinated him how people could drive miles in a car without crashing or being aware of how they had gotten to where they wanted to go.

As he glanced into the room, he wondered if his subconscious wanted him to return to fulfilling his pledge, or was it something different? Moving to his seat, Zander stole a surreptitious glance at Grace and knew the answer. It broke his heart to see the price her body was paying while it tried to fight off the virus.

When they had first met, he marveled at her smooth, supple skin. He would have guessed she was at least 10 years younger than her bio indicated. But now, lines of worry and pain marred her perfect features. A box of tissues at her elbow. She was every bit the trooper he expected her to be, but the toll on her was clear.

The cosmic irony of it all was not lost on him. At 45 years of age, he seriously doubted he would ever find that special someone. Now, he finds someone, and she has a 90 percent probability of dying within the next four days. Grace stopped her work and grimaced while rubbing her temples. Her obvious pain was a not-so-gentle reminder that if she was one of those unlucky enough not to shed the virus, her brilliant mind would be desiccated one cell at a time by it. Everything that made her vibrantly human would dim until she was no more.

Yesterday, they had a difficult conversation, and she had pushed him to vow she would not awake from Stage Four. She would be restrained, and if necessary, he would administer a lethally strong narcotic. He wasn't sure if he could kill anyone, let alone her, but he had agreed. *You can do it because it must be done. No one gets better.*

*Abby did it for my parents; you can do it for her too,* he thought in reproach.

At that moment, Zander's computer chirped, which startled him from his maudlin reverie. He tapped a key without thought, and the machine came dutifully awake. The aural alert had become one of the most annoying sounds he had ever heard. Initially, it had been a wonderful technological connection to his fellow networkers. Then, it morphed into something altogether different—an overwhelming chore. There were bits and pieces of information being shared by other scientists and doctors almost constantly, and it was his job to make sense of them. But looking at one bit meant he was missing five to ten others.

It was like finding a drop of water in a fully opened faucet. So, even though he was tempted to forgo looking at every single one of them, he could never forgive himself if he skipped the email that gave him the final piece of the puzzle. Zander had taken his earlier stroll because he had been caught-up, so the email in the inbox was the only one that hadn't been opened yet. The title read, "Vector acquired!" and the email's sender was from a prominent research team in Australia. This group had already come through several times in the past, and Zander hoped they could help the US scientists solve the final puzzle piece. So far, the world medical community has found a blocker that works on the virus aspect attacking the body. Still, they couldn't block the other element of the pathogen before it crossed the cerebral barrier and entered the brain.

For some reason, the hybrid contagion headed to the cerebrum quicker than its counterpart. So, their solution could inhibit the virus' attack on the body but not the brain. There were two promising angles for dealing with this final stumbling block, and the medical-science community hoped they could make one of them work in their serum. The first possible solution would involve creating a DNA modifier that could cross the brain barrier, thereby preemptively stopping the virus before it started replicating in the cerebrum and cerebellum. The more promising idea of the two was to speed up the circulation of the blocker within the body. If they could attack the contagion before it arrived at the brain, they could prevent any damage to the victim.

His pulse beat faster as he perused the email. Apparently, Dr. Anderson and his team went for the fast blocker approach. Essentially, they created a chemical cocktail that would 'goose' a human spleen so the organ would generate their blocker cells at a much more accelerated pace. A person's normal white blood cell count is 4,000 to 11,000 per microliter of blood. Their 'anti-virus-on-steroids' would force the spleen to create three to five times that amount for about a month. With those blocker levels coursing through a person's veins, the pathogen would be swarmed long before it could attack the host's immune system.

Health officials would have to continue administering boosters monthly until the virus ran its course, but the contagion would be contained. Everything else was a logistics problem that could be ferreted out later.

His triumphant smile fell as he finished perusing the test data. All of Dr. Anderson's initial results revealed that properly inoculated pigs rejected the virus. Unfortunately, upon autopsy completion, they discovered none of their blocker was found to have crossed the body-brain barrier. The scientific community had created a miracle in record time, but for now, their solution would have to be administered as a preemptive injection.

Half a dozen research groups were working on creating carrier molecules—"helpful" biologicals designed to pass through the brain barrier. But even the most enthusiastic of these teams insisted a breakthrough was at least seven years out. So, Dr. Anderson's solution could potentially arrest the pandemic, but for the thousands infected—it was worthless. The sad, cosmic irony for Grace and her valiant staff was they might save the world, but they were not going to share in the war's spoils.

Sadness threatened to overwhelm Zander, but he couldn't be selfish and hold on to this information for a second longer.

"Grace," he said.

"What's up?"

With a forlorn smile, he said, "Dr. Anderson and his group came through for us. They sent us the formula, and we could produce a preemptive anti-virus within the day. Forwarding the email now."

"That's amazing! Give me a minute to catch up," she enthused as she returned to her computer screen.

The minutes were interminable as Zander waited for her to assimilate the information, but he wanted her to corroborate his assessment. So, he picked up the phone and asked the receptionist to have Dr. Mack paged. "Tell him to report to the command center ASAP."

Seemingly seconds later, an obviously winded Mack came through the door. He removed his fogged glasses, bent over, and huffed. When he could breathe freely, he begged, "Give me some good news."

"Can do," Grace offered, "our good friends Dr. Anderson and company pulled a rabbit out of their hat." Then, she hit the salient points for him.

Mack's face fell. "So, we only have a preventative vaccine? That's wonderful, but what about us? Can we modify this so it can cure the virus? If not, the CDC computer models forecast that 90,000 people are infected. Which means we will have at least 81,000 fatalities if we stopped this thing today."

"Not to pour gas on that fire," Grace added, "but those numbers do not reflect the fact that you will soon have nearly one hundred thousand amped-up, homicidal killers on the loose."

"Oh my God!" Zander said in horror. Their only focus was on creating a solution that could save every infected person; he hadn't considered what their failure could mean to those who were not infected.

"Distributing the anti-virus during a city-wide scrum is going to be a bitch," Mack observed. "When I call the President, I will recommend bringing in as many soldiers and sailors as possible. Before I contact him, though, I need to know. Do we have all the ingredients we need for this anti-virus?"

"One step ahead of you, Mack," Grace said, "I just checked our material manifests, and Horizons has everything on the list except two of these compounds. I'm pretty sure we can procure them from a fellow pharma company here in Portland, with whom we do business extensively. Let me give them a call. If we can't work out something with them, I know Horizons could ship it in from Seattle or San Francisco, but it would require time we don't have."

"Sounds good. Let me know if I need to get the President to persuade some industry people to lend a hand." Mack turned to Zander and asked, "Can you create a document that lists all the particulars of the serum? I want to send it out on our intra-web within the hour so everyone in the building can start running models on this. The Aussies are a thorough bunch, but I want to know this is safe and effective before we get this into production and begin administering it to Americans."

"Will do," Zander said.

Struck by the moment, Mack walked over to them, put a hand on each person's shoulder, and looked them in the eyes while saying, "You guys did it." Grace and Zander both made to interrupt, but Mack continued, "Yes, yes, it was a group effort, yadda yadda—we all know if we pull this off, it is because of you. I just wanted you to know someone noticed." His voice hitched at the end of his compliment. Once more, he glanced at Grace in sympathy before shuffling to the door. "Got to make this call."

Mack pulled out his cell phone and was gone.

When Zander turned back to Grace, she smiled wistfully at him. "You know you don't need to treat me like I'm fragile." Zander made to object, but she bulled on through. "Really, I'm at peace with everything now. I'm not going to lie. I hope I survive this thing. But if I don't, I made a difference. My death will not be for nothing."

"But I don't want to lose you," he said angrily. It felt risky to reveal this to her. Like when a character in a movie uses the L-word before the other is ready for it. The consequence of not saying it to her, though, was he might never get the chance. "There has got to be a way, maybe induce a hypothermic coma or something. Please," he begged to anyone who would listen, "I can't take losing one more person I care about."

The grief over the losses he had suffered the past week rose up and nearly overwhelmed him, and the air refused to fill his lungs until he became aware of the gentlest of touches. With one hand, she lifted his face up to hers; with the other, she stroked it like a mother caressing her dear child's face.

"You're such a sweet man. I know you want to be my shining knight, but sometimes you must face it—the world is unfair. And when it doesn't play nicely, you don't have to feel responsible. Make no mistake, one of those two men being interrogated is. Promise me, don't hide your big heart because you fear to love again. This world desperately needs more people like you, someone not afraid to care and to feel."

Her chocolate brown eyes held him. "If only we had met sooner—"

"Shhhh," she said as she moved a forefinger to block his next words. "I feel the same, but saying anything more now will only hurt us. Promise me. If we make it through this. Then we may talk. Okay?"

*She was wrong,* he thought. *What they said or did not say would not matter.*

If he lost her, the void would return for him.

But he nodded in the affirmative for her anyway.

# Chapter 32



*July 9, Monday — 12:21 pm — Horizons Pharmaceuticals*

Grace fell almost three hours after they received the news about the Australians and their souped-up anti-virus. Grace had found several local sources for the compounds they needed as her time wound down. Mack had enlisted the President's aid in 'convincing' several larger sources to contribute further stores to the manufacture of the blocker.

One of the pharmaceuticals was in Beaverton, a suburb of Portland. Within minutes of making the call, a Black Hawk had been dispatched. The ingredients reached the production area not long after. With the supplies on hand, they could produce 400-500 doses of the virus blocker, which would be enough to work out the kinks on their fabrication lines. After this test run, they could begin mass production of the serum.

Technically, the anti-virus could have been produced by any number of pharmaceutical companies. Still, Horizons was reluctant to share their multi-billion-dollar anti-viral delivery system with literally everyone in the world. After some perfunctory negotiations, the President and his staff quickly tracked the appropriation and distribution of four mass production lines of equipment to the Horizons' Portland facility. Once installed, they could produce all the vaccines needed for the outbreak. The President secured a guarantee that they would be delivered and set up by the end of the workday tomorrow. Zander mused to himself, *Things are finally breaking our way—except one.*

With heartbreaking clarity, Zander thought back a mere 10 minutes ago when he was talking to Grace about an idea he had just come up with for isolating and attacking the cerebral virus element when her face lost expression. Simultaneously, her body slumped forward, and her face bounced off the keyboard before her—body turning as she fell out of the chair.

If not for Zander's quick dive to catch her inert form, her head would have hit full force on the substantial metal support for the table. Instead, he guided her body to the left of the brace and eased her onto the carpeted floor. After checking her pulse, Zander called Mack to tell him that Grace had gone into a coma. He thought it profane and counterproductive to leave her body lying in the command area while a dozen people tried to make the production of their blocker a reality.

So, he enlisted a passing guardsman's help to carry Grace to her office. There, they laid her on the couch, and the soldier excused himself. One of the nearby office doors proved to be a coat closet, which had two blankets and two pillows on the upper shelf. In moments, he had supported her head with the cushions, removed her shoes, and was tucking the blanket about her when he heard a tentative knock at her door. The door opened, and Mack poked his head in but remained mostly in the hallway.

"Come in," Zander said, motioning the man in with a wave of his hand. "She can't be disturbed."

"Came as soon as you called," Mack whispered like people do in a hospital. "When I didn't see you at the command room, I figured you brought her down here. What happened?"

"Everything was fine, and then she was heading for the floor the next thing I knew. Her vitals are depressed like all the others."

So far, six Horizons staff—besides Dr. Wu—had progressed to Stage Three, and they were being cared for in the make-shift hospital detention center located in the other building. The fallen were physically restrained and being watched by CDC doctors who had newly arrived from Atlanta. These physicians were easily distinguished from their peers because they wore cumbersome yellow hazmat suits, but they could shed them soon because they would be among the first to receive the new anti-virus serum. Both men sat in the two coffee table chairs facing the couch as if in mutual agreement.

The vigil over their fallen comrade was silent until Mack finally said, "We have all the ingredients we need for the short batch measured, and the production lines were almost completed before you called me. Wouldn't be surprised if we couldn't produce our first dose within the hour."

"Wonderful news," Zander said, but even he could hear how hollow his response sounded. It frightened him how little he cared about the final steps of putting his blocker to the test. *I'm so tired.* He rubbed his temples with his fingers. Hoping that at least one small part of him wouldn't ache or hurt. *She made me forget that for a while.* Now, he looked at her face again.

If he pretended, she looked asleep—peaceful, if only. Below her passive exterior, a war for her life raged.

"Take whatever time you need." Mack got up and said, "We will hold down the fort until you are ready to work again—"

Two large figures barged into the room without warning. Both wore hazmat suits similar to those of the CDC doctors, except their suits were cobalt blue, almost black. Neither spoke, but they moved toward Dr. Wu's prone form.

"Is this really necessary?" Zander said in indignation as he rose hastily and moved to intercept the mute intruders. "She entered Stage Three minutes ago. All our observations confirm she has 12-24 hours before she will move to Stage Four." Neither interloper seemed dissuaded in the least by Zander's argument, and one started to try to restrain him. Turning to Mack, "Did you approve this? You bastard!"

"There is nothing I can do about this," Mack waved his arms at the guards, "The CDC decided we needed new protocols to specifically address what happens to victims here at Horizons. Their instructions are as soon as someone succumbs to the third stage of the disease, they will be physically restrained and kept under armed supervision. Dammit, Zander, do you want what is happening on Portland's streets to happen here?"

"Of course not!" Zander felt his fury evaporate. "Not thinking clearly. Sorry."

"Understandable." Then, with a rakish grin, Mack explained, "Which is why when I found the command center empty, I figured you were bringing her here. So, I made these err. . . arrangements." Nodding toward the now motionless guards. "Otherwise, she would have to be placed in the hospital ward with the others. Restrain and guard her here were their only instructions."

Feeling a complete fool, Zander said, "Thanks." He left the rest unsaid.

Mack turned to the guards and said, "The doctor is correct. She doesn't need to be restrained this minute, but I want you to take care of it within the hour." Then he made eye contact with Zander and said sincerely, "Meant it before when I said this country owes the two of you a debt." Then he was gone.

Perspiration beaded on her brow and upper lip. Before he knew what he was doing, Zander had run to the washroom, grabbed a hand towel, and soaked it with cold water from the tap. It might have been his imagination, but it seemed her pinched face had relaxed after his tender ministrations. He spent a moment trying to etch her every feature in his memory. Unsure whether he would ever see her again. Then, in a rush, he left her.

Once again, he made an unconscious trip to the command center. As he entered the room, he headed toward his computer, but he stopped short when he saw a vacant floral-print couch that lined the left side of the room. His bone-deep weariness asserted itself. The couch was plush and comfy and within moments, Zander fell into a deep—but tortured sleep.

# Chapter 33



*July 10, Thursday — 12:01 am — Horizons Pharmaceuticals*

Awaking with a start, Zander tried to orient himself by looking at the time. No luck. The analog clock on the far wall had both hands pointing straight up, but darned if he could tell whether it was 12pm or am. The windowless room also provided no clue as to how long he had slept. But as the cobwebs began to recede, he recalled that Grace had succumbed to the virus in the afternoon. So, it had to be midnight. Sweet sleep had temporarily provided a salve for his wounded heart, but there was a sense of unease just beyond his understanding, which screamed to him that something was wrong.

Even feeling anxious, Zander was tempted to try and get a whole night's sleep. He closed his eyes again.

*"Get... up!"* A feminine voice boomed.

He launched himself off the couch and screamed, "What?! Who?!"

The few staff left in the room looked up in alarm. Then they surmised he had a nightmare, chuckled, and returned to their work. As he scanned the room for the speaker, he came to the same conclusion as those around him, and he relaxed. But the speaker interrupted him again. *"There's no time for this foolishness! Grab your friends Zander and get out of the building. Now! This way!"*

Without warning, his vision was replaced by an ultra-realistic image of the parking garage below the tower. This faded and was replaced by another panorama, this one of the front lawn of Horizons Pharmaceuticals. It was not a still shot because, as he watched, armed men in black body armor were stealthily approaching the building.

*"Come to me, and I will protect you,"* the woman declared.

The more he heard the voice, the more certain he was that it was the golden woman from the cavern. He was still baffled by his earlier encounters with her, but he was sure she meant him no harm. Besides, why would the mysterious woman warn him of danger unless she was trying to help?

Zander made his decision.

Running to the nearest telephone, he contacted the switchboard and learned Mack was at an office down the hall. The room's door was open, and Zander saw him talking on the phone. Zander sprinted up to him and made eye contact with the CDC director, who looked up and made a wait-one-minute gesture with his off-hand. Exactly five seconds later, Zander snatched the receiver from his hand and slammed it into the cradle.

"What the hell!" Mack said, not even trying to hide his indignation. "You're lucky I wasn't talking to the President."

"Don't have time to explain," Zander said as he seized the man's arm and dragged him out of his chair, "but we must get out of here now. Someone is attacking Horizons, and we need to leave *now!*"

"Listen," Mack said, giving Zander a look of pure empathy but also a touch of 'this man has truly lost his mind,' "we have at least 100 soldiers in the building, as well as a dozen or so special forces. I saw you sleeping in the command room, so I moved down here to let you get some rest. Did you just wake?" Zander nodded. "It was probably a bad dream. Don't worry. The President *won't* allow anything to happen to our efforts here."

Zander hated wasting time with this chit-chat, but he needed to make this man believe him. "Remember when I first told you someone in my lab was a saboteur, but we couldn't prove who it was?"

"Yeah," Mack said. "Well, the FBI had no luck in breaking either of them so far. They're still sitting in detention with armed guards. What of them?"

"Don't ask me how I know, but somehow, whoever distributed the virus here is not satisfied with merely stopping Horizons staff."

"Where is your proof? Why now?" Mack said with exasperation.

"I ask you the same question. Why would someone attack now?"

Mack pressed his glasses up his nose, and his brow furrowed in thought. "Someone on the inside told them we are producing a cure later today. Oh my God! But even if what you say is true, this is the United States of America. No one could be so stupid as to attack us and hope to win."

"Trust me, Mack. There is no time! They will destroy us and our work long before help arrives," he said with growing desperation as the minutes slid by. "If I'm wrong, we can have a good laugh at my expense; if I'm not, we could lose everything we have accomplished here."

It took the man all of a handful of seconds to reach a decision.

But decide he did. Taking out his cell, Mack pushed a button on his phone and auto-dialed a number. "Lieutenant, Dr. Mack, we have a code red. Lock everything down. Inform and coordinate with building security."

"Meet me at Grace's office," Zander said while Mack stuffed papers into his carry bag. Zander dashed to the command room, stowing his laptop in his shoulder bag. He slung it over his shoulder as he ran out of the door.

"Attention! Attention!" the internal loudspeaker system intoned. "This is a code red! This is not a drill. Code red. All non-combat personnel, please move to a secure area, lock the door, and await further instructions. This is not a drill."

When the message concluded, a klaxon, a dead ringer for the red alert signal on the original Star Trek series, came on. Looking at the nearest loudspeaker, Zander had to chuckle at the situation's absurdity. As he ran to Grace, he playfully shouted, "Nerds!" The moment of levity lasted only a moment before he reached the chaos of people rushing about in fear and purpose.

Zander wasn't sure what to do when he got to Grace's office door. Knocking at her door while sirens were going off felt a little ridiculous, but what could he do? So, he knocked once, waited a moment, and then opened the doors. The startled guards already had their weapons out, and he had the distinct impression that he was lucky they were not the jumpy kind.

"Easy, gentlemen," Zander said as he raised his empty hands, "I'm not the enemy."

The two soldiers looked at one another, unsure how to proceed.

A heartbeat later, Mack entered the room and said to them, "We need to evacuate the building, and you're with us."

The command in his voice triggered an automatic response in them, and the Guardsmen almost saluted until they realized their guns were still in their hands. Self-consciously shaking their heads, they holstered their weapons and awaited instructions. Zander moved to pick up Grace when a restraining hand grabbed his arm and spun him around.

"Not sure how you knew, but the lieutenant just told me you were right about the attack," Mack said. "I was willing to go out on a limb for you, but I won't allow you blunder about trying to be some hero for Grace. The President charged you with saving American lives. That hasn't changed. Stop thinking with your heart and start using your brain. How do we get out of this trap?"

An angry retort was on his lips, and then it died. Mack was right.

Taking a deep breath, he focused his breathing and then started to work the situation out loud, "The attack is coming from the front of the building, and the parking area is on the opposite side. From what I have been shown—" He forestalled Mack's objection with a hand-slicing gesture— "Later, I promise. So, if we go to the garage and—oh, wait a minute—almost forgot about Ben and Rohit. Need to grab them, too."

"Are you crazy?" Mack couldn't take it any longer. "You say we are under imminent attack and must drop everything immediately. But when we agree to follow you, you say, 'Hey, let's take a little side trip to pick up two men,' and may I add this insignificant detail— one who happens to be actively trying to *kill* you, me, and everyone in the world? For God's sake, *why?!*"

Zander's anger came to life like a careless match thrown on dry brush, "Why? Because I have given up everything to stop all of this!" He swept his arm in a broad gesture. "To you, this is all an academic exercise. Something you do for a career, but I lost my family, my home, and too many good friends. All I know is one of those men has done nothing but be my colleague and ally in trying to cure cancer all these years. Does he deserve to be interrogated and treated as a terrorist? Does he deserve to die here while I save myself? Don't ask me to sacrifice another friend because it's inconvenient, Mack." Zander softened his tone, "Lord knows I want you with me, but I can't lose anyone else."

The siren's pulsing wail kept time with an imaginary clock, tracking the waning moments left for them to escape.

"Fine," Zander said after enough time passed. He would go it alone. Grabbing Mack's restraining hand, Zander made to hoist Grace again.

Before he could lift her, Mack cleared his throat and said, "Damn you." Zander looked back at the man. "Why do I keep letting you talk me into shit? Never mind. I will probably regret this but damned if I can blame you for having a friend's back. You heard the man; we are heading to detention now. Assume guard positions."

The men nodded and headed to the hall to check for threats.

"Thanks," Zander whispered to Mack, "I owe you one."

"You're damned right you do!" Mack said with a growl. Cleary unhappy with being played by Zander. "Let's hope I live long enough to collect from you."

"Don't worry; you will." Zander unslung his bag and handed it to Mack.

Now that Zander was unencumbered, he moved to the couch and prepared to move Grace. Bound wrist to wrist and ankle to ankle with restraints, Zander guessed the cuffs wouldn't hinder their escape, so he didn't waste any precious time unshackling her. Leaning into her prone form, Zander tucked his shoulder under her torso and slung Grace over him in a fireman's carry. When her weight was distributed correctly, they left the office.

During Mack and Zander's absence, both soldiers had removed their bulky hazmat suits and seemed to tacitly agree that wearing their army issue face masks would hinder their ability to guard their assignments because neither unhooked them from their belts.

Eyes in constant motion, scanning the hall, and their weapons drawn, the bulkier of the two asked the CDC director, "Ready, Doc?" Mack shook his head and pointed in Zander's direction. Without missing a beat, the man seemed to shrug, turn toward Zander, and repeat, "Ready, Doc?" with perfect deadpan delivery.

"What's your name, soldier?" Zander asked as he shifted Grace's lithe body to find a more comfortable position.

"Sergeant Oliver Jennison," said the immense man, "but most call me Ollie."

Their bulky hazmat suits had made both men look like behemoths; now, they merely looked like they could bench-press a Mini Cooper. At first glance, the only distinction Zander could make between the two men was that Ollie was a bit taller and had brown hair—a few shades lighter than the other.

"This here is PFC Romanelli," Ollie said. "Trust me, it is impossible to get him to shut up." The twinkle in his eye gave away the lie.

"Well, Ollie," Zander said. "We need to get to the detention room. Isn't that close to the west elevator?" The sergeant grunted his agreement. "We'll stop on the second floor long enough to pick up the two men we talked about and then head down to the parking garage."

"Roger that," Ollie replied with practiced ease. "I have point. Follow my instructions and stay behind me."

The tight group was at the elevator in no time and was waiting for the car to arrive when the building shook like a wave crashing onto the beach. There was a small popping sound, followed by darkness. Within moments, the emergency generators must have kicked in because some lights flickered on.

"Breaching charge," Ollie said with a frown.

"Are you sure?" Mack asked. "It sounded like a firecracker."

The big man chuckled good-naturedly, "Two tours in Iraq and Afghanistan, doc. So, yeah. Pretty sure. It only sounds small because we are five floors up. Trust me; it would be much louder on the other side of the door they blew."

"Of course, you are right," Mack conceded.

The panel above their heads illuminated again, and the indicator showed the car resuming its upward path.

"The elevator is functioning again," Zander observed. "Do we stick with the plan?"

"If I were attacking," Ollie said, "I would target the backup generators to create chaos. The elevators are no longer a viable option."

As if to emphasize his point, a tense voice came over the intercom: *"The building has been breached at the north and west entrances. All forces converge in the main foyer."*

"Okay, it looks like we will get a little cardio in today; we take the stairs," Ollie said with practiced bravado as they headed to the access door 30 feet beyond the elevator.

As soon as they opened the stairwell access door, they could hear hundreds of rounds being fired. No one needed their guide to decode what they were hearing—automatic weapons fire—from somewhere nearby.

"Stay a floor behind me," Ollie said in a hushed voice. "If something happens to me, you should get out of this stairwell and have a go at a different one. Or you can attempt to hide in a room and hope they don't check every room. All I can tell you is, don't wait for me; I will either be dead, or I will try to catch up with you. Do you understand?" All nodded, and then Ollie turned to Zander and asked, "How are ya holding up, Doc? Don't want you to drop her in the middle of all this." His tone was not accusatory; he was just a man used to being prepared for every contingency a mission might throw at them. A consummate profession.

"Fine for now. Fortunately, I have a little adrenaline coursing through my veins now."

They all gently chuckled at his quip.

"Well, let me know if that changes," Ollie said, eyes crinkled as he smiled at him. "I prefer not leading an op with a bundle over my shoulder, but you should have seen some of the shit they made us carry in a war zone."

Without further discussion or hesitation, they started down the stairs in a perfect, nightmare, guard scenario—the point man had no cover or intel about what was coming toward him. Lucky for them, this was not Ollie's rookie mission. He preceded them in a semi-crouch; gun partially extended in front of him. Another smaller explosion shook the building when Ollie reached the fourth-floor platform.

This time the darkness enveloped them immediately. An eternity later, only the emergency lights, which lit each landing, came on, sharing their weak light. The intercom's power must have been cut at the same time as the backup generators because there were no further announcements about enemy movements or situation reports. If only the voice had warned him sooner. He thought, *I could have talked Mack into calling in reinforcements.*

Then he had an epiphany, *I bet whoever their inside man is he has fed the attackers all the info they need to take out this place.* Somehow the voice knew. These soldiers cannot hope to repel this assault; at best, they can hold them off until police and military reinforcements arrive. Wait a minute. The sound of frantic calls and instructions being given was now distinctly heard from below, as well as the pop and staccato crack of gunfire.

"We have to get out of here now!" Zander yelled over the cacophony below.

Mack turned to Zander, staring at him like he was insane, and asked, "What the hell do you think we are trying to do?"

Seeing them stop, Ollie returned to the group.

"Think about it, Mack," Zander said, "these guys intend to take on a whole company of National Guardsmen, but what is their end game? Say they take out all these soldiers. Then what? If the lieutenant called this in, I bet there are hundreds, if not thousands, of troops mobilizing to resecure this facility."

"Oh my God," Mack said, "there is no way this group can hold this building against the US Military. So, what is their move then?"

"If I was a terrorist," Ollie said, "I would want to destroy the government's ability to create an antidote, but why not just send in an explosives-laden truck?"

Just like when he sat in his office for a 'think,' the disparate pieces clicked together in Zander's head. "There is only one reason to make a surgical strike like this. The sergeant is right: tactically, whoever this is should just plant a bomb and blow up the place. Since they aren't doing that, and they can't hold the place, the only thing that makes sense is a smash-and-grab. Seems like a lot of work to rescue a grunt, so my bet is one of my 'friends' is much higher up the ladder in this organization than we might have guessed. Might even be their leader." Zander paused for a moment as another thought struck him. "Otherwise, why risk this attack?"

"Well, we have another justification for getting to the detention center ASAP," Ollie said.

"Lead on, MacDuff," Zander said, indicating the darkened abyss below.

Once the decision was made, there seemed little reason for undue caution, and they rushed down the stairs. It did not take many steps before his heart was pounding in his ears, and his breathing fell into his normal running rhythm. Preparation for those half-marathons was more useful than he could have possibly imagined because, otherwise, carrying this slight woman would have exhausted him very quickly. Thank God for small miracles—and miracles there were—because two men burst through the second-floor door just as Ollie arrived at the landing. A minute earlier or later would have been disastrous for the small party. As it was, it was merely deadly.

All the combatants hesitated for the briefest of moments before an explosion of movement made it difficult for Zander to determine what was happening in the low light of the 20x15 platform. It appeared that Ollie was the first to react.

In one quick motion, Ollie grabbed the nearest attacker's AR-15 and Ollie used it like a whip to launch the man into the concrete wall opposite the landing door. A loud *"humph"* was Ollie's opponent's only reaction, and the man seemed nonplussed by the collision with the solid surface behind him. The interloper brought up his long gun with surprising speed, but Ollie followed up his initial move with spin, which accelerated his elbow's impact to the man's throat—crushing his windpipe. The man dropped his weapon and vainly tried to get air through a destroyed trachea, which would never permit life-giving breath again.

During this skirmish, the second raider moved onto the platform while bringing up his weapon. He intended to use the party's distraction with Ollie's fight to allow the newcomer to spray the party with semi-automatic gunfire. Unfortunately for the man, Romanelli was on the half landing above when the two interlopers burst through the door.

With practiced ease, Romanelli rested both elbows on the tubular metal railing for stability and fired three rounds into the intruder's chest—the first missed entirely, the second and third did not, staggering the man. Even still, the trespasser tried to bring his weapon up a second time, but to no avail, because Romanelli expertly placed two bullets dead center of the man's face, which disintegrated into a gruesome confusion of tissue.

The handgun's loud report still seemed to be reverberating off the concrete stairwell walls, or maybe it was Zander's ears ringing. Ollie's opponent had slumped to the concrete platform, his movements were stilling, and his partner's body had fallen and held open the door to the second floor. The no longer gray door appeared to be a surrealist painting in the low light of the emergency floods.

In awe, Zander half-whisper to his guardian angels, "You guys don't get paid nearly enough."

The well-muscled man flashed him a hurried grin, "You have no idea, Doc. Stay back until I say it's safe."

Edging past the ruined corpse, Ollie squatted and quick looked around the corners of the stairway door alcove, first to his left, then to the right.

"It's clear for the moment," he said loud enough for the group to hear, but without turning his head. "I will take point again, and Romanelli has rear guard. Move unless we tell you to stop. Go!"

The party launched as one into the hall and ran like they had a pack of wolves at their heels. It was only 60 feet to the door of the makeshift detention room, but the hallway now made them feel naked and vulnerable.

Once inside, Zander was assaulted by the acrid smell of gunpowder and a slight, grayish haze in the room. As he moved farther into the room, he stumbled and nearly fell before he recovered. Shifting Grace's body to the side, Zander could now see he had tripped over a face-down body, which was near a table. His arms were aching, and he had to rest, so with care, he laid Grace on the carpeted floor. When he straightened up, he was shocked by the amount of blood spattered about the room.

"It looks like this man was standing guard in the hall," Ollie said, pointing at the man wearing guardsman fatigues. "Must have been shot with a silencer from down the hall because these two"—indicating the lifeless FBI agents— "didn't seem to know what was happening outside the room."

Apparently, both FBI agents had been sitting at a 3x15 wooden table facing away from the door. One officer had fallen forward with a hole in the back of his head, but the female had turned partway around before being shot in the head, too. Her body had slumped to the floor and had almost caused Zander's fall.

"Guess you were right about this being a rescue op, Dr. Parks," Ollie said.

"Zander? Is it you?" a mysterious voice from the back of the room asked.

Both soldiers ducked behind sparse cover and scanned the room with eyes and weapons.

"National Guard! Come out here with hands up, or we will fire!" Ollie commanded.

Ben and Rohit popped up, hands raised, from behind a table turned on its side.

"Don't shoot them," Zander said, "they're with us, sergeant."

The guardsmen lowered their handguns, and Ollie remarked, "Been a *civi* too long—getting sloppy." His tone was light, but his expression was self-recriminatory. "Shoulda checked the whole room when we got here."

Rohit let his hands fall to his sides, sidled around the table, and wrapped Zander in a big bear hug. Not sure which man was his betrayer, Zander decided the best course of action, for now, was to embrace the smiling man before him.

When they stepped apart, Rohit said, "They moved us from our rooms to here when the alarm went off. The FBI agents said we were safe, but then two men broke into the room and killed them. In the confusion and noise, I hit the floor and crawled as far away as I—" The poor man couldn't continue as he looked about the room.

By this time, Ben had also made his way to Zander's side and said, "We're lucky you came along when you did; those men in black fatigues had just undone our restraints, when they heard someone on the stairs. The men said they would check on things, and then they could get us safely out of here. Why would they want us?"

"Don't have time for this," Ollie said while looking up at the ceiling nervously. "Parking garage?" The gunfire was no longer just coming from below them.

"Yeah. Let's go," Zander said as he shouldered Grace again. The newcomers took up station behind him but in front of the Romanelli.

"Move!" Ollie bellowed.

The small party ran back to the stairs and down the remaining flight to the ground-level concrete apron in full flight. There were two clearly labeled doors, one leading to the offices and labs. The noise of a fiercely contested battle was obvious even from this side of that metal door. The sergeant bobbed his head at the door, and Romanelli nodded in reply.

"Stay here," Ollie said and disappeared through the door marked —Parking Garage. In no time, he returned and said, "The emergency lighting down here is for shit. It looks clear, but I wouldn't bet my paycheck on it. There were no intruders, but there were no guardsmen either. Can do a more thorough recon, but it's gonna take time."

A fresh burst of gunfire seemed to emanate from the other side of the door to the first floor, and Mack spoke up. "Nowhere in this damn place is safe; we should go now."

As Zander considered the options, the golden woman's warning came to mind. He said, "We stay together then. Let's find the first appropriate vehicle and get the hell out of here."

Murmurs of agreement and a possible "Hooah!" followed his suggestion. The parking garage looked like most others: five long lines of cars that radiated out from the elevator banks and their stairwell door.

Based on the map he had seen earlier, Zander knew there were other elevators and stairs that led to other directional points of the compass below the building. But for now, he had to strain to see beyond the first couple of cars. Ollie steered them to the far right, putting them in the row furthest from the exit.

As they followed the wall, the battery-powered emergency lights at the stairs faded into oblivion. Intermittent flood lights running at quarter power broke the darkness.

While passing one pool of illumination, Mack gasped and stopped. Pointing at a nearby building support pillar, he whispered, "Oh my God."

The small group turned as one and looked to where the man pointed. Even in this meager brightness, it was easy to see: some box was affixed to the concrete column. Only a hermit, who had never watched a movie in his life, would not know what he was staring at. But if Zander wanted to rent a shack in Montana and hide his head, Ollie would have none of it.

"Holy shit. If they are using that much C-4, they don't want to damage the building. This place could be a moon crater at any time. *Vamanos!*" he said as he resumed his search for a vehicle.

Ice ran down Zander's spine, and his legs refused to budge until he saw he was being left behind. As he made his way among the cars, the unnerving warning returned to him unbidden. Mistakenly, he thought they would be safe if they could avoid the soldiers attacking the building. Now he knew the lie for what it was: their existence could end any second with a gunshot *or* the push of a button.

Panic would have overwhelmed him if not for the fact that he was pretty sure one of his 'friends' was important enough for the enemy troops to effect a rescue before vaporizing the building. But what would happen if their foe had to abort the attempt?

A feeling of déjà vu came over Zander as the earlier golden-haired woman's vision overlapped with what he saw now. Coincidentally, Ollie decided he had found their ride: a black government suburban. The ponderous FBI transport was parked facing out and could easily seat their whole party. Staying low, Ollie hugged the front bumper while scanning the area. When Ollie thought everything was clear, he motioned Romanelli to check the vehicle. The private opened the door and located the keys in no time.

Holding them before his face, he jingled them on the keyring. Romanelli spoke for the first and last time during their escape, "Looks like we finally found a bit of—" The bullet tore through his throat and shattered the window of a car behind him. Tinkling glass and the round's report sounded as Romanelli's triumphant smile melted into an expression of confusion. The dead man's legs gave out, and his body hit the garage floor like a bag of grain.

There was silence for a few seconds.

And then there was none.

Bullets began ricocheting off the concrete and cars around them. The time for stealth was over. Ollie stowed his pistol and removed the long gun from his back. He commenced returning fire in short bursts.

Bellowing over the weapon's noisy racquet, Ollie shouted, "Someone go get the keys! Into the car now!"

Brilliant muzzle flashes appeared from the left and right of their SUV. Mack opened the passenger-side rear door, and he motioned to Zander to give him Grace's inert body. Zander ducked his shoulder so he could have her limp body fall forward into Mack's waiting arms.

As Mack transferred her to the back bench seat, Zander wasted no time shimmying across the middle cushion to Romanelli's side of the vehicle. Once there, he opened the door and sank to their wounded guardian's side. The soldier's staring eyes, and lack of a pulse told Zander everything he needed to know. Closing Romanelli's eyes, Zander hoped the man would find peace in the hereafter. After a quick scan, he found the PFC's forsaken gun and the keys. In the meantime, Rohit and Ben crawled through the door Zander had just exited and closed it.

The tinted windows made it difficult to see inside, but it looked like they had both ducked their heads down. Bullets were still flying, but Ollie's cover fire had kept them safe so far.

"Let's go, Ollie! Got the keys," Zander screamed. "Want me to drive?"

"No offense, Doc; I got this," Ollie yelled over the gunfire. "Get in the passenger seat. I might need a co-pilot!" Doing his best crab scuttle around the back of the vehicle, Zander opened the door. Hidden from view just ahead of him, Ollie asked, "Doc, can you shoot that thing?"

"Point and shoot, right?"

"Something like that. Cover me!"

Trying to use the door for protection, Zander began shooting the handgun in the direction of the enemy fire. Meanwhile, with surprising grace, Ollie launched across the front of the SUV, opened the driver's door, and threw himself into the seat. Zander seriously doubted his gunfire was even within a zip code of their attackers. Still, if he were to be brutally honest, he was ecstatic to maintain possession of the heavy gun. The recoil was insane.

The huge SUV's motor roared to glorious life, and Ollie commanded, "Get in now!"

Not needing to be told twice, Zander dove for his seat and shut the door. As he desperately tried to belt himself in, the vehicle surged forward like a space shuttle on launch day. Tires squealing, Ollie narrowly missed the van before them as he completed his turn and gunned it.

Even with the element of surprise, the gunman in their way still had time to dive in between parked cars to avoid being run down. But that terrorist was the least of their worries. They had to make three hard turns at high speed to escape their death trap, and Ollie was pushing the vehicle well beyond factory specs. The Suburban's tires squealed and smoked, but amazingly, it stayed upright as it bulled through the tight quarters of the garage. In a moment of surreal amazement, Zander mused, *This guy has a future in stunt driving—if we make it out of this alive.*

Of course, as soon as he dared believe they were home free, reality reared its ugly head. The well-muscled man literally stood on the Suburban's brake pedal to stop in time. The abrupt breaking maneuver brought angry curses from the back of the vehicle, and Zander hit his head on the dashboard. When his vision cleared, his heart sank. Instead of a path to freedom, they stared at a military half-track with at least half a dozen armed men waiting for them.

"Come out with your hands up!" one of the black-garbed men ordered.

*21 minutes earlier in an unmarked panel van parked in front of Horizons Pharmaceutical.*

In the best of times, Greg Mundst was not a patient person, and today wasn't even close to fine or dandy. They had sat in this van for the past nerve-wracking hour as they waited for the guards to be taken out, bombs placed, and the other team getting into place. Theirs was the most exposed part of the plan, so it had been decided they were to get there early and hunker down. So, while their comrades risked their lives and discovery, Greg and his team sat. But he was not still. Pent-up energy needs its escape, which happened to involve, for the moment, lifting his heels and bouncing his knees up and down rapidly.

It was unprofessional but dark, and his men could bite him if they didn't like it. After a few minutes, his fidgeting even annoyed him, so he placed a calming, firm hand on each knee and tried refocusing on their mission. The plan was simple—it had to be. Rescue Doc and demo Horizons.

The *Gaia's Children* strike forces were given five days to create a strategy integrating Alpha and Beta teams, drilling, and procuring all required equipment. If that wasn't a tall enough order already for his limited personnel, it was vital no one could leave the campus alive. So, they needed to assign guards to every exit before the charges went off.

Other cells were in transit to their location, but they couldn't wait for reinforcement. The directions Doc had given them gave no wiggle room. They were to begin the raid if he didn't make his regular twice-a-day check-in or if they learned the antidote was in production. The last call from Doc was expected six hours ago. Hence his impatient vigil in a van, waiting for a-go from Violet.

The GC teams decided a three-pronged attack would best accomplish the mission's parameters. Violet's Alpha team would split in two—each squad would be responsible for placing munitions under both Horizons' towers and then creating a blockade for each of the underground garages. This was the mission's most important aspect because Doc insisted that both buildings and everyone inside had to be destroyed. The last component of the attack would also be its trickiest.

It had been decided that Greg's team would blow the campus' electrical transformers, use shaped charges to gain access to their two entry points, and then 'hoof it' to the basement of the building and detonate charges around the generators, security system, and the com controls. Once they had achieved these objectives, they would split into smaller teams. The biggest—Greg's—would attempt to be big and loud to draw as much of the National Guardsmen's attention as possible.

Meanwhile, a two-man team was to stealthily 'acquire' intel about Craig's whereabouts and communicate their findings to Greg's group. The duo would try to extract the doctor, but if they couldn't, most of Greg's party would abandon their engagement with the guardsmen and join them. Bravo team's sole objective was to get Doc out and ensure no one escaped from the three doors not involved in the attack.

So, six of his badly needed team were assigned to babysit each door. No one inside should be able to escape. At least, that was the plan. Even with the element of surprise, at a minimum, dozens of things could cause the plan to go sideways in the next few minutes. Their enemy had over 100 soldiers in there, and even though most were essentially reservists, many were combat veterans.

Their enemy possessed a 5:1 troop advantage and knew the battlefield better. So, they needed to create a plan to meet all their objectives with minimal casualties. *Luckily, we don't have to hold the building for any length of time or kill all the soldiers here.* They knew that blowing the doors with surface charges was overkill. This was not a military installation; they could've easily bypassed the locks with a set of picks or a few whacks with a sledgehammer. But those methods didn't affect troops psychologically like an explosion— shock and awe, baby.

*Ask the Iraqis about that one,* Greg chuckled to himself. Between the surprise and the blast, most people's—no matter how sophisticated or battle-tested—first reactions are fear and freezing: primal human responses. Next, take out the lights. Yes, they probably have night vision goggles, but the dark will create confusion and play further on their fears. The coup de grace of the plan was cutting the defense-coordinating com system for the building and setting up a signal jammer.

Each of the enemy's soldiers working independently was far less effective than 100 with direct supervision. These measures should compensate for their numerical disadvantage, but then a more sober thought assailed him. *What if this battle plan is doomed from the start, and I die? It would take so little for this op to go south—one alert trooper seeing their early staging could ruin their whole element of surprise, a squad of soldiers diligently guarding the vulnerable back-up generators and com system, or someone could* tip them off and suddenly we are walking into an ambush.

The headset and mic headgear they all wore clicked on, and Greg's pre-battle jitters ended abruptly when he heard Violet's voice scream, "Go, go, go! All teams move out!"

The door to the van was opened, and their boots were on the ground as she finished her announcement. Wearing all black, including flak jackets and face paint, the soldiers made for the pharmaceutical building. After a few feet, four of his team peeled off and headed to the doors they would breach; they would set their charges and wait for Greg's group to achieve their separate objective—the transformer's cage.

There was a six-foot security fence surrounding the enclosure in the NW corner of the campus. Donna, his executive, made short work of the chains binding the door closed. It was then time for Jamie, his munitions expert, to place two loaf-of-bread-sized boxes on the west and east sides of the structure. The two groups dealing with the doors reported on their com channel: ready.

Switching to Violet's command channel, Greg whispered into his mic, "Team 2, packages are set to be delivered."

"Acknowledged," was the feminine terse reply. "Wait, one."

Greg made a move-out hand signal, and the team took off at an easy sprint to the west of the north door of the building, rejoining the door munitions teams.

"Begin phase two," Violet said on the command frequency.

Switching to his squad's channel, Greg said, "Brace yourselves, Bravo. Blow it now, Jamie."

The man pushed four separate buttons on the black box before them, and all the bombs went off in succession. After the near darkness and quiet of the last few minutes, the sound and light still threatened to overwhelm Greg's senses. Flames fifteen feet high rose above the transformers, and they combined with the blue arks of electricity. The building lights overhead, and the surrounding lamp posts dimmed and went out totally.

"Go! Go! Go!" Greg unnecessarily encouraged his troops over the squad channel.

Through the ragged wreckage of the door, they ran—down the hall to the nearest stairs and on to their destination. The other part of his team used a separate stairwell; with luck, they would reach their objective together. *At least we have a little redundancy,* he thought grimly as they advanced on the backup generators.

A roar from up ahead confirmed the backup diesel engines were nearby and coming online. The lights flickered around them, which was fortunate because they almost blundered into a couple of startled guardsmen. His point man—Eduardo—dispatched them with a short burst from his AK. Pausing long enough to make sure they were both dead, he led them to the generator's door and peppered it with bullets until the lock gave way.

The headset crackled, "GC2 command. Tango team, the package is in Room 214."

"Copy that. Almost at our next destination," Greg replied as Eduardo kicked open the door.

If someone was inside, they knew the squad was out there, so there was no use being subtle. As it was, there was no one in the room.

"It's all you, Jamie," Greg said. The diminutive man took two more bombs from his backpack, placed them beneath each giant generator, and gave Greg a thumbs-up signal.

"Let's go," their leader said. In seconds, the small band was pounding down the corridor.

The com snapped again, "GC2 command, Xray team, we have encountered resistance just short of the stairwell: about a dozen enemy troops pinning us down. Copy?" Greg could hear gunfire up ahead and an echo of it through his earpiece.

"Xray, GC2 command. Jerome, hang tight," Greg said. "We're moving to your position from below. We'll blow the generators before we engage. Have your night goggles ready, but wait for my signal. With any luck, we can catch them in a crossfire. Over."

"Affirmative GC2," came Jerome's steady reply over the continued gunfire.

Arriving at the stairwell, Greg could hear the metallic reports of weapons clearly from the other side of the door, and he rekeyed the command channel and reported. "GC1 command—GC2 command —ready for lights out."

"GC2; GC1 command—you're given the green light. Blow 'em!"

Greg switched to the all-call channel, made eye contact with his munitions man, and announced, "Activate goggles in 5...4...3...2...1."

Jamie pushed the button when Greg had gotten to 2. The blast behind them was more deafening within the closed spaces of a building than it was outside. The compression hit his chest like a hammer, and the heat wave from the explosion was. . . uncomfortable.

His men donned their night vision goggles as Greg contacted the other team, "GC Xray; GC2 command, give us 10 seconds. Watch for our fire."

"Understood GC2."

Giving Eduardo a thumbs-up signal, the point man pounded up the steps like a madman, and his comrades stayed in his wake. They swarmed through the door, some rolling across the floor and others acting like limpets on the walls, all spraying gunfire at the surprised guardsmen before them. It was all too much for the besieged defenders—between the massive explosions, the unexpected darkness, and suddenly finding themselves caught in a crossfire. They were overwhelmed. Both pincers of the GC attack moved forward in a rush. The slaughter was over in less than a minute.

As Bravo team checked the soldiers at their feet, Jamie said, "Poor bastards don't even have night goggles around their necks. No wonder they couldn't hit us. Looks like we nailed 14 of them."

"This isn't a contest. We get the package, and we get out. If we can do that without killing any more people or being killed, I will have fewer nightmares when this is over," Greg barked as bile rose in his throat at the smell of death. "Okay. Let's head up the stairs to the second—"

A roar swallowed his voice and then all semblance of thought with it. Before he could hope to make any sense of what was happening around him, a sudden, sunlight-bright light seared his eyes.

When Greg finally regained awareness, he had no idea how much time had passed. All he knew was that his disorientation was made worse because he could not see. He waved his hand in front of his face to test his vision, but his hand collided with the now useless night goggles.

Throwing them to the floor in disgust, Greg tried to see anything. Panic hit him. If he were blind, he would have no chance of escape. As he turned his head, he could perceive the dim glow of a distant emergency light. His relief was intense, but then he concentrated on his other senses.

Everything was muffled, and the ringing in his ears felt like he had attended a weeklong Metallica concert. When he tried to shout, all he felt were the vibrations of his vocal cords. As his thoughts started to clear, he was pretty sure someone tossed a flashbang grenade their way, but his biggest priority was to get away from whoever responded to his GC troop's invasion.

Bending down, Greg tried to use touch to identify his troops and help them out of the hallway. Just then, something hit him in the chest and caused him to lurch to the side. The corridor before him might as well be a void, but he could barely make out what seemed like muzzle flares. There was still no sound he could hear besides the ringing, but he didn't need to hear the incoming bullets to think falling to the floor and rolling against a wall was the smart choice.

Tapping the mic button to switch to the command channel, Greg shouted, "GC1 command, we finished off the first wave of enemy, but we have been incapacitated by a flashbang grenade and are taking fire from the reinforcements. I'm not sure who is left from my team. Over."

If there was a reply, he couldn't hear it. It was galling to admit the Guard had bested them, but his commander needed to know what happened to them. Blindly searching the floor, Greg found an assault weapon and began firing at his attackers in short bursts. There was no way he could effectively aim; he was hoping to keep them from closing on his position and massacring his men before they could get their bearings and try to complete the mission.

Like a blanket being lifted, Greg could now barely make out Violet shouting over the team channel, "Anyone left in GC2 should head to the stairs and accomplish your final objective. Get the package! Do it now!"

More guardsmen must be reinforcing their position because the rate of gunfire pouring down the hall was awe-inspiring. Any hopes of staving off this assault, even for a minute, were abandoned, and Greg crawled in panic the short distance back to the stairwell door. As he opened the door, searing pain lanced through his left arm and shoulder, and the kinetic energy spun him about so violently that he lost his balance and crashed to the ground before the door.

A prone teammate just inside the stairwell dragged him along the floor into the alcove. Thankfully, by his good arm. The enemies' bullets continued to pelt the steel door with a staccato beat while they crawled to relative safety behind the concrete wall adjacent to the door. The battery-powered light above the alcove provided enough dismal illumination that Greg could see his rescuer, Jerome.

"Where did you get hit?" Jerome asked as he felt Greg's torso, trying to find the wound.

"Left shoulder, arm, not sure if anywhere else." Nausea crashed into him for a second time, and he was losing touch with his surroundings. The wall behind him was probably the only reason he hadn't slumped to the ground yet.

"Hold on, Greg," Jerome probed the limb and quickly, but roughly, found the hole, which elicited a piercing scream from his patient. "Sorry about that, buddy," he said as he removed his belt and cinched it viciously above the wound. The blood flow slowed. "Can you move?" Jerome asked, "GI Joe is gonna be coming through the door pretty quick, and we don't want to—"

The door suddenly moved, Greg grabbed a .45 from his shoulder rig, and Jerome started to raise his AR-15 toward the intruder.

"Don't shoot! It's Donna," the woman screamed in desperation. Both men exhaled and lowered their weapons. After briefly scanning the scene, she asked with concern, "What happened to you?"

"Got shot." Greg tried to play it off by lifting his left arm for effect but nearly passed out from the show of bravado.

"Don't think anyone else's out there; we gotta go," Donna said.

But as Greg strove to reach his feet, his balance failed him, and he fell in a heap. The others each grabbed him about the waist and lifted him, moving his arms over their shoulders.

"Get out of here," he spit in frustration with himself, "I'll only slow you down, and like you said, they'll come through the door any second."

"Shut up," Donna said. "We don't leave behind our own. Now help us out a little, okay?" Winking at him, both his friends began pushing and pulling him up the stairs.

There was still a good amount of gunfire coming from the hallway behind them, but apparently, some of their team either couldn't hear the command to move out or were injured enough they couldn't disengage. By force of will they made it to the second-floor landing, and then onto Room 214.

Three dead government lackeys littered the floor, but there was no Doc. After a quick scan of the area, they found the rest of their team: Akiro's face was gone, and Logan's face was purple from asphyxiation. Whoever did this must have taken Greg's mark.

Keying the command channel again, Greg said, "Violet, Doc is gone, and his rescuers are dead." As FUBAR as the situation was, Greg figured using some coy code would mean nothing. "It looks like someone must have rescued him," he added ironically. "My guess is they'll try to escape through you."

"What is your status?" she asked.

"Big ol' hole in my arm. Not what you would call top fighting trim, but I have two of my team with me, though. They are in better shape than me. What are your orders?"

"Don't want anyone to get past me," Violet said, "if I go searching for them. I will maintain my troops at the parking entrance. Get down to the garage and put a little pressure on them. Be careful, though; I don't want Doc to accidentally get winged or dead. Beat the bushes, and we will take care of the rest."

"Understood. Heading down now. Good hunting," Greg said with more energy than he felt.

His two compatriots gave him a thumbs up and resumed their position on both sides of him as they descended. Fortunately, going down the stairs was much easier than going up, but it was still excruciating. Every jostling step felt like micro-explosions going off within his now-asleep arm. Jerome and Donna set him down in sight of the blockade; he would be useless in a fire fight, as he could barely stay conscious. Only two of his GC troops had made it this far. *One hell of a mess you made.*

"Go," he instructed as he drifted into the darkness.

The killers went in search of their prey.

*Current time — Government Escalade.*

"What do you think, Sergeant?" Zander asked, feeling totally out of his element.

"Not going to lie, sir. Not sure why they aren't firing at us. What would they gain in having a standoff with us?"

"Maybe," Zander said as the possibilities spun out before him. "They somehow have figured out that we have their guy with us. Attacking us might kill him. But I bet those people out there probably won't allow us to stall very long, especially if they know there must be a military response quickly converging on their position."

Even as Zander said this, the gunmen began moving toward the vehicle.

"Problem is, Doc, that thing," Ollie said, pointing at the half-track blocking their path, "probably outweighs us 2:1, so if we try to ram it, it will likely destroy the engine on this beast. We'll get whiplash, and they will take us anyway."

"So, we seem to agree, Ollie, 'damned if you do, damned if you don't.'" Zander tried to keep the lunatic smile off his face as he formally asked, "Sergeant, as our sole military liaison, which course of action would you counsel?"

The big man's feral grin was infectious, and he replied in kind, "I would advise that we use the laws of physics to rearrange their roadblock and hope we get lucky."

"Mack," Zander shouted to the back of the big SUV, "do you concur with the sergeant's recommendation?"

Insanity or bravado was in the air because Mack screamed in his best William Shatner imitation, "Scotty, bring the engines up to full ramming speed!"

Even for Zander, this was over-the-top, and yet who was he to squash a few seconds of levity before their likely deaths? *So, if you can't fight them,* Zander thought. *Join them.* "I'm surrounded by nerds." he said in mock horror. "Sergeant, I believe our mission commander just gave you a direct order."

"Aye, aye, sir," Ollie said with obvious glee. The gunmen were almost up to the front of the vehicle now, and Ollie yelled, "Seat belts on! This is going to be bumpy!"

With absolutely no warning, the Escalade accelerated madly forward. It was only in this moment that Zander realized Grace wasn't restrained by a seat belt. Moments ago, their bravado seemed like some cheesy Western gunfight to the death. His heart shrieked at the thought of her body being catapulted through the windshield and beyond on their impact with the military truck.

Every fiber of his being cried out at this last indignity, which almost transcended words, but he still screamed anyway, *"Graaaace!"*

The gap between the two vehicles shrank at an incredible rate, and Zander instinctually lifted his hand as if to ward off the inevitable impact between the two.

No one knew what happened next. The military truck was there one second, and then a massive gout of flame and force hit it. In less than a breath, the half-track was tossed 20 feet—up and away—from the garage egress like it was a feather. As it tumbled on its axis, the chassis transformed into a molten comet.

If Ollie was surprised by a four-ton military vehicle being thrown around like a child's Tonka truck or men suddenly bursting into flames, he didn't show it. With consummate skill, he 'drifted' the giant SUV as they left the campus thoroughfare and joined North Willamette Blvd.

Zander took a moment to glance in the rear-view mirror to make some sense of the barricade's demise, but he could see little besides a dozen black-clad people running around, waving their arms, and trying to put out the unquenchable flames.

Chuckling with glee, Ollie must have checked his mirror, too, because he said, "Don't they know they should stop, drop, and roll."

It bothered Zander more than a little that Ollie found comedy in these gruesome, excruciating deaths. He was a doctor who had spent most of his life trying to save people. Life was precious to him.

But how could he judge this soldier? He could only imagine what hell Ollie had to traipse through in the Middle East. If he had been through the same, might he also have such a black sense of humor? Besides, if those terrorists had survived, they would have happily killed their small party and allowed the virus to progress unchecked. The road was clear, and in no time, Ollie had greatly exceeded the local speed limit.

"What the hell happened back there?" Someone in the back-seat asked.

Even though he literally had a front-row seat, Zander was not sure how they were driving down this street unscathed. All he knew for certain was he wanted to save them all. As he raised his hands before himself in wonderment, Ollie gave him the briefest of appraising looks before refocusing all his energy on keeping the ever-accelerating Escalade on the road.

The survivors made it exactly four blocks from the pharmaceutical campus before they felt an explosive blast pick up the back end of their vehicle and drop it again. The roar came next and sounded like some great beast tearing at the sky. Checking the rear-view mirror a second time, Zander could see a colossal mushroom cloud expand and rise skyward. He was not a munitions expert but would guess nothing was left of the Horizons' complex except a crater. The reality of it made his stomach clench; the Horizons' staff, CDC personnel, and National Guardsmen—were gone.

Also, a tremendous tragedy, antidote production lines and the chemicals needed—were gone.

No one in the vehicle spoke. As if they read each other's minds, Zander and Ollie made eye contact and tacitly understood. One of the two men in their backseat just tried his damnedest to doom mankind and kill *them*.

The sergeant returned to his driving, but Zander examined his hands again. It was weird; they didn't appear any different from when they had 10 minutes ago, but something had changed. There were still no words to explain what was altered inside of him; he just knew he was different.

For the first time in his life, Zander felt like he had control over his fate, and with that feeling of power, he silently declared to the traitor behind him, *You have much to pay for.*

# Chapter 34



*July 10, Thursday — 12:50 am —*
*Portland, Oregon*

The adrenaline continued to course through Mack's veins unbidden. It would subside soon, and then he would crash hard. As he glanced about the SUV's cabin, he was amazed they were functioning at all. He had only been at it for less than a week and felt like hell.

But looking at the back of Zander's head, he understood that others had been through much more. Almost no sleep, insane stress, and a medical puzzle beyond unfathomable were the *rigors de jour.* And if that were not enough, almost half of the party was in the final stages of the deadly virus, and the other part had not fully recovered from the insidious pathogen. But deep down, Mack knew all his worry only served to mask what he desperately didn't want to face: he would soon succumb to the coma and most likely would degenerate into a mindless animal. That dark thought caused him to glance down.

Originally, he had lain Grace on the bench seat to his side, but after a few violent vehicle gyrations, which had nearly thrown her limp form to the floor or, even worse, into a bench support below, he had clasped her to him like a babe.

There was still no suitable way to put her into a seat belt, so he continued to hold her, head cradled in the crook of his arm. He dared not think what would happen if she awoke consumed with the virus, but he decided at this moment he would suffer the consequences if it happened.

Shaking his head, Mack still couldn't process how they got past the military vehicle. One second, they were going out in a delirious blaze of glory. The next, four tons of roadblock was a burning wreckage thrown about like it was so much tissue paper. The whole incident defied reality, but he wouldn't question a solid mark in the win column at this stage in the game. But even if he didn't understand everything, he had one last duty to fulfill before he could descend into the inevitable darkness.

"Um, guys!" Mack shouted above the road noise in the Escalade. "We need to pull over so I can make a phone call to the President ASAP."

Turning around in his seat, Zander said, "Not sure if we are being followed because of all the surface traffic here. If we stop and get ambushed, all this might be for naught. Can you make it as we drive?"

The point was decent, but Mack had some valid concerns, too. "I can, but is it wise?" He still couldn't believe how naïve the man could be about one of the men behind Zander, even after all they had been through. Without another word, he nodded his head toward Ben and Rohit.

The country doctor's face fell, and he said, "Well, if you call them and they want to risk us getting bushwhacked to have a secure conference, then they can tell you."

Exasperated with Zander's *laissez-faire* civilian attitude toward security but unsure what other option was available, Mack shrugged and hit the priority code that gave him access to the President.

Two rings were all it took. "Mr. President," he said before something could be said, which might compromise their plans, "I would like to put you on speakerphone so you can talk with Dr. Parks, Dr. Mayette, Dr. Tamboli, and me. Let me remind you that one of these men is a domestic terrorist, but we are concerned with our security if we stop. What would you have us do, sir?"

The President paused momentarily and then said, "Understood. Give me an overall report now, and we can chat later about more sensitive matters when we have privacy."

"Wait one, sir," Mack said and then spoke to Ollie, "Sergeant, would you please see if we can connect to the sound system?"

In seconds, they had made a Bluetooth connection.

"Ready, Mr. President," Mack said.

"Gentlemen," The President began, "it is *damn* great to hear from you! There has been scant intel about what happened at the lab. All we knew was there was an attack on Horizons. The Guardsmen's commander said they were under siege, but we lost the signal before we could get any particulars. Local officials reported an area explosion, and we feared the worst."

"Mr. President, this is Dr. Parks. Many para-military assailants attacked the lab. There was barely enough time for us to escape. While escaping, we saw enough C-4 to blow up the whole block."

"Glad you all made it out safely. Obviously, we will know more as emergency crews report back to us. My thoughts and prayers go out to the families in that lab, but I must be calloused and ask you an important question. Do you have all your virus blocker notes with you?"

"This is Dr. Mack, sir. Umm, Mr. President, why would you be so concerned that we have all our research with us?" Mack said in confusion. "The data was available to everyone on the web and was backed up on NSA hardware."

"The key word Dr. Mack was '*was*,'" the President's answer was short and clipped. "The strike on the Horizons' campus was not the only one of the day." He let that sink in for a moment. "Our research servers were the target of a sophisticated and devastating hacker attack. Ironically," his tone was dust dry, "a very nasty software virus initially took out the files on our server. Then, a computer worm went out to our medical science partners and infected their networks. Not all our data is lost, but enough to be severely handicapped. *Soooo,*" he drew out the word for a heartbeat, "do you have the formula with you or not?"

"Most of it, Mr. President," Zander said. "I have my computer, which contains all of my data and most of the coordinating research Dr. Wu and I did together."

"Wonderful news!" the President sounded like he could do a cartwheel. "Do we have enough to replicate your recipe for the blocker?"

"If we can get the Aussies to resend their spleen goosing formula," Zander said, "that would be a great start, but frankly, I only worked on parts of the formula. The other elements were on the worldwide net or Dr. Wu's machine. Losing the Horizons data is going to hurt us."

"Once again, I hate to sound cold," the President said quietly, "but Dr. Wu only has a 10 percent chance of survival?"

The expression on Zander's face said it all. "You are correct, sir; she is still in stage three, but we should know within the next 8-12 hours whether she is among the lucky few survivors or that she will literally try to kill us."

The President said, "Dr. Mack said Dr. Wu became a... friend during your close association. I'm sorry she has become another casualty of this thing. Let it comfort you that your work together can still save many lives. That and my family and I will pray for her recovery—and all of you."

"Thank you, sir," Zander said. "What do you want us to do now?"

"Well, we have most of the troops in place around Portland. The governor will declare martial law at a press conference within the hour. It kind of feels like we are trying to collect water with a sieve, but we can at least try to protect the innocent somewhat from the infected. So, you have less than 60 minutes to get out of the city limits and find a safe place to hole up. Are you in immediate danger?"

"Let me check with the driver, sir." Zander turned to Ollie and asked, "Sergeant, are we being followed?"

"Been watching since we left the campus, and damned if I can see a tail. If there is one, I can't see 'em. When we find somewhere to stop, we can double back and do some other evasive maneuvers to make doubly sure."

"Did you hear that, sir?" Zander said.

"Yes, I did, Dr. Parks. Dr. Mack," the President switched gears again, "touch base with me as soon as you reach your destination."

"Yes, sir," Mack said.

"Also, Dr. Mack, I want to make it very clear," the President paused to reinforce his point. "Under no circumstances will any person in your party try to use their phones to contact anyone. To do so will be considered a treasonable offense, punishable by summary execution. I expect to hear from you within the hour. Godspeed." The phone clicked.


*30 minutes later.*


After ending the call with the President, they decided to head south on I-5 to avoid the military siege of Portland. A few off-ramps later, they found a moderate-to high-priced hotel. It had two suites situated in a building separate from the hotel, near the pool. The rooms shared an adjoining door, and most importantly, they had doors and windows that gave direct access to the parking lot—an important consideration when moving their 'luggage' to the room.

In the lobby, Mack had joked with them about how he had an Uncle Sam credit card and knew how to use it. Everyone dutifully laughed, but their mood was one of confusion and fear. On the one hand, they were giddy with the knowledge that the hangman had come for them, and they had escaped him. On the other, between the traitor in their midst and the faceless soldiers who wiped out Horizons, they still felt a crosshair snugged between their shoulder blades.

Earlier, after numerous byzantine maneuvers, Ollie had assured them there was no tail, but that was little consolation considering an hour ago, they were supposedly safe as well. As they moved their few possessions into the rooms, Mack noticed more than one of his companions glancing over his shoulder as they left the relative safety of the SUV. There was no ambush, but they did have to worry about getting Dr. Wu's comatose form into their room. To say it would look bad if a group of men removed an unconscious, handcuffed woman from their black, mirrored vehicle and carried her into their room was a massive understatement.

Lucky for them, it was very late at night, and their choice of room location helped immensely. No other guests were the wiser. Mack held open the doors, Ollie and Zander carried Grace into a suite, and laid her on the master bedroom's king-sized bed.

As Zander walked from the room, Mack grabbed his arm and said, "We need to talk."

The sergeant acknowledged Mack's unspoken command and closed the door behind him. "Grace will be waking up within hours one way or another, and we need to be prepared for that. This mission is too important to have her kill us all because we have a soft spot for her."

The Zander's shoulders slumped slightly, but other than that, there was just a sense of resignation of the inevitable.

Finally, Zander broke the quiet, "I know; we should leave her restrained." More silence. "What is really troubling me is she made me promise—to anesthetize her if she becomes rabid after the coma. We assumed she would be at Horizons or a hospital somewhere, but not on the lamb, as it were. There are two doses of Ketamine in my computer bag. What happens if they run out? I can't afford to jeopardize the mission, but I don't know if I can give her a fatal double dose either." Zander looked like he was on the verge of breaking down. "How can I do that to her?"

"I know we haven't always seen eye to eye, but if I am still able I could..."

Zander grabbed Mack's arm and said, "I appreciate it. Really. But I must follow through with this."

"It's probably for the better. Not sure how much time I have left. But know that when I'm gone, the CDC won't be able to replace me in time. So, after my death, it will be up to you to coordinate the virus blocker's production. Can I count on you?"

"Hey, don't give up so quickly. If I can make it back, so can you. You have my word—I will do everything possible to finish this."

"Thanks, Zander. I will try, but we know 10 percent is not a good prognosis. One last thing." Mack made sure Zander was looking into his eyes. "I know you know this, but it must be said. Don't trust Rohit or Ben. If one or both are our saboteurs, your lives and the cure are in danger. At this point, I would love to tell you to tie them up and leave them behind, but if one is truly your friend, then I know that isn't an option. Do you think you can rely on Ollie?"

Thinking momentarily, Zander finally answered, "I think finding him was too random to be planned by our enemy."

"Agreed. Have him watch your back then," Mack said. "You don't have to tell him more than necessary, but tell him to stay on his toes with those two."

"As soon as we finish here, I will," Zander said.

"Good, then my last order as your doctor," Mack smirked at the joke, "after you speak with him, come back in here and deal with your grief." He raised his hands to forestall Zander's objections. "Whether it be for that wonderful woman there or for those you lost before." He shrugged. "The world needs your undivided attention. Take these last hours to say goodbye to Grace and others. If she survives, you will have only tried to get your emotional feet under you. Now go talk to Ollie; I need to contact the President again."

As Zander walked away from the man, he came to the terrible conclusion that he had misjudged Mack. Zander had seen him as a government lackey, a bureaucrat, a slave to rules, and someone who seemed to treat people as data rather than living, emotional beings. To be honest, this was all true, but it was also true that Zander had consigned him to that small box.

The advice Mack had just given him was every bit as insightful and heartfelt as he had ever received in his life. And because of that, Zander was ashamed. Here was a man trying his best to manage an impossible situation.

He would most likely die a continent away from his wife and children. He fervently hoped that Mack would make it. It would give Zander another chance to call the man—friend.

# Chapter 35



*July 10, Thursday — 2:10 am — Hilton
Grand Hotel Tigard, Oregon*

For what seemed to be the twentieth time in the past hour, Zander's eyes wandered to the nightstand, and he stared at the odious objects. Two clear syringes—with yellow Ketamine labels—sat before the room's clock. So innocuous, yet so *potentially* deadly. No good dwelling on that, he upbraided himself in the room's silence.

Even though he wanted to take Mack's advice and allow himself time to grieve his dead, sitting by her bed now felt too much like waiting for her to die. Arising from his seat, Zander began pacing the room nervously, when he noticed the open bathroom door.

*Five minutes later.*

The warm water sluiced over his neck and shoulders, and steam filled the tiny space. Tight muscles relaxed, and he started to feel his mood improve. But in a moment of inspiration, he knew that was not what he wanted. He grasped the smooth, silver handle and began to turn it to his left.

In increments, the water worked its way from rejuvenating to scalding. When he could bear no hotter; he turned around, put his head directly below the stream of water, and let it envelop his head and shoulders. The torrid waters tore away at the temporary barrier that he had erected so he could function the past few days. And in moments, that curtain shredded into millions of pieces and, just like his tears, swirled around the drain at his feet. Then disappearing.

Without witness or restraints, Zander's anguish crashed into him with surprising violence. What had once started as gentle tears became colossal wracking sobs. Zander had loved his sister beyond measure, but the hurt of her passing was an echo of what it once was. But now, the knife's edge pain of loss had returned manifold.

Crystal's death drew his remaining family closer. This bond remained particularly strong because he never searched for love beyond theirs. That and his friends and coworkers gave Zander all the love he needed. In the back of his mind, he knew his mother and father would precede him in death, but the suddenness and manner of their passing—shook him. But like most violent things in life—if energy is expended so explosively, it cannot last.

Just when Zander thought his chest was about to burst, the torrent of sorrow subsided to something more bearable. Zander found himself on his knees when he emerged from his miasma of grief. He rose and was about to turn off the shower when he decided to reduce the temperature to something more tolerable.

A bench was opposite the shower head, and he sat with his back to the wall. Closing his eyes, Zander allowed his breathing to slow, and he began to visit his dead. His grief in abeyance; he could scan their smiling faces, Lise, Abby, Wesley, Silvia, Pete, Roxy, even Crystal, moving before him like a video montage each seeming to offer him their love. For one blessed period, there was peace.

* * *

It took every bit of willpower for Craig not to scream and punch something—or, even better—someone. Earlier, Zander and the

Sergeant had spoken in whispered tones at the table in the kitchen area, but it didn't take a genius to figure out why the two kept making pointed glances in his direction. Whatever! He was safe until they figured out who was behind the virus.

After Zander departed for Dr. Wu's room, the sergeant suggested they all adjourn to the other suite. Dr. Mack took the couch, leaving him with one of the two recliners. The other men were sleeping in minutes, but that damned military man stood a solitary watch behind them. Besides brewing a full pot of coffee, the soldier's only goal was to bore a hole through the back of Craig's skull with his eyes. *Fine with me,* Craig thought, *I'm a patient man.* He finally caught a break 50 minutes later.

The TV was still on. It was gratifying for him to see his virus at work, but the newscasters began repeating themselves ad nauseam within half an hour. While he watched a particularly gruesome segment, there was a soft thump; Craig glanced to the side, without moving his head, and observed Dr. Mack's hand had fallen to the floor. Either the man had fallen into a deeper sleep, or he had succumbed to the next stage of the virus. But what caught Craig's eye was a silver gleam just above the man's pants pocket. Craig's only outward reaction was a haughty sneer.

As he waited for his chance, it felt like a lifetime passed, but he knew, it had only been minutes. Coffee, a diuretic, did its work, and Craig's *prison guard* got up from his watch post at the table, examined the front room and its occupants, and hurried to the bathroom down the hall.

There was no time to waste.

Turning the recliner toward the sofa, Craig lunged at the couch and grabbed the phone from Dr. Mack's pocket. As he suspected, the man reacted not at all. In no time, he was back in his chair and again turned toward the television. There was doubt in his mind that this was his only chance to fix this mess satisfactorily.

He was no hero, but if he didn't contact the GC now, he might never extricate himself from this band before he was discovered. The phone obediently lit when he pushed on the screen, and he thanked the gods above for giving Mack the foresight to leave his mobile unlocked so Zander could use it.

There was no time to attempt a call, so he texted the motel's address and room number to a prearranged burner. As he hit send, the sound of the bathroom door opening and heavy steps in the hall caused his heart rate to skyrocket. Craig could not risk being caught with the device. At the last second, he backhandedly slid the phone toward the couch. The sergeant scanned the front room, let out a small *"humph,"* satisfied nothing went awry in his absence, and resumed his seat at the kitchen table.

Once again, Craig smiled. And waited.

* * *

After his rejuvenating shower, Zander returned to Grace's side and picked up where he left off with his lonely vigil. Time passed unheeded until Zander could feel his legs tingling from sitting too long, so he got out of his plush brown recliner.

The lonely solitude had become too much. Zander went in search of some company. When he entered the kitchen, he could see Ollie visibly tense. But after seeing there was no threat, Ollie settled down and nodded to Zander. Bobbing an acknowledgment back, Zander continued to the living room area and found Mack passed out on the couch in front of the massive TV. Ben turned toward him, and Zander smiled at his friend. Ben swung the chair back around without returning the greeting. Shrugging, Zander shuffled into the room and noticed Mack's arm hanging over the side of the sofa.

The position of Mack's shoulders appeared awkward. Was it his time? Zander gently shook the CDC director but to no avail. With sadness in his heart, he moved Mack's lifeless limb, so it lay beside his body.

At that moment, Zander noticed a silver, metallic shape peeping out from below the couch. Reaching down, he grabbed what he now recognized was Mack's phone, and looked around the room nervously.

Snores were still coming from Rohit's direction, and Ben appeared oblivious to Zander's scrutiny. The mobile must have slipped out of the CDC director's pants when the man fell into his coma minutes after their talk. Another weary burden crushed Zander further, and he slid the phone into his pocket. The world dimmed again as companions about him continued to leave, and his earlier peace evaporated and turned to ashes.

Zander returned to the kitchen table, sat next to Ollie, and struck up a conversation with the powerful man, "We never had much of a chance to get acquainted with all the shooting, running, blowing up, and driving." Both chuckled, and then Zander held out his hand and asked, "Would you prefer I keep calling you Ollie, or would sergeant be more appropriate?"

"My name is Sergeant Oliver Jennison, sir. But honestly, Ollie is best."

"Private, I work for a living, so don't call me 'sir,'" Zander barked in his best drill sergeant mimicry. This time, Ollie brayed with gusto and something approximating a real laugh at that old military chestnut. "Seriously, I'm not in your chain of command, and I would prefer you call me Zander."

"Then, Zander it is." Ollie nodded toward the front room and said, "Nothing suspicious has happened all night, but they must know I'm watchin'. All three crashed soon after we settled down in this room, but Dr. Mayette woke a bit ago. Keeping to himself, though," Ollie said behind a large fist as he stifled a yawn.

"I can't tell you how much I appreciate you watching those two. Give me a few minutes to check on Gr—Dr. Wu, and then I will relieve you."

"Affirmative, *sirrrr*," Ollie said with a knowing smirk on his face.

Zander was going to say something but decided to wag his finger at the man and laughed instead. There was something about the man that reassured him in this situation's chaos.

Returning to Grace's room, Zander didn't notice any changes. She was still sleeping on her bed. He sat by her side and grabbed her wrist to check her vitals again. For the seemingly hundredth time, her skin was still somewhat clammy to the touch, but her heartbeat felt strong. Maybe it was Mack's moving onto the next stage or his emotions during his earlier solitary vigil, but he was reluctant to put her hand down. So, he used both hands to purportedly warm her fingers, but in reality, he knew he desperately needed to feel another human's touch.

Zander closed his eyes and was mid-sigh when he heard, "You do realize," a desert-dry feminine voice said in the room's silence, "that what you are doing is not considered to be proper medical bedside manner, right?"

Eyes bursting open, Zander studied her face, and nothing had changed. Maybe the imaginary voice was back. If it was, he was certain his sanity was dangerously close to the edge.

But as he started to doubt himself, she opened her eyes and gave him the most beatific, ornery grin he had ever seen. Time stood still as he stared at her—dumbfounded. Then, his mental gears finally slipped into place.

"You're alive!"

"Thank you for your expert diagnosis, doctor," Grace said with a smirk. "Are you finished checking my, um, pulse?"

Dropping her hand, Zander assumed a detached manor. "Ah, Dr. Wu, how nice to see you are not a mindless, hungry animal, who wants to kill me." But his straight face only lasted momentarily until he could no longer contain his elation at her survival. It was like he was given a reprieve, an eleventh-hour death row pardon. One important piece of his life clicked back into place. A welcome reversal of a recent terrible trend.

"Ahem," Grace said as she lifted her two shackled wrists, "if you're completely certain I'm of sound mind, would you be so good to take these off? For some reason, all my skin has been rubbed raw."

"Well," he said with a boyish, mischievous grin, "I'm not sure that would be prudent before I have a chance to run extensive tests. If I start now, I think I can decide within the next twelve hours or so."

"If you ever want to sleep with the certainty of waking again," Grace's smile was saccharine-sweet, "you will release me now."

"Though you appear crankier than your usual self, you seem hale enough. Let me go get the keys." Zander half-bowled to her and laughed with genuine laughter as he dashed out of the room.

Once he removed the handcuffs, he gave her a succinct rundown of what had occurred since she lost consciousness. Afterward, she handed him the shackles with a shudder, ushered him out of the room, and locked the door. Standing in the hallway outside her room, Zander considered going next door and putting the restraints on Mack but decided it could wait.

Everything in the adjoining suite was pretty much the same as before, except Rohit was now awake and gave Zander a small wave and a mumbled greeting.

On the vast flat screen, the Portland stations had switched to around-the-clock reporting—troop sightings, killings, and government updates—and the news reporters appeared increasingly frantic in their coverage of the metropolis.

Laying the cuffs on a side table in the kitchenette, Zander shouted, "Who's hungry?"

A hearty chorus of "I am" was all he heard, so he grabbed the room service menu and examined it. In no time, he ordered enough food to feed a high school staff *and* their students. Half an hour later, two heavily laden carts full of waffles, bacon, pancakes, biscuits and gravy, steak, and various fruits and vegetables, and two carafes of "Seattle's Best Coffee" arrived. The two waiters unloaded their bounty onto the kitchen table and left—after receiving a *very* generous tip courtesy of the CDC. Drawn by the wonderful aromas, Grace appeared in the suite doorway wearing a white, plush hotel robe, while she used a bath towel to dry her now clean, shiny, black hair.

"Oh my God, that smells so good. It feels like I haven't eaten in a week," she said as she snuck a piece of sourdough toast from one of the many dishes. The small party went about grabbing plates, silverware, and glasses from cupboards and drawers and arranging their places at the table. After everyone was seated, they all stared at one another, even though they were all starving.

Taking the initiative, Ollie bowed his head and said, "God, we thank you for our lives and these gifts. Amen."

There was an enthusiastic "amen" from everyone, and then all pretense that they weren't famished disappeared, and they all dug in. The conversation was sparse while they ate to their hearts' content, but Zander began to understand the soldier's way: eat when you have time. There will be time to talk soon, but first, bacon.

"Well, where do we go from here?" Zander initiated the discussion by ticking off points on the fingers of his right hand. We have some of our research, but not all of it. There are no Horizons' production facilities. There is martial law in Portland. The group that tried to stop us is probably still after us." He made specific eye contact with Ben and Rohit. "I open the table to discussion."

"I've been watching the news about what has been happening in Portland," Rohit said. "If it hasn't devolved into total chaos there yet, it soon will. Even if we could recreate our research in another lab in Portland, there is a good chance we wouldn't survive in the city long enough to distribute it."

"But we squander valuable time going somewhere else and then transporting it back. If we stay near the epicenter of this," Ben gestured arms wide, "then we can react much quicker. Time is of the essence; we can't afford to waste a second of it."

"Those are valid points, guys," Zander said while trying to remember that one of these men had a secret agenda.

"The President is bringing in soldiers from all over the country, but we just don't have enough boots on the ground to do what we are attempting," Ollie added. "If we could somehow bring in every grunt who could wield a gun, we would have 100,000 men and women to guard over 100 roads, highways, interstates, rivers, the ocean, and all the airports. Sounds impressive until we factor in those soldiers will be trying to coral two million people. It would be tough enough if these were ordinary civi's instead of amped-up virus victims. If they want to get through those blockades, they will. Wish I could tell you otherwise, but the President's move is a delaying tactic at best. Trust me; Portland will fall, and we would be crazy to return."

And there it was—in a few succinct words, their military liaison spelled out the gruesome reality facing Portland: two million people would be the victims of the virus. It would become a battlefield, a wasteland... a ghost town.

"If only we had the serum formula," Zander said, "I'm sure we could still save most of those people. The army could cordon off areas where we could inoculate people. It would keep the number of infected down to a manageable figure."

"Wait a minute," Grace said in confusion, "why don't we have the formula?"

Zander had forgotten to share the story of the hacker attack on the world network when he had debriefed her earlier.

Instead of dismay, she gave him a huge grin, "Give me your phone." Dialing a number, she listened momentarily and said, "This is Dr. Grace Wu from the Portland lab; I need to talk to Conrad immediately." The resulting silence was nerve-wracking, but finally, someone picked up her call, "Conrad, Grace. Yes, I know I'm not dead, but listen, I need to have your computer nerds check to see if our secure backup is intact. Yes, I can wait." Grace covered the phone's receiver with her hand and commented, "As you can imagine, what we don't announce to outsiders is that we make back-ups of our regional servers to our central server in San Francisco." Zander looked at Rohit and Ben and wished he could have stopped her from saying this in front of them. Unfortunately, there was no way he could have known about this until now.

"The labs do a burst of encrypted data," Grace explained, "once daily to the primary server. When the surge of data is done, they shut down the connection to the web. Each subsequent transmission is made to a new IP address, which only the company controllers know. With any luck, this worm will not be able to make it past our firewall."

"Everything is still there?" Grace asked to make certain. "You paranoid, security computer types are worth every penny! Would you be a dear and back that up onto an isolated hard disk for me? Thanks," she said as she hung up and handed the phone back to Zander. "*Voila,* one serum recipe."

Shaking his head in wonder, Zander took the mobile from her. He was about to call the President with the good news when he noticed a text message to an unlisted number. The only entry: the hotel's address and their room. With a puzzled expression Zander said, "What..."

Then, literally, the lights went out.

*** 

This wasn't the first time Ollie had been ambushed by an enemy, but he never got used to the gut punch: a buttload of adrenaline being dumped into his system in the space of a heartbeat. The only thing similar was when you are on a roller coaster heading up the first towering incline. . . then the bottom drops out on you, and your body is wrenched in all sorts of directions. Yeah, something like that. Fortunately, he was no rook. Even when he wasn't in a combat situation, Ollie would not sit with his back to a door or a window. Ever. Surprises get you dead. Which nearly happened earlier, and he was not a big fan of letting it happen again.

It was logical that the doctors were worried about serums and saving the world and all, but they weren't combat vets. Ollie had an itch between his shoulder blades, which wouldn't go away. There was just a sense he had that this war was far from over, and this meal was a short break before the next enemy salvo. From what little he saw, these GC nutjobs didn't seem like the type to just give up.

What he wouldn't have given for his body armor, but at least he had found a bag in the SUV's rear storage area. It turns out one of those feds was a fan of America having a fully armed militia. The bag held a Remington 870 shotgun with a shell holder, a Smith and Wesson AR-15, a Glock .45 handgun, and enough ammo to have an 'interesting' day. Not so coincidentally, that bag sat at his feet, under the table—open. Every weapon was checked and loaded.

His foresight was the only thing that kept the world from having a really 'bad' day—instead, it was merely awful.

The front door exploded inward, and an incoming figure in the entryway was outlined by the parking lot light behind him

As Ollie bent down to grab the shotgun, he shouted, "Get down! Now!"

He hated giving up his position, but unfortunately, his charges were a bunch of nerdy middle-aged doctors with no combat experience. The only thing that probably saved all their lives was that these jokers still wanted their guy alive. Otherwise, if they just wanted to kill them, it would have been safer and more straightforward to just spray the front of the suites with automatic weapon fire. But Ollie had counted on that, or he would have kept a better lookout on the parking lot.

In no time, he had the weapon pointed at the door and was firing. The concussion and muzzle flash were shocking in the nearly silent, dark room. His first target fell, and his second, as well, before the attackers knew what hit them. Subsequent raiders were much more cautious in their approach. They used cover and stayed lower than their foolhardier brethren.

Now that his element of surprise was over, Ollie entered a far more dangerous phase of the battle.

He didn't have clear targets without illumination behind them, so he might waste valuable ammo on something useless like a recliner or a doorpost. But if he conserved shells too much, they could gather, and bum-rush him. So, he continued to shoot at what he hoped were enemy troops. If one of the doctors was stupid enough to be anywhere but the floor, he couldn't check his fire. All too soon, the shotgun was empty.

Throwing it down in disgust, Ollie hefted the heavy gun bag over his shoulder, moved to take cover behind the kitchen island,

and grabbed the other rifle. Ollie fired short bursts of automatic gunfire at the door and front room, hoping to stymie their assault.

* * *

At first, Craig was exultant his troops had finally arrived. But his delight was soon replaced with raw fear. He had hit the deck without any need for prompting from the sergeant, and it was a good thing because the sergeant's mini cannon—or so it had seemed to him—had almost taken his head off.

How on earth had this man anticipated the attack and armed himself before his GC troops overwhelmed them all? Even from the floor in the dark, Craig could see the problem his people faced: the door was a choke point. They could not afford to wait until the police responded to this commotion, so they might have to risk returning fire. If that happened, then one Dr. Craig might end up being a casualty, and he wouldn't allow that. *Think.*

It was amazing how gunfire and possible death could focus one's thoughts immeasurably. An insane idea popped into his head, and before he could talk himself out of it, he began snake-crawling to the next-door room. The illumination from the room phone provided enough light to see his goal on the nightstand and grab it. In no time, he was back in the hellscape, which was lit by the sergeant's intermittent muzzle fire.

In no way did he want to be mistaken for the enemy, so he took the time to flank the Guardsman, and then approach him from behind. Removing the cap from the syringe, Craig closed the final two feet to Ollie, thrust the needle into his neck, and mashed the plunger with vigor. The soldier dropped his rifle and reached into his weapon's bag. He grabbed a handgun and tried to point it at Craig. Lucky for Craig, the powerful drug was already beginning to sap the big man's strength. Craig knocked the .45 out of Ollie's grip.

Calling out to his troops, Craig said, "Get in here; the gunman is down. And get the lights back on."

A minute later, the room was ablaze, and everyone in it was suddenly night blind. When Craig could see well enough, he picked up the .45 and smiled triumphantly.

It was finally time to come out of the shadows.

In the far background, three black-clad GC troopers stood among four or five of their dead brethren in the living room. Their guns were trained on the still-prone doctors, and he could see at least two more of his team in the parking lot. Acknowledging his followers with a nod, Craig made eye contact with Zander and savored the look on his face.

* * *

Since the Horizons tea poisoning, Zander knew his betrayer wasn't a low-level disgruntled tech but rather one of his oldest friends. But knowing had not prepared him for this. The man's face morphed into a mask of malevolence. If Zander had been standing, he would have taken a step back; so complete was his terror and amazement.

"Why, Ben?" was all he could croak out.

The ugly sneer appeared as if it were Ben's natural facial feature. "You can't know how long I have wanted to reveal everything to you. In fact, it has been a long two weeks, but I want you to know how laughable you all have been before I have the satisfaction of killing you."

After the Horizons attack, Zander knew someone wanted him dead, but with so many weapons pointed in his direction, the point was slammed home. The last thing he wanted to do in his waning moments was to listen to this traitor gloat, so he tensed, hoping to take Ben by surprise.

Something must have given him away because Ben said, "Ah, ah, ah. Don't be a hero, Zander; I would hate to see the little lady hurt." At that, Ben pointed his gun at Grace's chest.

Zander wanted it to be him if someone was going to get injured. Not her. So, he would wait. "Get on with it then. Why'd you join these goons?"

Ben's face grew hideous for the first time. "You are a fool; don't talk about things you know nothing about. These goons, as you put it, are worth ten of you; they are *Gaia's Children*. And I didn't go in with them. I was one of the founding members back when I was at the University of Washington." The anger seemed to dim a bit as he fell into what must have been familiar rhetoric for him.

"The GC started all those years ago because even then, we could see what was happening to our planet: corporations spewing their filth into the air, more and more cars and their carbon dioxide, nuclear power plants, and weapons built with no thought to the waste which takes thousands of years to become safe again, clear-cutting miles and miles of virgin forests with no thought to their delicate ecosystems, strip mining, dumping garbage in our oceans, 2-3 species going extinct per day, ozone layer depletion, and global warming.

"When I was young and idealistic, I used to believe humanity could change its ways if it only became aware of the danger around them. So, we put spikes in old-growth trees, sugar in logging truck gas tanks, sabotaged factories, protested nuclear plants, and such." Ben sneered. "What did all of that accomplish? Nothing. We were the fools then, thinking we could fix the system from within."

"If you were so disenchanted with everything, why did you come to work with me to cure cancer?" Zander wanted the answer to this maddening riddle.

"Like I said, I was a fool. Used to believe if humans had less pain and suffering in their lives, maybe they would care about anything except their selfish interests. So, I bought into your shiny dream, Zander. But I never gave up on trying to save Mother Earth.

"We are not your enemy," Zander said. He hoped to somehow find the man he thought he knew. "When have we or the lab done anything to damage our ecosystem? All we—all I wanted was to help people with Leukemia. I thought you did, too."

Ben seemed to consider Zander's points before saying, "I already told you that during my idealistic days, we wanted the same thing. It was . . ." Ben's mask fell away, and the hatred left his eyes. "It was so good at the start. It was you and me and Lise. You used to listen to my suggestions. We used to have wonderful skull sessions. Remember Zander? Even Lise didn't bring out your best ideas. That was me. Only me. I thought we would be partners. That we would run things together. And then you would always go back to her. No matter what I did, she was the one."

"Ben," Zander said, "I never knew you felt this way. You could've said something. We can still stop this virus and save millions of lives together."

Ben shook his head like a prize fighter after a punch. Anger replaced this show of vulnerability. "Why would I want to do that? We spent years creating the perfect disease. It spreads easily, and it promotes chaos, so there can't be an effort to contain it. We took your precious cure, and we will use it to exterminate most of the human population. The only souls left will be my Gaia's Children who've taken my vaccine. Everything is in motion now, this world is ending.

"Are you insane?" Rohit said with exasperation. "There are 7.5 billion people on the planet."

"Exactly," Ben said as if they were making the same point. "There are far too many humans for this Ecosystem to sustain, so we will remove her burden and give her a chance to regenerate."

"So, you're some Jim Jones cult wannabe?" Grace sneered with derision.

The backhand knocked Grace backward. The slap was as loud as any gunshot.

"You'll regret that," Zander said as he prepared his rush. There was no way he could outrun three bullets, but what other option was left?

Sirens were heard in the distance.

"How tiresome this has become; I thought you would at least listen and understand, but apparently, I gave you too much credit." Ben redirected the gun at Zander and pulled the trigger.

* * *

The scene before Grace a few seconds ago seemed so surreal: Ben was talking calmly with them, and then, the flare of the handgun, the concussive sound in the small room, and Zander's body being shoved back by the power of the large caliber bullet. But as astonishing as that all was, it was easier to explain than what she saw next: Zander's face contorted in fury, and a wave of force rippled outward from him. It knocked her against the wall, but she was relatively unharmed by the blast. The real target of his wrath was Ben and the other *Gaia's Children* in the room.

Like a child's pinwheel in a stiff breeze, Ben cartwheeled through the air and crashed through the big bay window to the left of the entry door. It appeared Ben was the lucky one, though, because all three of the GC troopers had been embedded in the far front room walls, their bodies at various wrong angles and very dead.

The sirens' volume strengthened as emergency vehicles approached. The two remaining GC helped Ben to his wobbly feet. A bright red slash ran diagonally across Ben's face, which was probably lacerated by the triple-paned window he had flown through.

Ben grabbed one trooper and screamed, "Don't worry about me. Kill them, and then join us." Ben and the other ran to the entranceway of the motel.

The first leaped to do his leader's bidding. He drew his weapon, entered the room, and pointed it at her chest. Staring up at her executioner, Grace's mind raced to come up with a way she could escape death. Nothing. Between her terror and the fact that she had just shaken off her coma an hour ago, all she could do was wait.

Suddenly, a figure screamed and hurled itself at the GC goon. But who was left? Then her brain finally engaged; Rohit had jumped into the scrum to save their lives: the two men were now on the ground, wrestling for the weapon. Embarrassed at her moment of indecision, she gave her own battle cry and leaped to aid Rohit.

It was lucky for them she had because as she got there, a single shot went off, and Rohit cried out in agony. Their assailant had almost wrested control of the gun from Rohit's weakening grip when she stamped on the GC's wrist. Bones audibly snapping like twigs.

The terrorist's cries joined the room's chorus of pain. The man was not cut out to be a martyr, though, because he was trying to move Rohit's limp form with his unbroken hand in order to escape. He would have made it too, if not for Grace's picking up the forgotten weapon and putting three slugs dead center mass of the fleeing man. The body painted a bright red stroke across the white door as it slumped to the floor.

Dropping the gun, Grace moved to Rohit's side and eased him from his side onto his back, her hand coming away slick with blood, but he was still alive.

"Don't worry about me," Rohit said in tremendous pain, but he tried to give her a brave face. "Check on Zander first."

"Okay, I will be back in a second," she said as she grabbed a small nearby seat cushion and placed it over the wound in his chest. The pale man resolutely put his hands over the pillow and grimaced at the torturous pain.

When she got to Zander's side, she was unsure if he was still alive. His skin was cold and clammy when she felt for a pulse. There was only the barest thrum below her fingers, but his eyes fluttered open, and he attempted to focus on her face. She might not be an ER doctor, but she knew this man had minutes, not hours, to live. And there was not a damn thing she could do to stop the massive flow of blood from the large caliber bullet's exit wound in his back. So, she did the only thing she could to give him comfort: she took his hands and held them.

Grace was startled by a weak chuckle, and she saw Zander's mischievous smile. How did he have the strength?

"Why, doctor, you do realize," he feebly mimicked her desert-dry feminine voice, "that isn't proper bedside manner?"

At that moment, she knew Zander needed to survive if they had any hopes of getting their blocker produced. That and just maybe there were the beginnings of something special. It was unfair: everything that took place in the past few days. It swept over her like a tidal wave, and she wept. Without thought, she kissed the back of his hand and wished with all her heart that he would live.

"Um, Grace, what are you doing?"

"What do you think I'm doing—" she started to reply tartly when she noticed her hands felt noticeably warmer.

Opening her eyes, Grace could see a soft, warm, yellow light emanating from her hands and enveloping Zander's prone form. The glow faltered, and pain returned to Zander's face. *What was I doing?* she thought. *I was desperately praying for him to live before it happened.*

Renewing her plea for him to stay with her, the warmth and luminosity around them reappeared.

It couldn't be happening, but it was. Somehow, she was healing him. Color returned to his cheeks, and his breathing became less labored. But how was she doing this? Then, her hands stopped glowing, and she suddenly felt weary, like she had run a marathon. Maybe she ran out of energy, or somehow, she knew Zander didn't need further mending.

Holding her breath, she lifted his shirt and gazed at a pink patch of skin where a bullet hole should have been. Her elation was cut short when she heard Rohit let out a painful cry behind them. How could she have forgotten her savior? She popped up and nearly fell; her legs refused to solidify below her. But she steadied herself by grabbing Zander's shoulder. She recovered quickly and found she had the strength to help Zander to his own wobbly feet.

* * *

For the second time in too few days, Zander marveled that he was not dead. This time, though, he had not slipped into death. With frightening clarity, he could see Ben's sneer and feel the bullet slam into his chest. The pain was mostly gone, but all his nerves were tingling, and it still felt like there was a giant hole in his back. All his wonder disappeared at the sight of his dying friend. Scarlet blood was specked on his face and seeped below the cushion on his chest. There was a whistling sound, and Rohit looked scared as he tried to breathe.

"Hey buddy," Zander said to his friend with false enthusiasm.

"How are you...?" Rohit's eyes traveled to Zander's chest and back up to his face.

"Not sure if we understand it ourselves; I think Grace somehow healed me." Zander thought for a moment, "Maybe it is like when I blasted that truck into the air. Or these men," he glanced up and grimaced at his handiwork. "Do you think you can heal him, too, Grace?"

"I will try. I'm not sure if I can. Healing you took a lot from me." She sat on the other side of Rohit. For a moment, she looked unsure of herself, but with sudden certainty, she grabbed Rohit's hands and closed her eyes in concentration. But for all her fervent wishing, Grace could not work a second miracle at this time. "I'm sorry; I wish I understood this more," she said with raw emotion. "You saved my life, Rohit."

"I'm sorry, too. I should've known it wasn't you," Zander said.

"Stop," Rohit said. "I don't have much time left, and I don't want to waste it with that drivel." His speech was broken by his gasping for breath and a rattle. "I went into medical school to save lives. You gave me an opportunity to save millions. I felt so lucky, I still do." Blood appeared on his bluish lips. "And if my death helps the millions in Portland, it was worth it." Rohit lifted his right hand, clasped Zander's neck, and drew him down so he could whisper, "I know I didn't always show it, but I have always loved you like a brother. I would have followed you anywhere."

Having said what he needed to. Rohit let go—arm falling lifelessly from Zander's neck. The only sound in the room was their mourning cry for Rohit, and the sirens still came.

* * *

Miraculously, Mack's unconscious body lay unharmed on the sofa in the room's ruins. Grace got up and sat beside him and tried to 'heal' him. Nothing happened. Then, a white fog seemed to envelop his body. The vapor slowly deepened in color until it settled on a brick-red hue. As the two of them shrugged, the mist rose in the air and dissipated into nothingness.

As the last of the ethereal substance disappeared, Mack shot up into a sitting position. Scaring the daylights out of them both. Once Grace could breathe again, she punched Mack in the shoulder playfully and went to check on Ollie.

The emergency vehicles arrived.

Much too late to do any good, the parking area was bathed with the blinding lights of several local police cars, a firetruck, and an ambulance. If the night hadn't already taken enough of a toll on the ragged survivors, it took Mack many stress-filled minutes before he could convince the local lawmen that the four survivors of Horizons were the 'good guys.' Zander had been cuffed and slid into the backseat of a squad car before Mack could make a quick call to the President and clear up any confusion for the local men in blue.

She still had no idea how, but Grace found she could remove the drug from Ollie much the same way she had coaxed the last bits of the virus from Mack's system. The grateful soldier clapped her a little too hard on the shoulder, and Grace's now mostly crimson motel robe shifted to give Ollie an unfettered view. Mortified, Grace adjusted the flaps of the garment and fled back to the other suite in search of more appropriate attire.

None of the GCs in the room had survived the brutal assault. More than a few rescue personnel had to beat a hasty retreat at the sight of the human wreckage.

After Grace got cleaned up, the four decided they needed some privacy to talk with the President and formulate a plan for what they would do going forward. Mack spoke to the hotel's manager and finagled a room that was not an active crime scene and had a front room window, not before assuring him that the US Government would cover all their damages.

*15 minutes later.*

The worn and battered, but nonetheless alive, band sat before Zander at the table. The big sergeant was to his left and was on the edge of his seat, spoiling for a fight he didn't get to finish. Mack was across from him, with sleep lines still on his face, but otherwise was clear-eyed. And lastly, Grace was to his right. Gone was the ghastly robe. Her old work clothes were redonned. Once again, somehow, she looked like she had freshly arrived for a day of work. Her sandalwood-colored skin was bright and unlined, and her luxurious hair seemed perfectly coifed.

Damned if he understood why, but it felt right that they were gathered around this table together, the loss of Rohit withstanding.

"Well, it seems like we are back to trying to figure out our next steps," Zander said to start the dialog. "I recommend we bring the President in on this conversation."

The whole group agreed, and Mack dialed the number, put it on speakerphone, and set it in the middle of the table. Once the President joined them, each relayed the different parts of the narrative they witnessed. In no time, their leader was up to date. Then, the party was placed on hold while the President made a few short calls.

Before long, he returned and said, "According to the FBI, they have a file on this *Gaia's Children* cult, but they seemed to think they were small potatoes. If we make it through this thing, I might have to rethink the leadership of an organization that misjudged this group so badly. For now, I will leave it to them to deal with these whackos. Have you thought about how we should proceed?"

"Frankly, sir," Mack said in a desert-dry tone, "we have been a wee bit preoccupied. Our Horizons' contact told us we have the recipe in a secure spot in San Francisco, but Dr. Mayette was present when the information was revealed. There is a high probability he escaped with this knowledge."

"Mr. President," Grace said, "Dr. Wu here. Have your computer people solved the hacker's attack yet? If so, I could authorize them to download the files to you directly."

"Wish I had good news in that regard, doctor; whoever created this nasty piece of programming spent enough time to make it damn hard to eradicate. Some of my networking advisors recommend we wipe the servers and start with a clean slate. The downside of doing something that drastic is it would take a great deal of time—something we don't have. So, if you sent us the formula, it would be corrupted again. Until our house is straightened out, we must rely on Horizon's desire for self-preservation." He laughed.

"Respectfully, sir, you have a dark sense of humor." Zander smiled as he said it.

"Between you, me, and the wall, you are not the first to say that," the President remarked with a tight laugh. "I'm finding out the hard way it's better to laugh than cry. Sounds like our best bet is to head to the Horizons' lab in San Francisco and try to get production up and running there. Isn't much we can do to help them produce the virus blocker, but—"

The President's speech faded, and Zander heard, *"You're wasting time. The spell will resolve whether you want it to or not. The only thing that matters is all of you must come south. There is much I need to tell you and get you ready for the transition. Head to Lake Shasta Caverns, and I will give you further directions. Come to me now. Next time, you might not be so lucky."* The golden-haired woman's voice was much stronger this time and had lost most of its ethereal quality. Zander was *convinced* she was present; he scoured the room for her. As he did, he noticed Grace and Mack were casting about the room looking for someone too.

"Doctors. Are you there?" the President asked in concern.

"Um, ah—yes, sir," Zander said distractedly. "Sorry, someone just asked me a question. Anyway, what I was going to say was that we want to be there to supervise the creation of the vaccine. Are you okay with us proceeding there?"

"Okay with it?" The President asked incredulously. "I'm glad you didn't make me beg you to do it. Do you want me to arrange transport for you?"

"How long will it take, sir?" Zander asked.

"Wait one," the President said, and the line went silent, until he resumed it a minute later, "We are using most of our MAC flights to bring as many troops as possible to reinforce the Portland blockade. A commercial flight could be arranged, but I am told it will take 14 hours to get from Eugene to San Francisco."

"If we get started now, sir, we can make it to San Francisco within 10 hours. So, we could shave four hours off the time." Ollie tapped Zander's elbow, vigorously shook his head, and held up eight fingers before him. "Errr, it sounds like Sergeant Jennison thinks we could do it in eight hours, sir. If it is okay with you, I would like not to waste any more time getting down there than we must. It is safe to assume Ben will try to stop us."

"Agreed," the President said, and then asked, "I suppose sending an armed convoy escort is out of the question?"

"You presume correctly, sir," Zander said to a chorus of nods. "Besides, we can be underway in less than half an hour, and what could possibly go wrong over such a short distance?"

"And now, who has the dark sense of humor?" the President said and laughed with them like an old friend. "Godspeed everyone and keep me in the loop."

"Affirmative," Mack said. "We will report back when we arrive."

"And I will call my people and have them start collecting supplies, Mr. President," Grace added.

"Before we finish, I want you to know how sad I am to hear about Dr. Tamboli's death. I'm told he was a good man."

"He was a hero, sir, and will be sorely missed," Grace said sincerely.

"If we come out on the other side of this thing, I assure you he will receive recognition from a grateful nation."

"Thank you, Mr. President," Zander's voice trembled.

"I don't want to hold you up. Just know you have the thoughts, prayers, and good wishes of me and my administration."

"Thank you, sir," Mack said. We appreciate everything we can get. Speak with you soon.

The line went dead.

"Are we going to talk about what happened during that conversation?" Mack asked as he glanced about the room nervously.

"With everything that has transpired in the past 12 hours," Zander asked in astonishment, "a telepathic exchange is what has you spooked? We will have plenty of time to analyze all the weirdness when we are in the car."

"What?" A confused Ollie said. "Are you telling me I'm going on an eight-hour road trip with a bunch of schizophrenics?" They all looked at him with trepidation until he broke into a broad grin and shouted, "Sign me up! Man, you guys are so easy." The big man's bravado was contagious, and they soon laughed at the absurdity of it all.

Exactly eight minutes later, their black Escalade was busily weaving among the travelers heading south on I-5.

Southern rock blaring from the speakers.

And Ollie exceeding the speed limit by more than a few miles per hour.

# Chapter 36



*July 10, Tuesday — 8:29 am — Lake Shasta Caverns, California*

It had taken Zander, Grace, and Mack nearly the whole Oregon leg of their southbound journey to convince Ollie that they needed to make a brief stop at the Lake Shasta Caverns in Northern California. Even those who had heard the voice were not entirely sure making this detour was what was best for the people of Portland or the world.

Ultimately, the deciding factor in the argument was that the caverns were only a few miles east of the Interstate. If this side trip was only a lark; the jaunt would only cost them half an hour's time. The voice directed them again as they left the freeway. They were to leave their car in the parking lot and continue south until they saw a tan, sandstone cliff side short of the lake. Everything was as she said, and they waited for their enigmatic host.

Without warning, a large section of the wall before them dissolved, and only darkness was beyond. After telekinesis, telepathy, healing and whatever the hell throwing a giant fireball at a truck was: an illusionary cliff face was one of the least weird things which happened to them lately. The group performed a collective shrug and made their way to the opening. It seemed ridiculous that this was a trap—but one couldn't be too careful—so Ollie took his hand-gun from his shoulder rig and led them inside.

Once they had all moved inside, the entrance disappeared and became solid again. Stretching out a hand, Zander touched the wall in wonder. "It feels like solid rock—not an illusion."

Mack took out his phone and turned on the flashlight function. In the meager light, Zander could see Ollie holster his weapon. It seems Ollie came to the same conclusion as Zander: What is the use of a gun against someone who can control matter? With no sign of their host, they decided to spread out and explore the area. After a few steps, Zander realized that he could see the room even as he moved away from Mack's device.

"Look at the floor," Grace commented, "the ground glows."

Glancing down at his feet, Zander discovered she was right. A dull sheen emanated from the stones they walked upon. Their illumination was low-watt florescent bulb-like. As their eyes adjusted further, they could determine the room was not vast; in fact, it barely held their company.

A tunnel opening appeared at the north end of the room, and they dutifully entered it. The passageway was only 100 feet long before it opened into an immeasurable space that they could only *sense* its actual dimensions. When they were all present, a bright light suddenly encompassed everything in the room, and Zander had to shield his eyes with a hand.

As he lowered it, he beheld the golden-haired woman in her full splendor. He shot a sideways glance at his party to see if they were seeing this angelic figure too. Mack and Grace were smiling and nodding in understanding. Ollie stared at her in wonder, and then he fell to his knees and wept.

The woman ran to him, crouched in front of him, and gently lifted his chin. As his tears continued to fall, she said in her multi-tonal voice, "Shhh, my son. There is no reason to fear. The change is upon you. I will hasten its progress."

Her hand seemed to glow golden like the rest of her person. Then Ollie was surrounded by a white aura, which became red just as Mack's had earlier. The soldier shook as someone waking from a dream and then he smiled and nodded like his counterparts had earlier and they both stood.

"Before we begin, a friend wishes to say hello," The gold-haired woman said.

Out of the shadows, a tall man wearing a worn Stetson sauntered into sight.

Zander's heart threatened to explode, "Pete! Can it really be you?" The newcomer moved entirely into the light, and they could see the distressed remnants of an Ontario police chief's uniform. The man removed his hat, and his face was no longer in shadow. A nasty group of red scars ran from his forehead to his chin, which looked like the damage raking fingernails might do, but otherwise, besides needing a shave, he seemed hale. "How are you?"

The man seemed not to hear the question for a moment, but then he broke out in a smile, closed the distance between them, and grabbed Zander in a bear hug. Grace, Mack, and Ollie looked on with amusement at the nearly hysterical men slapping each other on the back and talking too loudly. Finally, they broke the embrace.

"Damn, it's great to see you, Zander! I was starting to believe there would be no one left."

"There is *no one* beside Ben," Zander said through clenched teeth.

"I heard about that," Pete said as he nodded to the golden-haired woman. "I've had my own run-ins with *Gaia's Children*. They were not. . .pleasant. We'll have to swap stories sometime. Anyway, I was adrift until this lady contacted me. I figured nothin' holding me to Ontario any longer, so why not?"

"Roxy?" Zander asked. Pete shook his head. "I'm—"

Pete interrupted, "—Thanks, Zander, at least I got to see her—" It was then that two magnificent wolves charged from behind Pete. Ollie started to draw his gun again when Pete shouted, "They're with me! Athena and Deimos, sit." Both predators immediately sank their rears on the floor. Pete went to them and affectionately ruffled their fur about their ears like they were pups.

"What?" That was all Zander could say.

"Told you," Pete said, "we've got a lot of catching up to do. Let's save it for later because our host has kept me in the dark as much as you, and I can't wait to hear this tale."

She nodded in welcome to Pete and said, "My friends, my name is Solaurum, and I welcome you to this place—Portus." Though her voice was familiar, it now held a strength and vigor which was not evident before. "I know you must have many questions." She looked at Zander with knowing eyes. "I'm sorry for your loss. Rohit was a virtuous man, and he should have joined us here today. My only excuse for not saving him is I'm still not at full strength. That and you are not the only ones in my care. The prehistoric spell has not yet relinquished its power over the world, so I do my best."

Stepping forward, Zander dared to ask, "Spell?"

"I'm glad to see that even though your forms are different, you're still the same in essence, Zander." They looked at her in puzzlement. "There I went and did it. I have a millennium to prepare this speech and still get ahead of myself."

Grace asked, "Millennia?"

"Millennia," the gold-haired woman assured. "But during the great darkness, I have only been dimly aware of your world. You see, I am supernatural, but your world has no magic. Therefore, if I was to survive; I had to create this haven: Portus is an enchanted bubble separate from your time and reality."

"But something is altering our world now," Mack ventured.

"Essentially correct," Solaurum said. "You always had a sharp mind, Mac. When I last knew you, you went by Mac rather than Mack. I wonder which you will choose now.

"I've always fancied Mac as a nickname." He wrinkled his nose and said, "It's much better than Latrelle. No one calls me that besides my mom." Mack laughed at his admission, but then the group joined in.

"Mac it is then. In answer to your earlier question, yes, your world is changing, but not something new. Rather, it is reverting to what it was before." She approached him, snatched his glasses, and threw them into the dark recess of the room. Solaurum passed her hand in front of Mac's eyes and stepped back. Mac protested the loss of his glasses briefly until he looked around in wonder. He broadly grinned.

Zander's world spun again. The past few days have been extraordinary: the visits with this 'woman,' the truck's demolishing, throwing men about with a thought, and Grace's miraculous healings. *I thought I was losing my mind. Things that couldn't be real. But now? What I thought was real is essentially a lie?*

"It's not a lie, dear heart," Solaurum said with tenderness and understanding as Zander's eyes boggled. "Yes, I can hear your thoughts, and I do many other things you will say are impossible."

"Solaurum," Zander said, "you keep acting like you know me. How is it possible? If I have lived my whole life in a world you can't interact with; how would you know I love to search for answers?"

"Well, you should remember me, but fate has stepped in the way." A single golden tear fell from her eye as she spoke, and the tonal melody of her voice moved into the minor key.

She waved her arm, chairs appeared behind them all, and she motioned for them to sit as she did. When her whole audience was settled, she began her recitation, "Let me tell you the story from the beginning. But because you are temporal beings, let me give you some frame of reference. This tale occurred at least 10,000 years ago. The world today looks very much as it did back then. It was called Gaia." Her listener's eyes went wide. "Yes, the word is the same in both worlds. Inexplicably, quite a few things from the 'old world' bled into this one.

"Gaia was a world of magic and creatures you can't even begin to imagine. But it was not one of peace and harmony. The discord you have experienced throughout your human history is, unfortunately, nothing new." Solaurum disclosed this with a touch of resignation.

"Without too much simplification, the world was split into two main factions. From what little I have observed in this world, it is much the same." The group nodded in bitter understanding. "Anyway . . .the first group—the Lucian Conclave—was founded by a quorum of magic users. Not everyone in Gaia can use magic, but to one extent or another, most people and creatures are innately magical. Whether it is someone who can heal," Solaurum nodded to Grace, or someone resistant to magic." This time, she nodded to Ollie. As you can imagine, the more powerful users tend to wield more influence, sometimes whether they want it or not." She stared into his eyes until he shifted his weight and looked down.

With these ideas in mind, the Lucians created a society that sought truth, respect, understanding, and peace. Lofty goals—and sometimes they met them. But, as Pete said, 'There will be time for stories later.' In fact," Solaurum said with a gleam in her eye. "I hope a memory or two of yours will pop through the veil soon.

"I'm doing a rather poor job of succinctly summarizing the past. I had spent so much time rehearsing this that I thought I would do better," she clicked her tongue and continued, "No doubt you can probably guess what the other clique—the Nyxians—wanted: wealth and supreme power.

"There were many wars and battles fought between the factions, but for the most part, there was equilibrium between them. Neither dominated long over the other. . . until the Nyxians, in their lust for power, created a spell that they believed would destroy the Lucians' magic."

"Let me guess," Grace said, "it didn't go how they hoped?"

"Correct," Solaurum acceded. "Neither your world nor mine was meant to have only good or evil. Both worlds contain many balanced extremes, such as day and night, sound and silence, and life and death. Each of these is a part of a grand design that can never be removed."

"Got a bad feeling about what comes next," Ollie groused.

"As well you should," Solaurum agreed. The incantation the wizards from the Nyxian Cabal unleashed started to undo all magic in my world, not negating just the Lucians' power as they had hoped. To their credit," To Zander, Solaurum didn't sound like she wanted to do any such thing. "Instead of just waiting for the end of our world, they came to the Conclave of Light and proposed a truce between the factions to allow everyone to temporarily combine resources."

"If I were one of these Conclave guys, I would assume it was a trap," Pete observed.

"And they did. But after viewing the Nyxian spell configuration, they discovered for themselves that magic was failing. An alliance was formed, and they got to work on trying to avert an apocalypse."

"Excuse me, ma'am, but it sounds like you were there to witness it," Ollie said.

"Some of us have long lives and memories: when time began. The coalition came to me for advice on how to solve the crisis and believe me; I had a stake in its success." She looked at Zander and said, "Perhaps that is why you enlisted my aid."

"Why would I? How could I?" Zander was so flummoxed he couldn't even form the question.

"Because you were the Primoose—or head—of the Lucians," Solaurum said.

If Zander thought his world was upside down before, now it felt like he was in a naughty child's snow globe being shaken violently. "How... how?"

There was no reply, but a light appeared 40 meters to their right, and Solaurum nodded for Zander to inspect the illuminated table. There was only one thing on the table: a six-foot staff. As he reached for the rod, it flew the rest of the way to his hand unbidden. The wood was dark brown and of a grain he did not recognize. It looked like a branch, but on closer inspection, the stave was made of vines with branches interwoven in a complex pattern. Glassy and smooth, the rod radiated a faint warmth. With an unconscious movement, Zander clasped the staff in his right hand. The weight and feel of the thing felt natural. There was no doubt it was his.

"This is mine," he said in wonder. "I remember holding this. How is that possible?"

"It is possible because you have ruled the Lucians for one hundred and twenty of your years. We believed everyone's memories would gradually return after the spell was resolved. Maybe that was wishful thinking on our part. Still, I'm glad you remember holding the staff of your office—Docerilum. Does it trigger anything?" Zander shook his head in the negative. "No matter. Back to my tale, you and Grace were the ones who came up with a way to avoid our destruction. However, I think Zander just rode Grace's coattails," she ribbed him.

"I'm a Lucian, too?" Grace asked.

"Of course, my child. All of you were. I try not to summon the two groups here simultaneously—for obvious reasons." She paused for any further questions, but when none were forthcoming, she continued, "Your solution was simplistic and elegant: minutely change the world."

Eyebrows went up throughout the company.

"If magic—or the supernatural—was removed from the world," Zander reasoned, "the magical world they had described in the Nyxian spell would no longer exist, and the world could not be destroyed." His eyes opened wide. "Much like what we attempted to do with our virus masker."

"Maybe I was wrong to think Grace was the only brains in your partnership," she teased good-naturedly. Then she switched tacks. "Can you see the pattern now? There is a correlation between your world and the one of magic, for example, can you figure out who was the Nyxian in your world?"

"Ben," Mac guessed, "he wants the world all to himself and his followers."

"Quite right, and he is Zander's counterpart: ruler of the Nyxians—The Pontiarc. He was also the principal author and proponent of destroying all 'white' magic. How sad that he is as misguided in this time as he was back then. Ironically, his plague is the tool that will bring about the removal of the last vestiges of his original perversion. Of course, that is of little consolation for the losses you have suffered."

Just like in Zander's office brainstorming sessions, the disparate pieces began to order themselves and fall into place. He asked, "Since we are alive and discussing this, I guess it's fair to say our plan worked?"

"The spell was cast just before the cataclysm could occur. The only enchanted objects in this world are contained here in Portus. The only way we could keep the invocation from affecting me was to limit my life energies to almost nothing. It is one of the reasons I knew very little about your world or what was going on about me.

But you assured me I would regain my birthright as an elder being as the old world reasserted itself. I'm glad you were right."

"So am I," Zander said. "But why is the spell dissipating now?"

"There is the insightful mage I used to know," she beamed. Grace hypothesized that the initial spell would not have the power to last as long as the new one cast by the alliance. Therefore, our counter spell was designed to last for a finite number of years. If she was correct, the previous spell would be spent, and our world could safely return."

"I know it is a moot point," Ollie said, "but what if you all had been wrong?"

"Then we had prolonged the world for a score of millennia before the final apocalypse and had lost nothing," their host said.

"Valid argument," Ollie agreed.

"Wait a minute," Grace said as she screwed up her face in concentration, "if Ben was the instrument to bring back our world…"

"Then Ben was technically the 'good guy,'" Pete said as he applied air quotes to the phrase, "and we almost stopped him from ending the spell. Ouch! This is so twisty it hurts my head."

"And yet the parallels are uncanny," Ollie recognized. "You guys" —pointing at Mac, Grace, and Zander— "finding each other, working on an anti-virus to save the world's population, and choosing careers benefiting people. The spell must not have been able to modify people much."

"Well, the spell was primarily designed to eliminate magic, not to adjust a person's personality," Solaurum observed. "If you recall, my messages were always aimed at helping you survive and never to assist with creating the anti-virus."

"Strange, I hadn't thought about it that way," Zander said, "I was so sure we were on the right side of all this."

"Most people do," Solaurum said. "I would speculate that Ben thought he was in the right as well. He wanted to save the planet. Unfortunately, he was willing to kill billions to achieve that goal."

"So, Ben is the agent of change for the spell, but how long will it take for the world to switch back to the original?" Grace asked.

"The transfer is almost complete," Solaurum assured them.

"*What!*" They all exclaimed at once.

"Why are you surprised?" the golden-haired woman asked. "When we started this conversation, I told you time does not act the same way here as in your world. Our chat has lasted nearly six of your months. It is imperative you leave Portus immediately."

"What is the hurry?" Ollie inquired.

"As we discussed earlier, the world needs balance. The Nyxian Cabal has an unfair advantage over you: most of them were in *Gaia's Children.* So, Ben is organizing his followers as we speak. The Lucians are out there, but the spell does not guarantee their survival. Fate brought you to the end of this world, but what happens now is up to you. Go, lead your people."

"Are you coming with us?" Grace asked hopefully.

"I will escort you out, but for now, I must remain. Someday, I can rejoin the world," she said, "but for now, my job is to redistribute all the items entrusted in my care." Another table laden with various weapons and equipment appeared before them. "These were placed in my keeping; I will faithfully discharge my duty to all when their owners retake possession. Much like Zander's staff, you will know yours."

"You said your job was to redistribute all enchanted property to their owners. Do you have the Nyxians' belongings, too?" Grace challenged.

Chuckling, Solaurum noted, "I forgot how hard it was to get anything past you, but I made a promise to impartially hand all magical weapons, jewelry, and tomes, whether they be of light or dark magic. Beware, if you try to stop me in this duty, I will destroy you." As she made this threat, her face became a terrible mask, and her eyes glowed hotly.

Holding both hands palms out, Ollie said in a somber tone, "Let me speak for everyone here; we don't want to be destroyed today. He boldly approached the table and grabbed an item without hesitation. "This little claymore is calling my name, and now I'm stepping back slowly."

The 'little' claymore was more accurately described as a piece of dark metal about 4 feet in length with a grass-green wrapping about its handle and an intricately designed but stalwart crossing guard. The sword gleamed as he hefted it, and he broke out in a childlike grin when he saw the leather scabbard and rigging. Without hesitation, he donned it and put both hands on his hips in a classic pose. The laughter that followed was pure and reverberated throughout the chamber. Each moved to the table in turn.

Grace grabbed a golden pendant, which resembled an ankh with the top loop closed, and put the long gold chain around her neck. It fell over her heart and between her breasts. Grace smiled and nodded at the woman.

Next, Mac moved to a black leather-bound book and took it. It seemed to pulse with energy as he took it, and it continued to glow lightly. He looked like he burned to open it, but when he looked up, it appeared he would wait for a more private time. He, too, nodded to the woman in respect.

Lastly, Pete bee-lined to a well-wrought crossbow. The wood was so dark as to appear almost black, and it was accented with purpleheart about its grip and along its planer surfaces. Five ebony arrows with red flashing were stashed along its body. Before using its rig, Pete removed his gun and belt holster and placed them carefully on the table. Then he donned the mini crossbow across the front of his chest. He did it so efficiently that it looked like he had done it thousands of times, which he had if what the lady had said was true. The former policeman bowed to her, and she returned the nod.

Possessions returned, and Solaurum had kept their ancient covenant. She motioned for them to proceed with her from the cave.

The sunshine was shining brilliantly, or maybe it was their return to natural daylight. Whichever, Zander needed to close his eyes for a moment and then squint when he opened them, which is why he was immediately startled when he saw—her.

As they left Portus, the beautiful woman began to glow and shimmer. As her form became less concrete, she increased to gigantic proportions. If he were forced to compare her size to something, she reminded him of a brontosaurus skeleton he saw in a museum as a child. In fact, body-wise, she was similar in musculature to the herbivore. In awe, Zander's eyes continued to examine the impossibility before him: four incredibly muscular legs tipped with talons, an elongated tail that lazily twitched side to side, a neck sinuous and tall, and two enormous, pale yellowish-red wings that were tucked against her body like a bat's. But after briefly examining her breathtaking and grand features, it was her face that drew the eye. It was covered with golden scales, like the rest of her body, but they were finer and looked almost like human skin. Two massive horns wound with grace and symmetry behind her head, and though she was the most inhuman creature Zander had ever seen, she was every bit as comely as her human avatar.

They all gasped in awe at the golden creature before them. And then she spoke. When she did, her voice did not match the movement of her massive jaw, but her human guests did not seem to care.

"Forgive me, my friends, and please shut your mouths. That's good," she said with humor. "You are the first mortals to view my true form in many millennia. I wanted to reveal myself to you so you could take heart and remember me in the dark days to come." She shook her prodigious head from side to side. "No. I can't reveal the future more than I have already. Is there anything else I can help you with before you begin your journey?"

They continued to stare in awe for a time before Zander could ask, "Do you have any advice for where we should go?"

"After everything you have heard today, you probably believe fate is real: that life has handrails which you may not veer from. But your having a predetermined destiny is simply not true. Yes. The spell somehow led your essence to this time and place to fulfill its overall conditions, but what you make of your lives from here on out will be up to you," Solaurum said thoughtfully. "Gaia—our world—has been restored to us, and now *we* must decide how to remake it. In a way, this was Ben's dream. I hope you have more wisdom than him. Lastly, be on your guard. The world and its denizens are not as you remember them."

With this blatant dismissal, Grace stepped forward and dared a kiss on the golden dragon's foot and said, "Thank you for your faithful, lonely vigil."

With a nod, Solaurum turned from them and disappeared through the cliffside.

The small party returned the way they came and found their Escalade unmolested. The only telltale difference from their arrival was an 8-inch dusting of snow all about them.

"Hold tight, everybody," Ollie said, "and I will have her purring in no time." True to his word, Ollie coaxed the engine to life after a short wait. "All aboard."

"Gotta leak, be right back," Mac said.

Ollie got into the driver's seat. Grace, Pete, and Zander sat on the bench seat directly behind the driver. Mac hurried from his business back across the blacktop to the vehicle. The back door was still open, so seeing the three in the back, Mac assumed he had 'shotgun.' Upon opening the door, Mac discovered a pair of sky-blue eyes. That and a 120-pound wolf. Mac hesitated. The apex predator bared its teeth and growled softly. Mac closed the door, ducked inside the entrance, and aimed for the second bench seat. A pair of orangish-red eyes accompanied another terrifying growl.

"Don't worry, Mac. They won't hurt you."

Apparently, this did not comfort the man because he 'chose' to sit in the last bench seat.

Once everyone had chosen a seat, they made their way to the nearby town of Shasta Lake. Ollie wanted to top off the tank before they headed out. There was no telling how hard it would be to find fuel.

The informational sign at the entrance to the city said: Population 10,164, but Zander doubted it was true any longer.

As they drove down the street, they saw not another living soul. Houses had broken windows and open doors, cars were stacked together in gridlock, and they could smell smoke in the air.

"It looks like Solaurum was right," remarked Zander to the other passengers in the SUV. "The world has continued on without us."

After a few tries, they found some gas. After Ollie filled the tank, Zander asked, "Anyone have a suggestion for where we should head?

"If the old world no longer needs our help," Everyone nodded, "then, there is no use in heading to San Francisco any longer. Besides," Pete pointed at the gridlock heading south. "That direction's not really viable. But there is someone back in Oregon who can help us with that." The wolves growled in agreement.

The road leading north had a smattering of cars but otherwise looked passable to Zander, "I know I'm supposed to be some grand-poopa, but I'm not feeling very dictatorial today. What do you guys think?"

"Let's see where that road takes us," Grace said. Everyone else agreed with her.

They had barely started their grand journey when Zander shouted, "Stop!"

The startled sergeant jumped on the brakes, and they came to an abrupt halt. Zander opened the passenger door and ran into the nearest building. No one knew what got into their friend, but they figured he would call if he needed them.

Just when Ollie was about to check on him, Zander appeared in the convenience store's doorway. As he made his way back to them, he pulled a package of spearmint gum from his pocket, unwrapped a stick, popped it in his mouth, folded up the wrapper meticulously, placed it on the vehicle's console, and smiled the smile of a contented man.

"That was close," Zander said in all seriousness.

Everyone laughed as Ollie turned up some Lynyrd Skynyrd and gunned it. The future was uncertain, but they would face their imminent adventures.

Together.

A.P. Vandy is a retired English/Creative Writing teacher pursuing his writing career full-time. He is an avid Science Fiction/Fantasy reader, which helped keep things light when he was reading 'the classics.' He was born and raised in Oregon, the setting of his first two novels. He resides in Hawaii with his wife, Shannon, of 30+ years and his pug-mix, Zoey.

Visit A.P. Vandy at his website:
www.apvandy.com

Explore new horizons with us as we sail
onto shores of latest products, events,
great titles, and beyond.

Visit us:

www.oceaniacom.com


OCEANIACOM PRESS

www.ingramcontent.com/pod-product-compliance
Lightning Source LLC
Chambersburg PA
CBHW011218190726
48287CB00008B/2656